NO MORE REGRETS

"You're a good man, Mitch Mathews."

Mitch huffed, because he didn't feel particularly good. He felt stupid in a lot of ways. And helpless. But he was willing to put himself out on a limb for a chance to make things right with the woman in his arms. "I'm no angel, sweetheart. I've done plenty of dumb shit in my life."

"I'm sure you have, but you've got a good heart. That doesn't change. You're going to make a great husband and father someday."

It just won't be today. Or with me.

He heard the unspoken words as loud as if Simone had screamed them. And inside, everything he'd been holding back, all his plans to keep things light between them, whooshed right out of his head. Along with what was left of his common sense.

"You're damn right I am." He gripped her by the jaw and turned her face up to his. Surprised dark eyes met his. Eyes that had captivated him from the first. "But not someday."

Then he lowered his mouth to hers.

Titles By Elisabeth Naughton

Aegis Security Series
(Romantic Suspense)
EXTREME MEASURES *(2014)*
SINFUL SURRENDER
FIRST EXPOSURE
ACAPULCO HEAT *(in the Bodyguards in Bed Anthology)*

Against All Odds Series
(Contemporary Romance)
HOLD ON TO ME
WAIT FOR ME

Stolen Series
(Romantic Suspense)
STOLEN CHANCES
STOLEN SEDUCTION
STOLEN HEAT
STOLEN FURY

Eternal Guardians Series
(Paranormal Romance)
TWISTED *(2014)*
BOUND
ENSLAVED
ENRAPTURED
TEMPTED
ENTWINED
MARKED

Firebrand Series
(Paranormal romance)
POSSESSED BY DESIRE
SLAVE TO PASSION
BOUND TO SEDUCTION

Anthologies
SINFUL SECONDS
WICKED FIRSTS
DARK NIGHTS--DANGEROUS MEN
BODYGUARDS IN BED

HOLD ON TO ME

ELISABETH
NAUGHTON

EN

ISBN-13: 978-0-9889862-9-9
ISBN-10: 0-9889862-9-9

Cover art and design by Patricia Schmitt/Pickyme
Copy editing by Linda Ingmanson

For all readers,
young and old,
who have experienced the joy of love
and the heartbreak of loss.

Chapter One

Simone Conners had done some really stupid things in her life, but she was pretty sure what she was currently contemplating topped all of it combined by at least a mile.

"Ladies and gentlemen, we're about to make our final descent into San Francisco. Please bring your trays and seat backs into the locked and upright position."

She shifted in her seat, gripped the armrest, and looked out the plane's window. A thin layer of fog hugged the coastline, but for once she didn't care about the incessant cold and perpetual fog on the West Coast. She wanted to get home. She wanted to see Mitch. She wanted to tell him…

Tell him what? Tell him she missed him? That she'd spent the last week thinking about the future? That she was ready for that next step? A wave of nausea washed through her, the same one she'd been dealing with for days, and she pressed a hand against her stomach. The answer to every single one of those questions scared the crap out of her.

"I don't know what young people are thinking these days," the white-haired, eighty-something woman seated to Simone's right muttered as she flipped through a gossip magazine. "Look at this couple here. Divorcing already after only a month. And they're so attractive. People just don't commit like they used to. It's ridiculous. They should just stay single and avoid the whole mess."

Simone could care less about some Hollywood power couple. Managing a "Hm," she went back to looking out the window. Her seatmate had talked nonstop through the entire flight from DC, and more than once Simone had cursed herself for forgetting her earbuds, but she'd been too wound up to tell the elderly woman to stop chattering. Because right now, commitment was foremost on her mind.

What if it was too soon? She'd grown complacent, but then…why shouldn't she? Ten years had passed since her life had been upended, and her husband was now dead. Whatever Steve had been afraid *might* happen when they were married was no longer a threat. She'd been living half a life since she'd lost him. Wasn't it time she started living the whole thing? Taking chances? Being happy? Wasn't that the next step?

Her heart told her it was. But in the back of her mind, she couldn't stop worrying that if she took that step, if she made that leap of faith, that something would go wrong. And the worst thing she could envision was that in a month from now, Mitch could change his mind about what he wanted. That would kill her more than never taking the risk.

Simone's chest prickled with a rash of nerves as the city spires grew larger in the window. She didn't know who'd she'd be today if she hadn't chosen to run away with Steve, but part of her was thankful she didn't have to wonder. Because if she hadn't been that reckless girl she barely even remembered, she'd never have met Steve in the first place. She wouldn't have her daughter, Shannon, now. She wouldn't be worrying about a future with a man who made her so crazy sometimes she could barely think straight.

Mitch…

Warmth gathered beneath her ribs and sent that flutter through her belly she felt every time she thought of him.

The woman beside her slapped the magazine closed and sighed as she tugged her glasses off to hang from the chain around her neck. "You're smart to still be single at your age, young lady. Mark my word. A man will rip your heart out and trample all over it if you let him. These women in this magazine are the perfect example. Better to be savvy, successful, and single rather than miserable with a man who will only disappoint you in the long run."

Savvy and successful hadn't done anything but remind Simone just how alone she'd been since her husband's funeral. Was two and a half years long enough to mourn? What would Shannon think? Simone hadn't been avoiding relationships since Steve's death, but she hadn't been looking for a man either. Mitch Mathews had simply stumbled into her life.

No, whirled into it was more like it. Just like a tornado, sucking up everything around him and drawing it all in, including her.

Tuning out the old woman's muttering, she closed her eyes as the plane's wheels touched down. Mitch's goofy smile flashed in her mind, his shaggy, unkempt hair, and the way he could always make her smile, even when she'd had the day from hell or Shannon was in the midst of one of her preteen tantrums.

That flutter in her stomach grew larger and more insistent.

The plane came to a stop, and a bell dinged, indicating it was okay to get up. Stomach still swirling, Simone gathered her bag, muttered good-bye to the woman next to her as she pushed out of her seat, and reached into the pocket of her slacks for her cell. As she followed the rest of the passengers off the plane and up the Jetway, she turned on her phone and waited for the screen to load.

Four unread messages flashed, the first from the man she'd just been thinking of.

> MITCH: *You'd better already be on a plane, sweetheart. My hand and I have gotten way too reacquainted during the last week. Get home soon! I promise to make it worth your while.*

A wicked-hot sensation rolled through her belly, and a smile spread across her lips. No, he wasn't the kind of guy who would disappoint her in the long run. She knew it in her heart. He was the kind of guy who could make a woman happy. Blissfully so.

She moved through the terminal and read his next message, telling her he was watching her plane on the airline's tracking website and couldn't wait to see her. Who did that? Monitored flights because he was so anxious? Not any guy she'd ever dated. Not even her own husband.

Yards from security, she caught sight of a man with shaggy brown hair, dressed in jeans and a gray sweater, standing on the other side of the glass, holding a handful of flowers. Simone's pulse picked up speed, and all that excitement she'd tried to keep tamped down rushed in on a wave of emotion that stole her breath.

Her feet picked up speed. She hurried through the security gate only to realize…it wasn't Mitch.

Her steps drew to a stop. Disappointment dropped her heart into the pit of her stomach. Beside her, a woman squealed, held out her arms, and ran into the man's waiting embrace.

And in that moment, as Simone watched the romantic reunion, she realized…that was what she wanted. That was how she felt. The disappointment was quickly replaced with a fire that sparked in the center of her chest and spread outward through every limb and vein and cell until her entire body felt alive.

She loved Mitch.

She loved him more than any man she'd ever known, even Steve. This crazy, maddening, spur-of-the-moment man who'd completely flipped her world upside down and inside out and left her so frazzled some days she wanted to scream. She loved him, and she wanted him, even knowing her past might one day come back to bite her in the ass. But for him—for *them*—she was willing to take that chance.

Her palms grew sweaty. All other thought fled, and her head grew so light, she was afraid it might fly right off her shoulders.

She looked down at the cell phone in her hand, wanting, *needing* to text him back to tell him that she felt the same way. That she'd missed him more than she ever thought she could, that she was on her way to see him right this very moment…that she *couldn't freaking wait.* But before she could hit Reply, her phone buzzed.

"Mitch."

Excitement bubbled like champagne in her veins. She fumbled with the phone and pressed it to her ear. "Mitch?"

Silence, then… "No. It's William Holdt."

Every cell in Simone's body went cold. She hadn't heard that name in years. Hadn't expected to hear from him in just as long.

Sweat broke out on her forehead, but she worked to keep her voice calm. "Will? This is a surprise."

"I know." There was no humor in his voice. No friendliness either. The man who'd been in charge of Steve's relocation had always been at least cordial. "I'm sorry. I didn't mean for them to find out. I made a mistake. I trusted the wrong person. I thought enough time had passed."

"What are you talking about, Will? Who found out what?"

"*They* found out where you are."

All sound vanished. The terminal spun around Simone, travelers brushing by her in a whir. But she didn't see or hear or feel any of it. All she knew was an icy chill rushing straight down her spine.

"I'm sorry," Will whispered. "I—"

Distant voices echoed across the line, and Will shouted something, but it was muffled, and Simone couldn't tell what was going on. Seconds later, a thunk echoed, followed by a grunt and the sound of some kind of commotion.

"Will?"

Silence.

Fear clamped a frigid hand around Simone's throat and squeezed. "Will? Talk to me."

More silence. Her pulse beat fast and hard in her ears as she waited.

Finally, a scraping echoed, followed by Will's low voice. "If they come for it, don't give it to them. You remember what I told you, right? Don't forget it and you'll be okay."

The phone clicked dead in her ear.

Simone stared down at the cell in her hand. Disbelief raged like an inferno inside her. Hand shaking, she hit Redial. The line went straight to voice mail.

No.

No, no, no, no, no.

Air clogged in her lungs, and the terminal spun faster until she couldn't focus on a single thing.

Ten years. She'd gotten sloppy. She'd thought enough time had gone by and that no one would care where she was. That everything she'd gone through had buffered her from the past. But it hadn't. And now, when she was finally ready to start over with Mitch, that past was finally catching up with her. Threatening her one chance to be truly happy.

Shannon.

Her ten-year-old daughter's smiling face flashed behind her eyes and brought the spinning terminal to a standstill.

Her feet shuffled forward. One foot in front of the other, slowly at first, then faster until she was darting around passengers, heading for the exit. Only one thought revolved in her mind. Only one thing mattered.

She had to get to Shannon before they did.

Thanks for taking Shannon tonight." Mitch Mathews popped the top on the beer in his hand and took a long swallow.

"You owe me." Ryan Harrison scowled over his own bottle. "An extra kid in the house cramps my style. Now I have to wait to give Katie those padded handcuffs I got for her on my last trip to New York."

Mitch cringed. "God Almighty. Stop already. I don't want to know about your kinky sex life with my sister."

Ryan chuckled and moved from the kitchen counter toward the slider to look out where Shannon and Julia were swaying on the tire swing Mitch had hung from an old oak in his backyard. It was November in the Bay Area, but the weather had been unseasonably warm the past week, and thankfully, it wasn't raining, so the girls could be outside.

A slow smile spread across Ryan's face as he looked at the girls playing together, and without even asking, Mitch knew Ryan was thinking about his wife. He'd had that same sappy grin ever since Annie—now Kate, thanks to her amnesia and five years away—had come back into his life. Oh, he was still the same master-of-the universe, high-strung CEO and controlling son of a bitch he'd always been, but these days Ryan smiled more, he laughed more, and for the first time in years, he actually looked…happy.

Mitch eyed his cell phone on the counter, willing it to buzz, but it just sat there, cold and dark against the granite, mocking him with every look. He hadn't talked to Simone this morning, and for reasons he couldn't explain, he needed to know she was okay. She'd been in meetings all day, and her plane had landed in SFO—how pathetic was it that he tracked her flight?—but she had yet to text him. He knew she was probably just busy, but he couldn't stop thinking about how distracted she'd sounded on the phone last night. He'd just feel a thousand times better when he saw her and talked to her in person.

He glanced back toward Ryan looking like a stupid, sappy schmuck, and reached for the bottle again. Nerves bunched and rolled through his stomach as he took a long pull. Was that what he looked like when he was thinking about Simone? Shit, could Simone see it? Was that why she'd sounded so off last night? What if she wasn't ready?

He knew what it was like not to be ready. He was thirty-six years old and was just now at a point where he was willing to take a chance again. Simone knew how he felt about her and Shannon, but in the six months they'd been together, she hadn't once told him she loved him. Maybe it was too soon after her husband's death.

"Christ, Mathews." Ryan turned away from the window. "I can hear you stressing all the way over here. Give it a rest."

"I'm not stressing."

One corner of Ryan's lips curled. "Like an expectant father."

"Whoa. Back that train up. That's your department, numbnuts, not mine."

"You will soon."

Those nerves kicked up higher. Mitch downed the rest of his beer and glanced back at his phone. *Come on, already…ring!*

"She'll say yes," Ryan said in a quiet voice.

Mitch wasn't so sure. "She never does anything I expect her to do."

"Which is why you love her. Easy-going, brainless hotties don't interest you anymore."

Mitch frowned again and tossed his empty bottle into the recycle bin under the sink, then reached for another from the fridge. Ryan was right. And when the hell had that happened? He'd be way better off if he could just fall for a submissive, timid woman. But no, he had to go and take a header for a woman who liked to argue until she was blue in the face and was so damn independent he wasn't sure she'd ever truly need him the way he needed her.

He closed his eyes and drew in a steadying breath. Shit, he was in so far over his head he didn't know which way was up.

"I sure do like watching someone else being put through the wringer," Ryan said with a lift in his voice. "It's a nice change of pace."

Mitch raked a hand through his too-long hair. "I'm so glad I could entertain you. Now take these kids out of my house. I've got things to do before Simone gets here."

Ryan chuckled and pulled the slider open. "Girls, time to go."

The girls giggled and ran into the house. As they swept past Ryan and Mitch and grabbed Shannon's bag in the foyer, Ryan pulled the keys from his pocket and muttered, "Assuming you don't fuck things up tonight, Mathews, bring Simone over tomorrow morning, and we'll do brunch to celebrate the end of your bachelorhood."

If I don't fuck things up… And yeah, what if he did?

"Okay," Mitch managed, walking Ryan to the door, not wanting to think too much about that possibility.

The girls were already standing out front, waiting for Ryan to unlock the car. As soon as Mitch stepped outside, Shannon rushed over and wrapped her arms around Mitch's waist. "Good luck tonight. Don't let Mom get all lawyerly with you."

Shannon's words eased a place around Mitch's heart. He knelt down so they were eye to eye. He'd never wanted kids of his own, had never really dated any woman who had kids, but he was crazy about this ten-year-old girl with her wavy red hair and big brown eyes. And every time he thought about being her stepdad, a big ol' lump formed in his throat. "I'll do my best to argue our case."

Shannon grinned and slid her arms around his neck. "She's gonna love it. She's such a sucker for anything shiny."

She smelled liked cotton candy, and her hair was silky soft against his cheek. Mitch closed his arms around her. "I'll try to remember that. Be good for Ryan and Kate."

She eased out of his arms, waved, and ran down the path after Julia, who was already waiting in the back of Ryan's Mercedes.

Mitch pushed to his feet and waved back, feeling oddly nostalgic.

Just nerves.

Man, he needed to see Simone. To hold her and kiss her and lose himself in her sexy scent. Then everything would be good again.

Ryan clamped a hand on Mitch's shoulder, then slipped on his sunglasses and moved down a step. "You should get a haircut. Women don't like the scruffy look. And maybe shave for a change. You are trying to make a good impression, you know."

Mitch tucked his hands into the front pockets of his jeans and shot Ryan a look. "I'm not taking advice about women from you."

"Why not? I'm two for two on the whole proposal/marriage thing since your sister married me again. And zero divorces. You won't find better stats than that."

"Get the hell off my property. And don't lock my sister up in handcuffs," Mitch called as Ryan made his way down the front walk. "That's just freakin' wrong."

Ryan chuckled. "Good luck, buddy."

The girls waved wildly from the backseat while Ryan climbed into the car and started the ignition. And as they pulled away from the curb and headed down the street, Mitch had the strangest sensation that a small part of his heart was going right along with them.

Alone, all those nerves came slamming back. He closed his eyes and drew in a deep breath.

She had to say yes. She just had to.

Because he wasn't sure what he'd do if her answer was no.

CHAPTER TWO

Simone cut the engine of her Volvo outside Mitch's house in Pacifica and gripped the steering wheel. Panic made it hard to think—hard to breathe, for that matter—but she needed to keep it together and stay calm. It was the only way she was going to get through this.

After freaking out in her car, she'd finally relaxed enough to think through the steps she needed to complete. First and foremost was getting to Shannon. Common sense told her it had been ten years. If the "*they*" Steve had run from were really interested in finding her, they'd have tracked her down six months ago when she'd foolishly let the cameras catch her face during Kate and Ryan's press conference.

That had been a stupid move on her part. Though she'd known Kate's amnesia case was unique and that taking her on as a client would generate a little interest, she hadn't expected the firestorm that had erupted in the press when reporters had discovered that pharmaceutical tycoon Ryan Harrison's dead wife was really alive. Simone had known her face had been caught on camera—Ryan had been, after all, one of San Francisco's most eligible bachelor's— but no one had recognized her, and when weeks went by with zero threat or so much as an inquiry directed her way, she'd dropped her guard.

She wasn't dropping it now, though. Yes, she had time—no one was coming after her right this minute, were they?—but that didn't mean they weren't on their way. She'd already put her and Shannon's lives in jeopardy. She couldn't jeopardize Mitch's too.

Mitch…

Her eyes slid closed. A few hours ago, she'd been so excited, ready to take a chance and start over with him. Now…

Now that was nothing but a wasted dream. She didn't know where she was headed yet, but she knew she had to get out of San

Francisco. But just the thought of leaving caused her stomach to churn, made her chest cinch down tight, and sent a pounding ache straight behind her eyes.

She dropped her head against the steering wheel and focused on breathing. In and out. One breath at a time. And for a fleeting moment, she thought about telling Mitch a half-truth. That the "*they*" coming after her were disgruntled past clients, set on revenge. Only… She knew she could never do that. She'd never be able to live with herself if something happened to him because of Steve's past. And she was going to have a hard enough time keeping Shannon safe as it was.

Dammit… She'd known… She'd known not to get involved with anyone.

And damn Steve not only for dying on her, but for putting her in the middle of this nightmare to begin with.

Tears she wasn't going to let fall—not yet—burned behind her eyes. She had to stay focused on what to do next. Only when she knew Shannon was safe...then she'd let the emotions in.

She drew in a ragged breath, lifted her head, and peered across the lawn with its big trees toward Mitch's craftsman-style house. Lights burned in the front windows, and some kind of muffled music echoed from inside. Shannon had stayed with him while Simone had been in Washington, DC on business, and she'd known from the phone calls during the week that the two had had a ball together.

Her chest tightened even more. Someday, hopefully, she'd make him understand. But right now she just needed to make this as quick and painless as possible. The less he knew, the better off he'd be.

Like you?

She pushed the irony in that thought aside, drew in one last breath, then pushed the car door open and crossed the dimly lit street toward his front lawn. Since Mitch usually went in and out through the garage, she knew the front door was locked. Wishing it was open, she lifted her hand to knock, then waited for Shannon's excited voice to echo through the house.

The only sound that met her ears was a very familiar string melody.

Van Morrison. He was listening to the present she'd given him for his birthday last month. He was listening to the song she'd played when she'd given him his *other* birthday present: her, in the little red leather number she'd promised him months ago.

"These are the Days" slowly played out behind the door, and her heart contracted as she remembered the gleam in his eyes while she'd danced seductively around her bedroom in the ridiculously tight outfit. Followed by the frantic way he'd kissed her when she'd finally gotten close enough for him to grab.

Like a man starved. Like she was his everything. Like he'd never let her go.

She closed her eyes on a wave of emotion that burned everywhere. She wasn't going to be able to do this. She wasn't—

The door pulled open. Startled, Simone looked up. A slow and seductive smile spread across Mitch's rugged face, and in his eyes, a dark, rolling heat brewed. One she knew oh so well.

"Mitch—"

His arm snaked out around her waist and pulled her tight against him. And before she could catch her bearings, he slid his other hand into her hair, then lowered his mouth to hers.

Warmth. Safety. Bliss. She felt herself moving, felt him tugging her inside the house, kicking the door closed, and pressing her back against the hard wood. But all she could focus on was the way he all but devoured her whole with those sweet, tempting, masculine lips.

Desire and need—so much need—bloomed inside her. She opened on reflex, pressed her hands against his warm chest, and groaned when his tongue slid into her mouth. He tasted like wine. Like spice. Like the same damn hunger consuming her. Slowly, he changed the angle of the kiss, stroked his tongue against hers in a languid way, lifted both hands to gently cradle her face as if she were the most precious thing.

Thought fled. Reason disappeared. All she felt in the moment was wanted, desired, cherished.

He eased back slowly and stared down into her eyes. That slow, sexy, wicked smile she loved so much spread back over his lips. "Hi."

"H-hi."

He brushed his thumb across her oversensitized cheek. "I missed you."

She'd missed him too. So much more than she'd realized until this very moment. She swallowed hard, unable to move, to think, to do anything but stare into his fathomless eyes. "I-I see that."

Gently, he tipped her chin up again, kissed her lips delicately as if she were made of glass, then trailed his tantalizing mouth across her jaw to feather whisper-soft kisses against her earlobe. A shiver raced down her spine, and a moan slid from her lips before she could stop it, followed by her head tipping away, giving him more access.

"Mitch…"

The music in the overhead speakers shifted to the gentle notes of "Someone Like You." And then they were dancing, turning an easy circle through his entryway, moving smoothly down the hardwood floor toward his great room.

Her hands inched up his chest. His mouth found hers again. He was wearing her favorite black T-shirt and the faded denim jeans he'd worn the first night they'd met, when she'd agreed to have drinks to talk about his sister. Memories spiraled in as his tongue brushed hers again, as his hips pressed against her belly, as his knee slid between her thighs.

"Mitch…"

"God, you taste good," he murmured against her mouth, continuing to gently move her to the beat of the hypnotic music. He was so damn sexy, so hot, so *hers*, and the way he moved… He took her breath away. "I've been looking for someone exactly like you," he whispered, echoing the song. "Just you."

Her heart swelled, and she gave herself over to his mouth, his hands, his incredibly wicked touch. Her fingers slid into the silky soft tendrils at the nape of his neck, pulling him closer so she could kiss him deeper. He answered by tightening his arms around her waist until his erection pressed into her belly.

Yes, yes, this. Just this.

She had the vague impression of candlelight, of flames flickering in the fireplace across the room, but all she could focus on was him. Only him.

The music faded way before she was ready to let it go, and as the song ended and he eased away once more, she saw the pleasure in his eyes, the happiness, and the relief. Relief that she was back and finally in his arms.

Reality spiraled in. A cold slap she wanted to ignore but couldn't. Her hands trailed down to his biceps, and she swallowed hard, hating what she knew was coming next. After the greeting he'd just given her—after the way she'd reacted—how could she walk away from him?

"Wh-where is Shannon?" she managed, looking down at his chest so she didn't have to see those gorgeous eyes. Eyes she knew were going to haunt her for a very long time.

"Spending the night with Julia. I want you all to myself."

That was all she wanted too—him, all to herself. But she couldn't have him. Not now. And oh God, Shannon wasn't even here. Her eyes slid closed, and pain lanced through her chest.

"Hey," he whispered, concern replacing the sexy timbre of his voice. "What's wrong?"

Indecision roared while she fought back the tears. Maybe she should just tell him the truth. But if she did…she'd be putting him at so much risk.

"The less you know, the better off you'll be. Trust me."

How many times had Steve said that to her? Too many to count. She understood why he'd done that now, but it didn't make what she had to do any easier.

Her stomach rolled, and that pain grew sharper.

Focus. Plan. Execute.

She mentally repeated the words and pushed out of his arms. Words that had gotten her through the agony of leaving her old life behind. Words that had saved her after Steve's death. Words she would depend on now. His brow dropped when she pulled away, but she ignored it and gathered her courage, pulling up every wall he'd worn down over the last six months.

Behind him, she spotted the table set for a romantic dinner for two, and noticed, for the first time, the delicious Italian scents in the air.

He'd cooked. *Shit.* The man never cooked.

She quickly looked away from his manly kitchen with its black granite counter and cherry cabinets and refocused on him. Then realized he'd shaved—something else he didn't often like to do. His wavy hair had that sexy tousled look where she'd run her fingers through it, and he was barefoot.

Her walls started to crumble. Why the hell were his feet so damn sexy?

Focus. Plan. Execute.

Right. She could do that. She straightened.

"Simone?" He reached for her hand, but she took a step back so he couldn't touch her. If he touched her, like he'd done at the door, she'd never get through this. And she had to get it done and over with so she could get to Shannon.

"I'm leaving, Mitch."

"What? You just got here."

"I don't just mean right now. I mean…I'm leaving San Francisco."

Panic filled his eyes. Panic that was going to wear her down if she didn't get out of fast.

"My dad isn't doing well," she lied. "Shannon and I are moving back to Connecticut."

"Okay," he said slowly.

Okay? Her own panic slithered in.

He raked a hand through his hair, sending his already disheveled locks sticking out all over, and looked down at the floor. She could practically see the gears working in his brain, trying to figure out how they were going to make this work on opposite coasts.

His gaze lifted to hers, and he reached for her hand. Strong, steady, everything she wanted but couldn't lean on. "Tell me what you need me to do. I'm here for you."

She didn't want him to be there for her. Not now. Not when she knew what it could cost him.

She pulled her fingers from his and moved out of his reach once more. "I don't want you to do anything. I just wanted you to know."

"Simone—"

He stepped toward her, and she moved back again. "I've thought about this a lot, and this is the right decision for me and Shannon."

"For Shannon? Look, I understand needing to be with your family if your dad's sick. If my dad was in trouble, I'd be the first one on a plane to Seattle, but permanently uprooting Shannon isn't the answer."

"You don't know what's right for Shannon."

He held up both hands to calm her down, and she knew her voice was starting to rise, but she couldn't stop it. "I'd never tell you what's best for Shannon, I'm just saying…there's no reason to do something drastic. I can take some time off from work. We can all head to your parents' place. Ryan can get someone to look after your house."

"Mitch… No."

Confusion swirled in his eyes. "Why not? Simone, talk to me. I'm here for you. What's really going on?"

She stepped back when he moved toward her. Her mind spun. Sweat broke out all over her body. She couldn't seem to think clearly. And she hated that he was pushing her toward doing something she didn't want to do. Toward saying something she didn't want to say.

"It's not... I can't..." She brushed both hands through her hair and dropped them. "I never wanted this. I told you I don't do relationships. It's too much responsibility."

"Okay. Okay," he said, holding up his hands again. "Just...relax for a minute. I'm not trying to push you. I'm just trying to help."

But he wasn't. Couldn't he see that? She looked up at him. Saw the rolling emotions in his eyes. And in the silence between them, her heart broke. Just cracked and shattered at her feet, because she knew she wasn't going to be able to make this break clean and easy like she wanted. She was going to have to hurt him to ensure he didn't try to follow her.

"Mitch, I'm not changing my mind. Simone and I are leaving. I only came here tonight to say good-bye."

"Good-bye," he repeated in a low voice. "And you don't care what I have to say about it?"

"No, I don't. This doesn't have anything to do with you."

In the seconds that followed, she watched his eyes harden, his jaw clench, and his hand drop to his side as the reality of what she was saying finally sank in. "So that's it. You're leaving for good. No discussion."

She swallowed hard and told herself this was the only way. "No. I mean, yes. No discussion."

"All because your dad's sick?" Disbelief flashed in his eyes. "I don't get it. What's *really* going on? This isn't like you, Simone. There's something you're not telling me."

There were a thousand things she wasn't telling him, but he was better off not knowing. *Like a Band-Aid. Rip it off.*

"This is what's going on."

"Don't lie to me. Just tell me the truth. You owe me that much."

Every emotion she'd been fighting back slammed into her, forcing her voice higher and her nerves humming. "You want to know what's really going on? Here it is. I had a husband, Mitch. I'm not looking for another. I should have ended this a long time ago because I knew you wanted more, only I didn't because I was selfish. I liked being with you. But this last week I realized…it's too much. I don't want you to be Shannon's father, I don't want to play house, and I don't want to have to worry about you when I make decisions. This situation…with my parents… It just reinforced this is the perfect time to end things before either of us gets any more involved in something that never should have started."

His eyes narrowed. "So earlier, when you kissed me—"

"That was physical," she said quickly, desperate now to get this over. "Physical between us has always been good. It's just everything else that's not working for me."

Hurt flashed in his gorgeous green eyes. "Physical," he repeated. "That didn't feel like physical to me. That felt like a whole lot more."

It felt like a whole lot more to her too, only she couldn't tell him that now. She swallowed hard. Knowing there was one thing she could say that would end things for good. Only saying it…

Bile pushed up her throat. *Oh God…*

She swallowed hard. "I'm sorry but I just…" *Shit.* "I don't…love you, Mitch, not the way you want me to."

His face paled, and he took a big step back. Wiping one hand across his mouth, he rested the other on his hip and looked quickly away.

And in the silence, the pain of a thousand burning suns scorched through her, because the sick look rushing over his features wasn't one of just shock, it was pure and utter betrayal.

"Ouch," he said after several seconds. "That hurt more than I expected. You, ah, sure know how to drop the gavel, Counselor. You should have been a judge."

Pinpricks of heat stabbed at every inch of Simone's body. *No, no, no. I lied. I take it back!* Thoughts spun out of control and mixed with emotions she hadn't expected to feel. She had to do something to make this better. She had to fix this before it was too late. She stepped toward him. "Mitch—"

"Don't." He moved back and held up a hand, this time to stop *her* from touching *him*. "I, ah, I get it. Loud and clear. You don't have to say it more than once."

A sob pushed up her throat. It wasn't supposed to be like this. She had to tell him the truth. She didn't care if it was breaking the rules or if it put her in more danger. Admitting she wasn't who he thought didn't even compare to the pain of knowing he believed she didn’t love him.

"Mitch." She’d been so careful not to say the words these past few months. Afraid of losing control, of giving up a part of herself. Now… Now she wished she’d said them a hundred times so he’d know she was lying. “Wait—”

He gripped a kitchen chair and moved behind it, putting it and the table between them so she couldn’t touch him. “You need to leave, Simone.”

She faltered, and panic spread through her. A desperate need to make him understand urged her forward. “Mitch—”

His head swiveled her way. He gripped the chair back with both hands, his knuckles turning white. But when his eyes locked on hers, she drew up short. Hard, cold, blazing eyes. Eyes she’d never seen before. “Are you deaf? I said get out!”

A buzzer went off in the kitchen, and Simone startled. It took several seconds to realize it was the timer on the oven.

Dinner. The romantic dinner he’d made for her was ready. He didn’t break eye contact, didn’t move to turn off the timer. In the silence between them, candlelight flickered off his hard jaw and chiseled face, and she realized she’d been wrong. She’d spent the last hour worrying what he’d think of her when he learned about her past. What she should have been afraid of was this. What it would feel like when he hated her.

A chill swept over her body, and heartache lanced through every cell. In a daze, she stepped back, then turned for the hallway, her pulse a roar in her ears that drowned out Van Morrison’s voice as he sang about crazy love.

Hand shaking, she found the doorknob and somehow managed to get outside. Cool air whooshed around her when she stepped onto the front porch. The door slammed at her back, and as the sound echoed in her ears, the dam finally broke. Every emotion she’d held back since Will’s call flooded in and knocked the wind right out of her body.

She covered her mouth with her hand to keep from screaming and ran for her car. She’d done exactly what she’d planned when she’d left the airport. But she hadn’t expected it to burn like this.

A burn, she now knew, that would leave a scar she’d carry with her forever.

CHAPTER THREE

Mitch waited until the sound of Simone's car faded into the darkness before he let go of the chair.

His body vibrated as if an electrical current ran through it. Crossing the room, he punched off the stereo so he didn't have to listen to Van Morrison's fucking voice anymore, then moved into the kitchen and flipped off the oven.

The special dinner he'd made forgotten, he grabbed a glass and the Jamison he kept above the stove. After walking into his living room, he poured a generous shot and downed it in one long gulp, then stared into the flickering flames of the fire.

"I don't love you."

Anger and stupidity whipped through him, so hot it singed every vein. He dropped the bottle on the coffee table, then hurled the tumbler toward the fireplace, a perfect pitch that shattered the glass against the bricks into a thousand pieces and did shit to calm the storm raging inside. Body still humming, he extinguished every candle he'd lit to set a romantic mood, flipped off the lights, and stalked upstairs to his bedroom.

Everywhere he looked, he saw Simone. Lying across his bed, smiling that sexy grin. Sitting on the counter in his bathroom, watching while he shaved. Perched on the window seat in his bedroom, wearing his favorite Mariner's T-shirt and nothing else, her dark hair a sexy mess around her face, her lips swollen from his mouth, her eyes wicked and seductive as she crooked her index finger and tried to coax him to come her way.

Holy hell, he was such a moron. He'd been so head over heels in love with her, he'd completely ignored the signs. The way she refused to talk about the future. The way she wouldn't discuss her feelings. The fact he'd had to argue like a freakin' lawyer just to get her to leave Shannon with him for the week. And the kicker—the giant neon warning sign he should have clued in to long ago—the fact she'd never once told him she loved him.

His legs gave out, just dropped him on his ass on the carpet like a big ol' wuss. And his chest cinched down so tight it stole his breath.

Holy shit. *This* was why he was still single. Because nothing in the world was worth the pain currently stabbing through every inch of his body.

The future rolled out in front of him like a long, unending carpet while he braced his hands on his knees and sat there for…he didn't know how long…just trying to breathe. Not a future with a family of his own like he'd envisioned this morning, but him alone, as he'd been for years. Looking out for the only thing that mattered: himself.

He needed to get the hell out of San Francisco. He had to get away from the memories before he lost it for good.

Before he could change his mind, he pushed to his feet, crossed to his closet, and yanked out his bag. He didn't pay attention to what he pulled from the hangers, just stuffed clothes inside, then went into his bathroom and gathered his toiletries. After throwing on his boots, he came back into the bedroom and bent to zip his bag. Something sharp poked into his hip.

Slowly, he reached in his pocket and pulled out the ring, then just stared at the shimmering diamond. Another wave of agony washed through him, but this one was quickly followed by a burst of anger at his own gullibility.

There were very few things in life a man could control. His heart, however, was one of them.

Fuck relationships. And most definitely, fuck happily ever after.

He grabbed his bag and headed for the door.

Laughter echoed from inside Ryan and Kate's house in the Sausalito hills. Simone's pulse beat hard and fast as she stood on the porch, knocked on the door, and waited.

Tears still threatened, but she swiped at her cheeks to clear away the remnants of her breakdown in the car and worked up an impassive expression.

The door pulled open, but one look was all it took for Simone to realize she hadn't done a thing to fool anyone.

"Simone?" Ryan asked. "What's wrong?"

Oh no. She wasn't going to lose it in front of him too. "Nothing," she said quickly. "I just came to get Shannon."

"Katie!" Ryan yelled, swiveling his head toward the hall. Then to Simone, softer, "Come inside."

Simone pushed the hair back from her forehead as she stepped into the foyer of Ryan's big house. Kate's voice echoed from the direction of the kitchen, followed by girlish giggles. Her skin prickled with heat. All she wanted was get to Shannon and get the hell out of here.

"What happened?" Ryan asked, closing the door behind her.

"Nothing." She didn't want to get into it with him. Not only was Ryan Mitch's brother-in-law, they were best friends; had been since college. "Everything's fine. I-I just need Shannon."

"Simone?" Kate's concerned voice from the hall brought Simone's head around. Her friend's worried eyes darted from her to Ryan and back again.

Shit. She was going to lose it if she didn't leave now. "I just came to get Shannon."

"But I thought—"

"It's okay," Ryan said quickly. "Simone, I'll go grab Shannon's stuff."

He squeezed Kate's arm as he passed, heading for the great room at the back of the house, where the girls were laughing.

Stepping close, Kate rested both hands on Simone's upper arms. "What happened? What did that brother of mine do to upset you like this?"

"Nothing." Simone shook her head and swiped at her cheek. Dammit, she felt like she'd cried more in the last hour than she had in the previous year. "He didn't do anything. It was me. It was all me."

"Oh, Simone," Kate said softly.

Okay, that was it. As much as she could take. Her talk with Will, the scene with Mitch… It all came barreling in and robbed her of what little strength she had left. "I can't talk about it. I just need Shannon."

"Sure. Whatever you need. We're here for you."

Ryan came back down the hall with Shannon's bag. Shannon followed quickly at his heels, along with Julia, and the two were speaking quickly, obviously curious about what was going on. But the moment Shannon spotted her mother in the entry, her entire face fell, and her feet faltered.

No *I missed you, Mom!* No *I'm so glad to see you!* Just hard dark eyes, so much like Steve's, staring back at her. The kid obviously knew something had happened. She was way too perceptive. And she'd already lived through way more than any ten-year-old should have to experience.

"I thought Shannon was going to spend the night?" Julia asked, looking from one adult to the other.

Thankfully, before Simone could think of something to say, Kate forced a smile and looked down at her daughter, then to Shannon. "Not tonight. Shannon's mom missed her. We have lots of time for sleepovers. We'll just reschedule. Shannon, are your shoes in the front closet?"

"Yeah," Shannon mumbled, but she didn't look Kate's way. Her gaze was fixed solidly on Simone, and it was filled with both frustration and disappointment.

I'm doing this for you Simone wanted to shout but knew it would do no good. She'd let everyone down today, and she couldn't handle one more confrontation. At least not right now. "Say thank you, Shannon." She took the bag from Ryan. Then she turned toward Kate. "I'll call you."

But would she? Probably not. The lies were coming so easily now.

Kate gave her a quick hug. "I'm here for you. Whatever you need."

Tears threatened again, so Simone pulled quickly out of her friend's arms and turned for the door. She was aware of voices behind her, but she didn't care what they were saying. She couldn't. Not anymore.

She climbed into the car while that depressing thought sank in and waited for Shannon to slide into the front seat and latch her seat belt. She knew Kate and Ryan were standing on the front porch looking after her, wondering what had happened, but she didn't look back. Shoving the car into Drive, she pulled away from the curb and didn't glance at her daughter either. If she did, she was afraid she'd break. And she'd already broken way too many times today.

They drove in silence back toward the city. Lights rushed by as they crossed the Golden Gate Bridge. Only when they were over the water and heading up the steadily rising hills did Shannon finally shift in her seat to Simone's right.

"You said no, didn't you?"

Simone's pulse picked up speed, and she chanced a look at her daughter. "No? Said no to what?"

Shannon crossed her arms over her chest and looked straight ahead. But in the dim lights from the dash, Simone caught the hint of tears in her daughter's eyes. "I knew you'd say no. You always mess everything up."

Suddenly, the music, the candles, the special dinner Mitch had prepared, and the reason he'd arranged for Shannon to spend the night with Julia suddenly made sense.

No. *No, no, no…* He was going to propose tonight?

A sob pushed its way up Simone's throat, and she pursed her lips to hold it back while she focused on driving through the blur of tears filling her eyes. This wasn't happening. This wasn't her life. In a matter of hours, she couldn't possibly have managed to mess everything up so very badly.

Shannon rolled toward the passenger window and rested her head against the seat. "Sometimes, I wish you weren't my mom."

Simone blinked again and again and gripped the wheel, unable to even think of a single thing to ease her daughter's pain.

Because Shannon was right. She deserved a mother who wasn't a complete and utter mess.

Ryan."

"I know." Ryan wrapped his arms around his wife and pulled her close on the front porch of their house, not knowing exactly what had happened between Mitch and Simone, but so very thankful it wasn't happening to him. "She'll be okay."

"She's not the one I'm worried about," Katie whispered.

No, Simone wasn't the one Ryan was worried about either. Simone was one of the strongest women Ryan had ever met. She could handle anything life threw her way. And even though she looked like she'd just had the wind knocked out of her, he was pretty sure she'd pick herself up and keep right on going, just like she'd always done. Mitch was another story.

He rubbed his hand down Katie's back and glanced over her shoulder. Julia stood just beyond the open door in the entry, watching them with worry and a whole host of questions brewing in her eyes. From the direction of the great room, Reed's laughter echoed. He was still watching the movie, oblivious to everything that had just happened.

Ryan nodded for Julia to go back into the house with her brother.

She frowned but was smart enough to listen. Though she was old enough to know what was going on, he didn't want to talk about her uncle in front of her. The two had a special relationship, one he didn't want tainted by any of this.

The door closed softly behind Julia, and Ryan drew back from Katie, looking down into her soft green eyes. "I'll go check on Mitch."

"I should go with you."

He brushed his thumb across her silky cheek. "I can guarantee he won't like that."

"But—"

"I know a thing or two about how a guy's feeling when he's just lost everything, babe." When her eyes darkened, he added softly, "Trust me on this. He's not going to want to talk to you or anyone else. I've been where he's at."

"Oh, Ryan."

She moved back into him, wrapped her arms around his waist, and pressed her face against his chest. And as he held her tight, her heat seeping in to warm him from the outside in, he remembered all those years after he thought she'd died, when he'd wanted to die himself just to get rid of the pain. The only thing that had saved him was Julia. Mitch had no one.

He pressed his lips against her temple and told himself this was different. And Mitch was a thousand times stronger than Ryan had ever been. "Whatever happened, he'll be okay," he whispered, more for his own peace of mind than for hers. "If I survived losing you, he can survive this."

She leaned back and looked up, but her expression said she wasn't so sure.

Mitch had a gentle heart. Though he acted like he didn't give a shit about most things, they both knew it wasn't true.

Ryan tucked a lock of curly hair behind his wife's ear and kissed her lips. Lips he once thought he'd never taste again. Lips he was thankful for every single day. "Wait up for me?"

"Always." Her hand slid down his arm as he moved away, clasping his fingers when they reached hers, then finally letting go.

God, he loved that woman. More every day. So much more than when he'd married her the first time. Pulling the keys from his pocket, he crossed the yard toward his car in the drive and thanked God all over again that she'd come back to him.

Mitch's house was dark when Ryan pulled onto his street thirty minutes later. A wave of foreboding washed over him as he killed the engine.

The front door opened, and Mitch stepped out, a bag slung over his shoulder, keys in his hands. He took one look at Ryan's Mercedes and scowled.

Shit. That was not a good sign.

Ryan parked at the curb, popped the door, and climbed out of the car. Mitch was already at the back of his dusty Land Rover parked in the drive, throwing a bag in the back when Ryan reached him. "I don't need a babysitter, Harrison."

Yep, definitely didn't want to talk. Ryan tucked his hands into his pockets. "Going somewhere?"

Mitch tossed his winter coat into the back, then slamming the back shut. "British Columbia."

"I thought they didn't need you at the job site just yet?"

Mitch huffed, a humorless sound. "They needed me three weeks ago. I just kept putting it off."

Because of Simone. The unsaid words hung between them. Dammit, if Mitch was running, things were worse than Ryan had suspected. "Mitch—"

"Don't." Mitch raked a hand through his already wild hair. "I'm not in the mood. And no, I don't want to fucking talk about it."

Oh yeah. Definitely worse.

Mitch drew a deep breath. "Look, I don't know how long I'll be gone, but if you'd have someone check on the house now and then, I'd appreciate it."

"Sure. You know that's no problem."

Mitch looked at him. Seemed to want to say something else, but turned and headed for the driver's side of his vehicle instead.

Ryan moved around the side of the car as Mitch pulled the door open. And though he knew he shouldn't push, he couldn't help himself. Because Mitch had been there for him all those years after he'd lost his wife. If it hadn't been for Mitch's pushing, Ryan wouldn't be where he was now. "Are you gonna be okay?"

"Me?" Mitch stood with one hand on the open car door. "Sure. I'm always okay. Haven't you figured that out yet?"

Before Ryan could call him on the bullshit he was spewing, Mitch pulled something from his pocket and tossed it Ryan's way. "There is one more thing you can do for me. Get rid of that. I don't want to see it again."

Ryan caught the small velvet box with both hands.

Mitch climbed into his Land Rover and slammed the door. He backed out of the drive, his headlights casting a wide path of light over the dark neighborhood. When he reached the street, he shifted into Drive, glanced once toward Ryan but didn't wave. And there was no missing the anger and pain swirling in his eyes as he pressed down on the gas.

The car disappeared around the bend. Alone, Ryan popped the top on the box and stared down at the princess-cut diamond—the one that had to have set Mitch back at least three months' worth of his salary—sparkling under the light of the full moon.

CHAPTER FOUR

Are you sure?" Shannon rolled to her belly on the queen-size bed in her room and lowered her voice to just above a whisper. "This totally isn't going to work."

"Trust me," Julia said on the other end of the line, all confidence and maturity. Maturity, Shannon did *not* have. "No one's going to catch on unless you act like a baby."

Shannon glanced toward the open door. She could hear Melody, her babysitter, opening and closing drawers in the kitchen, making dinner, which meant for the moment, at least, she was safe. She really hoped Melody was making mac and cheese and not that healthy stuff her mom was always forcing her to eat.

She pushed up to sitting, crossed her long legs, and cradled the phone between her ear and shoulder. Her pink nail polish was chipped away from gnawing on her fingers, and her pants had a hole in the knee where she'd picked at the loose threads. "No one's ever going to believe I'm twelve."

"They will if you act like it. Look." Julia huffed. "You're ten now, which is practically eleven, which almost the same as twelve. And you're tall."

Shannon sighed, but inside, her stomach was a knot of nerves. She didn't have Julia's confidence or worldliness. One look and the TSA officials were going to call her mom and tell on her. Or maybe worse…send her to airport jail for lying. "What about security?"

"Security's a snap. You don't check a bag, you print your boarding pass at home, and when you get to the front of the line, you just pick someone in the crowd waving to a family member leaving, and wave back. If security asks, you just say 'That's my mom.'"

It sounded foolproof, but Shannon wasn't convinced. "What if no one's waving?"

"Someone's always waving," Julia said. "It's a huge airport. Besides, if the security guys ask, all you have to do is say 'Of course I'm twelve. Do you think my parents are stupid enough to send me on a plane by myself without a chaperone if I wasn't?'"

This all sounded so complicated. Shannon bit her lip, and her palm grew sweaty against the phone in her hand.

"Where's your mom?" Julia asked.

Shannon shot a look toward the hall again. She could just see the banister on the curved staircase and the dozens of framed photos hanging on the two-story wall. Ones of her and her mom and her dad and a time when they'd been a happy family and her mom hadn't been a giant stress case all the time. "At her office. She went in for a few hours to do some kind of work."

"How long will she be there?"

"I don't know. She arranged for Melody to spend the night. Said she might be there most of the night. She's been crying all day while she's been packing."

"Definitely not a good sign."

No, it definitely wasn't. Shannon's mom wasn't a crier. Even after her dad had died, Shannon could only remember a handful of times her mom had gotten teary-eyed. That ball of nerves twisted tighter.

"There's a flight out of SFO at ten p.m. Do you think you'll be able to get there in time?"

Shannon's stomach rolled. "Yeah. Melody spends most of the time on her phone with her boyfriend. If I tell her I'm tired and going to bed early, she won't care."

She'd need to have her backpack all ready and call a cab from her cell phone. And she'd have to walk across the park in the dark, which her mom *never* let her do. Those nerves jumped all over again.

"Put a pile of pillows under your covers," Julia said. "Make it look like you're sleeping."

That was what Shannon had planned to do. But saying it out loud made it all so real. "Julia, I don't know if this is a good idea. What if…?"

"No 'what ifs,' Shannon. Whatever happened between Uncle Mitch and your mom was bad if your mom's been crying. You have to do something drastic to get their attention."

Shannon knew that was true. Especially since Mitch had left without saying good-bye. Her heart pinched, and all the fears that had kept her awake last night came spiraling back. What if he'd decided he didn't want a kid after all? She wasn't cute like she'd been as a baby. She was just long-legged and gangly. And she had a big red bump on her chin. Mitch probably didn't want a daughter who had pimples.

Fear pushed in strong, making it hard to breathe. "How do I know he'll even be there?"

"Trust me. He'll be there. My dad's friend Tate called this morning. He and my dad and Uncle Mitch all went to college together. He's got this great big house up in the San Juan Islands. And he's super cute. I heard my parents talking about Uncle Mitch before breakfast. He showed up at Tate's house late last night, got drunk, and passed out. He's obviously moping about whatever happened with your mom."

Shannon couldn't picture Mitch moping. Or drunk. In all the months her mom and Mitch had been dating, she'd never seen him have more than two beers at any one time. "I don't know, Julia—"

"Look. Do you want to move away forever and never see me again?"

Shannon's belly clenched. "No."

"Don't you want Uncle Mitch to be your dad?"

More than anything. Shannon's pulse picked up speed, and all those daydreams she'd had about having a dad again popped back into her head. Her gaze strayed to the picture of her real dad on her nightstand. She loved him—always would—but he'd been gone so long, sometimes she forgot what he looked like, and she couldn't even remember what his voice sounded like anymore. She wanted to be like the other kids at school. The ones with dads who took them to baseball games and amusement parks and who were always telling them to do their homework. All the things Mitch did when she spent time with him.

Tears filled her eyes. "Yes."

"Then you have to do something to get them back together. Trust me, this plan will totally work if you follow my directions. Uncle Mitch just needs a kick in the butt. Now, get a pen. When you get to Seattle, you'll need to take a taxi and then a ferry. The ferries in Seattle are just like the ones here. I'm gonna tell you which one will take you to Tate's house. But just remember, he's mine, so hands off. Once I'm old enough, I'm gonna marry the guy."

Julia's bluntness eased the sting around Simone's heart, just a little, just enough so Shannon didn't freak out. "Don't you think your dad with tell you no?"

"Duh. I'm not telling him until right before the wedding. He'd have a cow if he knew. Tate's like a bazillion years older than me. But he's rich and he sings and he's really cute for an old guy. And he thinks I'm cool. He says so every time we see him. Okay, I'm going to book this ticket."

Shannon's nerves hummed again. "How am I going to pay for it?"

"I've got you covered. I swiped my dad's credit card. Do you have enough cash for taxis and Kit Kats?"

Between what she'd pulled from her piggy bank and the slush fund her mom kept in the cookie jar, Shannon figured she had plenty. Or, at least, she hoped. "Yeah."

"Okay, grab a pen then."

For a moment, Shannon thought she was going to be sick. They were going to get in so much trouble when their parents found out what they'd done. But she climbed off the bed and picked up a pencil and notepad from her desk like Julia said. She didn't care about getting in trouble. She didn't care about this Tate person Julia couldn't stop talking about. She just wanted to see Mitch. And convince him she'd be the most perfect daughter ever if he'd just give her mom a second chance.

"Okay, I have it."

"Good. Now write this down. When you get off the plane at Sea-Tac, head for baggage claim…"

Simone tossed her keys on the entry table in her foyer and rubbed her tired eyes. They hurt, not just because she hadn't slept in over twenty-four hours, but from crying. She had to get a handle on these useless emotions. She was not an emotional woman. She'd learned the hard way that tears never fixed anything.

She glanced up the dark stairs toward the second floor. No sound. Shannon was—thankfully—fast asleep. It was close to two in the morning. She'd been at the office wrapping up her current cases, getting everything together to transfer to her partners. She felt bad about leaving them in the lurch, but her daughter's safety was more important than any job. And she still had enough cash in the bank from Steve's life insurance policy for her and Shannon to start over somewhere else.

The thought of running sent her stomach swirling, but she took a deep breath and ignored it. Quietly, she moved down the hall toward the great room. She was going to miss this house. It was the first place that had felt like home in a very long time.

Melody lifted her head from the pillow on the couch and pushed up, rubbing her tired eyes. "You're back."

"Yeah." Simone looked toward the muted TV, flickering images of a rerun of *The Simpsons*, then glanced back at the seventeen-year-old. "I'm sorry I'm so late. Is everything okay?"

"Yeah, fine. No problems."

Simone breathed a sigh of relief. Will's phone call echoed in her mind, and she reminded herself if something bad was imminent, he would have urged her to grab Shannon and run. The fact he hadn't told her she had time. Not that she was pushing that luck, but it meant she didn't have to disappear right on the spot. Yet. "How's Shannon?"

"Fine. She went to bed around eight. Said she was really tired. I checked on her once. She was sound asleep and didn't even move when her door creaked."

Shannon slept like the dead. When she was exhausted, nothing could rouse that kid. And considering she hadn't slept much the night before, it made sense tonight she'd be zonked out.

Simone smiled weakly, hating the reason her daughter hadn't slept. Hating even more that she was hurting as much as Simone. "It's late. Why don't you just spend the night?"

Melody reached for her shoes from the floor. "No, that's okay. I told my folks I'd be late, so they're expecting me. And it's only a few blocks, anyway."

A whisper of relief passed through Simone. Being responsible for one more person was a burden she was thankful not to have to bear tonight. "Okay. If you're sure."

She waited while Melody gathered her things—backpack, laptop, cell phone, charger—the girl traveled with an entire mini office. After walking her to the door, Simone handed her the cash—and a big tip. "Can you come by on Friday? I'll be packing all day, and I'm sure Shannon would love the company."

"Sure thing. I'll see you then. Just text me the time."

Simone watched the teen climb in her car and drive off, then closed the door. Turning, she looked down the dark hall.

A tension headache kicked up behind her eyes. She pressed shaky fingers to her temples and told herself to stay calm. *Focus on the most important things.* Like where the hell she and Shannon were going to go. Maybe they should head north, to Washington, or perhaps northeast, toward Montana. Shannon probably wouldn't mind seeing snow again.

God, Simone hated snow.

Thoughts spun out of control as she forced her feet up the stairs. She wasn't going to sleep again tonight, she could already tell. Every second she stayed here was one more second they were closer to finding her. And she wasn't about to let that happen.

She stopped at Shannon's bedroom door, cracked it open an inch, and gently pushed. The heavy wood creaked, and she peaked inside. Her daughter lay curled under a pile of blankets, so many Simone couldn't even see that telltale red hair that was just like her father's.

A sigh escaped her lips. Shannon was still so mad at her. They hadn't talked much since she'd picked Shannon up from Ryan and Kate's, and she knew her daughter was hurting over the fact Mitch had cut and run, but Simone couldn't do anything about that now. Someday, though, hopefully, Shannon would understand why she'd done everything. Someday maybe Mitch would too.

She pushed thoughts of the man who'd distracted her way too much over the last few months from her mind and crossed soundlessly to Shannon's queen-size bed. The mattress sagged when she sat, and love for a daughter she'd never even wanted warmed the cold space in her chest.

"I love you, Nannon," she said softly, using the nickname Steve had given Shannon because she hadn't been able to say her own name until she was three. "Even if you don't think I do. We have to stick together, baby. Everything always turns out okay when we do."

She ran her hand over the lump beneath the covers. But instead of the hard shoulder she expected to touch, her hand sank into softness.

"What the…?" She tugged the blanket back and stared down at a lump of pillows.

A gasp ripped from her chest, and Simone pushed to her feet. Scenarios—mostly bad—filled her mind.

They'd been here. They'd taken her daughter. Panic dragged the air from her chest. She'd wasted valuable time at the office when she should have just grabbed Shannon and run.

A shimmer of white on the floor caught her attention, and she stopped feet from the door. Leaning forward, she picked up the folded sheet of paper and opened it.

Her daughter's curvy handwriting was scrawled across the page. A sixteen-digit number was separated into four groups. A credit card number, she realized. Followed by an expiration date. And below that, times. One next to the word "out." The other beside "fairy."

Her chest rose and fell with her quick breaths while she tried to make sense of what she was reading. Fairy…fairy… Shannon was a terrible speller. Had she meant to write ferry?

Oh holy God…

She was running away? Because she was so miserable? Because Simone was such a horrible mother? No, that couldn't be. Simone stared at the number again. She didn't recognize it, which meant it wasn't hers. And Shannon didn't even know how to use a credit card. Besides, she wouldn't be stupid enough to run off by herself right now when they were packing to move, not without…

Everything inside Simone went cold. And in her mind, links clicked into place.

Not without help.

Did you hear that?" Kate lifted her head from the pillow and looked toward the door.

Beside her, Ryan tossed a leg over her thigh and wrapped his hand around her waist. "I don't hear anything. But since you woke me at this hour…"

He nuzzled her neck and pressed his rapidly growing erection against her hip. Tingles spread through Kate's entire body, but the banging from somewhere downstairs overrode her simmering desire. She pushed against his shoulder. "That. You heard it that time, didn't you?"

He stilled, lifted his head. When it happened again, his handsome features tightened. "That time I did."

He tossed back the covers and tugged on the pajama bottoms she'd yanked off him only hours ago. "Stay here."

Like that was happening.

Kate glanced toward the bedside clock as he jerked their bedroom door open and disappeared down the stairs—2:35 a.m. Pulling on her own T-shirt and pajama bottoms, she followed.

Cool air spilled into the entry hall. Ryan's concerned voice floated up the stairs. "What's wrong?"

A flustered and windblown Simone swept into the house. "I called several times, but you didn't answer. Is Shannon here?"

"Shannon?" Kate moved from carpet on the stairs to tile in the foyer. Light from the chandelier cascaded over her friend's messy dark hair. Simone's jacket hung off one shoulder, her eyes were red and bloodshot, and Kate was pretty sure the usually calm and collected attorney was wearing two different colored shoes. "No. Is she supposed to be? We haven't seen her all day. What's happened?"

"I don't know." Simone lifted her arms, then dropped them on a huff. "I think she might have run off. We had an argument last night, and today I've been at the office getting everything finalized. Melody—our babysitter—was with her. I already talked to her, and she said Shannon was in her room at eight." She pressed the palm of her hand against her forehead. "But that was like six hours ago. She could be anywhere by now. I have to find her."

"Okay, calm down." Ryan reached for Simone's shoulders and turned her to face him. He was so good in a crisis. Kate loved that about him. Loved that when she felt ready to flip out, he was the calm to her crazy. "Where would Shannon go besides our house?"

"I don't know. But I found this on the floor in her room." Simone held out a slip of paper. "It was just lying there like she dropped it. I don't know whose credit card number that is—"

"I do." Ryan looked up from the note in his hand and frowned.

He handed the note to Kate, exasperation reflecting clearly in his features. "Wait here, both of you. I have a feeling I know what's going on."

He disappeared up the steps. Kate turned Simone for the living room. "Do you want coffee? Something to drink?"

"A lobotomy, if you have it." Simone dropped onto the couch and pressed her hands against her head. "She's never run off before. I don't understand. I know she's mad at me but…"

Simone's voice trailed off, and sensing her friend was at the end of her rope—and knowing what that was like because she'd been there herself—Kate sat next to her and wrapped an arm around Simone's shoulder. "It's going to be okay. Shannon's a smart kid. I'm sure she's fine. She's probably staying at another friend's house. We'll find her."

"You don't understand." Simone dropped her hands and looked Kate's way. And in her brown eyes, Kate saw heartache and anger and fear—true fear. The kind that can change a person in drastic ways. "There's so much you don't know."

"About what?" Kate whispered.

Simone stared at her. Seemed to want to say something. Didn't. Long seconds passed, then Simone's eyes fell closed, and she lowered her head back into her hands. "You wouldn't understand."

There was more going on here than Simone's breakup with Mitch. Kate rubbed a hand down Simone's back, hoping to soothe her friend, but knew instinctively that she couldn't. Footsteps from the direction of the stairs brought both their heads up.

Ryan and a very sleepy Julia stopped in the archway to the living room. "Katie? The note?"

Kate pushed from the couch, handed him the paper, and glanced at their daughter. Julia's long hair was a mess of curls around her face, and her pajamas were wrinkled and pushed up one leg. She scrubbed at her eyes, but guilt was already slithering over her features.

Ryan handed the paper to Julia. "You wanna explain what this is?"

Hesitantly, Julia took the folded page, turned it over in her hands, and looked down. "It's paper."

"Don't get smart with me, missy." He opened the note and pointed at the writing. "Explain why Shannon had my credit card number."

Julia's eyes shifted back and forth. She looked everywhere but at the paper in her hands. Silence settled over the room, and Kate could all but feel the tension crackling higher with every passing second.

Finally, Julia looked up at her dad. "Okay, don't get mad."

Ryan wrapped one arm around his waist and pinched the bridge of his nose with his other hand. “Why do I cringe whenever you use that phrase?”

"I don't know." Julia shrugged. "Maybe because I deliver it so well?”

“Julia,” Kate cut in, sensing Ryan’s waning patience. “Focus, and maybe we’ll reconsider grounding you for the rest of your life. Where is Shannon? Her mom’s worried sick.”

Julia’s guilty eyes darted to Simone, still seated on the couch, then shifted back to Kate.

“You’re already busted, so you might as well fess up.” Ryan crossed his arms over his chest and glared down at her. "At this point, your only hope is to throw yourself on the mercy of the court."

Julia cringed. “You're not gonna like the answer."

"Talk," Ryan snapped.

Julia sighed. "In Washington. She’s probably already on Whidbey Island by now. She went to find Uncle Mitch.”

CHAPTER FIVE

Tate Kendrick leaned back in his chair and looked across the mom-and-pop bar. "*That*, my friend, is exactly what you need to take your mind off things."

Mitch turned to watch the leggy blonde in the short skirt and apron Tate had been eyeing most of the night head across the room. She turned and sent Tate a wicked smile, licking her lips to draw attention to her plump mouth.

"Not interested." Mitch looked back at their table and poured another inch of Jamison into the tumbler in his hand. He swirled the golden liquid in the glass, then downed it in one swallow that burned a path of heat straight to his gut. "I'm done with women."

Music from a jukebox across the room echoed classic eighties music. Pool balls clacked in the adjacent room. Dragging his attention from the blonde at the bar, Tate grinned Mitch's way. "Done with women? Fine. But don't get any ideas. You're not sleeping in my bed tonight."

Mitch rolled his eyes. "I know this might come as a shock, Kendrick, but not everyone on the planet thinks you're a rock god."

Tate chuckled and went back to watching the blonde. "Only the ones who matter, old man."

Sighing, Mitch leaned back in his seat and looked down at the empty glass. A little voice in the back of his head told him he should really stop drinking, but at the moment, he couldn't find a legitimate reason to listen. He was supposed to be heading to British Columbia and the work site, but he'd gotten off the plane in Seattle instead and hopped a ferry out to Whidbey Island. He and Tate had been friends since college, when the freshman upstart had joined the baseball team and he and Ryan had decided to take Tate under their wing during their senior year. He was a few years younger, a whole lot cockier, and ever since his band, Kendrick, had taken off the last few years, a hell of a lot more obnoxious. But if there was one person Mitch knew he could get drunk with and not have to spill his guts to about everything that had happened with Simone, it was Tate.

Not that Tate wouldn't understand. But thankfully—at least for Mitch—the guy didn't do emotions. In fact, in all the years Mitch had known him, he couldn't remember a single time he'd heard Tate talk about anything deeper than how much he loved his stupid band.

"You look like shit, you know," Tate said, lifting the Corona bottle to his lips while he continued to flirt with the blonde. "You go up to BC looking like that and every one of your big-oil coworkers is gonna know you got your ass handed to you by a girl."

Mitch frowned and reached for the bottle again. It wobbled in his vision, but he wrapped his hand around the cool glass and slowly lifted it so he could pour again. "Thanks for the advice. You're not so hot either, music man. That soul patch looks like something died on your face."

Tate chuckled and rubbed his thumb over the patch of hair on his chin. "The chicks dig it.

"The chicks dig your money and celebrity status. Trust me, they hate the pubes on your chin. They're just too starstruck to tell you."

Simone had said that to him one night. When they'd been cuddled up on his couch watching Kendrick's debut on SNL. A vicious sharp pain lanced his chest at the memory and sent waves of misery outward. Before it could consume him, he poured another inch of Jamison in his glass and tossed it back.

"You better go easy on that stuff or you're gonna get sick," Tate muttered.

Mitch swiped his mouth with the back of his hand and set the glass on the table. "News flash, brainiac. I'm already sick."

Sick of women, sick of love, sick of making a fool out of himself.

"God, you're a breath of fresh air." Tate pushed back from the table, the legs of his chair scraping the ground as he stood. "Come on. Let's get the hell out of here before you ruin my reputation."

Mitch pushed up to his feet. The room swayed, and he caught himself from going down by bracing his hands on the table. "Your reputation was shot the minute you hung out with me."

Did he slur those words? And, wow, the room was really spinning now.

"Yeah, yeah." Tate grabbed him by the arm and turned him for the entrance of the small bar. "Your hero status is shot. I just want you to know that. Playing Mr. Mom with Ryan these past few years obviously killed your tolerance for booze. Who will I look up to now?"

Mitch stumbled into the back of an empty chair. "I can still drink."

"Uh-huh." Tate dragged him toward the door. "Like a lightweight little virgin."

"Tate." The blonde he'd been flirting with the whole night materialized out of nowhere, dragging Mitch's feet to a stop. "You're not leaving yet, are you?"

Mitch's eyes widened. He blinked several times to see her clearly. Couldn't seem to focus on anything more than a fuzzy yellow halo around her head. Luckily, Tate didn't let go of his arm. Maybe this was exactly what he did need, a woman to take his mind off Simone. Except, whoa… Now there were three of her.

"Yeah, unfortunately, I gotta get this old guy home," Tate said somewhere close. "Way past his bedtime."

Three sets of eyes looked Mitch's way, but all three were obviously more interested in the music man. She stuck out her full bottom lip—all three of them. "I was just about to take my break."

"Next time, baby-doll. I promise."

She rose up on her toes and kissed Tate's scruffy cheek. "I'll hold you to that."

Tate grinned once more as he pushed the door open to the parking lot and pulled Mitch through. Stopping on the other side, he turned and looked back. "Hey, Aubrey. You like the soul patch, right?"

Slapping the bar rag in her hand, Aubrey shrugged. "Sure. It's kinda cute. I'll see you next time."

She waved and disappeared back into the bar.

The door snapped shut, and cool air washed over Mitch. He chuckled. "See? Told ya."

Tate frowned and pulled Mitch toward his truck. "Cute is for bunny rabbits and panda bears. I am *not* cute."

The world didn't seem to want to stop spinning even out here in the cool night air. Mitch climbed into Tate's souped-up Dodge, closed the door, and leaned his head back against the plush seat.

When Tate climbed in next to him, he muttered, "If I hurl, I just want you to know it's not personal."

"Fuck that," Tate muttered. The window at Mitch's right went all the way down, and crisp air rushed over him as they pulled out of the small parking lot. "I swear to God, if you get sick in my truck, Mathews, you'll regret it."

"I already regret it." Mitch's eyes drifted closed, and he fought back the waves of nausea as the rig bounced over ruts in the road. "Why did you let me drink so much?"

"Hell if I know," Tate mumbled. "Maybe because I know what it's like to get your teeth kicked in by the woman of your dreams."

Mitch's eyes drifted open, and he looked across the cab toward his friend, pretty sure he'd imagined that response. Dim green light from the dashboard illuminated Tate's set features and the mop of dark brown hair that was already brushing his shoulders. The guy dated a lot of women, but Mitch couldn't remember a single one who had lasted more than a month.

Not that he cared right now. He tilted his head back and closed his eyes again, focusing on deep breaths, in and out, so he didn't get sick. Some sappy country music floated out of the speakers, and Tate hummed along as he drove.

Mitch floated, hating the music, hating the way his stomach tossed, hating life in general. "Country music is so freakin' depressing."

Tate grinned. "That's because it's deep."

"Thank God you don't play it."

"Are you saying my music lacks substance?"

"Any substance in your music's hidden behind heavy bass and that tricky guitar shit you do."

"I totally take offense at that."

Mitch crossed his arms over his chest. "That's because you listen to crap like this that makes a person want to blow their brains out."

"You are a total peach tonight, you know that, Michelle?"

It was a familiar joke, one they'd started in college and that had lingered over the years, calling each other by their girlie counter-names. A tiny smile tugged at the corner of Mitch's lips. "As peachy as you, Tara."

They made several turns on the island, and the music shifted to a song about football. Still country, but at least it wasn't a depressing monologue about a man's regrets. As the song echoed in the cab, Mitch mentally tried to figure out where they were without opening his eyes but finally gave up as his mind drifted away from his rolling stomach and floating head and resettled on the scene at his house last night with Simone.

Holy hell. He was such a fucking moron. He totally should have seen that coming. Couldn't believe how far he'd bought into that whole stupid fairy tale.

"Damn, Mathews." The rig drew to a stop, and Tate's voice cut through Mitch's self-defeating thoughts. "When you said this Simone chick was younger than you, I thought she was at least *legal.* Even I don't push those boundaries."

Mitch's eyes drifted open, and he looked over at his friend. Tate's gaze was locked on something out the front windshield.

Blinking several times, Mitch turned his head, then froze.

Every muscle in his body contracted, and he sat forward. "Holy shit."

He was out of the truck in seconds, his hiking boots hitting the asphalt drive while the cool air and adrenaline rush cleared his foggy head, enough so he didn't fall over. "Shannon? What the hell are you doing here?"

Illuminated by the headlights of the truck, Shannon swiped at her runny nose with the sleeve of her hoodie as she sat on the front steps of Tate's new house. Tears tracked down her cheeks, and she rubbed at them with her sleeve. "I… I…"

Confusion snapped to worry, which morphed to a burst of excitement rushing through Mitch's veins. His gaze swept from Shannon to the fancy new house, then around the parking area surrounded by trees. Simone had to be here.

"D-don't be mad. Please?" Shannon sniffled, drawing his attention. "I just… You didn't say good-bye. And I…" Tears streamed down her cheeks. "Mom doesn't know I'm here. I-I…" Wide, wet, red-rimmed eyes looked up at him. Pleading eyes. "Just…just please come back. I promise I'll be good. I won't get in the way."

A car door slammed behind Mitch. Footsteps echoed. But he knew it wasn't Simone. It was Tate, wondering what was going on.

All that excitement fizzled. Simone wasn't here. She hadn't changed her mind. She hadn't come after him. But instead of the heartbroken anger he'd felt earlier, guilt consumed him. Guilt for not thinking about anyone but himself.

"Shit." He sat next to her on the steps and wrapped an arm around her. When she threw herself against his chest and started sobbing, he just held her close, not knowing what the hell to do or say.

Tate's footsteps drew to a stop. "How come every girl you're with ends up crying, Mathews?"

Mitch glanced up at his friend, frowned, and flipped him the bird.

Tate chuckled.

Shannon's sobs died down. She sniffled, then drew back and looked at Tate. Glancing at Mitch, she said, "Is that…the music guy?"

"You know Kendrick?" Mitch asked, one arm still around her.

"Yes. I mean, kinda." She sniffled again. "Julia told me about him."

"Julia," Mitch mumbled. "That explains how you found me. But I'd still like to know how the hell you got all the way up here on your own."

Shannon sat up and swiped at her cheeks. A sheepish expression crossed her features. "Julia helped me."

"I figured. Keep going."

She cringed. "She, ah, used her dad's credit card to get me a plane ticket."

"You're ten."

She bit her lip and looked down at her shoes. "I know. She, ah, also told me how to act like I was older so I could travel without an adult."

Tate chuckled. "Damn, but I love that kid."

Mitch frowned. "That kid's going to be grounded for life when her parents find out what she did." He looked down at Shannon. "And so are you, sweetheart, when your mom realizes you're gone."

Tears filled Shannon's eyes all over again. "Please? Please, can we not tell her right away? If you come back, she won't be so mad at me."

She collapsed into sobs against Mitch's chest again, and he rubbed her back, knowing he should be pissed but having a hard time finding the energy.

"Bring her into the house," Tate said. "If she gets sick out here in the cold, her mom's really gonna hate you."

"Her mom already does." Mitch hefted Shannon into his arms and followed Tate inside.

A great room with a huge rock fireplace and dark wood accents opened to a kitchen beyond and stairs that led up to the second floor. Mitch sat on the leather couch in the middle of the room and held Shannon while she cried. Tate disappeared somewhere in the kitchen.

"It's gonna be okay," he said, rubbing her back, not knowing what else to do to console her. Julia was never emotional like this. Instead, she just got mad and yelled. Part of him preferred the yelling, but a tiny piece liked that Shannon needed him. God knew, her mother didn't. "I'll call your mom and work everything out. She might be a little mad, but she'll get over it."

"No, she won't." Shannon sniffled. "I've messed everything up. First I made you leave, and now this."

He drew her away from him and looked into her eyes. "Listen to me. You didn't do anything wrong. And I didn't leave because of you. I left because…" How the hell did he explain this to a ten-year-old? He was still struggling with it himself. "Listen, Shannon. Sometimes things just don't work out. It's not anybody's fault, especially yours. You're a great kid, and I…" *…wanted to be your dad. I still do.* He swallowed the emotions closing his throat. "It was wrong of me to leave without telling you. I'm sorry."

She laid her head on his chest and cried again. And, feeling like shit, Mitch just sat there and held her, knowing there wasn't a damn thing he could do to make her—or himself—feel better.

Eventually, Shannon's sniffling died off, and she grew limp in his arms. It had to be close to three a.m. Realizing she was asleep, he laid her on the couch and pulled a throw over her, then looked down at all her curly red hair fanned out around her and remembered why he'd never wanted to have a family of his own. Because this kind of stuff killed him. The highs he could totally manage, but the lows… He wasn't strong enough to deal with reality when the bottom fell out beneath him.

The scent of coffee beckoned from the direction of the kitchen, and he headed that way.

Tate—always a night owl—was sitting at the counter, tinkering on his laptop, when Mitch walked into the room. Darkness pressed in from outside, just a twinkle of lights across the water reflecting in the glass. Tate leaned back in his chair. "She finally go to sleep?"

Mitch opened a cupboard and pulled out a mug. "You mean pass out from crying? Yeah. Finally."

Tate chuckled. "Gotta admit. All those years you spent helping Ryan with Julia, I never saw you as the father figure. Not until tonight."

Mitch scowled as he poured coffee into his mug. "Don't get used to it. She's not my kid, and her mother has made it more than clear she doesn't want her to *be* my kid. I am not, and never will be, dad material."

Tate was silent for a moment. The strong, bitter coffee went down hot, but at least it cleared the last of the cobwebs from Mitch's brain. He took another sip, wishing it would clear away that lingering ache in his chest too.

"What are you gonna do?" Tate asked quietly.

What he wanted to do was drink himself into oblivion and pass out just like Shannon. What he *had* to do was call the woman who'd just shit kicked him in the groin and tell her her daughter was over eight hundred miles away. With him.

"Consider moving to a deserted island." He pulled out his cell and cringed when he saw seven missed calls from Simone.

So much for passing out.

He punched in Simone's number. Then drew a deep breath and steeled himself for what was about to happen next.

Simone answered on the first ring. "Mitch? Is Shannon with you?"

Just the sound of her voice caused his stomach to tighten with a mixture of pain and stupidity. He clenched his jaw. "She's here. And she's fine."

"Oh, thank God. I've been going out of my mind. Put her on the phone."

"She's sleeping."

"Well, wake her up. She's in some serious trouble for this stunt."

He leaned back against the counter. Across the kitchen, Tate watched with interest. "No."

"This isn't funny, Mitch. Put her on the damn phone."

Simone was good and fired up. The woman rarely swore. But that only fueled Mitch's own rage. "It's three o'clock in the freakin' morning, Simone. She's tired and upset and already feels like crap, thanks to you. So forgive me for not waking her so you can lay into her and make her feel worse."

"*Wha—?*" Shock reverberated through the line. Then, steadier, Simone said, "Where are you? I'll come get her."

Bullshit. She wasn't coming up here and fucking up any more of his life. She'd done enough of that already. "I'll take care of it."

"What? No. Just put her on a plane in the morning, and I'll meet her in San Francisco."

She didn't want to see him. Yeah, that made this all the more fun. "And leave her feeling abandoned all over again? I don't think so. I'm pretty sure we've both fucked things up for her enough for one week. I'll call you tomorrow when I know our flight time."

"Wait, Mitch. Have *her* call me."

Now she didn't even want to talk to him? Oh yeah, this was just so fucking *excellent.*

"Not if she doesn't want to. And right now, you're like the last person on the planet she wants to talk to."

"Mitch—"

"You know what, Simone?" He rolled right over her, his own emotions melding with Shannon's, leaving him vibrating with anger. "You're just gonna have to learn to deal with disappointment. I sure have."

He clicked End before she could protest and slid the phone into the back pocket of his jeans. A tension headache—or maybe it was a hangover headache—was taking up space right behind his eyeballs. He rubbed two fingers over his brow.

"That sounded like it went well," Tate said from the table.

"About as well as a car crash on the 101." Mitch tossed his coffee in the sink and headed for the living room. "I'm tired. If Shannon wakes, make sure she doesn't escape, would ya? The last thing I need is her mother all over my ass because she got away."

"At one time, you would have liked that."

Yeah, he would have. And part of him still did. But as he'd told Simone, disappointment was something he was learning to live with.

"That's because I'm a sick son of a bitch." Mitch turned for the stairs. "But like you, Kendrick, thank the stars above, I've finally come to my senses."

"Yeah," Kendrick muttered from the kitchen in a less than enthusiastic tone, "we're regular old rocket scientists, aren't we?"

Simone stared at the phone in her hand in utter disbelief.

He'd hung up on her.

"She's with Mitch?" Kate asked where she sat next to Simone on the sofa. "Oh, thank God. What did he say?"

"He—" Simone was still too shocked to think. She knew Mitch was pissed at her after the scene at his house, but this was different. He'd all but accused her of being a terrible mother. Which, she couldn't help but agree, she was. She swallowed hard. "H-he said he's bringing her back to San Francisco tomorrow."

Kate and Ryan exchanged glances. She saw it from the corner of her eye. But she was too upset to care what they were thinking.

"Don't worry, Simone," Ryan said. "Mitch has been taking care of Julia for years. He's very responsible. I'm sure everything's just fine."

From the leather chair across the room where she lay splayed over the armrest, Julia huffed. "Sure. Responsible. That's Uncle Mitch. He's only forgotten to pick me up from practice and school and stuff five, maybe six times. The best was the time I had to wait at the softball fields, in the rain, for two hours because Dad was on a trip and Uncle Mitch totally spaced me off."

"Julia Anne Harrison," Ryan snapped. All eyes shot his way, and his jaw clenched as he visibly tried to hold back his temper. "That's not helping."

Kate pushed from the couch. "I think it's time Julia went back to bed." Her mother shot the girl a look. "Before she's grounded for a second lifetime."

Julia heaved out a sigh but stood and shuffled toward the stairs, her chestnut hair a wild mop of curls around her face, her fuzzy pajama bottoms too long and dragging on the floor. She paused with one foot on the bottom step, one hand on the newel post, and turned to look back into the living room. "For what it's worth, we didn't mean for anyone to get mad. We were just trying to help."

Her mother sighed. "Julia—"

"No. Wait." Emotions shot through Simone's chest, pushing her to her feet and forcing her to step into the entryway. "How on earth could you or Shannon possibly think running away would help anything?"

"Shannon wasn't running away. She was just trying to fix things. Like what happened with my mom and dad."

Ryan moved into the entry behind Kate. "What do you mean?"

Julia's gaze settled on Simone. "It's like when my mom left after all the reporters were bugging us. My dad was really upset, see, but he didn't go after her. And we didn't know if she was coming back, even though Dad said she would eventually. But Mom got to the airport and saw this other family, and when she came back, she said looking at them made her realize what was important. That *we* were important. But Uncle Mitch doesn't notice people in the airport, so he wouldn't realize the same thing. And Shannon and I decided he needed someone to, you know, make him see what was important. That's why she went up there. Not to run away, but to make him come back."

The room was quiet except for the tick of a clock in the adjacent living room, and Simone's stomach churned with a mixture of regret and sadness that nearly did her in.

Kate looked up at Ryan, standing behind her, and whispered, "How does she do that?"

He blew out a breath and moved around his wife toward his daughter on the stairs. "I don't know. She's too smart for her own good." He laid a hand on Julia's shoulder and nudged her up the stairs. "Come on, Miss Smarty pants, it's time you went back to bed and stopped acting like a forty-year-old."

"Dad, you're not even forty."

"I know. Don't remind me."

A tiny smile curled one side of Julia's mouth as she slipped her hand into her father's. "Am I still grounded for the rest of my life?"

"The jury's out on that at the moment."

The pair moved up the stairs and disappeared, and, dazed, Simone sank onto the couch in the living room once more. Resting her elbows on her knees, she dropped her head into her hands and just focused on breathing, because it was the only thing she could do at the moment. "I've made such a mess of everything. Mitch hates me. Shannon hates me. There's no way this is ever going to get better."

Kate sat next to her and rubbed a hand down her back. "It will. I know it doesn't seem like it now, but it'll get better. If there's one thing I've learned after everything Ryan and I went through, it's that nothing is impossible. If you love someone enough, you'll find a way to work it out."

Loving enough wasn't Simone's problem. It was everything else getting in the way of that love. She dropped her arms. "You don't understand what's happened. Mitch is never going to forgive me."

Kate's features softened. "Mitch is one of the most understanding people I know. You just have to talk to him, Simone—really talk to him—and tell him the truth about whatever's going on with you. He'll understand. Give him a chance."

Simone wasn't so sure. Maybe once, but not after she'd lied about how she felt. Why would he ever trust her again? She barely trusted herself.

She rubbed a hand over her aching head, her heart and mind at war against each other, her body caught in the middle. "The only thing I'm sure of right now is that I need to fix things with Shannon. Only then can I think about Mitch and making things right with him. Or at the very least, civil."

A sad smile turned Kate's lips. "Is there anything I can do to help?"

Simone pushed to her feet. At this point, she feared there was nothing anyone could do. Least of all her. "No. But thanks. He's so mad at me, I'm not sure he'll even call me in the morning, so if he calls here—"

Kate rose. "I'll be sure to let you know." She squeezed Simone's hand. "Try to have faith. Mitch is hurting right now, but he's not vindictive. And he still loves you. He'll listen to whatever you have to say."

Simone wasn't so sure. Pulling her hand from Kate's, she turned for the door and the darkness beyond that had become her life. "I'll talk to you tomorrow."

CHAPTER SIX

"Ladies and gentlemen, we've begun our final descent into San Francisco. Please turn off all your electronic devices and bring your seat backs to the upright position."

Mitch reached over and hit the button on Shannon's armrest, drawing her seat forward. "Time to say good-bye to Candy Crush."

Shannon frowned and powered down her iPod. "One of these days, I'm going to beat this level. Just wait."

"Only if your mom doesn't confiscate that thing. Might want to get used to the fact your life could be hell for the next few months."

Shannon frowned but didn't argue. Instead, she turned off her device and pushed it into her pocket, then looked out the window at the city growing larger with every passing second. "Are you absolutely sure you can't find me a job with your oil company? I'm really good at organizing stuff."

One corner of his lips curled, but the smile didn't reach his eyes. He hurt, not just for her but for him too. "Pretty sure they have things called child labor laws that prevent companies from hiring ten-year-olds."

Shannon sighed and focused on the seat in front of her. "Darn lawyers."

Mitch's stomach knotted. He'd always thought that about lawyers too. Until he'd met Simone.

Actually, he was thinking that again.

A sharp pain stabbed through his chest, and he drew a deep breath, then shifted in his seat to try to take his mind off what was coming. He really didn't want to see Simone again so soon. When he'd called her this morning to tell her they'd be on the afternoon flight, she'd been quiet and agreeable, not combative and stressed as she'd been the night before. But he knew nothing had changed between them, and having to look her in the eye after she'd ripped out his heart only two days ago wasn't something he was particularly looking forward to.

The sound of the landing gear descending echoed through the cabin. Mitch reached over and tightened Shannon's seat belt, then closed his hand over hers on the armrest. Her palm was already sweating, but he knew it wasn't from the flight.

"Will you stay with me until we find my mom?" she whispered, not looking his way. "I-I don't want to have to find her on my own."

He squeezed her hand. "You betcha. I'm not going anywhere, sweetheart." At least not until he had to.

She didn't answer. But when she leaned her head against his shoulder and closed her other hand over their joined fingers, that heart that Simone had already cracked crumbled right at his feet.

No, he'd never really wanted kids of his own, but he'd sure fallen for *this* kid. And the knowledge that he wasn't just losing the love of his life in this whole mess, but also a family he'd never expected to want, caused that pain in his chest to multiply by ten.

The plane came to a stop at the gate, and, reluctantly, he let go of Shannon's hand and pushed to his feet. Nerves showed clearly on her face while she pulled her bag from beneath the seat in front of her, but there was nothing he could do to ease either of them at this point. Passengers began filtering off the plane. When Shannon slid the straps of her bag over her shoulders, Mitch asked, "Ready?"

Shannon shrugged, but her sad eyes didn't meet his. "I guess."

They headed off the plane and up the Jetway. The terminal was a buzz of activity, just like always. Travelers rushed by. He grasped Shannon's hand to keep from getting separated. With every step they moved toward security, his adrenaline shot up another notch.

Shannon rubbed the sleeve of her free arm over her eyes, and Mitch knew she was upset, but he was tapped out and didn't know how to console her. They moved through security without speaking, and when they cleared the checkpoint, Mitch's nerves hummed as he scanned the faces waiting expectantly for arrivals.

Simone moved out from behind an excited family hugging a returning soldier, and Mitch's first thought was that she didn't look like the confident, put-together lawyer she always was. Her hair was clipped up in a messy do, dark circles showed beneath her eyes, and worry was etched across her face. But even mussed and obviously stressed, she was still gorgeous, dressed in slim jeans and a loose white T-shirt. And his heart did a flip—just like it always did when he saw her—then dropped like a stone straight into his belly.

Shannon's feet drew to a stop beside him, and she tugged on his hand, stopping his forward momentum. He looked down at her. Watched tears fill her eyes. And had an overwhelming urge to wrap her in his arms and hold on to her, since he knew he could no longer hold on to her mother. But before he could do just that, the tears spilled over her eyelashes, she pulled free of his hand, dropped her backpack on the ground, and sprinted toward Simone.

Simone fell to one knee and caught her in a tight hug. Shannon held on for dear life and sobbed. Mitch couldn't hear what Simone said to her daughter, but the relief and love rushing over Simone's features told him everything he needed to know.

He was the outsider here. He'd gotten so caught up in the whole idea of having a ready-made family, he hadn't paid attention to what was right in front of his eyes. Simone and Shannon were a unit. They needed each other, just like Julia and Ryan needed one another. And though they'd let him into their circle for a little while, their world wouldn't crumble without him. Even if things hadn't gone to shit between him and Simone, he always would have been the outsider, looking in, wanting to be a part of something that, frankly, wasn't his to want.

That realization sliced right through the center of his chest, but he clenched his jaw, picked up Shannon's bag from the floor, and forced his feet forward. He stopped two steps from mother and daughter, still tangled together, and cleared his throat. All he wanted now was to get the hell out of here, but for Shannon's sake, he stood still. And waited.

Simone looked up at him. Tears glistened in her eyes. Tears a part of him wished she'd shed, just once, for him. "Thank you," she whispered.

He nodded. Couldn't seem to find anything else to say. Cleared his throat again. "Shannon, I need to get going."

Shannon turned in her mother's arms. Blinked several times. Then swiped her sleeve over her damp eyes. "Already?"

"Yeah."

Simone pushed to her feet. "Are you heading back to Seattle right away?"

Small talk. Mitch could handle small talk, for Shannon's sake. He shifted his backpack on his shoulder and tucked one hand into the front pocket of his jeans. "No. Tomorrow. I need to pick up a few files I left at the office."

Simone nodded and placed both hands on her daughter's shoulders. "I-I'm...sorry we interrupted your plans."

"Shannon is never an interruption."

Shannon's eyes filled with tears again, and that was all Mitch could take. He had to get out of here, before he said or did something he'd regret later. Before he begged.

"Anytime you want to talk, Shannon, just call. I have my cell on me most of the time. And don't give your mom too much trouble. She loves you, even when you don't think she does."

A tear spilled over Shannon's lashes, and she nodded.

"Mitch," Simone whispered, stepping around Shannon.

Yeah. No. He was *not* about to reopen wounds that were already oozing.

Mitch gripped his backpack at the shoulder and turned. "I gotta go."

He pushed his feet forward one step at a time. Refused to look back. Forced himself to head across the long, wide hallway toward the doors to freedom. Two days ago, he thought his heart had shattered when Simone had told him she didn't love him, but today he knew no matter where he went in his life, it would never be whole again.

"Mitch!"

He stopped at the sound of Shannon's voice and glanced over his shoulder. Shannon darted around Simone and streaked across the airport. Tears streamed down her cheeks. She held her arms out wide.

He dropped to his knees, caught her in a tight hug, closed his eyes, and held her close.

"I love you," she sobbed.

"Ah, sweetheart." His chest squeezed tight. "I love you too. That's never going to change."

"But you're leaving."

"I'll be back, Shannon." He eased away just enough so he could swipe at her tears. Swallowed back his own. "I have to leave for my job, but that doesn't mean I'm not coming back. I'll always come back."

Her shoulders shook with her heart-wrenching sobs.

God, this was killing him. He brushed the tears from her cheek once more. "Tell you what. Opening day, just you and me. I need my best girl to cheer on the Giants with me. What do you say? Is it a date?"

She sniffled. Rubbed her eyes. Seemed unsure. "O-okay."

"Okay." He had no idea if she'd even be here on opening day, if Simone was staying in San Francisco or leaving like she'd told him she planned to do. But he'd do whatever he could to make this easier for her. Even if it killed him just a little bit more. "Okay. See? There's nothing to be sad about. This isn't good-bye. Before you know it, I'll be back from British Columbia, and we'll be heading to AT&T Park."

She sniffled once more. Drew up her shoulders and swiped at her tears. "Promise?"

He forced a smile for her, knowing there was no way he could ever love his own kid more than he loved her. "I promise."

She sucked in a deep breath, then slowly let it out. And as her own lips curled into a forced smile, he knew nothing, not even nearly dying from a head wound, compared to the pain he felt at this moment.

Tears threatened, and he knew if he didn't leave now, he might not be able to without making a total ass of himself. Careful not to look at Simone, he grabbed his bag from the ground, tapped Shannon on the nose, and beat feet for the doors.

Then told himself he was better off without them. Even if in his heart he knew that was a total lie.

Nothing eased the ache that had settled deep within her chest.

Simone set her mug of tea on the kitchen counter and ran her hand through her hair, replaying the scene in the airport for the thousandth time. The look on Mitch's face when Shannon had raced after him and he'd caught her in that hug was something she was never going to forget.

She looked toward the stairs. Boxes littered the hallway that ran from the kitchen to the entry. After returning home from the airport, she'd told Shannon they didn't need to resume packing, at least not yet. They'd talked some—about what Shannon had been thinking going up to Seattle, about how dangerous that had been, and about why it was so wrong—but Simone hadn't laid into her daughter as she'd planned. Instead, they'd cuddled on the couch and watched a movie, and even now, after putting Shannon to bed, Simone couldn't bring herself to box up anything else.

Was she jumping the gun? Uprooting Shannon and herself all because of her own stupid fears? Will had said they *knew* where she was. And not to give them anything *if* they came after her. That didn't mean someone was actually coming after her, though. No one had shown up in the last two days, had they? It was highly possible all that meant was that someone was keeping tabs on her, for safety's sake, even if she didn't understand why. Besides, if someone *had* been looking for her, they could have easily found her the last three years. It wasn't like she'd been in hiding. If the people Steve had turned on really wanted to find her, they could have done it long before now.

But the question still remained—why would they want to? She didn't know anything. Steve had been careful not to tell her much about the case that had pushed him into running. And she'd hooked up with him after the fact anyway. That was why Will, the US marshal assigned to her case, had assured her it was okay for her and Shannon to leave the program after Steve's death.

Her mind drifted back over the call as she dumped what was left of her tea into the sink and washed out her cup. She'd tried to call Will several times since then to get answers to her questions, but his phone kept going to voice mail.

"You remember what I told you, right? Don't forget it."

Her memory flashed to the day she'd had the moving van packed, ready to head west with Shannon. Will had come by to wish the two of them good luck. He'd placed his big hands on her shoulders, looked down at her and said, *"Fear is the biggest enemy. Remember that and you'll make it through anything. If you jump without thinking, then they win. And the truth is, you're nothing to these people. You're not a threat."*

Relief whipped through her, the kind that gave her strength. The kind that brought hope back to life. She'd been so freaked out by Will's call, she hadn't really listened to what he'd been telling her. Sure, she still wasn't positive what had been going on in the background of that call, but he worked in law enforcement. It could have been any number of things. And in her gut, she knew if Will had wanted her to run, he'd have told her that outright. Instead, he'd been warning her to stay on her toes, just like he'd trained her and Steve to do when they'd been living in hiding. And she'd been so stupid, she'd reacted without thinking, just as he'd told her *not* to do all those years ago.

God, she'd made a mess of things when what she should have been doing was being thankful Will was reminding her not to get complacent.

Hand shaking, she wiped her palms on a towel and quickly moved through the kitchen and into the entryway, glancing up the curved stairs toward the second level, where Shannon lay sleeping. It was after eleven p.m. and part of her wanted to go up and make sure Shannon was still there. Another part told herself what Shannon had done, she'd done to try to help matters, not hinder them. If Simone wanted to repair her relationship with her daughter, she needed to start by trusting her.

She also needed to trust herself. Running wasn't the solution she'd thought it to be only days before. Neither was yanking Shannon out of school and away from her friends, not when she'd finally acclimated to life without Steve. And as much as Simone had tried to convince herself over the months that her relationship with Mitch hadn't yet impacted Shannon, she knew now that was a lie. There was no way she could tear Shannon away from Mitch after the bond she'd seen between them today at the airport.

Mitch…

An ache spread beneath her ribs and twisted hard. The same damn knot that had taken up space there since she'd told Mitch that terrible lie.

She had to tell him the truth. She had to try to set at least some part of this right. Kate had said Mitch was one of the most understanding people she knew, and Simone believed that herself. If she could just talk to him and explain things, maybe then she could fix it. If not for her, then at least for Shannon.

She looked up the stairs toward Shannon's open door. A dim green light from Shannon's alarm clock shone through the darkness, followed by the steady deep breaths of her daughter, lost in sleep.

Before she could change her mind, Simone headed for the kitchen and reached for her phone from the counter. Paging through her contacts, she found the one she was looking for and clicked Call.

Her nerves hummed as she waited. She only had a few hours to make this work. If she missed the window and Mitch left for British Columbia, she might never have a chance to make it right.

"Melody?" she asked when the girl answered. "No, everything's fine. I'm sorry to call so late. Listen, I was wondering"—hope spiraled through every cell in her body—"are you free for a few hours?"

Two dive bars in two nights was a little much, even for Mitch.

He swiveled on his seat and rested his forearm on the smooth bar top as he looked toward Mara—Lara? God, he couldn't even remember her name—chatting with the bartender at the far end of the long mahogany counter.

She was new at the office. Pretty. Big blue eyes, long blond hair, a small waist and killer legs. He'd seen her a few times over the last few weeks but hadn't paid her much attention. He was pretty sure she was an intern, but he couldn't remember in what department. And honestly, before tonight, he hadn't even cared.

He lifted the beer in his hand and took a long swallow as he watched her flip that mass of blond hair over her shoulder and laugh at something the bartender was saying. Pool balls clacked in the adjacent room, and some kind of '80s rock filtered from speakers hidden in the ceiling.

Jetting up to Seattle had been a spur-of-the-moment decision—and not a particularly smart one—but now that he was back in San Francisco, this time he was checking out the right way. They did need him up at the work site in British Columbia for the predrill assessment, but they needed him with his head screwed on right, not half-cocked and emotionally strung out as he'd been when he'd flown up to see Kendrick. So, after leaving the airport, he'd swung by the office to pick up his files and tell his boss he was finally heading up to the job site, and on his way out the door, he'd run into Lara or Mara or whatever the hell her name was. They'd chatted for a few minutes, then somehow he'd gotten sucked into having a drink with her before heading home.

He downed the rest of his beer and reached for the froufrou girly mixed drink she'd left sitting in front of her seat, then took a long swallow of that too. Vodka. He scrunched his face at the taste. He hated vodka, but it was better than nothing. He wasn't looking to get drunk, but every time the girl laughed, it was like fingernails running down a chalkboard. Mitch couldn't figure out just what it was about her that set him on edge, because she was totally hot, but tonight he didn't want to care. Tonight he wanted to get a little drunk, a lot laid, and forget about Simone for good. Because after that scene in the airport, he was pretty sure that was the only way he was going to get his life back on track.

Lara smiled, said something to the bartender Mitch couldn't hear, then locked eyes on Mitch and headed his direction. Her legs seemed to stretch for miles in those formfitting black skinny jeans, her breasts the perfect size as they peeked out from behind the tight pink blouse, and the predatory fuck-me gleam in her eyes told him if he wanted a wife for a night, she was all his.

His stomach tightened, but not in a good way. Not in the way it always did when Simone sent him that same smoldering look. He reached for Lara's drink and downed the rest of it, barely even tasting the alcohol.

To his left, the bartender set two shot glasses on the bar and reached back for a bottle of Patron.

Lara placed both hands on his thighs and moved in close between his legs. Heat permeated his jeans but didn't come close to exciting him. "I've been looking forward to this all day." She lifted one hand from his leg, reached for the first shot, and handed it to him, then picked up her own. Clinking glasses, she said, "Here's to new experiences. Cheers."

She was talking about him leaving for three months to oversee the job site in BC, which they'd talked about on the drive to the bar. Or maybe she was talking about the two of them hooking up. Regardless, Mitch downed the shot in one swallow. The tequila warmed his chest and settled hard in the pit of his stomach. Heat rushing all through his belly, he set the glass down. Before he could say anything, Lara laughed. To the bartender, she said, "Another."

Voices and music echoed around him. The combination of beer and vodka and tequila was definitely spiraling to his head. When Lara chuckled at Mitch's facial expression after the second shot, he realized her laugh wasn't all *that* bad. And her hand still resting on his thigh, slowly stroking the soft denim, was absolutely having some kind of impact on his libido, even if it wasn't the shot of wicked-hot desire he always felt whenever Simone barely touched him.

Simone…

His chest squeezed tight, and that same ache he'd been living with the last two days reformed right beneath his breastbone, stealing his breath.

Shit. She doesn't need you. She doesn't want you. If she regretted anything, she could have tried to talk to you at the airport, but she didn't. Don't think about her. Just focus on the hot bod all but sitting in your lap, offering to fuck your brains out right this very second.

He slid his arm around Lara's waist and pulled her in closer. Her hair tickled his nose and some floral scent filled his senses. "You wanna get out of here?"

She eased back and smiled a sexy, I'm-gonna-rock-your-world grin. "Oh yeah. After one more."

She hollered at the bartender, and the guy lined the glasses up again. This time doubles. A little voice in the back of Mitch's head said this was a bad idea, that Mara or Lara or whatever her name was could obviously drink him under the table and that he should be careful, but he ignored it. Reaching for the glass, he downed the double in one long swallow.

Before he'd even set the glass down, she closed her hand over his on the bar. "Let's go."

He let her lead him out of the bar. His head spun as he stepped through the open door into the cool November air, reminding him hard alcohol wasn't his friend. Beer he could do. And wine. But shots had a history of getting him in trouble.

He must have swayed, because Lara plucked the keys from his hand. "I'll drive. We have to go to your place, though, because my roommate will be at mine."

For a split second, Mitch considered calling a cab, but Lara was already pushing him toward his Land Rover. He slid into the passenger seat and shoved it back to make room for his long legs. Lara climbed into the driver's side and closed the door. The floral scent of her perfume filled the interior of the vehicle, sending a shot of nausea through his stomach.

"Where to?" she asked.

He didn't trust his direction skills after the Patron. Tugging the smart phone from his jeans pocket, he opened the navigation app and squinted until all the little boxes stopped spinning. "You don't know where I live? Would'a thought with your access to the personnel files, you'd be able to tell me."

She shoved the gearshift into Reverse and slowly backed out of the parking space. "I might'a had a crush on you for weeks, but I haven't stalked you. Yet."

The "yet" brought his head up, but the wicked smile across her lips told him she was playing. Or so he hoped.

He typed in his address and set the phone on the front of the console. She flipped on the radio, fiddled with the station, then shoved the stick shift into first.

Pop music echoed out of the speakers, some boy band he couldn't name and didn't want to listen to. But instead of switching the station, he leaned his head back against the seat. "Careful. This'ing sticks in second."

"I've got it." She shoved the clutch down and tried to shift gears. The grind of metal echoed through the small space.

At one point, Mitch might have cared that she was hurting his baby—he rarely let anyone drive the old 1990 Defender, especially someone who wasn't good with a stick shift—but tonight the alcohol was doing its job. Tonight he had only one thought in his mind: oblivion. Pure, sweet, blessed oblivion. And if this blonde chick whose name he could barely remember could take him there, he didn't even care if she trashed the transmission of his pride and joy.

She hummed along to the music, slid one hand across the console and onto his thigh. He tensed for a second, then forced himself to relax as she drew her fingers up and down the denim, working her way higher with every pass.

He'd fooled around with Simone in this car only a week or so ago, just before she'd left on that trip to DC, when he'd driven her home after their date. Shannon had been with a babysitter, and he'd tried to get Simone to invite him in for the night, but Simone always had those strict rules about no overnights when Shannon was around. So instead he'd settled for making it to second base in the driveway of her house right here in this car before he'd finally let go, sweaty and aching for more as he'd watched her disappear into her big old Victorian house.

The arousal he'd been starting to feel from Mara's—no, Lara's—teasing fizzled and died. That damn ache resettled beneath his ribs. He was still sober enough to realize they needed to get to his house fast before he changed his mind or before the alcohol wore off for good.

Lara turned onto his street, then pointed toward his house, completely dark and silent. "This one?"

"Yeah," he managed. "Driveway's on the other side."

She pulled into the drive and shoved the car into first. Metal ground against metal once more, and Mitch cringed. After stepping on the parking brake, she shut off the ignition. He reached for the door handle but was surprised when she whipped his way, grasped the front of his shirt, and dragged his mouth toward hers.

Her lips were cold, a little too firm, and tasted like that strawberry lip balm Shannon had made him buy for her last week. The scent of her perfume wafted around him—not really roses, but not citrusy either. Actually, it reminded him of his grandmother's house. A little too old-fashioned, a lot too nauseating.

She pulled her mouth from his. "Mm, I've been wanting to do that for weeks." She reached for the door handle. "Come on. Let's take this inside."

Mitch's stomach rolled, but his head was still light enough where he wasn't paying attention. Or was trying hard not to.

Don't think. You want this…

He opened the door and swayed. Lara laughed and ran up to his side. Her arm slid around his waist. "Come on, big guy."

She led him toward the house and used his keys to unlock the door. In the entry, she stopped and looked around at all the old wood paneling he'd restored. "Wow. This place is awesome."

"Thanks." He took the keys from her, tossed them on the entry table, and shut the door. The room spun, and he braced a hand against the solid wood to hold himself up.

Maybe three—or had it been four?—shots of Patron was a little much. He'd been able to hold his own back in college, but these days he rarely had more than a couple of beers in one sitting.

She grasped his hand before he could catch his bearings and dragged him down the hall. "Your bedroom's through here, right?"

His stomach tightened. Thoughts of Simone pinged around in his fuzzy head. What had seemed like a great idea moments before was suddenly turning his stomach.

Lara drew up short at his open bedroom door, grasped his shirt at the front, and shoved him up against the door. Shock registered, but before he could react, her mouth closed over his. A little too forcefully. A lot too wet. He tasted the fruity drink she'd sucked back earlier and what was left of the Patron.

Don't think. Just feel.

The fingers of her free hand slid into his hair, and she pulled his mouth more firmly down onto hers, kissing him deeper. She didn't kiss at all like Simone. This wasn't sweet or sexy or even arousing. It felt…forced, and a little bit brutal.

She pulled him away from the door. The room spun again, and he stumbled. Air whooshed over his back, and he felt himself going down. Then the soft cushion of his mattress met his spine, and the dominatrix at his front landed on top of him.

This wasn't right. He wasn't into it. And dammit, how fucked was he that he couldn't even screw a hot chick climbing all over him?

He rolled her to her back to get her claws off him, and told himself it was the alcohol. That was the reason he wasn't the least bit turned-on. It had to be, because he wasn't going to let this be about Simone.

Mitch pulled his mouth from hers. "Lara, you're hot and everything, but I don't think this is going to work tonight."

Excitement flared in her eyes. "You think I'm hot?"

Good God. Of all the things for her to get stuck on. Mitch's mouth fell open to try to smooth things over, but before he could, she flipped him to his back again.

The mattress bounced. He grunted. A predatory glint sparked in her eyes. She climbed over him like a lioness ready to devour her prey, and Mitch tensed.

"The name's Clara, by the way, not Lara. Get it right." She lowered her mouth to his throat. "But don't worry. Whatever's broken, I can totally make it work. I'm good at that. Trust me, I'm very, very good."

CHAPTER SEVEN

Mitch's car was parked in the drive of his house when Simone arrived. Relief spiraled through her—that he hadn't left for BC yet, that he was home, that she still had a chance, even if that chance was only a meager explanation.

Her stomach tossed and turned as she parked behind his dusty Land Rover and climbed out of her BMW. The light across the street had gone out, and the other houses in the Pacifica neighborhood were dark at this hour. Behind Mitch's house, a green space opened to a park, and the tall, dark trees blocked city lights beyond.

She loved his house—the setting, the neighborhood, the fact he'd taken a rundown ranch and remodeled it into a craftsman dream home with dark woods and big windows and his own unique masculine style. She loved it more than her own Victorian because it had the kind of character she'd never pick for herself—a lot like Mitch. He was not the sort of man she usually went for, and he was nothing like Steve. He was rugged and rough and way too laid back. And she hadn't realized just how much she needed all of that until it was too late.

She stopped inches from the front door, lifted her hand to knock, then hesitated. Her bracelet slid from her wrist to her forearm, pinching her skin, but she barely noticed. The door wasn't completely closed. It looked like it had been shut but hadn't completely latched.

Mitch rarely used the front door. He always went in through the garage. Her adrenaline shot up, and all kinds of dangerous options raced through her mind. But she squashed them by reminding herself no one was really after her, which meant no one would be the least bit interested in hurting Mitch.

She pushed the door open and stepped into the dim entryway. A look toward the dark kitchen and living room told her he was probably already in bed.

And why wouldn't he be? It was after midnight. If he had an early flight up to Canada in the morning, he'd be sound asleep by now.

She slipped off her shoes so they wouldn't squeak on the hardwood floor and set them beside the door. Moving quietly, she headed down the hallway toward the bedrooms. The house had three—in addition to an office. One of which was Mitch's, one he used as a guest room, and the third was where he stored his various backpacks and hiking gear and all those geological instruments Simone couldn't name and would never be able to operate.

Her feet drew to a stop outside his bedroom. A pillow was tossed haphazardly against the end of the open door, but it was the man sound asleep on his back, lying diagonally across the middle of the bed, that drew her attention.

Her heart stuttered, stopped, then felt like it came to life all over again as she stood in the doorway, watching the slow rise and fall of his bare chest. His left hand was up by his head, his watchband just barely covering the scar he'd gotten camping as a kid. The other lay across his chest, right over the spot she loved to rest her fingers against as she fell asleep in his arms.

Tears filled her eyes. Tears she blinked back. She was so stupid to think she could ever let him go. If he'd give her a second chance, she'd do whatever she could to make it up to him.

She crossed the floor and gently sat on the edge of the bed, as close to him as she could get. "Mitch," she said softly.

He didn't respond, so she laid her hand on his warm thigh and said it again. "Mitch."

He shifted his head her direction, but his eyes still didn't open. God, he had the longest eyelashes. They looked like curved, light brown feathers against his tanned skin. Her gaze ran over him, from the rumpled, slightly too-long hair she loved to sift her fingers through to the scruff on his chiseled jaw.

Her hand drifted up to his hair as if it had a mind of its own and combed through the thick, curly locks. When her fingernails scraped his scalp, he groaned in what she knew was pure pleasure.

Her skin warmed, and her stomach tightened. She raked her fingers through his hair again, just as she knew he liked. Common sense told her she should pull her hand back, that she should wake him, but she'd been dying to touch him since she'd walked away. No, that wasn't right. She'd been dying to touch him like this since she'd left for that trip to DC.

"Mm, Simone." His voice was a throaty purr. He still didn't open his eyes, but every nerve in Simone's body jolted as if she'd been shocked by an electrical current. "Love that."

She loved it too. Loved him. She leaned closer. "Mitch. I need…" *to talk to* "…you."

She wasn't sure why she left the words out. It wasn't that they weren't true. It was simply that right now she did need him. Only him.

He drew in a deep breath, and his eyes opened, just a sliver, just enough so she could see his unfocused, soft green gaze. It held on her, and the tiniest smile curled one side of his mouth, showcasing that deep dimple in his cheek she loved. His hand lifted, slid into her chin-length hair, and tugged her mouth down to his.

Home…

The word spun through her mind, ricocheted through her body, and echoed through every limb.

He didn't give her a chance to say no, and frankly, she didn't want him to. His lips were firm and insistent. His scent, masculine and so familiar. And when she opened to him and he kissed her with that warm, wet tongue like he couldn't get enough, every protest she knew she should voice slipped right out of her head.

She sank into the kiss, stroked her tongue against his, ran her fingers through her hair and stretched out against him. Warmth permeated her body, slithered through her chest, and heated the cold space around her heart she'd been living with since that awful night.

"Mm…" He pulled her over him, then rolled her to her side. His hand streaked down her neck, across her collarbone, and closed over her breast.

Electrical sensations shot from beneath her bra to her belly and lower. Simone moaned into his mouth and wrapped her arms around his shoulders as he continued pushing her back into the mattress. He answered by kissing her deeper, by stroking her tongue harder. Spreading her legs to make room for him, she felt his arousal pushing into her, and her pulse picked up speed, knowing he still wanted her.

It wasn't too late. She could fix everything she'd broken. All she needed to do was explain why she'd been ready to run.

"Mitch…" Her fingers toyed with his hair. "I'm sorry. I'm so sorry. I shouldn't have lied to you. I didn't mean it."

He groaned and moved fully on top of her. Sweet, heavenly bliss radiated outward from her pelvis where he rubbed against her, but the stab of something sharp in her shoulder made her pull back from his mouth and gasp. "Ouch. What's that?"

His hand landed against the mattress near her head. He pushed away just enough to look down. He blinked several times, then his unfocused gaze slowly sharpened and held on her face. "Simone?"

"Something's sticking into me." She pushed up just enough so she could wiggle to the side. Reaching back, she grasped the small metal object stuck in the fabric of her shirt and looked down at it in her hand.

Darkness made it hard to see what the object was at first, but then she realized it was an earring. A long, dangly silver thing she'd never be caught dead wearing.

Mitch scrambled off her and pushed upright, swaying on his feet, looking more than a little dazed and seriously confused. "What the…? How did you…? What the *hell* are you doing in my bed?"

The accusation in his voice brought Simone's gaze up. And the stark mixture of surprise and anger in his features told her he hadn't been fully awake when he'd started kissing her.

"I—" She looked down at the earring in her hand, her mind flipping back and forth between a logical explanation and shock over what she'd found. "I came to talk to you."

"That wasn't talking." Mitch grabbed his shirt from the floor and quickly tugged it on. "What kind of games are you playing? You haven't fucked with my head enough for one week?"

Animosity radiated from him in waves, and Simone's mouth fell open, an explanation hovering on her tongue. But then she looked down at the earring in her hand again. "I… What is this?"

His gaze snapped to her hand, and surprise flickered over his features, followed by a shot of guilt, which was quickly masked by a scowl. He rested his hands on his hips and glared at her. "Nothing that really concerns you, now does it?"

Everything inside Simone went cold. Ice cold. He'd fucked someone else, right here in this bed, hours—maybe even minutes—ago. Only two days after their breakup.

Her chest felt like it closed in on itself. Pinpricks of heat stabbed at every inch of her skin. She couldn't breathe. Didn't want to feel. Shaking, she pushed quickly to her feet. "Well, it's nice to know you're not pining away for me. Clearly, you've already moved on."

She dropped the earring on the floor and rushed for the hall. He stepped in the way of her path and braced his hand on the doorjamb, blocking her exit. "*I* moved on? *I moved on?* You're the one who dumped me. And now I'm the one who's supposed to feel guilty about that?"

She wasn't thinking clearly. She knew that. Her emotions were way too hot for her to remain calm and rational. The reckless college girl who'd fallen into an affair with Steve, gotten pregnant, and given up her life on a whim was threatening what was left of her sanity. "Get out of my way."

"Why?" His eyes narrowed to thin points, and a vehemence she'd never seen before reflected in their depths. "You came all the way over here in the middle of the night to tell me something. Go ahead and say it."

Emotions bubbled up inside her—anger, heartache, disbelief—but the one that won out was betrayal, even if a tiny voice in the back of her head said she had no right to feel that way.

She whirled on him. "You have no *idea* what I was willing to do for you. You have no *idea* what I've been through. I came here to explain, but there's no point now."

She ducked under his arm and rushed down the hall toward the door and freedom. Somewhere deep inside, she knew she was being irrational. *She'd* broken things off with *him.* Whatever and whoever he'd done since had nothing to do with her, and yet even though her head understood that, her heart was having a really hard time accepting it. Because for her, things hadn't been over. And she doubted they ever would be.

"Hold on. *What you've done for me?*" He grasped her by the arm and swung her around to face him in the entry hall. Moonlight spilled in through the sidelights by the front door, illuminating his enraged features and disbelieving eyes, the T-shirt molding to his muscular chest, the loose-fitting jeans and his gorgeous, bare feet against the hardwood floor. "You're the one who ended things.

You're the one who said you didn't care. As I recall, your exact words were, 'I don't love you.' So why the fuck would I believe you'd do anything for me when I already know you just don't give a shit?"

She wanted to lash out, to make him hurt the way she was hurting, to tell him he was right, that she really did no longer give a shit. But before she could get the words out, the glass in the far sidelight shattered, sending shards flying through the entryway.

Simone screamed. Mitch threw her to the ground face-first and covered her with his body. Pain echoed through her hipbones and hands and anywhere she hit the hardwood. But the sound of something small and hard digging into the siding, the door, shattering windows and pinging off metal echoed all through the house, distracting her from the pain.

She pushed against him, but he held her firmly to the ground. "Stay down," he growled. "Those are bullets."

Bullets? Simone's adrenaline shot up. *Bullets?* Fear clamped a cold, hard hand around her throat and squeezed. Bullets meant...she'd been wrong. They *had* been following her.

The flight-or-fight response kicked in, and flight won out. By a landslide.

She struggled against Mitch, this time with every ounce of strength she had. "We have to get out of here. They found me. Move. Right now, *move*!"

She managed to shove him off her, pushed to her feet, and sprinted away from the gunfire, down the hallway toward the back of the house. Mitch muttered a curse but grasped her arm just as she reached the back door.

"Hold on. You don't know who's out there." He pulled her tight against him and sank back into the shadows, peering over her head out the slider in the back room he used as his gym. Exercise equipment surrounded her. Gunshots still echoed from the front of the house, but through the glass, the backyard looked empty.

His heart beat fast and hard against hers. He had one arm around her shoulders, one at her lower back, holding her still. Shaking, she chanced a look up at his face and saw his intense gaze sweeping over the backyard.

"I think it's clear," he whispered, still not looking at her. "Sprint for the park. Don't stop. Don't look back. No matter what. You got it?"

All she could do was nod. But that guilt swept in again. Guilt for hurting him, guilt for dragging him into this, guilt for making such a mess of everything.

He let go of her, then quietly slid the door open, and whispered, "Go."

"What about you?"

"I'm right behind you."

Simone's entire body vibrated with fear, but she nodded, looked both ways. When she hesitated, Mitch nudged her from behind. "Go now."

She wanted to grab him, to drag him with her, but his gentle push forced her out the door before she could. And once the cold air washed over her, that flight response kicked back in. Her muscles burned as she streaked across the backyard. She didn't even register the fact her feet were bare until she hit the bark dust on the far side. Since Mitch didn't have a pet, there was no fence to slow her down, and she ran from his property into the safety of the trees of the park without slowing. Behind her, a voice rang out, followed by the ricochet of bullets hitting the dirt, then a hard thunk, as if someone or something had gone down.

Terror brought her feet to a skidding stop. She turned and looked over her shoulder. She'd run so far and so fast, she could only just make out the dark shadow of Mitch's house through the trees.

He wasn't behind her. She scanned the forest. Nothing moved in the dim light. Her adrenaline shot up even higher, and horror vibrated in every cell.

Oh, shit. Mitch. Her heart leapt into her throat. *Mitch!*

She fought from screaming for him. Looked through the trees again, her blood turning to a roar in her ears. Quietly, she picked her way back the way she'd come, moving slower this time, searching everywhere for him, hoping, praying…

He couldn't be dead. They couldn't have gotten him. This wasn't supposed to happen. A hard lump formed in her throat. Tears burned behind her eyes.

And then she saw it. The dark silhouette of a body, lying at the edge of his property.

A scream rose up in her mind.

"Mitch!"

Mitch's head hurt like a motherfucker where he'd been nailed, and his right arm was on fire. He darted around trees and bushes, heading the direction Simone had disappeared.

Rocks and twigs dug into the soles of his bare feet. He made it twenty feet into the cover of the trees, when he realized Simone was yards from him, heading back toward the house, running in the wrong damn direction.

"Son of a bitch." He cut to his right and zeroed in on her. He'd taken one guy down who'd been lurking in the backyard, but from the sounds of gunfire that had died down at the front of the house, there were bound to be more in mere seconds.

He grasped Simone around the waist with one arm and covered her mouth with his other hand. She gasped and jerked against him. Pulling her back into his body, he tugged her into the shadow of a tree and whispered, "Stop fighting me, dammit."

She immediately ceased struggling. Her hands closed over his forearm at her waist. "Mitch," she mumbled against his fingers.

"Who the hell did you think it was? God Almighty, you're gonna get us killed."

Her fingers closed over his against her mouth, and she tugged his hand away. Whipping around in his arms, she placed both hands on his face, feeling for him in the darkness. "I thought that was you on the ground. Oh my God, I thought—"

"We have to get out of here." Mitch didn't look back. Didn't want to see the guy he'd dropped or wonder whether he was alive. His stomach rolled. "Now."

There was just enough light for him to see Simone nod. She didn't put up any kind of fight. Didn't try to tell him what to do. As he pushed her ahead of him into the darkness, her words inside when the gunfire had started pinged through his mind.

"They found me."

He kept looking over his shoulder, but no one seemed to be following. His adrenaline slowly came down the farther they moved away from the devastation, but with every step, questions churned in his brain.

Her strange behavior lately, the fact that even after six months he knew very little about her past, the way she'd acted when those bullets started flying… It all started to make a sick sort of sense.

She was involved in something—something bad. And she'd sucked him into it without any kind of warning.

Confusion slowly gave way to an anger that he couldn't seem to contain. Thanks to her, he'd had his heart ripped out, his mind fucked with, he'd been shot—if the burn in his arm was any indication—and now his house was full of holes. *And* she hadn't once said she was sorry. For *any* of that shit.

They didn't stop until they reached the far side of the park behind his house. A small strip mall with a Laundromat, copy store, and barber shop faced them, every window dark. Barefoot, Simone stepped off the curb and waved toward an approaching taxi.

"I don't have any cash," Mitch mumbled. He patted his pockets. Shit, he didn't have his wallet, cell phone, not even shoes.

"I've got it." The cab slowed and came to a stop. Simone whipped out her ID from her back pocket, a credit card, and cell phone.

One of them was prepared. Not that that made him feel any better. What the hell was she involved in? And why had she been at his house? It obviously wasn't because she wanted him. She'd made that more than clear the last few times he'd seen her.

She climbed into the cab and gave the driver her address.

And that was all Mitch could take.

"What the hell do you think you're doing?" he asked in disbelief, shutting the door after him.

"I have to get to Shannon." Her voice rose as the cab pulled away from the curb. "She's at home with a babysitter."

Screw that. Mitch plucked the cell out of her hand and dialed. Holding it to his ear, he gave the driver a different address.

Simone's mouth fell open. "What are you—?"

"Hey, Simone." Ryan picked up on the second ring, trying to mask a groggy voice. "I didn't expect to hear from you."

"It's not Simone. It's Mitch." And this was a call Mitch never expected to make. "Listen, you gotta get someone over to Simone's house right now and pick up Shannon."

"Why?" Ryan's voice tightened. "What's going on?"

Mitch shot Simone a look. He wasn't about to be softened by the worry in her eyes. Not after what he'd just been through because of her. "Because my house has so many holes in it right now, it looks like Swiss fucking cheese."

"What? What are you talking about? What the hell happened?"

In the background, Mitch heard his sister ask, "What's going on?"

Mitch rubbed his throbbing forehead. "I don't know. Simone showed up at my place, someone followed her, then all hell broke loose. She's obviously involved in some kind of shit she never bothered to tell me about, and we barely got out of there alive."

Simone stiffened next to him, but Mitch was beyond caring at this point.

"Holy shit," Ryan muttered. "She's with you?"

With him? No. Simone had made it perfectly clear she didn't want to be *with* him ever again. "We're in a cab heading toward your building downtown. It was the only place I could think that had security."

Ryan was the CEO of a multinational pharmaceutical empire, and he owned an entire building downtown where his company was headquartered. "I'll call John at the front desk and let him know you're on the way. And don't worry, I'll get someone to pick Shannon up right now."

Relief trickled through Mitch, if only for a microsecond. "Thanks, man."

"Hold tight."

Hold tight? Right now he was just trying to hold on to what was left of his sanity.

Mitch clicked End and tossed the phone to Simone. "Ryan's getting her."

He leaned back in his seat, looked out the window, and tried to settle his raging temper.

Simone was silent next to him, but after several minutes of city lights streaking by and the vehicle bouncing over dips in the road, she said, "I'm sorry."

The words ignited a firestorm inside Mitch. He turned on her before he thought better of it. "You're *sorry*? For what? Fucking up my life, destroying my house, or nearly getting me killed? Tell me, what are you *really* sorry for, Simone?"

"Mitch—"

The placating sound of her voice caused his emotions to bubble up and over before he could stop them. Everything he'd been through the last few days—the stress and the misery and the loss—was all because of her. "What the hell are you involved in? Is it an irate client? Or is it just the last guy you fucked over coming after you because you ruined his life too?"

The cab driver's curious glance reflected in the rearview mirror, but Mitch ignored him. Then wished he'd ignored Simone too and hadn't seen the color fade from her cheeks. He wasn't the one who should feel guilty here, dammit. He hadn't fucked everything up.

"That's not fair," she whispered.

"Not fair? *Not fair?*" Mitch pushed away from the seat back and leaned toward her. "I'll tell you what's not fair. The fact I gave up six fucking months for this shit. If I'd known this was what I was going to get out of it, I never would have stepped foot in your damn office."

His hands were shaking, and realizing he'd reached the end of his rope, he shifted back in his seat and looked out the window again so he didn't shake some serious sense into her. Yeah he was being a dick, but he honestly didn't care. He'd lost his house tonight, and very nearly his life. All because of her. That went ten steps beyond ripping out his heart, which she'd already done.

Silence filled the cab. But as they pulled up in front of Ryan's building and the car drew to a stop, Simone quietly said, "I was wrong about you. You're more like your brother-in-law than I thought. You obviously learned how to be an ass from the very best."

CHAPTER EIGHT

Simone stood in the elevator of Ryan's building, staring at the numbers as they passed floors, heading toward Ryan's office. Mitch was leaning against the back wall of the car, seething, but she was too worried to care. He hadn't given her a chance to explain, he hadn't wanted to listen, and right now all she could think about was making sure her daughter was okay.

The elevator pinged, and the door opened. A security guard with dark hair, one Simone knew she'd met before, greeted them and unlocked Ryan's office door. "Mr. Harrison said he'd be here shortly and to just make yourselves at home."

Right. Like that was going to happen.

She managed a "thank you" and clenched her hands into fists as she stepped into the lavish corporate office. A view of the twinkling city shone through the wall of windows ahead, just past Ryan's sleek desk. To her left, a sitting area with couches and tables and a wet bar faced a large flat screen TV, and on her right, double glass doors opened to a spacious conference room.

Mitch went right for the wet bar, but Simone was too keyed up to drink. Instead, she spotted the bathroom door on the far side of the room and made a beeline straight for it.

Ryan's private bathroom was as swanky as his office. Marble, mirrors, and a huge stone shower filled the space. Bracing her hands on the counter, she stood in front of the mirror and stared at her reflection. Dirt was smeared across her forehead, her hair was a mess of brown strands around her face, and her eyes held a wild, frightened look she'd only seen once before. Everything she'd been afraid of when she'd first gotten that call was coming true and there wasn't a single thing she could do to stop it.

Her mind flashed back to that day Steve had told her where he was. And the gut-wrenching moment she'd had to decide to either go with him or say good-bye forever. That, at least, had been her decision. Her stomach tightened when she realized Mitch might not have the luxury of that choice. Not if the people who'd been after Steve had already connected Mitch to her.

A lead weight landed hard, right in the center of her chest. Hand shaking, she reached for a towel from a shelf beneath the sink, flipped on the water, and ran it under the stream. After wiping the dirt from her skin, she splashed cool water on her face and reached for a fresh towel to dry.

A door opened and closed in the outer office. Voices echoed beyond the bathroom walls. Simone froze, and when she heard Shannon's exuberant voice, bolted for the door.

Mitch was kneeling on one knee, holding Shannon in a tight hug when Simone stepped into the room, his eyes closed, his hair a sexy mess around his face. As he held her daughter, the anger he'd directed Simone's way seemed to seep away, leaving behind only relief and…joy.

Shannon hugged him hard and whispered, "I can't believe you're here. Why are you here? Where's my mom?"

"Nannon."

Shannon turned her head at the sound of Simone's voice and looked her way. She pulled out of Mitch's arms and sprinted across the room. "Mom."

Simone dropped to her knees, closed her eyes, and gathered her daughter close. Yesterday, she'd been livid that Shannon had run off. Today all she could do was thank God she was safe.

Shannon eased back, her curly hair caught in the neck of her hoodie as if she'd just thrown it on. "Are you okay? Why is your shirt ripped?"

Simone glanced down at the tear in the shoulder and along the hem. She shook her head, not wanting Shannon to worry. "It's nothing. I just caught it on something." She placed both hands on Shannon's cheeks. "Are you okay?"

"I'm fine, Mom." When Simone started inspecting her, Shannon rolled her eyes. "I told you I was fine. I was asleep when Mr. Harrison came over and woke me and Melody up."

Melody.

Simone's gaze snapped to Ryan, standing near the wet bar, and, Kate, who was picking up a soda can from the counter and tossing it in the trash. "Is Melody okay?"

"Fine." Ryan tugged off his jacket and threw it on the end of the couch. "We took her home. I have a couple of guys at your place keeping an eye on things to see if anyone shows."

"What about Julia and Reed?"

"My folks are at the house," Kate answered.

"Shit," Mitch muttered. "Mom and Dad are here? I thought they weren't coming until next week."

Simone blew out a breath of relief, the first time since those bullets had started flying. For now it seemed like tragedy had been averted, but that wouldn't last.

"They changed their plans." Kate glanced her brother's way, and her eyes widened. "Oh my God, you're bleeding." She grabbed a towel from the bar and stepped toward Mitch, pressing the cotton against his upper arm. "What happened to you two?"

Simone's relief was short-lived. She pushed to her feet, rested her hand on Shannon's shoulder's, and looked at Mitch's arm. "You got shot?"

"*Shot?*" Shannon asked in a frantic voice, turning beneath her mother's hands. "What?"

"It's okay." Mitch sent Simone a *don't worry her more* look, then focused on Shannon, his expressions softening. "It's nothing."

Kate looked toward her husband. "Do you have a first aid kit in here?"

"Yeah." Ryan moved toward cabinets on the far wall, and Kate followed.

Mitch held the towel against his arm, and for the first time, Simone noticed the dried streaks of blood on his forearm and the smears across his T-shirt. "I'm fine, Shannon. It's just a scratch."

"Just a scratch, my ass," Kate muttered as she came back.

Ryan wheeled his desk chair over and pushed on Mitch's good shoulder. "Sit. Before your sister flips out."

"It's nothing," Mitch said to Kate, pulling back his sleeve so she could get at the wound. "It barely grazed me."

It being the bullet. Simone gripped Shannon's shoulders and fought back the bile sliding up her throat.

Kate dabbed at the wound with an alcohol pad. "Mom and Dad were right to be worried about you."

Mitch clenched his jaw. "Mom and Dad wouldn't be worried about me if someone didn't have loose lips."

"I'm not the one who blabbed," Kate tossed back. "Thank your friend Kendrick."

Mitch's gaze shot to Ryan, standing on his other side. Ryan shrugged. "Sorry, man. Your mom called our house, and Julia must have told them you were staying with Kendrick, then your mom called him wondering why you hadn't just come home if you were in the Seattle area. I swear he's the one who spilled, not us."

It took a moment for the conversation to sink in, but when it did, Simone realized they were talking about her. The reason Mitch's parents were worried about him was because of their breakup.

The room started to close in. The air felt hot, and her skin tight. Mitch's gaze snapped to hers and held, but before she could find any words, he looked down at Shannon, who stood in front of her.

"I'm fine, Shannon," he said again. "It's nothing."

"But…but you got shot."

He motioned with his good arm, and hesitantly, Shannon eased out from under her mother's grip and stepped toward his chair. He wrapped an arm around her waist and pulled her to his side. "Kate, take that off for a minute."

Kate pulled the alcohol pad back to reveal the skin that had been stripped away.

"See?" Mitch said to Shannon. "Not a big deal. Just a scratch. Not even as bad as when you crashed your bike last month."

"But…who would shoot at you?"

Mitch looked over Shannon's head toward Simone again, and his eyes narrowed, but his voice remained just as calm as it always did when he stepped in to diffuse a situation with Shannon. "No one. They weren't after me. It was just a random drive-by thing." He looked down at her again, his face softening once more. "You know that stuff happens in the city sometimes, right? We saw it on the news a few weeks ago, remember?"

"Yeah." Shannon watched Kate clean and bandage the wound, but her one-word answer said she still wasn't sure.

"Everything's okay, Shannon. Trust me."

He pulled her in for a one-armed hug, and Shannon leaned against his chest. Closing her eyes, she whispered, "I'm glad you're okay."

"Me too, sweetheart."

Mitch might be okay, but Simone wasn't. Her pulse picked up speed, and her head felt light. Everything that had happened tonight spiraled in to suck the air out of her lungs.

"Mom? Are you okay?"

The room spun. Simone swayed.

Dimly, she heard Kate say, "Ryan?"

"I've got her."

She registered Ryan's arm around her waist, his hand on her arm, felt her sluggish feet moving but couldn't seem to focus on any one thing. Something soft pressed against her spine and the backs of her legs. From across the room, she recognized Shannon's panicked voice but couldn't find the words to respond.

"That's it. Just breathe," Ryan said in a reassuring voice. "You're okay."

"Mom?"

"She's fine," Ryan said again in that same calm voice. "Just give her some room."

"I'm done here," Kate said. "Shannon, why don't you and I go down the hall and get some coffee going? You're out of coffee here, aren't you, Ryan?"

"What? Yeah. Coffee. Right. That's a good idea."

"But my mom—"

"She's fine, Shannon," Kate said. "Some people get queasy at the sight of blood, that's all. Let's just give her some space, okay? We'll be right back."

The door opened and closed. Slowly, the room seemed to slow its crazy spinning, and Simone felt air filling her lungs all over again. When she lifted her head and managed to open her eyes, she focused on Ryan's face, just in front of hers.

A slow smile spread across his lips. His hands were resting on her biceps, and he was kneeling in front of the couch where she was sitting. "There you go. That looks more like the girl I know."

The girl he knew…

That was the problem. He had no idea who she really was. None of them did. That familiar panic pushed in again, but she fought it back.

She hadn't had a panic attack in years, and she wasn't giving in to one again. Not now.

Focus. Plan. Execute.

"I-I'm fine." She pulled her arms from his grip and ran her hands through her hair. "Mitch…" Her throat closed, and she swallowed hard. "Mitch is the one you should worry about."

Ryan looked to his left. "Dog-breath is fine. Aren't you?"

From the edge of the bar where he was standing, Mitch flipped Ryan the bird. “No thanks to you.”

Ryan chuckled, then turned to Simone. His face sobered. “We need to call the police. But first, why don’t you tell me what happened.”

She chanced a look Mitch’s way. His eyes were focused solely on her, his arms hanging loosely at his sides, the bandage and the blood on his T-shirt drawing her attention and reminding her of everything that had happened.

She closed her eyes to block out the memory. “The police aren’t going to be able to do anything. We need to call WITSEC. But even that…” She opened her eyes and stared at Ryan’s shocked expression. “I’m not sure I can trust the US marshal assigned to my case.”

CHAPTER NINE

Mitch had to have heard Simone wrong.

"WITSEC? US marshals?" He gave his head a small shake, afraid the blow he'd taken when he'd been fighting that guy in his yard might have done some serious damage. "What the hell are you talking about?"

Simone gripped the couch cushion at her thighs, and opened her eyes. "Shannon and I left the witness protection program two and a half years ago after Steve died. I thought we were safe, but I was obviously wrong."

Ryan moved to sit on the long arm of the leather sectional. "Witness protection? Holy cow."

Simone didn't look Mitch's way. "I met Steve my last year of college. He was an accountant, working for a big company on the east coast."

"Wait," Mitch said from the direction of the wet bar. "I thought your husband was a lawyer."

Simone flicked a guilty look his way, then refocused on the floor in front of her. "Technically he was both. His specialty was corporate tax law. He passed the bar, but after he was hired by his firm, they encouraged him to get his CPA license. He spent more time doing their books than practicing law."

Mitch felt like he'd been sucker punched all over again. She hadn't just lied to him about her feelings, she'd lied about her entire life.

Stunned, he leaned back against the counter, thankful it was there to hold him upright. Part of him wanted to run and not listen to any more. Another part needed to hear the truth.

"I honestly don't know much about the case," Simone went on. "Steve and I had just started dating when it was all happening, and he told me the less I knew, the better off I'd be. All I know is that the managing partner of his firm was some bigwig in the northeast, and somehow Steve had come across evidence proving the firm was laundering money."

She ran a hand through her hair, sending the already disheveled dark locks to fall against her pale cheeks. "It was a big case, with far-reaching implications that went beyond the firm, though Steve would never tell me where. And when his life was threatened before the trial, prosecutors offered him protection via WITSEC."

Ryan braced his forearms against his thighs and clasped his hands together in front of him. "But you weren't involved?"

Simone shook her head. "I didn't know anything about it until much later. Steve had been acting funny, and we'd only been together a few months, so I didn't know what to make of it. I went to talk to him one night and found him frantically throwing things in a backpack, getting ready to leave. That's when he gave me a brief explanation of what was going on. And offered to take me with him."

Mitch could barely believe what he was hearing. The calm, composed, totally reserved attorney he'd fallen for would never leap without looking. At least she never had with him. He crossed his arms over his chest. "I'm surprised you went."

Simone finally looked his way, and he saw a mix of emotions in her eyes—hurt, regret, anger—he just couldn't tell which one was meant for him. "I wouldn't have. Not normally. But I'd just found out I was pregnant with Shannon. That's why I went to talk to him that night. And I was already freaking out a little. When I found out what was going on, the marshals gave me five minutes to make a decision. Go with him or never see him again."

Disbelief pulsed through Mitch's veins. This woman he *thought* he'd known had given up her life for a man she barely knew, whereas all these months they'd been together, he'd had to fight tooth and nail to get her to do something as impulsive as blow off work for the day and hang out at the beach.

Ryan rested his hand on Simone's arm. "Tell us what happened after the trial."

Simone looked back down at her hands. "The three main managing partners were sentenced to fifteen years. But when Steve tried to step back into his old life, those far-reaching arms I was telling you about tried to have him killed. So they relocated us to Atlanta. I had Shannon, Steve got a job in financial planning, and when things settled down, I decided I wanted to go to law school.

By the time I graduated, everything seemed…normal, so when I was offered a job in the Baltimore area, WITSEC gave us the go ahead to relocate. They got Steve another position, and everything seemed fine…until he got sick."

She closed her eyes briefly, gave her head a swift shake, then opened them again. Her hands tightened around the seat cushion once more. "He wasn't sick long. It came out of nowhere, and at first we didn't know what was wrong. Test after test. When he finally got the diagnosis of pancreatic cancer, things went fast. Three weeks later, he was gone."

She blinked several times and released her grip. "Since I was never involved in the case, WITSEC gave me the choice of remaining in the program or leaving. I had never been mentioned in any of the threats against Steve, nor was there ever any indication anyone from his old firm knew about me or Shannon. It had been nearly eight years with no incidents, so I opted to leave. We kept our new identities, moved out here, and started over. And I thought we were safe but"—she lifted her shoulders and dropped them in defeat— "now I know I was wrong."

"Why do you think what happened tonight has anything to do with Steve's case?" Ryan asked.

Simone slanted Ryan a look. "What else would it have to do with?"

"I know." He smirked. "Dumb question. But humor me. You, yourself, said you weren't a witness and that no one even knew about you."

"Because I got a call a few days ago. The day I came back from DC. William Holdt was the US marshal assigned to my case. He sounded frantic. And he was apologizing for the fact they'd found out where I was."

The day she'd come back from DC. Mitch thought back to the night she'd flown home. That was also the day she'd stomped all over his heart.

"What else did he say?" Ryan asked.

"Not a lot. But I freaked out. All I could think about was keeping Shannon safe. That's why we were leaving. But then Shannon ran off, and a few days passed without anything happening, and I thought… stupidly…that maybe I'd overreacted. So I went over to your house tonight"—she motioned toward Mitch but didn't look his way again—"to explain, when all hell broke loose."

Something inside Mitch's chest drew tight. Lies weren't something he could usually forgive, but even he could see why Simone hadn't been totally honest about her past. And when he thought back to the way she'd abruptly broken things off, her excuse about leaving town because her father was sick, and how frantic she'd been to get Shannon back, that anger inside started to crack.

"So you think the same people who were after Steve are now after you," Ryan said.

Simone closed her eyes again. "I don't know. All I know is if they were trying to flush me out, they did a damn good job, don't you think?"

Ryan looked Mitch's way, and Mitch caught the serious look in his brother-in-law's blue gaze. Ryan believed her. And if the buzz growing in the pit of Mitch's belly was any indication, he believed her too.

Which he wasn't particularly thrilled about. Because as his brain spun, trying to find a solution to this, only one thought latched on and wouldn't let go.

Whoever was after her now knew about him. They'd blown *his* property to pieces, not hers. He'd seen the face of one of the attackers, a face he was never going to be able to forget. Whether they'd targeted him because of his relationship with Simone or were simply following her and she'd inadvertently led them to him, he was now as embroiled in all of this as was she.

"Why can't you call WITSEC and tell them what happened?" Ryan asked.

"I could," Simone answered. "But…it gets complicated."

"Complicated, how?" Ryan asked.

Simone flicked a wary look Mitch's direction. And all that resentment reignited an anger he only barely held back.

"Because of me," Mitch said. "Because as soon as you contact them, they're going to put you and Shannon into protective custody again and recommend I go as well."

"They know who you are now," Simone said quietly. "These aren't the kind of people who just…forget a name."

Mitch crossed his arms over his chest. "I'm not giving up my life for this."

"What are we talking here?" Ryan asked. "Mafia?"

"Sort of," Simone answered. "Steve told me they were like the Mafia, but he never explained."

"*Like* the mafia?" There was a whole lot more she wasn't saying. And the fact she was holding back now only spurred Mitch's growing frustration. "You're a fucking lawyer. You should have asked a few key questions."

Simone pushed to her feet, and for the first time since he'd awoken and found her kissing him, he saw anger instead of doubt. "I did ask questions, but Steve always evaded them. The less I knew, the better. That was his standard answer every time. Do you think I wanted any of this? I've been working my ass off to make the best of things since the moment I met him. And I tried to keep you out of all this. I told you I wasn't looking for a relationship, remember? But you wouldn't take no for an answer. You're the one who pushed your way into this mess when I tried to keep you out of it."

"Okay." Ryan stood, holding out his hands to try to defuse the situation. "Relax. No one's blaming you for anything, Simone."

"You're not, but he is."

Ryan shot Mitch a scathing look, then turned and gripped Simone's arms again, forcing her to focus on him. "Why don't we call the marshal assigned to your case—Holdt?"

She flicked another irate look Mitch's way, then drew in a calming breath. "I tried. More than once. His phone keeps going to voice mail. I didn't think it was a big deal before, but after all this…" She swiped a hand across her forehead. "I'm not sure who to trust. If he gave someone my location, who else in WITSEC is compromised?"

"Why don't you let me try," Ryan said.

Simone stiffened. "You can't tell him where we are."

"I won't."

Simone hesitated, looked up at Mitch. But after several seconds, she pulled her phone from her pocket and paged through screens until she found the contact. "Here."

Ryan pulled out his own cell, dialed, then held it up to his ear. After several seconds, he said, "Yeah, I'm trying to get in touch with Marshal William Holdt. No. Yeah, I can hold."

As they waited, Mitch crossed to the floor-to-ceiling windows and looked out at the sparkling lights of the city far below. Witness protection. Mafia. His head was spinning. And every time he closed his eyes, he saw his house being blown to pieces.

"Okay, thanks."

Ryan lowered the phone, hit End, and sighed. "Well, that's not going to help us."

"What did they say?" Simone asked.

Mitch turned from the window.

"William Holdt died yesterday."

"No." Simone's eyes fell closed. Her face paled, and she lowered herself to the couch. "No, no, no."

"It could just be a coincidence," Ryan said quickly.

Simone huffed out a sound that held no humor. "Not unless my luck has changed."

Ryan looked toward Mitch, and in his eyes, Mitch saw the same thing he was thinking. There was more to this than she was saying.

Ryan tapped the phone against his palm and looked back at Simone. "You were right to come here. We'll figure something out."

No, Mitch had been right to bring her here. Though at the moment, he wasn't overjoyed by that decision.

"I don't feel like it," Simone muttered. "I feel like I just put you and Kate in danger too."

"We'll be fine. Don't worry about us. Let me do a little research on Holdt and see what I can find."

Simone didn't answer, just nodded and rested her head back against the couch. And in the silence, Mitch wrestled with a mixture of anger and helplessness and feelings of utter stupidity.

The mafia? He really hoped to hell that wasn't what this was, because he wasn't giving up his life.

That anger and betrayal popped and sizzled while he pulled out another soda. The door opened before he took his first sip, and Kate stepped back into the room, followed by a smiling Shannon, carrying a large plastic bowl.

Shannon crawled onto the L-shaped leather sectional near Simone and tugged on her mom's hand, forcing her to scoot toward her. "Mrs. Harrison found popcorn and said we could watch a movie. Can we, Mom?"

Simone looked over her shoulder toward Kate. Kate closed the door and wrinkled her nose. "Thought the movie might help her drift back to sleep."

"And the popcorn?" Simone asked.

Kate frowned. "Considering you look like you haven't eaten in days, I figured some kind of food—even popcorn—wasn't a bad midnight snack."

Mitch paused midswallow and looked over the soda can at his lips toward Simone. Kate was right, and he'd been so pissed these last few days—last few hours—he hadn't noticed just how pale and hollow her cheeks looked.

Guilt crept in. A guilt that warred with the anger he wanted to continue stoking.

She'd lied to him, broken his heart, and blown apart his house.

But she'd also been protecting her daughter for years. She'd given up her life, uprooted herself from her friends and family, moved clear across the country and started over. And she was right… She had tried to keep their relationship platonic. But he'd pushed until he'd fallen head over heels in love with the woman and was already planning a marriage she didn't want.

Her words from earlier sifted through his mind. Words he thought he'd dreamed but now wasn't so sure.

"I'm so sorry. I shouldn't have lied to you. I didn't mean it."

Confusion slid back in, replacing the anger and melding with a knot of unease that formed a hot ball of nerves in the middle of his belly. Just which lie was she sorry for? Not telling him about her past? Hiding the fact she'd been in the witness protection program and that people could be trying to kill her? Or what she felt for him?"

Those nerves twisted and rolled until his skin grew tight and tingly.

"Mitch?"

Startled, he looked toward his sister, standing on the other side of the room, watching him with a perplexed expression. Her curly chestnut hair, a lot like his but longer, was tied in a neat tail at the back of her head and swayed when she moved. "Are you okay?"

He glanced around the room in a daze. Simone and Shannon were snuggled on the couch with their popcorn, watching some animated movie on the TV, the lights dimmed and the sound on low. Simone had her back turned his way and didn't seem the least bit curious about what he was doing. His gaze flicked the other direction, to Ryan's desk, where Ryan was leaning back against the mahogany surface and Kate was standing in front of him with her arms crossed over her chest, listening to whatever he'd been telling her.

They both stared at him as if his head might twist off and explode.

Good God. How long had he been standing there? Mitch rubbed a hand down his face and set the soda can back on the bar with a hand that was way more unsteady than he liked. "I'm fine."

The look Kate sent him said she didn't think he looked fine. She obviously thought he looked fucked. Which was exactly how he felt. "Why don't you go take a shower and get cleaned up while Ryan fills me in on everything? By then, maybe Shannon will be asleep, and we can all decide what to do next."

What to do next. Yeah. Like that was a simple decision.

Mitch nodded, barely registering his feet moving as he crossed the office toward Ryan's fancy corporate bathroom. He didn't have a clue what to do next. But one thing was certain: he needed to clear his head and think.

Because if he didn't stop being ruled by his emotions, he wasn't sure where he'd end up. Or who would be leading him.

Hey, Counselor. How are you holding up?"

Simone looked up when Kate sank into the chair to her right. Mitch called her that too sometimes—counselor—and she'd always liked it, but right now all it did was make her feel like a fraud.

She lifted Shannon's head from her lap to the couch and shifted closer to the short arm of the sectional so she and Kate could talk quietly. "I'm fine."

"It's okay not to be fine, you know, considering all this."

"No. I'm fine. Really."

Kate's small smile said she didn't believe her. "I wish you'd told me some of what was going on. I don't know what I could have done to help, but I do know what it's like not to have anyone to talk to. I would have been there for you."

Simone didn't want to think about how isolating her life had been because of all this. After she'd left New England, she'd accepted the fact she'd never have any close girlfriends again. Over the years, she'd made acquaintances, but she'd never let herself get attached to anyone. Not until recently.

She blinked back the tears threatening and leaned on the armrest of the sofa. "I'm sorry. I should have told you. It's just…not something you can blurt out, you know?"

"I know." Kate's hand covered hers on the armrest. "And I'm not upset that you didn't tell me. I understand."

Simone frowned. "I wish others were as understanding."

"Mitch is just…shell-shocked right now."

Yeah, Simone knew all about 'shell-shocked.' But it was more than that. She'd seen the look in his eyes when his house—and life—had been destroyed, all because of her.

"He has every right to be upset with me."

"That doesn't mean it's okay for him to be a jerk," Kate countered.

Simone huffed a sound that was part laugh, part exasperation. "Maybe. But it doesn't change the truth."

"Just give him some time. He'll get over it."

Simone wasn't so sure. And right now, she didn't even know if she wanted him to get over it. She'd seen a side of him tonight she hadn't known existed. And when she thought back to that earring stabbing into her back…

Her stomach rolled, and a sick feeling slid up her throat.

She closed her eyes tight, then opened them again, fighting back the nausea. "I can't think about Mitch right now. I have too many other things to worry about. Shannon and I have to leave."

"Simone—"

"No, don't." Simone held up a hand to stop her friend from protesting. This was going to hurt no matter how she did it, but it was better just to get it over with. "I've thought a lot about it while you and Ryan have been over there whispering. I voluntarily left the witness protection program. My case, according to WITSEC, was closed. But even if they would take me back, I'm not sure I'd want to go. Whether Will leaked my information or not doesn't really matter. It's out there. And with everything that happened, I obviously can't stay here. I'd go now, except"—her gaze strayed to her daughter's angelic face—"Shannon's been through so much tonight, I wanted to give her one good night's sleep before we leave."

Kate was quiet for a moment, then finally said, "Where will you go?"

Options raced through Simone's frazzled mind. Options she'd considered over the last few days, then abandoned. "I'm not sure. Somewhere far from here. That's all I know."

"Don't jump without thinking, Simone."

Simone looked to her friend. "I'm not. But if it was Reed's and Julia's safety on the line—"

Kate sighed. "I'd do the exact same thing."

Simone knew her friend would.

Kate squeezed her hand and pushed to her feet, then reached for a blanket Simone hadn't noticed on the coffee table. "I brought this for you and Shannon. If you're really leaving in the morning, you need your rest too."

Simone took the blanket and looked up at her friend. "You're not going to try to stop me?"

"No." She glanced across the room to where Ryan was busily searching his computer monitor. "But that man of mine is trying to come up with some other options for you. If he finds something, will you at least listen?"

Simone frowned. "I don't know what he could possibly find that would change my mind."

"Let's just see what he discovers. He has been known to surprise us, now and again."

Ryan Harrison, CEO of the universe, come up with something game changing? It could happen, but Simone doubted it. This situation wasn't something his money or fame or billion-dollar pharmaceutical company could fix.

She forced a sad smile she didn't feel and looked back at her friend. "Sure. But I'm not getting my hopes up. They've been crushed to rubble before."

"Have a little faith, Simone. Sometimes, it's all you really need."

Simone flicked off the TV, spread the blanket over her daughter, and lay down on the other arm of the sofa, so their heads were touching on the pillow they shared. She used to have faith, but even that had failed her. She'd lost her identity, lost her husband, and now she was losing not just the family she'd come to love here in San Francisco, but she'd lost Mitch. The only other person besides Shannon she would risk all of this for.

In her case, even faith seemed miles out of her grasp.

CHAPTER TEN

A wave of steam preceded Mitch when he stepped out of the bathroom after his shower. The room was dark, the TV was off, and the only people he could see were Simone and Shannon, asleep on the leather sectional.

Emotions rolled through his chest. His body urged him to go over, gather them both in his arms, and hold them close where nothing could hurt them. But his pride and that searing betrayal still simmering in his gut wouldn't let him.

The light in the adjacent conference room was on, so he moved that way. Through the glass doors, he saw Ryan sitting behind his laptop, the screen reflecting in his reading glasses as he pointed to something for Kate, who was standing next to him, her arms crossed over her chest, her head dipped low.

He didn't like that worried look. His sister had already been through too much. And he disliked the serious expression on Ryan's surly face even more.

Pushing the door open, he forced his shoulders to relax and tried to keep things light. God knew they'd all had too much heavy to last them the rest of their lives. "Something tells me you're not watching porn in here."

Kate's head shot up, and she quickly masked the fear in her eyes. She dropped her hands. "How are you feeling? Are you okay? Do you need me to rewrap that bandage?"

The last thing he needed was her fawning all over him. "No, I'm fine. Though I could use some of that coffee you brewed earlier. I don't think I'm sleeping much tonight."

She smiled, but it wasn't one of her normal happy smiles, and that dimple they both shared didn't even wink his way. "I'll get it." She turned to her husband. "Babe?"

"Yeah, I'll have another cup."

She grabbed his mug from the table and crossed the room. When she reached Mitch at the door, she rose on her toes, wrapped her arms around his neck, and gave him a tight hug. "You scared me. Don't do that again."

He hugged her back. "I'll try not to."

She dropped to her feet, smiled again, then disappeared out the door. When they were alone, Mitch looked at his best friend and frowned. "Your acting skills suck. I can totally tell whatever you found is gonna fuck up my life even more."

Ryan leaned back in his chair and chuckled. "I never claimed to be Oscar worthy."

"Woulda thought you'd picked something up, all those years dating models and actresses." He crossed the room and looked at the screen over Ryan's shoulder.

Ryan swiveled his leather chair at the head of the conference table and glanced up at Mitch. Behind him, out the wall of glass, city lights twinkled against a black sky. "They weren't exactly giving me acting lessons."

No, they hadn't been. In the years after they'd all thought Kate had died, Ryan had gone through a two-year depression where he hadn't done much of anything besides work. Then, after much prodding—mostly from Mitch—he'd started dating again. But he hadn't gone for normal women. No, the women he'd picked had all been flashy, self-centered, and not a single one had lasted more than a few weeks. He'd done his best to date every single woman who was the opposite of his dead wife, and not a single one had done anything to make him forget.

A lot like Mitch had done by bringing that girl, Lara—no Clara—home from the bar.

The memory of Simone finding that girl's earring in his bed flashed in his mind. He knew she thought he'd slept with her, and the decent part of him whispered he needed to come clean. But another part—the part that was still really pissed at her—wouldn't let him.

He focused on the screen. "What did you find?"

"Pull up a chair." Ryan angled the laptop so Mitch could see it. "Simone told me her husband's name before reidentification was Graham. I did a search, and this is what came up."

He paged back up to the top of the article. It was dated over ten years ago and had been written by a reporter covering the case against Reynolds, Palmer, and McMillian, a high-powered law firm in Hartford, Connecticut. Mitch scanned the article, which outlined the state's case, including charges of racketeering. The article mentioned Simone's late husband by name as the accountant for the firm, and that he'd agreed to turn state's evidence against his employers in exchange for immunity from prosecution.

It was the same information Simone had told them earlier. With two exceptions. This made it sound like Simone's husband had received immunity from prosecution in exchange for his testimony, and the article hinted at a link between the firm and a secret organization with ties to the "power elite."

A buzzing sounded in Mitch's brain. The article was familiar. Too familiar. He read it from the beginning again, scrolled down, then froze when he saw the sketch the reporter had done of a symbol linked to this "power elite."

Everything inside him went cold. Ice cold. He stared at the image of the three daggers, one pointed down, the other two perpendicular to the first, both pointing outward to form a cross, and above, a circle at the top, filled with two numbers and one letter.

"Oh fuck," he whispered. "Fuck me." This was not happening. No way was this happening.

"What?" Ryan asked.

The air closed in around Mitch. He pushed back from the table and dropped his head between his knees, focusing on drawing a breath. Simone's panic attack suddenly seemed like nothing compared to this.

"Mitch?" Ryan asked again. "What the hell's going on?"

Without lifting his head, Mitch turned the laptop so Ryan could see the screen.

"Yeah? So?" Ryan said. "Is that supposed to mean something to me?"

Slowly, because his hands were shaking, Mitch unlatched the watch he always wore on his left wrist and lifted his arm so Ryan could see the mark—no, not a mark, a brand—he kept hidden.

The room went stone-cold silent for several seconds, then Ryan whispered, "What the fuck is that?"

Mitch strapped the watch back to his wrist and pushed back from the table. He couldn't sit. He had to walk. He had to think. "You know exactly what it is."

Ryan sat stunned in his chair while Mitch paced the length of the conference room. "You joined a secret society? When did this happen? And why the hell didn't I know about it?"

"Because it was secret, dumbass. That's the whole point of a *secret* society."

"But…how? When—?"

"In college. And you didn't know because you were too busy hitting on my sister at the time to give a rip about what I was up to."

Ryan was silent for a minute and then said, "You got tapped by a secret society our senior year?"

"That's usually when it happens."

"Why you? I mean…I was the one involved in a dozen different organizations on campus. I was the one with the higher GPA. I was the captain of the baseball team, and the one—"

"Holy hell, Harrison. Get over yourself, would you?" Mitch stopped and stared at his friend in utter disbelief. "This isn't a competition over who was the better man in college."

"They obviously thought you were if they tapped you and not me," Ryan muttered. "Man, they really screwed the pooch there."

"Son of a bitch." Mitch raked both hands through his hair. "Focus, moron. This is fucking important."

"Yeah, yeah. Okay, sorry." Ryan held up a hand. "I'm just…surprised, that's all. I mean…wow. They tapped you. I seriously did not see that coming."

Ryan's jealousy was the least of Mitch's worries right now. "Trust me, it hasn't been a cakewalk."

"What do you mean?"

Mitch glanced through the glass doors toward Ryan's office, where Simone and Shannon were sleeping. The room was still dark, and there was no movement, so he doubted they were awake, but he lowered his voice just in case. "Look, it was a trip senior year, even I'll admit that. Money, parties, girls… They lavished it all on us. But once college was over, things got real."

He turned to face Ryan and gripped the back of a chair in front of him. "The Cyphers are not nobodies. They're exactly what that article states. The Power Elite. Three of the last twelve US presidents have been members of Cypher and Dagger. Company CEOs, research specialists, military leaders… If you can think of a job that's important in this country and has the power to shape society, odds are fairly high a Cypher's in one of those key positions."

Ryan looked back at the symbol on the screen and drummed his fingers on the long table. "How do you figure into all of this?"

"I've not been an exemplary member. The Cyphers got me my job with PreCorp, but once they started pushing me up the ranks, I found reasons to turn down the promotions, which pissed them off. See, they want people in power positions so the Society can dictate policy, and an oil-and-gas conglomerate? Nothing shapes the direction of the world more than oil. But you know how much I hate being behind a desk. I like being out in the field, traveling, and being on site with my team when they're in the identification stage of an oil reserve, even when they're doing the initial excavation. I wasn't built to be a suit. So by turning them down, I was putting myself in some hot water with the society."

"What happened?" Ryan asked.

"What happened is…we lost Kate." Mitch looked at his friend. "This is going to sound really shallow but when Kate's plane crashed, that gave me a reason to stick close to home. You and Julia needed me, and I was able to convince my boss—who also happens to be a Cypher and is my contact within the company—that I needed to *stay* close to home."

"Wait. Chris Murdoch's a Cypher?"

Mitch nodded. Ryan had met Chris, the president of the US division of PreCorp, a dozen times. They'd even all gone to a few ball games together.

"Shit," Ryan muttered.

Shit wasn't even the half of it. Mitch resumed pacing. "I do the bare minimum. I go to one meeting a year, and I schmooze it up like I'm supposed to, but then I come home and pretend like it didn't happen. And most of the time I convince myself they don't care about where I am or what I'm doing. But that's obviously not the case anymore."

"What do you mean?"

"I mean," Mitch said, turning to face his brother-in-law. "I don't think Simone was the target tonight. I'm pretty sure it was me."

"Whoa. Whoa. Whoa. Hold on a minute." Ryan tugged off his glasses and pushed out of his chair. "Simone's late husband turned state's evidence against these people. Even if they are linked to the

Cyphers, which this article can't even confirm, that doesn't mean someone coming after her has anything to do with you."

Mitch closed his eyes and pressed his fingers against his suddenly aching forehead. He'd give just about anything to go back to that drunken state of oblivion he'd been in earlier tonight, but he knew now that was no longer an option.

"You don't get it." He dropped his hand. "I remember this case, Ryan. I remember it because the society made sure every member learned a valuable lesson during it. All three of the managing partners of that firm were Cyphers, and they got caught doing something illegal. The Society didn't care whether they broke the law or not. They only cared that the Society's name was tarnished in the press because of it. They cut those three loose. And I don't doubt they put out a hit on Simone's husband if he was the one who turned over evidence against them. The Society comes before everything else—work, family, women—and those three went against the code. You don't go against the code. Ever."

Ryan leaned back against the table, fingering his glasses. "So you're saying—"

"I'm saying, if the Cyphers were watching Simone, wondering if she knew something, or if Steve had given her something that could still implicate them in some way, then they'd know I was dating her. And I'm already a fuck-up in their eyes. I don't think that hit was meant for her. If it was, they could have taken her out at any time at her own house. I think they came after me. Because I got in too deep with the enemy. I went against the code."

"But you didn't. Not knowingly, at least."

Mitch sighed. "They won't see it that way."

Ryan pursed his lips and looked at the computer screen in stunned silence. After several moments, he lifted his head and pinned Mitch with a determined look. "We don't know that for sure. You and Simone have been dating for over six months. This still could be about her."

"Not if they just now caught up with her. She was in the WITSEC program. Even though she left, she didn't assume her old identity. It'd make sense it would take them time to track her down."

"Maybe." Ryan shook his head. "But it's still just a guess. There's no logical reason for them to want to get rid of you. You didn't technically do anything against them."

Ryan saw things in terms of profit and loss. He was a numbers guy, always had been. But Mitch knew how these people worked. To them, there was always an acceptable loss, no matter the cost. "I thought for myself. I've already gone against what they want dozens of times. They'd see my dating Simone as the final straw."

Ryan frowned and tossed his glasses on a stack of papers on the table. "I don't buy it. I still think there's something else going on. I'm gonna give all this info to my PI and see what he can find. There has to be more to this than just you."

Mitch wasn't sure what Ryan thought he'd find, but the emotional toll of everything was starting to take effect. He pulled out a chair and dropped into it, resting his elbow on the arm and rubbing his head. "It's a waste of time."

Holy hell, he couldn't believe he was thinking it, but disappearing into the witness protection program wasn't looking like such a bad idea anymore.

"Time's about all you've got left," Ryan said. "Let me research this before you do something you can't undo."

Ryan obviously knew what he was thinking. Mitch leaned his head back and stared up at the ceiling. In one night, his life had been shot to hell, just like his house. Reluctantly, he nodded.

The door pulled open, and the scent of fresh-brewed coffee filled the room. Kate set a mug in front of Mitch. "I had to brew a second pot. Sorry it took me so long."

Forcing a smile he didn't feel, Mitch looked at his sister, then reached for the steaming cup. "It's okay. Thanks."

Kate handed the second mug to Ryan, then looked between the two, her brow wrinkling with every passing second. "What did I miss?"

Ryan glanced at Mitch. Lifting the cup to his lips, Mitch shook his head. He didn't want Kate worrying more than she already was, and diving into the whole Cypher connection? Yeah, that would only stress her out more.

Ryan's features softened when he looked back at his wife. Reaching for her hand, he squeezed her fingers then pulled her close. "Not much. I'm going to have my PI do some digging. In the meantime, until we figure out what's going on, Mitch is going to take Simone someplace where no one can find them."

Mitch's head came up. He looked over the mug toward his brother-in-law. "I'm *what?*"

Ryan grinned, clearly in CEO mode. "Kendrick has that house in Tahoe he just finished building. He and I talked a lot about it because I was thinking of doing the same thing for Katie and the kids."

Kate's eyes widened. "You were?"

One arm wrapped around her waist, Ryan smiled down at her. "Surprise. I've been shopping for some property up there. Figured it'd be a good place for us to get away from the city."

"It's too expensive."

"Babe." A *you're worth it* smile spread across his face. "There is no such thing where you and the kids are concerned." He leaned down and kissed her.

Mitch glanced quickly away, refocusing on his coffee. Most days he was thrilled the two had found each other again and that they were so happy, but tonight all it did was remind him he was never gonna have that. At least not with the woman he was still pathetically in love with.

Ryan looked toward Mitch again. "Kendrick's house isn't listed under his name. He bought it through a shadow corporation so his crazy stalker fans couldn't find him. There's no way anyone would link you to Kendrick at the house. It's the perfect place for you two to hole up until I can gather more info."

Hiding out in a snowy cabin in Tahoe with Simone. A place deep inside Mitch leapt with excitement over that thought. Another place urged him to run now. He was still pissed at her for everything she'd done and omitted, but now that he knew what was really going on, he just couldn't blame her. And when he thought about the fact she could have been killed tonight, all because of him, a knot of regret lodged in the middle of his chest and made it hard to breathe.

"Simone will argue against this," he said quietly

"Probably." Ryan slid his free hand into the pocket of his jeans. "But if she knows we're working on a solution that could keep her in San Francisco so she doesn't have to run, I think that'll change her mind. Because I get the impression she doesn't really want to leave."

"Me too," Kate said. "This is home for her now. She's having a hard time with the thought of leaving. I don't know what happened between the two of you, Mitch, but it's killing her. She doesn't want to go, and a big part of that has to do with you."

That knot twisted tighter. Mitch didn't want her to go either. Regardless of whether or not she loved him, she obviously felt something for him. She wouldn't have come to his house tonight if she didn't.

"I don't think Shannon should go with you," Ryan said. "Until we know what's really going on, I think it's safer if she's not even in the picture."

Mitch agreed. "What are you thinking?"

Glancing down at his wife, Ryan said, "I'm think my parents should disappear with all the kids for a while. Kendrick gave me the name of an elite security firm he's used. They're supposed to be the best of the best. I want them where no one can find them."

Ryan had obviously already realized the Cyphers would make the connection between Mitch and his brother-in-law. And having lost his family once before, he wasn't about to let it happen again.

"Are you sure about this?" Kate whispered.

He leaned down and kissed his wife's wrinkled brow. "Don't worry, Katie. Nothing's going to happen to the kids. And I'm pretty sure my folks will be thrilled to have them all under foot for a while. Even Shannon. They adore her."

"Simone will never agree to letting Shannon out of her sight," Mitch cautioned.

"Yes, she will," Ryan said. "If we all convince her it's the safest thing for her daughter."

Kate wrapped both arms around Ryan's waist. "I'm ready for things to just be normal, you know?"

"You and me both." He hugged her back. "And they will be. Soon."

She drew back, ran a hand over her curly hair, and sent Mitch a weary look. "I'm gonna go lie down. Something tells me I'm going to need my rest for tomorrow."

Ryan reluctantly let go of her hand and watched her leave the conference room with a sappy, *I'm head over heels in love* look on his face.

When the door closed behind her, Mitch asked the question that had been foremost in his mind since Kate had stepped into the room. "What about her?"

"No one's touching her," Ryan said with dead calm. "She and I'll get out of the city until we know more too. I'm not about to let anything happen to her either."

Mitch glanced down at the half-empty cup in his hand. Ryan's plan made sense, but there was one very major flaw.

"You have to tell her the truth," Ryan said quietly.

Yep. That was the flaw. Mitch knew Ryan was talking about Mitch's association with the Cyphers, but right now all he could think about was the look of utter betrayal on Simone's face when she'd found that earring. "I will."

"I'm serious, Mitch. If you've learned anything from me, it's that secrets—big ones like this—can destroy everything. I nearly lost Katie because I thought I was protecting her by not telling her the truth. Don't make the same mistake I did. Tell Simone everything. Up front. No holds barred. She'll understand."

Mitch wasn't so sure. And he couldn't take the risk. Not yet. The first thing he needed to do was get Simone to agree to leave with him so they all had time to figure out what was really going on. If he let loose about his association with the Cyphers too soon, she'd cut and run faster than Speedy Gonzalez.

"I will."

"This is important, Mitch. You gotta tell her everything."

He looked up. He and Ryan had been friends for years, since long before Ryan had started dating his younger sister, and in all those years, he'd never flat-out lied to Ryan. But tonight he did. Because telling Simone the truth wasn't an option. At least not yet.

"I will," he said again. "I'll tell her everything. Don't worry. I'm not as dumb as you."

A sad smile spread across Ryan's lips. "You are. You're just too stupid to realize it. Now, let's call Kendrick and wake his ass up so you can get into his house."

CHAPTER ELEVEN

Simone wasn't sure how she'd let herself be talked into this stupid idea.

She looked out the passenger window of the sleek black Audi SUV Ryan had arranged for her and Mitch and watched the forest rush by. Her skin felt prickly, her head too jumbled with what-ifs, and whenever she chanced a look at Mitch beside her in the driver's seat, wearing those faded jeans, that loose gray Henley, and the black knit skullcap Ryan had gotten for him, she was reminded of only one fact: he was the last person she should be with.

Nothing had been resolved between them, he was still as pissed at her as before, and each time she closed her eyes, all she could see was that earring she'd found on his bed. Being alone with him was like waiting for a bomb to detonate.

"I think we should go back." She turned away from the window and fixed her gaze on the snazzy console of the new vehicle, so much nicer than that interior of the beat-up old Land Rover he loved.

"We've been over this a hundred times already."

Frustration welled inside her. He wasn't even bothering to look at her. "I know. I just… Shannon would be better off with me." Where Simone could see her and touch her and make sure the girl didn't do something stupid, like run off again.

"Shannon's safer where she's at. Ryan's people will make sure no one finds her. End of story."

His voice was blunt and unyielding—a lot like Ryan's when he set his mind on something—and Simone didn't like it. Crossing her arms over her chest, the red cable knit sweater Kate had brought her scratchy against her skin, she looked out the windshield and worked to keep her temper in check. A light rain had started falling the farther they drove into the California mountains heading east, and she was starting to worry it might turn to snow before they got wherever it was they were going.

God, she hated snow. And she did *not* want to be snowed in anywhere with Mitch.

"I want to call her." They'd been out of cell phone range for twenty minutes, and every second she was unable to talk to Shannon was wearing against Simone's already frayed nerves.

Mitch heaved out a sigh, rested his elbow on the windowsill, and rubbed his forehead. "You're gonna be a joy the next few days. I can already tell."

She looked his way, then wished she hadn't. A few locks of his hair peeked out from behind the knit cap, and the dark stubble on his jaw from three days without shaving was so damn sexy, she had to fight the urge to run her hand over it like she'd done a thousand times before.

Forcing her gaze back out the windshield, she ground her teeth. A week hiding out in a cabin alone with him while Ryan's PI looked for information on Steve's case? She'd never survive it. Especially not with her conflicting emotions where he was concerned.

Dammit, those raindrops were definitely turning to snowflakes. Her anxiety shot up another notch. "No one said we had to spend time locked up together. In fact, I think it would be easier if we weren't. If we go back now, I can find my own place to hide until Ryan's guy gets back to him with more information."

Mitch slanted her a *yeah right* look. "Not a chance, sweetheart. I let you out of my sight, and I know exactly what you'll do. You'll cut and run. And I'll be left with those Delta Team-wannabes all over my ass. No, until we figure out what's going on and how to get out of this mess, you're stuck with me."

Her frustration grew to exponential levels. It was all she could do not to snap at him. Then a thought occurred.

She bit her lip, but figured, what the hell. It was worth a chance. "There is a way out that doesn't require either of us to be together."

"Witness protection? No, thanks. I happen to like my life. Besides, you said your case manager was compromised."

"Not witness protection. People disappear every single day. With Ryan's resources, you could do just that for a while. At least until things calm down. Take a few months off and go somewhere. I'm sure you have plenty of vacation time banked."

He looked at her, his features a blend of disbelief and incredulity, then refocused on the road and shook his head. "It's still abandoning my life, and sorry, sweetheart, but I'm not interested."

Simone's frustration bubbled up and over. "Dammit, Mitch—"

"Look, we're not making any decisions until we know more, so just deal with it. You got me into this mess, you can stick around until we can figure a way out of it. In a week, if we still don't have any answers, you can argue your case until you're blue in the face."

"It's only worth the effort if the opposing party will listen," she snapped, "which we both know you won't."

She huffed and looked back out the front window. The man was exasperating. He didn't want to be with her any more than she wanted to be with him, so why was he agreeing to this? And on top of all that, the snow was getting thicker, the skies darker, just like her mood.

"Hey." He shifted lanes to pass a semi. "I can be as agreeable as the next guy."

Simone gripped the armrest at her side. Why the man couldn't use a blinker, she'd never know. Most days, that fact only irritated her. Today, on slick roads that were already turning white, it terrified her. "Yeah, I know how agreeable you can be. I felt it stabbing me in the back."

He turned to look at her, and her skin grew hot, but she didn't meet his gaze. Couldn't. Because she could still feel that earring pressing into her flesh, followed by the bitter bite in her chest when she'd realized what it meant.

"Do you *really* want to go there right now?" he asked in a low voice.

No, not now. Not ever. She'd decided late last night that breaking up with him had obviously been a good idea, considering how fast he'd turned to someone else, and even though she regretted how she'd gone about that breakup, at least now she knew she'd saved herself—and Shannon—from heartache somewhere down the line. Better to do it now, rather than when Shannon was really attached to him.

Right. Like Shannon isn't already head over heels in love with the guy, just like you.

She shifted away from him, leaned her head against the headrest, and closed her eyes, fighting back the misery. "I'm going to sleep. Wake me when we get there."

So I can hide from you in my bedroom for the next few days. And pretend my life is not a total disaster.

Yeah, this was turning out to be a brilliant plan.

This is the house?"

Mitch could tell from the tone of Simone's voice that she wasn't impressed. He drove slowly forward and glanced in his rearview mirror at the gate closing behind them. Ahead, a three-car garage sat below an A-frame style log cabin. Trees and brush butted up to both sides of the garage, preventing a view of the rest of the property. There was no front door, no path, nothing but what looked like a tiny cabin.

"Worried?" he asked.

Simone crossed her arms and shrugged, avoiding eye contact like she'd been doing the whole trip. "When Ryan mentioned your rock star friend owned this place, I expected something a little…I don't know…fancier."

By fancier she meant bigger. So she could get away from him. For a second, Mitch considered turning around and finding someplace small so they *would* be right on top of each other. That, at least, would force her to deal with issues still unsettled between them, but common sense told him that was a bad idea. No one knew they were here, no one could link this place to either one of them, and Kendrick's security was top of the line. Which, right now, they needed.

The gate opening had signaled the security monitor, and without even having to let anyone know they'd arrived, the middle bay of the garage rolled upward.

Lights illuminated the large garage as they drove in and parked. White walls surrounded them. A brand-new silver Range Rover took up the first bay; a dusty black Yukon took up the third. Four different ski pairs hung off hooks along the back wall, and a variety of different size boots were lined up below.

Mitch shoved the car into park in the middle bay and popped his door. "I guess you'll find out in a minute, won't you?"

As they were climbing out of the car, a door on the left side of the garage opened, and a man with dark hair, wearing jeans and a sweater, waved their way. "Welcome. I'm Ben Ford. I hope your drive up wasn't too bad."

Mitch shook his hand. "Thanks. I'm Mitch. This is Simone. The drive was fine. Snow's picking up a little now though."

Ford held his hand out to Simone, who accepted it hesitantly. He rested his hands on his hips. "We aren't supposed to get more than an inch and it'll probably melt by tomorrow. Why don't I show you around, then I'll come back and get your stuff."

"We can grab it," Simone said.

Ford smiled, a twinkle lighting his eyes as he focused on Simone, but she didn't return the smile. "All part of the job." He turned and headed back for the door he'd come through. "Follow me."

So she wasn't just being cold to him. Mitch wasn't sure if that was good news or bad. He made it to the door, but Simone's hand tugging on the sleeve of his Henley drew him to a stop.

"Who is this guy, and how do you know we can trust him?" she whispered.

Heat permeated his shirt where she touched him, and the sweet citrusy scent of her perfume wafted in the air around him, reminding him of every second they'd spent together the last six months. Part of him wanted that back, but an even bigger part just wanted answers. "He's part of Kendrick's permanent onsite security team."

"And Kendrick's rarely here," she countered. "That doesn't exactly put me at ease."

They were barely on speaking terms. If he had any hope of getting through the next few days so he could get the answers he wanted, he needed to work on being civil and stop being such a smartass.

"Look," he said, forcing the animosity from his voice, "I know you're nervous, but there's no one I trust more than Kendrick—except maybe Ryan. If Kendrick trusts Ford, then I trust him."

The look in Simone's brown eyes said she didn't feel the same, but she pursed her lips. "Fine. For now. But let's not give him any personal information. The less he knows about us, the better."

Mitch nodded. "Agreed."

She let go of his arm, and a cool brush of air replaced the warmth, sending a shiver of disappointment all across his skin. He wasn't sure what was going on behind the scenes, he wasn't even sure what Ryan's PI would find, but he was sure of one thing: he wasn't over her. And at the moment, he wasn't sure what to do about that—or if he even *wanted* to do anything about it.

Stepping back so she could walk in front of him, he watched as she brushed her dark, shoulder-length hair back from her face and headed through the door. Her body brushed his as she moved, and his stomach tightened just being close to her again.

Shaking his head at his pathetic weakness, he followed her through a small hallway. A set of stairs disappeared up and to the right. Ahead, Ford reached for a parka from a line of hooks along the left wall, shrugged it on, then punched a code into the keypad next to another door.

"The garage is separated from the house for privacy," Ford announced. "So be sure to bundle up before you come out here for anything." He pushed the door open and led them across a curved walkway that angled toward an enormous log-style house, already lit up against the darkening sky.

"Wow," Simone whispered.

"This more what you were expecting?" Mitch asked her.

Simone's gaze skipped over the two-story monstrosity. Pine trees rose to the gray sky, and around the side of the building, Mitch could see the beach and lake beyond.

"I guess," she answered. "This is insane. No one can even tell this place is back here from the road."

"That was the goal." Ford stopped at the front door and slid a key into the lock. Mitch and Simone waited while he unlocked the door, then pushed it open. "After you."

Mitch followed Simone into the house. The walls were decked out all in wood, the ceiling with rounded beams. He glanced around while Ford typed a code into the security system, his gaze skipping from the wide staircase that led up to the second floor, to the archway that opened to an office on his left, then ahead to a short hall that opened to an enormous great room and kitchen with a two-story rock fireplace that rose all the way to the ceiling and a wall of windows that looked out over the lake.

Ford led them into the kitchen. "I stocked the fridge earlier. If there's something you want that's not here, just let me know, and I can get it for you. The bedrooms are all upstairs. There are four.

All have views of the lake, so use whichever one you like best. Every door and window is wired, so be sure to use the code before you go in and out. There's a hot tub on the patio and a small pier accessible from the yard, but keep in mind that there are sensors that alert us when someone moves from the beach to the yard, so if you plan to go down to the pier or the beach, be sure to deactivate that sensor or let me know so I don't think we've had a breach."

Simone turned a small circle, taking it all in. "Which bedroom do you use?"

"I don't stay in the house," Ford answered. "Security's set up in an apartment over the garage. You'll barely even know I'm here, unless we have an issue." He looked from Simone to Mitch, then stepped back and motioned with his hands. "Follow me."

He led them through an archway and into a library. Bookshelves lined two adjacent walls. A couch and two plush chairs filled the space, angled toward the fourth wall and built-in entertainment center. But instead of pointing out the features, Ford pushed on a section of the bookshelf molding. A click sounded, then the entire middle shelving unit opened outward with a hiss, revealing a thick steel door. Lights came on in the room behind.

"This is the safe room," Ford announced, stepping into the small space no bigger than Mitch's laundry room at home. The walls were all concrete. Three were bare. The fourth was decked out with a counter holding a computer keyboard and joystick, cabinets below, and a series of monitors mounted to the wall above. "If an unauthorized person steps foot on the property, you'll hear my voice on the intercom instructing you to go to this room. Once inside, lock the door and wait for my instructions. These monitors are linked to mine in the security center so you can see what's happening on the property."

"What about the joystick?" Mitch asked. "Doesn't look like Nintendo."

Ford moved the joystick and pushed a few buttons on the keyboard. From somewhere in the house, a door slammed. "You can close and lock any doors in the house with this. Comes in handy in case we do have an intruder."

Mitch looked over at Simone, and flashed her a *See? Nothing to worry about* look. Her expression said she didn't agree.

"Impressive," Mitch said, refocusing on Ford. "Has Kendrick had to use any of this?"

"Not yet. Directions for everything are in the cabinets, along with supplies should you find yourself in here longer than a few minutes."

"Let's hope that doesn't happen," Mitch muttered under his breath.

Ford led them out of the safe room and closed the bookshelf door. "It's just a precaution. Things have been quiet here." He turned to face them. "Do either of you have any questions about local activities, rentals, etcetera? We're kind of between seasons now, but I can get a list of restaurants and spas in the area if you're interested."

"No," Simone said quickly. "We won't be leaving the house."

A slow smile spread across Ford's face. "A cozy romantic vacation. I totally understand."

Simone opened her mouth to correct him, but Mitch cut her off by sliding an arm around her shoulder and pulling her close. "Yep. Just that."

She flashed him a startled look, but Mitch only tugged her in tighter and lifted his brows, telling her to play along. She was the one who'd said she didn't want to give Ford any personal info, just in case. Admitting they weren't a couple would only raise flags for the security guard. If he thought Kendrick had loaned the house to friends for a romantic getaway, then Mitch wasn't about to give the guy any reason to wonder about the contrary.

"We drove down from Klamath Falls," Mitch said. "It's nice to get away, isn't it, sweetheart?"

Confusion flashed in Simone's eyes, but it quickly cleared. She fixed a pleasant look on her face and slid her arm around his waist. Heat flared wherever she touched, but her body remained taut, as if just being close to him put her on the defensive. "Yes, it is. Kendrick was so nice to let us use his house. Your childhood friendship has finally paid off." She focused on Ford. "We just want to relax and not have to worry about other people. At all."

"Well, you picked a perfect place. This is one of the most romantic spots on the planet. And if you get the urge to tie the knot, there are even a few wedding chapels down in South Lake Tahoe."

Simone released a startled choking sound, and Mitch just couldn't help himself. He rubbed her shoulder and smiled down at her. "Hear that, honey? We could avoid the whole engagement thing and just run off and elope. Sounds like a plan to me. Saves me from having to buy a ring."

Simone's fingers dug into his side, and Mitch bit back a wince as she laid her head sweetly against his chest. "Now, honey. That wouldn't be fair to your three ex-wives considering all they got was a civil ceremony at the county courthouse, and here I would be getting an actual wedding in a real fancy chapel. And you know how disappointed your mother would be if we ran off and eloped. She said this time she was really hoping you'd finally wear that baby-blue tux she saved from your high school prom."

A smile cut across Mitch's lips, even with the pain radiating from his side where Simone was still pinching him. This was the woman he remembered before things had gone to hell between them. The one who could take his crap and dish it right back.

Ford glanced between them with a confused expression, then dropped his arms. "I, ah, think I'll just go get your bags."

"Thank you," Simone said in that saccharin sweet voice.

When he disappeared down the hall and they heard the door open then close, Simone quickly pulled her arm from Mitch's waist and stepped away. "A wedding chapel? You're hilarious."

He rubbed at his side. "You're the one who said you didn't want to give him any personal info." Damn, the woman was strong. "And how did you know I wore a baby blue tux in high school?"

Simone rolled her eyes and crossed to the fireplace, which was already roaring with a generous fire. "It's no surprise you wore an ugly tux to your prom. You have nonconformer written all over you."

Mitch chuckled, feeling more relaxed than he had in days. "The shirt was the best part. It had ruffles."

"Why does that not surprise me?"

The door opened and closed again, followed by Ford's voice from the entry. "I'm just putting your bags upstairs."

"Thanks," Mitch called.

Ford's footsteps echoed up the stairs. While Simone stared at the fire, Mitch moved into the kitchen. He glanced over the contents of the fridge, and his stomach rumbled, reminding him he hadn't eaten since last night.

"Y'all have a good night," Ford called from the entry again. Before either of them could answer, the door opened and closed behind him.

He'd said he'd be scarce. Mitch scratched his head beneath the back edge of his knit cap and told himself he should be happy. But one look at Simone's rigid shoulders, and he could already see the tension returning.

He needed to keep things light. Yeah, she was uncomfortable around him, but she didn't have to be. The last few minutes had proved they could still get along like they used to. "How about some dinner? I could cook a couple of steaks."

"I'm not hungry."

That cold, emotionless tone was back in her voice. The one he'd heard the whole drive up here. "You should eat something."

"I'm not interested." She dropped her crossed arms and turned for the entry. "It's been a long day. I'm going to bed early."

Running. She was good at that. She'd run from him the night she'd shattered his heart, had run from him last night when she'd found that earring, and she was doing it now.

He quickly stepped out from behind the counter so he could look after her down the hall. "You can't hide from me the whole time we're here, you know. You're gonna have to talk to me at some point."

She paused with one hand on the newel post, one foot on the first step. But she didn't look his way, and the tightness in her shoulders told him loud and clear that she'd keep on running until he forced her to stay. "Not if I can help it."

CHAPTER TWELVE

Simone awoke to the tantalizing scent of frying bacon.

Her stomach rumbled, reminding her she hadn't eaten much yesterday. Blinking several times, she sat up and looked through the tall glass windows over the clear blue lake and the snowcapped mountains beyond. Awe rippled through her. It had been nearly dark when they'd arrived last night, so she hadn't gotten a good view of Lake Tahoe, and now that she saw it for the first time she couldn't help but be impressed. For years she'd been meaning to bring Shannon up here but kept putting it off. Like she kept putting off a lot of things.

She pushed that depressing thought aside and rose from the comfy bed in the smallest bedroom, which she'd purposely picked last night, the farthest from the master where Ford had left their bags. Sunlight streamed through the tall windows, but it didn't ease the chill in the room. Rubbing her arms, Simone crossed to the bag Kate had packed for her, drew out a Stanford sweatshirt and tugged it on over her T-shirt.

A thin layer of snow covered the ground, but the skies were blue, not a cloud to be seen, and she remembered what Ford had said last night—that they weren't expected to get any major snow, at least not today.

That was probably a good thing, in case they needed to get out of here fast. Glancing at the clock, she realized it was almost ten a.m. She couldn't remember what time she'd finally fallen asleep, but it had been late. Instead of sleeping, she'd rolled around everything that had happened with Mitch the last few days and couldn't stop thinking about his comment last night about not being able to avoid him.

Her stomach tightened, but this time not with hunger pains. Avoiding him was all she wanted to do at this point. Not wanting to think about that too much, she moved into the adjoining bathroom, brushed her teeth and combed her hair, then stared at her reflection.

She looked like hell. Dark circles were clearly evident beneath her eyes, and her cheeks looked hollow, her skin pale. She needed to take better care of herself for Shannon's sake. When she got out of here and she decided where she and Shannon were going next, she'd make a point to eat better. Or simply just eat.

The scent of frying bacon drifted through the air once more, intensifying those hunger pains. She needed to eat now. But eating meant facing Mitch. And at this point she didn't know what to say to him.

Running her fingers through her hair, she decided enough was enough. She found socks in her bag, slid them on, then headed for the hall.

Some football game was playing on the flat-screen TV when she stepped into the great room. Bacon sizzled on the stove, and the aroma of fresh brewed coffee hit Simone for the first time, waking up her senses in a way they hadn't been before.

Mitch looked up from the stove, a spatula in hand. His heated gaze slid over her, then quickly moved back to the pan. "I didn't expect to see you today."

Okay, she had that coming. Steeling her nerves, Simone fingered the gold bracelet on her wrist and moved into the room. "I smelled coffee."

Liar.

He stirred scrambled eggs in the pan. "Help yourself."

He hadn't looked at her since she'd first walked into the room, and though she told herself that was a good thing, a tiny space in her chest pinched. Lifting her chin, she moved around the island, drew a mug out of the cabinet, and poured a cup of the steaming brew. The bitter liquid went down like a bullet, but it gave her a strength she'd been missing, and just this one small normality felt like a slice of control she'd lost.

Turning, she leaned back against the counter and looked toward Mitch. He'd obviously been up for a while, had already showered and was wearing loose-fitting jeans and a Mariners sweatshirt. No matter how long he lived in the Bay area or how many Giants games he went to, he would always be a Pacific Northwest boy, and the Mariners would always be his team.

He was right. She couldn't go on avoiding him. They were stuck here together for at least the next few days. Instead of fighting it, she needed to at least be civil. And try not to make both of them miserable in the meantime.

"I apologize if I came across as rude last night. I was tired, and it had been a long day, and…" *I don't know how to be around you anymore.* She swallowed hard. "…and I was a little overwhelmed by everything. I didn't mean to take it out on you."

Mitch's hand stopped moving over the pan, but he didn't turn to look at her. "Apology accepted."

Simone waited for him to say more, but he didn't. And she figured she had that coming too. She took another sip for courage, then lowered her cup and worked like hell for normal. "Have you seen Ford this morning?"

He moved the eggs to a plate and added the eight slices of bacon he'd cooked. "Nope."

He took the plate and his coffee to the table and sat down. Simone looked from him to the pans on the stove, which were now empty, then back to the table, which was only set for one. Her stomach rumbled.

"Oh, did you want breakfast?" Mitch asked.

Simone stiffened. He hadn't cooked extra for her. But then why would he? She'd told him last night she didn't want to be around him. But still, a tiny place in her chest pinched again. "No. I'm fine."

A slow smile spread across Mitch's face, and that damn dimple in his cheek that she always loved winked at her. He pulled an empty plate from beneath his and set it on the table across from him. Then he tugged an extra fork and napkin from the pocket of his sweatshirt. "Your lips may lie, but your stomach tells another story." He scooped half the eggs and bacon onto the second plate. "Sit and eat. You can be annoyed with me later."

The relief coursing through Simone's veins felt stupid, but she saw the olive branch he was dangling, and she took it.

She sat and dove into her meal. Mitch smiled and lifted his fork. After several bites, Simone nodded toward the TV. "Who's playing?"

"No one. They're replaying an old game. 1991 Rose Bowl. What should have been the championship game."

She looked closer and realized it was Washington playing, their purple uniforms standing out against the green field. He was from the Seattle area, and he was married to the Mariners. Yet he'd ended up at school in California. They'd dated long enough for her to know he loosely followed Husky football, but she didn't know why.

She lifted her coffee. "Do you know someone who went to the University of Washington?"

"My parents." He lifted a bite of eggs. "They met there."

How had she never known that? "You didn't want to go there too?"

He shrugged. "I wanted to play baseball. Cal gave me a scholarship."

That was where he and Ryan had met. At Berkeley, where they'd both played baseball. "And Kate followed you there."

He shook his head and nodded at her sweatshirt. "She went to Stanford. As she explained it, Stanford had the better geology program."

"Do they?"

Mitch shrugged again. "Both programs are ranked in the top ten nationally. But no, they don't."

A small smile tugged at the corner of Simone's lips. Not because they were making small talk, but because she remembered the dozens of times she'd heard Mitch and Kate bickering about geology. Kate loved to razz Mitch about the fact he wasn't doing important work shackled to an oil-and-gas company. And he loved to point out the world's economy would come to a screaming standstill if people like him weren't doing their jobs.

Appetite satiated, Simone pushed her plate back and leaned her forearms on the table as she looked past Mitch toward the view of the lake. It was just as beautiful downstairs as it had been from her room. The house was situated in such a way that all you could see were the trees and beach and lake… Not another house or person unless you specifically looked.

"Have you heard anything from Ryan?" she asked.

"No. He said it would be a few days."

Simone knew that, but part of her had been hoping for news already. She felt helpless sitting here, doing nothing.

"I talked to Shannon this morning."

Simone's gaze snapped to Mitch. "You did?"

"Yeah." He leaned back and crossed his arms over his chest. "Does that bother you?"

"No." Did it? Yeah, okay, it did. A little.

"She called my cell around eight. You didn't answer yours."

Simone closed her eyes briefly. No, at eight a.m. she'd been sound asleep because she'd been awake the whole night thinking about the man next to her. "Is she okay?"

Mitch reached for his coffee. "She's fine. They were getting ready to head to the boat. Said she'd call later."

Simone nodded. Ryan's parents had taken the kids to Hawaii, and they'd rented a boat, which they were going to sail around the islands until it was time to come home or until Simone went to get her. Simone had been against the plan until she'd found out what a seasoned captain Ryan's father was—he owned his own marina up in Puget Sound—but she still worried. It was her job as a mother to worry.

"So I have a proposal," Mitch said, his strong, familiar voice cutting through her crazy thoughts.

Cautiously, she looked his way. She couldn't read his expression. He didn't look especially happy, but he didn't look pissed either, as he had the night his house had been shot up. "What kind of proposal?"

Thoughts of Ford's comment from last night flashed through her mind, warming her skin in a way she didn't expect.

He set his mug down and leaned his forearms on the scuffed wood table. "We're stuck here together for a few days. The way I see it, we have two options. We can go on ignoring each other and both be miserable the entire time, or we can make the best of it."

She wasn't sure where he was going with this. "What do you mean by 'make the best of it'?"

"I mean…I think we should forget about everything that happened before this morning and start over."

Start over? Was he serious? Simone's brow dropped even lower. How could they possibly start over after everything that had happened between them? Why would he even want to? Conflicting thoughts flashed in her brain, followed by a warmth in her stomach she didn't want to feel.

Mitch frowned. "I've obviously confused you. I meant start over as friends. And if not that…then at least not enemies. I don't want to spend the next few days fighting with you or ignoring you. We got along once without the romantic stuff. I think we could do it again. At least for a couple of days, if we tried. What do you think?"

That warmth went ice cold, and her stomach rolled all over again, but this time not from hunger. This time the pain was from knowing everything between them was truly over for good.

Which was the best thing all around, she reminded herself. The sooner he got away from her, the better off he'd be.

She lifted her shoulders and straightened her spine, telling herself this was the only way it could be. Even if they could somehow fix things between them—and that was a big *if*, considering everything that had happened—honestly, she wasn't sure her heart could take another blow like the last.

"Yeah," she managed. "I think we could do that."

His smile widened. Not a heated smile. Not a come-get-me smile like she'd seen on his lips so many times before. But a friendly, I'm-making-the-best-of-it smile. One that made her feel even worse than before.

He pushed his chair back and reached for the plates. "Good. Why don't you go get dressed, and I'll clean up the kitchen. Then we can decide what we're going to do with the rest of the day."

Simone nodded and rose from the table. But as she made her way for the stairs, she couldn't help but feel as if something inside had died. Something that had come to life the day Mitch Mathews had barreled into her life. Something she was sure she'd never find again.

Mitch watched Simone head for the stairs and clenched his jaw to keep from calling her back.

When he heard her bedroom door open and close upstairs, he set the plates on the counter in the kitchen, braced his hands against the cool granite, and drew in two deep breaths.

This was going to be harder than he'd thought. Act like nothing had happened? Yeah, he could do that. Act like he didn't still want her, mind, body, and soul? No way. He was already aching with the need to touch her, and they'd only been here one night.

God, he was fucking pathetic.

The new cell phone he'd picked up on the drive to Tahoe buzzed, and he grasped it from the counter, anxious for word from

Ryan. But when he saw the number on the screen, everything inside him stilled.

Chris Murdoch. His boss. His Cypher contact within the company.

His pulse picked up speed, and sweat gathered against his palms. It could just be about work. Chris was probably wondering why he hadn't shown at the job site in British Columbia. But something in Mitch's gut said this call had nothing to do with work. It had to do with what had happened at his house. And why the hell Mitch wasn't already dead.

Mitch hit Decline, then chewed on the inside of his lip and debated his options. At some point he had to call Chris, but he wasn't ready yet. Not until he had more info and knew how to play it.

He cleaned up the kitchen, loaded the dishwasher, and poured himself another cup of coffee. By the time he was done, Simone was just coming back down the stairs.

He looked up when she stepped into the room, then nearly swallowed his tongue. She was wearing slim-fitting jeans, a loose white sweater with a ballet collar that showcased her toned shoulders, hung to her hips, and covered all but the tips of her fingers. Her hair was loose around her face, hanging in a fall of chocolate to her shoulders, and her face was clean of makeup except for a little mascara.

He'd seen her dolled up in expensive gowns for several charity events. He'd seen her in her lawyerly business suit, the picture of confidence. And he'd seen her first thing in the morning, when she'd roll over, all rumpled hair and smelling like him and the night before. And each of those times he'd thought she'd been at her most beautiful. But he'd been wrong. Walking into the room with the sunlight streaming over her, wearing that simple white sweater that shouldn't be sexy but made him ache to touch her, he was pretty sure she'd never been more beautiful than she was right now.

"I heard your phone ring," she said. "Was it Ryan?"

"No." He fought back the need to reach out for her and tossed the dishtowel on the counter. "Someone from work."

"You didn't answer it, did you?"

"No. And I don't plan to."

Her shoulders relaxed. "Good." She dropped onto the couch, rested her elbow on the armrest, and rubbed her forehead. "I don't mean good. It's not good that you're having to interrupt your life for all this." She dropped her hand. "What I meant is—"

Mitch moved into the living area. "What you meant was…not to say anything. We're starting over, remember? This is what it is. We're both dealing with it. So no more apologizing, okay?"

She sighed and dropped her hand in her lap. But her eyes softened when she looked up at him. Not in the way they had been before, when they'd been a couple, but in a way that told him she was relaxing, if only a little.

He'd take that for now. Because…the sad truth was, he didn't know what he wanted. His head was still a mess, and he was trying to sort things through in his brain. And he didn't know what she wanted or if there was even still a chance for them. But this was more than he'd had yesterday. And until they heard from Ryan, it would be enough.

Or so he hoped.

"I think we need to do something to take our minds off everything." He swiped his sweaty palm against his thigh and moved for the cabinet in the entertainment center he'd discovered earlier.

"I don't think I'm up for watching a movie. If it was baseball season, I'd totally watch a game with you, but football really isn't my thing."

No, football definitely wasn't her thing, and that didn't bother him in the least. He only watched it this time of year because there wasn't much else on after the World Series wrapped up. Memories of the games he'd taken her to at AT&T Park ricocheted in his brain, especially when he'd surprised her with tickets to see her beloved Orioles. And the way she'd thanked him after when they'd celebrated the Birds' win over the Giants back at his house.

"Um"—he swallowed the lump growing in his throat—"I wasn't thinking of a movie." He grabbed the box in the cupboard and turned. "I was thinking of something a little more involved."

Simone's brown eyes widened when she saw what he was holding. "You want to play Monopoly?"

"We've got hours to kill. What do you say?"

Simone eyed him like he had a second nose smack in the center of his forehead. And yeah, maybe it was a stupid idea, but if he didn't do something with his hands soon, he was going to reach for her, then all his plans about keeping things platonic so she'd stop avoiding him would be shot to hell. And if that happened, she might run before he had his answers.

"Come on." He tipped his head and shot her his most devastating smile. "Unless you're scared I'll win. In which case, we could just call me the champ right now and find something else to do."

Her eyes narrowed, and he saw it then—that flash of challenge, of interest, of strength. And in that moment, it was like looking at the old her. Not the victim he'd seen the night his house had been attacked. Not the one who was afraid to hold on to what she wanted. And definitely not the one who was ready to give up her life and run. No, in that second, he saw a spark that told him the confident, take-charge woman he'd fallen in love with was still in there.

She leaned slightly forward and pinned him with a look. "You do not want to challenge me at Monopoly. Trust me."

His smile widened, and he set the box on the coffee table in front of her. "Why not?"

"Because Shannon and I play this all the time, and I never lose."

"You take advantage of a ten-year-old? I'm pretty sure I can hold my own."

"That ten-year-old will probably end up with an MBA. When it comes to Monopoly, she's got claws as sharp as Ryan's. Regardless, though, if you insist on playing, I will destroy you. Be forewarned."

Mitch's heart squeezed tight, and his smile faded. *Sweetheart, you already did that.* He pushed the hurt down and flipped the box lid open, then sat in the chair across from her and worked to keep things light. "We'll see. Here. You can be the dog. I know how much you like to bitch at me. I'll be the car."

She lifted her brows and took the piece he handed her. "Good thing it's not a minivan."

His hand hesitated over GO. Yeah, good thing it wasn't. There was a time he thought he was minivan material, but that was slowly drifting away. And right now, he wasn't sure how, or if, he ever wanted it back.

CHAPTER THIRTEEN

North Carolina Avenue with one hotel…" Simone looked down at the back of her card. "You owe me one thousand, two hundred, and seventy-five dollars."

Sitting on the ottoman with his elbows resting on his knees, Mitch glanced over the measly stack of Monopoly money on the coffee table in front of him, then frowned across the board at her.

"What?" she asked with an adorably innocent, one-sided smile. "I warned you before we started. I always win."

He was not going to let her win, even if it did brighten her eyes and bolster her mood. He counted his money, then flipped over his three yellow properties. "I had four houses on each of these and they cost a hundred and fifty each, so that's—"

"You're selling properties?"

"—seventy-five times twelve equals…nine hundred bucks. Hand it over, JP Morgan."

Her smile widened, and she counted out the money, then slid it across the coffee table. "You still owe me three hundred and thirty-five dollars. You know, you could make this easier on yourself. I'll forgo the rent this time if you give me Boardwalk and Park Place."

He snatched up the money. "You are higher than a kite. I'm not giving you the best properties, especially when you're about to come around. I've got you just where I want you."

She laughed, the sound like silver bells, and brushed her dark hair back from her face. "You can't win this, Mitch. Look at the board. You're going down fast."

He was. Even he could see it. The woman was more ruthless than Ryan and Julia put together, but at least when he played Monopoly with *them* he could hold his own, because they were usually going after each other. Simone the shark was another story. He wasn't ready to give up the fight yet though. He was having too much fun. And sitting on the floor cross-legged across from him, smiling up at him like she hadn't in days, Simone seemed to be having fun too.

He grabbed what was left of his cash and threw the entire bundle at her. "There you go, miser. If I could pay you in pennies, I would."

Her hands darted out, she laughed again, and Monopoly money went flittering through the air all around her. "You are such a sore loser."

"I haven't lost yet. It's your turn. Roll the damn dice."

"This is Ford in the security center." Simone's hand froze over the board. They both looked up at the sound of the voice coming from somewhere in the ceiling. "We've had a security breach on the property. Quickly make your way to the safe room."

The color drained from Simone's face. She jerked to her feet, sending the Monopoly board and pieces flying. Mitch shot up and grasped her arm at the biceps. "Come on. Hustle."

They jogged into the library. Mitch felt all over the center shelf molding and couldn't find the release. "Dammit."

"Bottom of the third shelf." Simone's panicked voice drifted to his ears. "Hurry."

His fingers slid over the button, and he pushed it. The shelving unit angled out with a hiss. Grasping Simone's hand, he tugged her in after him.

He let go of her hand and pulled on the metal bar, then turned the handle, locking them in. One look at the monitor showed Ford wasn't making shit up. Someone was on the grass on the east side of the property, heading for the house. Someone he didn't recognize.

"Oh God." Simone shuffled backward, and Mitch looked her way just as she hit the cold cement wall. Her eyes slid closed, her hands landed against the cement at her sides. What little color was left in her features was draining away quickly. "I told you to leave. I told you you were better off without me."

She was panicking again. Like she'd done in Ryan's office. He crossed to her, cradled her face in his hands, and slid his fingers into her hair, tipping her face up to his. "Look at me, Simone."

She shook her head and squeezed her eyes, but he only held her tighter. "Open your eyes and look at me."

Fear swirled in her chocolate irises when she finally did. The same fear he'd seen the night his house had been shot up. The same fear he'd noticed the night she'd come back from DC, but which he'd ignored because he'd been too hurt to do anything but focus on his own misery.

"I told you," she whispered. "I *told* you not to get involved with me."

His pulse, which was already fast, took off, and pinpricks of heat raced down his spine. Because this fear wasn't for her—it was for him.

Holy shit, she still cares.

"No one's getting in here." His voice was thick. His hands damp. Dammit, why hadn't he figured this out before?

Because you were too pissed to do anything but mope.

But he wasn't now. Now he was thinking clearly. And knowing she'd called their relationship quits because she was worried about him changed everything. "No one's getting to us. Nod your head so I know you hear me."

She closed her eyes again, but he held her firmly. "Simone, focus. No one's getting in here. Nod for me."

Slowly, she did, and a lone tear escaped from beneath her lashes, then slid down her cheek.

All those walls he'd erected to protect himself came crumbling down. He let go of her with one hand, slid the other to the back of her head, and pulled her in close, wrapping himself around her. Her head rested against this chest, just under his chin. Her arms closed around his waist. The beat of her heart pounded against his, reminding him of every moment he'd held her like this in his bed, in her bed, anywhere he could get her.

"You're okay," he whispered. "We're both okay. Nothing's going to happen."

She sniffled, and he felt the wetness of her tears soaking into his shirt. "I hate this. I hate being this weak, helpless female. This isn't me."

But it was her. This vulnerable side he hadn't known existed was as much a part of her as was the strong, confident lawyer. "You're not weak."

"I feel like it." She let go of his waist with one arm and swiped at her cheek. "I'm on the verge of a breakdown when I should be running."

He eased back, slid his hands to her face again. "No more running. If you do, they'll just follow you wherever you go."

He saw the defeat in her features. "Mitch—"

"No. We're in this together now, and I'm not letting you give up your life again for these people. They're just trying to scare you. We will figure it out and find a way to beat them. Do you hear me, Simone? This isn't the end. It's not even close."

Her eyes held his, damp, worried, filled with so many emotions, he felt every one in his very soul.

She did care about him. He saw it in her features, felt it in the way she held him tight, and knew it in his heart. Even in the midst of all this chaos and uncertainty, hope bloomed in his chest. A hope that he could win her back, that they could fix everything that was broken between them, that maybe they could somehow—in some insane way—have that minivan future he'd thought was gone for good.

Heat encircled him, and his gaze flicked to her lips, held. Her pulse sped up beneath his fingers, her breasts rose and fell with her shallow breaths, and the need to kiss her, to taste her, to make her his again, overpowered every sense.

A click echoed in the room, stopping him from doing just that.

"All clear," Ford said through a speaker somewhere near the monitors. "The situation's under control. You can both come out now."

Mitch didn't move, and neither did Simone. They just continued to stare at each other. And in the thick, sultry air, one thing became crystal clear.

No matter what had happened, no matter how far they'd strayed from where they'd once been, she still wanted him, still needed him, still craved him with the same soul-deep intensity that he craved her. The hope he'd felt before exploded inside, giving him the strength and purpose he'd been missing. Because that meant he only had one thing left to do.

Before he confessed his secret, he had to convince her she was still his.

A crazed Kendrick fan.

That was how Ford had identified the man who'd stumbled onto the property from the beach. According to Ford, the guy had seen a car pull through the gate the night before and had heard

Kendrick had a house here, and had put two and two together, hoping to find the rock star at his retreat home.

Instead, he'd found the police for trespassing.

Wrapped in a plush white towel fresh from a shower, Simone stood in front of the mirror and swiped the steam from the glass with a hand towel. Her eyes still looked tired this morning, and she wanted to blame another restless night on what had happened yesterday, but she couldn't. While yes, all that did weigh heavy on her mind, and she was happy it had turned out to be nothing, the truth about her insomnia had to do with only one thing. One man. One aggravatingly, sexy, incredible man she wanted with every inch of her being.

An image of Mitch in his room, stepping from the shower, filled her mind. His skin golden from hours outdoors beaded with water, his hair damp, the muscles in his arms flexing as he wrapped a towel just like hers low around his lean, sexy hips. The breadth of his muscular chest, the cut of his strong, carved stomach, and that thin line of dark hair that started at his belly button and stretched downward, like an arrow pointing toward what she wanted most.

A low, pulsing ache kick-started in her breasts, spread to her belly, then radiated all through her hips. Breathing deep, she braced her hands on the cool granite and dropped her head.

Coming here with him had been a bad idea, just like she knew it would be. She'd barely been able to be around him last night after the way she'd leaned on him in that safe room, and he'd obviously been able to sense her anxiety. Every minute they spent together made it harder to resist reaching for him. And it wasn't just about sex—which with him had always been mind-bendingly incredible. No, when he pulled that protective knight-in-shining-armor stuff like he'd done yesterday, she lost all ability to think rationally. Even after everything they'd done to each other, her treacherous heart and body still wanted him, still needed him. And if she didn't do something to counteract that quick, her teetering mind was going to give in and ruin everything.

She lifted her gaze and stared at her reflection, already growing foggy again as steam continued to roll through the room. Okay, so she'd admitted that. Now she just needed to toughen up. She wasn't someone who needed saving. In her life, *she* was the one who found the solution and made it work. Yes, she'd been thrown off-kilter this whole last week, but she was done being the victim. She was done leaning on Mitch in a way that would just get him in more trouble. All she had to do was remember why she'd broken things off with him in the first place. And get through the next few days without jumping his bones.

A groan echoed through her body at that thought, and, disgusted with herself, she turned out of the bathroom, picked up the small suitcase Kate had packed for her, and dropped it on the bed. Deciding a turtleneck was her safest choice—*thank you, Kate, for packing for cold weather*—she grabbed it, a fresh pair of jeans and a thick sweatshirt. Maybe if she wrapped herself in enough fabric, she could protect herself from his heady looks and casual touches.

Yeah, right.

She dried her hair, slapped on lip balm and a thin layer of mascara, and figured that was good. She wasn't getting gussied up for him. As it was, if she hadn't already agreed to be cordial to him, she'd barricade herself in her room and not come out until it was time to leave.

Still not a bad option…

She shook her head and frowned. He'd only hunt her down if she tried that, and the last thing she needed was him here in this cozy room with her and that giant bed. Pushing the thought—and the fantasy—aside, she headed for the hall.

No sound echoed from the kitchen when she reached the stairs. No scents of breakfast cooking either. Which was a good thing, she figured, because if she'd beat him to the kitchen, at least cooking would give her something to do with her hands so she wouldn't be tempted to grab him.

Surprise drew her feet to a halt though when she reached the great room. Mitch was already up, sitting on the couch, leaning over and tying his boots. He was wearing jeans and a thick blue-checked flannel shirt. And the same black-knit skullcap he'd worn when they'd driven up here.

He must have sensed her, because his head came up, and she saw then that the tips of his curly hair peeking out from beneath the cap were wet. The image of him stepping from the shower filled her mind again and sent heat careening through her veins to condense between her legs.

A slow smile spread across his scruffy face, crinkling the skin around his green eyes in a way that made them sparkle. "Good morning."

She didn't like that heated look in his eyes, the *I've been waiting for you* look. And she liked the flutters in her stomach because of that look even less. "G-good morning."

She pulled her gaze from his and moved around the island, heading for the coffeepot. *Please let there be coffee.* That, at least, would go one step further in settling her raging hormones.

Mitch went back to tying his dusty hiking boots. "I'm glad you're already wearing something warm. Saves me from telling you to go change."

She reached for a mug from the cabinet. "Why? Are you expecting the heat to go out or something?"

He pushed to his feet. "We're getting out of here."

Her cup clattered against the counter, and she whirled on him quickly. "Did you hear from Ryan?"

"No." He rested his hands on his lean hips. "Sorry. I didn't mean like that. I meant…we're getting out of here for the day. I can only be cooped up so long before I go stir-crazy."

Simone glanced around the living area. "It's only been a day."

Mitch scratched the back of his neck. "Yeah, well, I need some exercise, so unless you can think of something sweaty and physical we can do right here in the house together…"

His unfinished words lingered in the air, and Simone didn't miss the innuendo. Neither did her body, which felt like someone had just fired up her internal burners and switched them to SMOLDER.

She cleared her throat and turned back to the coffeepot. "I can't think of a single thing."

His sexy chuckle drifted across the room, igniting a tingle deep in her core, one that messed with every inch of her resolve. "You're quick, Counselor. I bet if I give you some time, you could come up with something."

Her pulse shot up, and a memory of the last time they'd been together, when he'd done that crazy thing with his tongue that had made her see stars, ricocheted through her mind. Heat erupted all through her body, and a thin layer of perspiration dotted her spine. She wanted that. Needed it. But she couldn't have it. "Mitch—"

His boot steps echoed across the kitchen floor, and she tensed as he drew close, afraid if he touched her right now, she'd give in. The warmth of his body permeated the air around her, and his fresh, masculine scent drifted to her nose, causing that heat to turn into a full-blown blaze. Her fingers shook against the mug in her hand. No, if he touched her right now, she *knew* she'd give in.

But the touch never came. Instead, a clatter echoed at her feet, and, surprised, she looked down to see another pair of leather hiking boots lying against the hardwood floor.

"These should be your size," he said, close but not close enough. "I've already packed us some food and a fresh thermos of coffee. Grab some breakfast and meet me out at the garage."

He moved away, and she turned quickly, surprised—and disappointed. "You're serious about getting out of the house?"

He stopped near the hall and looked back, all sexy, rugged, outdoor man she never thought she'd be attracted to. "Unless you want to get down and dirty on the kitchen floor right now, yeah."

Her cheeks heated, and she opened her mouth to respond but couldn't find the right words. Because *hell, yeah, right now* would totally work. And doom him for all eternity.

His sexy, throaty chuckle slid across the room toward her again. "I didn't think so. We're going hiking. I want to show you something."

"Mitch." She crossed the kitchen before he could get more than a step or two down the hall. "Are you sure that's a good idea. After what happened yesterday—"

He turned back toward her. "That guy yesterday was nothing more than one of Kendrick's crazy fans. You heard Ford. It had nothing to do with us. No one knows we're here. And where I'm taking you, no one would ever think to look for us."

Simone wasn't so sure.

"Trust me, sweetheart. You need this. And you're gonna like it." That sexy, mischievous smile slinked across his lips again. "Ten minutes. If you're not out there in ten, I'll assume you'd rather go the kitchen route."

He left before Simone could stop him.

Alone, she frowned and looked down at her mug. She didn't particularly want to go hiking. She and the great outdoors weren't exactly friends. Her gaze slid to the hardwood floor beneath her feet. And before she could stop it, a bone-deep craving pushed that ache deep in her belly to a throbbing need she could only just contain.

Lifting the cup to her lips, she ignored the fact that her hand was shaking.

Okay, hiking. She could do this. And thankfully, at least, they were heading someplace cold, which would be enough to keep her blistering hormones in check.

Or so she hoped.

CHAPTER FOURTEEN

The crisp mountain air was exactly what Mitch needed.

He paused along the snowy trail, drew in a deep breath, and turned to look for Simone. She was still ten yards back, breathing heavily as she climbed the steadily rising path toward him, lifting her snowshoes with every step as if they were lead weights attached to her feet.

Okay, not *exactly* what he needed, but a strong second. If she'd taken him up on his offer back at the house, he'd have gladly locked himself inside for one more day and made sure they were both thoroughly sweaty and exhausted in the sweetest way. But part of him was glad she hadn't. Because sex between them had never been a problem. It was everything else—the secrets, the omissions, the holding back—that had done them in. And this excursion at least gave them the chance to spend more time together and hopefully bridge the gap they'd created between them.

Lodgepole pine, white fir, and spindly aspen that had just lost their leaves stretched to the gray sky. He'd thrown snowshoes in the back of the rig before they'd left, just in case, and was now glad. Though most of the snow from the earlier storm had melted down by the lake, up here a layer of white still covered the ground and hid the trail. He'd made Simone pull on snow pants, boots, and the snow shoes before they'd left the car, which she'd bitched about, but once she'd gotten the hang of it, she'd stopped complaining. For the most part. Of course, watching her try to navigate the terrain with all the gear was thoroughly entertaining, and every time she sent him one of her adorably irritated looks, it only made him smile wider.

Simone reached him, her cheeks rosy, her chest rising and falling beneath the thick jacket, her breath making tiny wisps of steam all around her. "You didn't bother to mention this hike was uphill the entire way."

Before he could stop himself, he tugged the white knit cap farther over her ears so they didn't get cold. She had no idea how cute she looked right now—his own personal Stay Puft Marshmallow girl. "Think of it this way, it'll be downhill the entire trip back."

Her frown told him she was less than impressed. "This looks like it could be a road."

"It is in the summer." Reluctantly, he let go of her and moved back up the path, slowing his pace so she could keep up with him. "The gate where we parked is usually open when the weather's good."

"You mean we could have driven all the way up here and missed out on all this fun?"

He laughed. She was such a city girl. Usually that was a major turn-off for him, but every single thing about her turned him on. It always had.

"I'll take that as a yes," she muttered. "I successfully managed avoiding the outdoors with you all these months, and the first time I cave, it's in the middle of winter, when I'm freezing my ass off. Yeah, this makes sense." Louder, she said, "Speaking of the weather. Is it just me or does that look like trouble?"

The clouds moving up from the southwest looked like trouble to Mitch too, though "trouble" was subjective depending on one's interpretation. He'd glanced at the weather report before they'd left. He knew that the storm moving in wasn't going to be a big one. The worst that could happen was they'd get stuck out here for a night, if that.

The thought of being stuck with Simone pinged around in his brain and heated his blood. Being locked in Kendrick's giant house together was one thing. Being trapped alone together in the great outdoors where they'd have to huddle together to stay warm took on a completely different meaning.

"Mitch?"

Her voice brought him around. He glanced her way and realized she was ten feet in front of him on the path, watching him carefully. "Yeah?"

"Should we go back?"

Go back and walk on eggshells around each other, or stay here and see where it went. He glanced from her worried eyes to her gorgeous lips. Her cold, pink, perfect lips he wanted to kiss now more than yesterday.

"We're fine." He moved toward her, his stomach tightening with every step, his awareness of her inching up the closer he drew. "It's not much farther."

He stopped in front of her. Even with the elevation and her standing uphill, he was still taller than her. Her chin lifted, and her chocolate eyes narrowed in a way he'd seen her do in the courtroom when a witness gave an answer she knew was false. "Why do I get the feeling you're up to something?"

Because she was as keen as a bloodhound, and because she knew him. Really well. But tonight he wanted her to know him a whole lot better.

One side of his mouth curled in a smirk. He stepped around her, careful not to touch her. There'd be time for that later. Hopefully. "Now what could I possibly be up to out here in the middle of the wilderness?"

"You tell me," she said. Then, in a whisper: "Um, Mitch?"

He stopped and turned back. She wasn't looking at him. She was staring at something off in the trees. "What now?"

"Please tell me that isn't what I think it is."

His gaze slid past her and into the trees, to the large, four-legged creature ambling parallel to them at least a hundred yards away.

Slowly, he made his way back down to her. "Don't make any loud noises."

"Oh. My. God," she whispered.

"Your chances of being attacked by a bear are less than your chances of being hit by lightning," he told her, trying to diffuse her anxiety. She'd gone rigid next to him, her eyes wide with fear. Grasping her gloved hand in his, he slowly tugged her up the path. "He hasn't looked our way, which is a good thing. Come on."

She followed but kept glancing over her shoulder toward the bear, which was now moving away from them. "Have I ever mentioned I hate the great outdoors?"

He chuckled.

"There's no way I'm going back down there now."

He smiled, loving the way she gripped his hand tightly in his, loving the way she was now plastered to his side. "I may need to send that bear a fish basket to say thanks."

She frowned, a sexy little pout that turned her lips and made him want to kiss them all over again. "The view up there better be worth it."

It probably wouldn't be—at least to her—but finding a way to fix things between them? Yeah, that was totally worth whatever the cost.

Simone paused along the trail to catch her breath.

The air was a lot thinner than she was used to, and it seemed to take twice as much energy to go half the distance as it did at sea level. As she braced her hands on her knees, she drew in large breaths, hoping to ease that low burn in her lungs while she turned to look down the path again.

Still no sign of that bear. A bear, for God's sake. Mitch owed her. Owed her big-time agreeing to this crazy activity. She didn't even like bears in zoos.

"We're almost there, sweetheart. Don't give up now."

Lifting her head, she glared up the trail toward Mitch, who stood near the trunk of a pine tree, seemingly unfazed by the elevation or the fact they could have been lunch. Granted, it wasn't a difficult hike, and that bear hadn't even looked their way or tried to follow them. But still… It was a bear!

She glanced up at the sky again. It was definitely growing grayer, the air temperature dropping. She could barely feel her nose anymore. They'd gotten a later start than she'd thought, mostly because Ford had insisted on finding all the snow gear for them, and she wasn't sure of the time, but it was definitely heading toward late afternoon. Going back down would probably be a lot faster than coming up, but there was no way she was going down until that bear had plenty of time to disappear.

She looked back at Mitch, who didn't seem the least concerned about anything other than his precious hike. Her eyes narrowed. He was definitely up to something. The red parka he was wearing brought out a ginger hue in his beard she hadn't noticed before, but it was the sparkle in his green eyes and that lopsided grin accentuating his dimple that made her suspicious. And revved her pulse.

Slowly, she made her way up to where he stood waiting for her. When he handed her the water bottle, she took it and downed a generous sip. "How far is 'almost there'?"

"Two hundred yards, if that. It's just up around that bend."

Two football-field lengths didn't seem that bad. He pointed up the hill, and Simone looked past him at the snow covering the ground, then to the cloud behind her, which seemed a whole lot closer than it had only moments before. "We're not going to freeze to death out here, are we?" She faced him again. "I know you've been mad at me, but I'm starting to worry you dragged me all the way up here to make my death look like a random accident. Hypothermia, starvation, being lunch for some giant beast.... The possibilities are growing by the minute."

Mitch laughed, a throaty, sexy sound, and took the water bottle back from her. His hand grazed hers in the process, and for a fleeting moment, she wished neither of them had been wearing gloves.

Which was just asinine. She knew better than to go there with him. And as much as she'd grumbled about this hike, it had at least given her something to do rather than daydream about him all day.

His brow lifted beneath the rim of his cap. "The only kind of bears around here are black bears, and they're more scared of us than we are of them. Trust me. No beast is going to eat you. At least not the bear kind."

The spark in his eyes sent her blood humming, but she tamped it down, not wanting to go there. "Okay, so you're not planning to kill me by bear. That only eliminates one possibility."

His smile widened. "If I didn't know you better, Counselor, I'd think you were nervous."

Of course she was nervous. She had every reason to be. She'd lied to him, broken his heart, ruined his future. Any sane woman would be worried he could be plotting some kind of major payback, but when she was with him, she didn't feel sane. She never had. The minute Mitch Mathews had stepped into her life, sane had flown straight out the window.

Regardless of everything she'd done, though... This was Mitch. He was as rugged and rough around the edges as any outdoorsman, but his heart was made of gold. And after the way he'd held her in that safe room, she knew he'd never hurt her, even if she had it coming.

Stomach tight, she pulled her hand away. Words hovered on her tongue, an explanation she knew he deserved, but she couldn't get them out. Call it pride or self-preservation or even just the simple fact they'd agreed not to discuss anything that had happened, but...she didn't want anything to ruin this moment.

She'd never admit it to him, but he'd been right—she did need to get out of that house—and part of her was actually enjoying this, even if she was still worried about bear attacks and freezing to death and all other kinds of impending doom.

She frowned, because even to her, that reasoning sounded idiotic. "Better be careful, or your lips will freeze in that stupid Joker grin."

He leaned in so close, his minty breath warming her cheek, taking her completely by surprise. "Better be careful, or I'll find something physical to do to keep my lips nice and warm."

Her gaze shot to his lips. To his plump, masculine lips she knew felt like heaven against her own. A deep, dark craving rolled through her core, sparking electricity in her belly, sending waves of heat all through her hips that radiated down between her legs and up to her breasts. Her limbs fell slack, her stomach caved in, and she sucked in a breath, watching as his smile widened into a sexy, Cheshire cat, *I know exactly what I'm doing to you* grin.

"Message received," he whispered. Then, easing back, "Come on, sweetheart. You don't want to miss this. I promise it's going to be good."

He headed up the path again. And as Simone tried to settle her thumping heart, the first snowflake flittered through the air in front of her.

Oh boy. She was in big trouble here. She had no doubt whatever he planned was going to be incredibly good. The question was, could she resist it? Because after today, she knew for sure that he was no longer pissed at her. And while part of her was relieved by that fact, another part was deathly afraid. Fighting her own desires was one thing. Fighting his when he turned on the Mitch Mathews *I'm gonna make you mine* charm? Something entirely different.

He'd already rounded the bend by the time she got her act in gear and started moving again. When she reached the corner, she caught sight of the Martis Peak fire lookout and slowed her feet. It was still a ways ahead, up the steepest part of their hike, but it was more than she'd expected.

The small square building with a pointed roof sat on top of a rock outcropping. A deck ran all the way around the lookout, and a flagpole, void of flag, stood tall against the darkening sky.

Mitch had already made it to the base of the rocks and was waving for her to catch up. Steeling her resolve, she lifted her foot so the stupid snowshoe wouldn't get stuck. By the time she reached him, she was sweaty, shaking with nerves, and more than a little ticked she couldn't seem to get her own stupid emotions under control.

"These may work, but they totally slow you down." He knelt in front of her to unhook her showshoes. "No wonder it's taking you forever. Your buckle snapped."

She looked down at the latch he held in his hand and realized that was why it had felt like she was dragging the damn thing. "I told you the great outdoors and I don't get along."

He chuckled and unlatched her other snowshoe. "There's never a better time to change that." Rising to his feet, he grasped her gloved hand with his and tugged her up the stairs. "Almost there."

If she hadn't been worried about slipping on the ice-and-snow-covered steps, she'd have pulled her hand free. As it was, she bit back the protest on her lips and yanked the collar of her jacket up to block the bite of wind rushing over the deck of the small building. But when she saw the view, her mouth fell open, and all thought slipped from her mind.

"Oh…wow."

"Too bad this weather's moving in," Mitch said at her back as she stepped up to the railing. "I bet the view this morning was pretty stellar."

With the light snow falling and the thickening clouds, she couldn't see much more than the outline of the lake below and the snowy mountains on the Nevada side; the California side was already blanketed in white, blocking the view. But it was enough. The lake was huge, the water a deep crystal blue she'd never seen before. Her gaze skipped over the north edge of the lake, and she searched for Kendrick's house but couldn't see it. On a clear day, she was sure you could see all the way to Heavenly Ski Resort in South Lake Tahoe.

"This side isn't quite so bad."

The sound of Mitch's voice on the far side of the building drew her from the view. She followed the decking around the corner of the building. From here, the view stretched to Truckee and the white-capped mountains beyond. Several lakes dotted the landscape, and a long road stretched across a valley.

"What's that?" she asked.

"Truckee-Tahoe Airport. Kendrick usually flies in and out of there. Faster than driving up from Sacramento. Those mountains make up the Granite Chief Wilderness."

"And that?" She pointed to another, smaller body of water to the northwest.

"Donner Lake."

"We passed that on the way here, didn't we?"

He glanced sideways at her. "You have good eyesight when you're asleep."

Oh yeah. She'd been pretending to sleep on the drive to Tahoe. She'd forgotten that. Her cheeks heated.

He tugged her to the east side of the lookout, his face like that of a kid in a candy store, eager to share what he'd already found. "On a good day, you can see almost all the way to Reno. You've got almost a three-hundred-sixty degree view from up here." He frowned and looked up into the clouds, his cheeks as rosy as hers, his nose a soft shade of red. "I wish you could see it."

She believed him. And she wished she could see it all too. Walking around the other side of the building again, she watched as the clouds slowly moved over Lake Tahoe, smothering it in a field of white. There was no one around. No sound except the wind curling through the trees. No one who could see her or care about what she was doing. And for a moment, she felt as small as one of the snowflakes floating in the air. The people who were chasing her, everything that had happened in the last few days… None of it seemed to matter when she was looking at a view as vast and awe-inspiring as this.

"Pretty cool, huh?"

He moved up behind her, and she sensed he was close, even though he didn't touch her. "Yeah. Very cool. I can't even see the bear that was following us."

His laughter echoed on the breeze and slowly died off. "This is what I love most about hiking. Getting to the top and realizing…you're a part of something really amazing. You might not be able to see it all the time. You might not be able to feel it. But it's all around you. And it's always there when you need a little reassurance that the world isn't so bad after all."

Her throat grew thick, her eyes damp as she looked out over the steadily shrinking view. All these months she'd repeatedly turned down his requests to take her hiking, she hadn't realized he'd been trying to show her a piece of who he was inside. Not just the laid-back, carefree, sexy man she'd been dating, but the real him. And to share with her that what he felt for all this was similar to what he felt for her. That to him, what they had was just as amazing and awe-inspiring as what was always around them.

"You're shivering," he said softly just behind her. "Let's go inside and get warmed up."

Yes, she was cold, but she wasn't shaking because of the temperature. She was shaking because even with all the awful things she'd done to him in the last few days, she knew he still loved her. No one had ever loved her like that. Not her parents or Steve or even Shannon. Not to the point that they could put aside their own hurt and forgive the way he did. The way he was doing right now.

He grabbed her hand and pulled her around the side of the building. Pushing the door open with his hip, he drew her into the square room with windows on every side that looked out at the view. It was still cold in here, but the bitter bite of wind was gone, and for the first time she realized how frozen her cheeks were.

He dropped his pack on the floor and pulled her into his body, rubbing his hands up and down her arms to stimulate circulation. "Maybe this hike wasn't such a good idea. We left later than I thought we would."

"I-I'm fine," she stuttered. But was she? She wasn't sure anymore. Even in the middle of all the craziness, things had made sense. When she knew what she had to do, when she focused on a goal like getting Shannon somewhere safe, she could convince herself she was doing the right thing. But these last few days with Mitch… Nothing made sense anymore.

"We should have turned around when I noticed the clouds getting darker."

He continued to rub her arms, but he wasn't looking at her anymore. He was focused on the steadily darkening view. Worry tingled over her nerve endings. "Are you saying we're…that we're going to get snowed in up here?"

His focus slid back to her. And in his soft green gaze, she saw confidence. A confidence that calmed her in a way nothing else could. "Not exactly. This storm won't dump more than a few inches. But it's getting dark. We have two choices. We can head down now, although we won't make it to the rig before dark and there's no telling how long it will take with your broken snowshoe—"

"Going back now means we could run into that bear, though, right?"

An amused smile turned his lips. "Probably not. I'm sure he's long gone."

"What's our other option?"

"We can stay here for the night."

Stay here? Overnight? In these close quarters? Her nerves jumped all over again as she looked around the small room, but this time it had nothing to do with the fear of freezing. "H-here? Can we d-do that?"

His hands ran up and down her sleeves. And oh, what that smile did to her insides… "This lookout's on forest service land. They leave it unlocked for snow backpackers and campers, just like us."

Just like them.

A thought hit, and her eyes narrowed on that wicked grin. "You didn't plan this, did you?"

He feigned shock. "Planned *this*? The storm and darkness and your busted snowshoe?"

"Don't forget the bear."

He chuckled. "I'd have to be pretty talented to plan all that and make it work. We both know I'm not that organized."

He could be, though. When he put his mind to something, she had no doubt he could be successful at whatever he wanted. And that thought only excited her more, because she both loved and feared the idea of being stuck up here alone with him.

"Assuming I vote for staying," she said, her stomach a mass of nerves, "that doesn't solve the problem of hypothermia. We're out of the wind, but it's already below freezing." And it would only get colder. Which meant they'd have to rely on each other for warmth.

A tingle ran down her spine at the thought.

"I've got that covered." Letting go of her, he knelt in front of his pack. He yanked off his gloves, set those on the ground, then extracted an LED light that looked like a cross between a flashlight and a lantern and flipped it on, illuminating the darkening room. After setting that on the floor, he pulled out a silver blanket folded into a ten-by-ten square and handed it to her. Finally, he extracted a round grill-like looking thing with a neck, a one-pound propane tank and connected the two. He reached into his pocket and produced a lighter, which he used to light the contraption. Seconds later, the inside of the round grill turned a red-orange color, and warmth seeped from the device.

"Heat?" Simone yanked off her gloves and knelt to place her hands in front of the small portable heater. "You brought a heater with you? What else do you have in that magic pack?"

Mitch attached a circular base to the heater and set it on the floor. "A few things to tide us over. I don't usually pack the heater, but this was a short hike, and I wasn't sure how cold you'd get."

Right now, Simone didn't care if it made her look like a wimpy city girl or not. She was simply thankful for the warmth.

While she warmed her hands, he set up the folding table in the room—the only furniture in the place—and moved his pack to the surface. Outside, the snow was definitely picking up, and the light was fading, making it impossible to see the lake below anymore.

"We won't be able to run the heater all night." Mitch set a canteen, trail mix, a handful of granola bars, and a package of beef jerky on the table. "That tank will only last about five hours. But we can run it off and on, enough to take the chill off until morning."

Simone glanced over the measly selection, not particularly hungry but knowing she needed to eat something. She opted for a granola bar and a bit of jerky.

Settling herself on the floor in front of the heater, she unzipped her jacket and began eating. The room was already growing warmer, and whatever worry had been lingering was now gone. At least any worry over the temperature.

"Have you stayed up here before?" she asked, working for normal when she felt anything but.

He grabbed his own granola bar and sat cross-legged on the floor next to her. "No. But I've always wanted to. Beats the hell out of a tent in the middle of the snow."

Simone chewed and figured that had to be true. "Did you ever bring Ryan up here?"

"Once. He bitched the whole way. And it was summer. You've got bigger balls than he does, that's for sure."

Simone couldn't help it—she laughed, then covered her mouth. Mitch grinned and ripped open his granola bar. From inside his jacket, he produced a flask. He unscrewed the top and handed it to her. "I think you've earned this."

She took a small sniff, then a sip that warmed her insides all the way to her belly. Brandy. Wiping the back of her hand over her mouth, she blinked several times, then handed it back to him. "I think you solved the food-and-warmth problem."

"Not exactly." He took a sip of the brandy and then screwed the lid closed. "It's going to get cold in here once we turn off the heater. Which means if you're opting for staying, we're going to have to find another way to generate heat."

All those nerves came screaming back to life, and Simone's cheeks heated. She could suddenly think of several ways to generate heat with him. And not a single one was safe.

Mitch glanced out the windows, which were now almost completely black. "Better decide soon, or Mother Nature's going to decide for you."

Simone's gaze followed. And though it went against everything she'd been telling herself these last few days, she knew she didn't want to be anywhere else tonight but right here with him. "It looks to me like she already decided."

CHAPTER FIFTEEN

Keeping his hands to himself tonight was going to be nearly impossible.

Huddled together under the two-person Mylar thermal blanket, Mitch wished Simone hadn't taken off her coat so there was more padding between their bodies. Not that he didn't like feeling her up close and personal, but her subtle curves molded against his body made it damn hard to keep his hands from wandering over and under her soft sweatshirt to her silky skin beneath. And while he wanted nothing more than to do just that, he didn't want to do anything to spook her. They'd just gotten to the point where they could be civil to each other. If he moved too fast, he'd send her running.

And since she was obviously a pro at running, it was all he could do not to give her a reason to do just that.

She sighed and laid her head against his chest, her heat seeping into his pores, reflecting back at him under the safety blanket, making him even hotter with every passing second. "'Annie's Song.'"

"What?"

She rested her hand on his chest and spread her fingers. Tingles rushed over his flesh everywhere she touched, even through his thick flannel shirt. "You were humming it."

He hadn't realized he'd been humming. Nervous energy, obviously. He looked across the room but couldn't see anything in the darkness. They'd extinguished both the lantern and heater for the time being to conserve energy. "You know John Denver?"

"Not personally." She laughed. "My mom used to listen to his Christmas album every year. I got to know a lot of his songs that way."

"My dad used to sing it to my sister when she was little. When she and Ryan got married, Dad played it for her during the father-bride dance."

"I didn't know that."

"I think there's a lot about each other we didn't know."

Simone was silent, and in the darkness, Mitch cursed himself. He'd agreed not to mention the past, at least for the next few days, and he'd already crossed his own damn line.

"I didn't have a wedding," Simone said quietly. "Steve and I got married in a courthouse. We didn't have to. I mean, WITSEC had already given me my new identity as his wife, but he wanted it to be official."

She didn't say more, and Mitch couldn't quite tell if that was a good or bad thing. But man, he wanted to ask. Wanted to ask a thousand things about her dead husband. She'd rarely talked about the guy in all the months they'd been together, but he sensed if he pushed her for too much too soon, he wouldn't get any of the answers he needed.

"It was a month or so after we went into the program," she finally went on. "I didn't really want to get married. Steve was the one who pushed it. Said he wanted everything to be official. For Shannon."

"For Shannon," she muttered. "'For Shannon' was his excuse for everything. No one knows this, but I didn't want to have a baby. That probably makes me a terrible mother, doesn't it? I didn't want to get married, didn't want to have kids. And I resented him for it, because in one split second, I gave up my whole life. For a man I wasn't even in love with. Lust, yes. Love? No. I didn't even get to say good-bye to my grandmother."

Mitch wasn't sure what to say. But his mind drifted to her parents, who'd flown out a few times from Baltimore to spend time with Shannon. "What about your parents? I met them."

Simone shifted against him. "No, you met our neighbors. Ray and Betty lived next door to us in Baltimore. They sort of adopted us, and when Shannon was little and started calling them Grandma and Grandpa, none of us corrected them. My dad died in a car accident when I was little, and my mom raised me in a small town in Pennsylvania until she died from heart disease I was sixteen. After that, I lived with my grandmother until I left for college. Her health wasn't good, and I didn't get to see her as often as I should have. I think that's part of the reason the US marshals let me go with Steve. I didn't have much of a family to miss me. A year after we went into the program, my grandmother had a stroke. I couldn't go to the hospital to be with her. Shannon was only a couple of months old then."

Mitch didn't know what to say. So many lies. But he couldn't judge her or be angry that she hadn't told him the truth. Because if he'd been in the same position, he'd likely have done the same.

Simone pushed up. All he could see were the whites of her eyes, but they were sad, and a small part of him broke, knowing the lies had hurt her way more than they'd ever hurt him. "I never blamed Shannon. She gave me a reason not to dwell on the negatives, and in a lot of ways, she saved me. And even though I never wished for any of this to happen, it taught me patience and the importance of thinking things through. I don't regret the choices I made. But I do regret that I couldn't talk about them. I think..." Her eyes drifted down to her hand, still resting against his chest. "I think maybe if I'd been able to talk about it...things might have been easier."

Things between them. She didn't say the words, but he sensed them hovering in the air between them. And his pulse picked up speed, igniting a flutter—that hope—in his belly he'd felt when he'd held her in the safe room.

She laid her head back against his chest, and her fingers gently brushed his shirt. Tingles flared all over his skin again, and he worked like hell to keep his pulse from racing. She was sharing secrets—things most couples talked about way earlier in their relationship. And though he couldn't tell her his biggest secret—at least not yet—he knew he could give her something.

"I almost got married once."

Her hand stopped moving against his shirt. "You did?"

He hadn't told anyone this—not even Ryan—and though he'd never planned to air his vulnerability, part of him figured maybe it was time. Maybe if she understood what he'd been through, she could understand why he'd reacted so badly when she'd lied to him. "It was about two years after we lost my sister. Ryan was just starting to come out of his fog. I'd been putting off working in the field because of him and Julia, but I was antsy to get out of the Bay Area. So when a site was identified in South America, I jumped on the chance to be the first geologist to start taking samples."

He hadn't really been in the market for a relationship, but looking back on it, losing his sister had definitely made him rethink what was important in life. "She was part of the team sent to Ecuador to evaluate the site. We met a few days after I got there, hit it off. One thing led to another, and before I knew it, we were a couple."

More than a couple. They'd spent every waking moment together. Rachel had been everything he thought he'd been looking for in a woman. Outdoorsy, able to hold her own with the other guys on site, and totally hot. The first time he'd seen those long, shapely legs of hers in cargo shorts and dusty hiking boots, he thought he'd found nirvana. He'd never been so completely wrong in his life.

He cleared his throat and shifted his back against the wall where he was leaning. "A few months went by, and things were great. Neither of us wanted to leave, but when our analysis of the site was finished, we didn't have much choice. I came home, and she went back to Dallas. We made plans for her to come to San Francisco to visit, but a week went by, and I didn't hear from her. I tried to call her, but it kept going to voice mail. So after a few days, I got worried and flew out to Dallas to see her."

"What happened?"

He shook his head, feeling like a complete idiot all over again. "Turns out the joke was on me. Her husband answered the door."

"Oh boy."

"Yeah, there was one of those. Seven-year-old. And a girl who looked to be about five. Rachel was out shopping when I got there. Her husband looked as shell-shocked as I felt."

He could feel Simone cringe against his chest. "What did you do?"

"Said I was from the office and pretended to be dropping off some files for her. Then I got the hell out of there. But I think he knew what was going on."

"That's awful. Did you ever hear from her?"

"A day later. She called after I was back in San Francisco."

"What did she say?"

"Not much. There wasn't much she could say. Just that she didn't know how to tell me the truth and that she never wanted me to get hurt."

Simone didn't answer, and in the silence, Mitch realized those were the same things Simone had told him the night she'd come to his house and those thugs had shot up his property.

Except…in Simone's case, at least she'd been sorry. Rachel had only been sorry she'd been caught.

A shiver racked Simone's body, and, reflexively, Mitch pulled her in closer. "Are you cold? We can flip the heater on for a bit to take the chill off."

"No, I'm fine." She huddled close, so the length of her thigh was against his, heat seeping from her into him, sending tingles of awareness all across his flesh. "I'm sorry she did that to you. That…wasn't right."

Mitch stared off into the darkness, remembering how upset he'd been. Ironically, the pain of that humiliation didn't even compare to how he'd felt when Simone had left him. "I wasn't really in love with her. I think I wanted to be. After we lost my sister, I realized that family is the only thing that really matters. I think more than anything I just wanted to know what it was like to have a family of my own. She was the wrong one to want that with, though."

And Simone was the right one. He just wasn't sure how to convince her of that fact.

"You're a good man, Mitch Mathews."

He huffed, because he didn't feel particularly good. He felt stupid in a lot of ways. And helpless. But he was willing to put himself out on a limb for a chance to make things right with the woman in his arms. "I'm no angel, sweetheart. I've done plenty of dumb shit in my life."

"I'm sure you have, but you've got a good heart. That doesn't change. You're going to make a great husband and father someday."

It just won't be today. Or with me.

He heard the unspoken words as loud as if she'd screamed them. And inside, everything he'd been holding back, all his plans to keep things light between them, whooshed right out of his head. Along with what was left of his common sense.

"You're damn right I am." He gripped her by the jaw and turned her face up to his. Surprised dark eyes met his. Eyes that had captivated him from the first. "But not someday."

Then he lowered his mouth to hers.

Simone sucked in a breath and froze.

Mitch's lips pressed against hers, soft, firm, cool like the air in the small lookout, but warming from a heat that was flaring to life between them. Like a fire sparking against black embers and slowly turning to a full-blown blaze.

He groaned, the sound echoing through his chest and into hers, sending fingers of awareness tingling through her core. He eased the pressure on her mouth, tilted his head, and kissed her again. Her pulse sped up. Electricity raced all along her skin. Panic—or maybe it was excitement, she couldn't tell which—clouded her mind, making it hard to think, to act, to know what to do.

The hand at her jaw slid up into her hair, and his fingers spread, cupping the back of her head, tugging her even closer. She grabbed a fistful of his flannel shirt—to push him away or pull him closer, she wasn't sure which—but right now she was glad he'd taken off that heavy coat, that she didn't have to fumble with layers of fabric, that he wasn't giving her time to think.

"Give in to me, Simone," he mumbled against her lips. "You know you want to."

Oh, but she did. It was why she'd gone to see him that night at his house. Why she'd come all the way to Tahoe with him. Why she'd agreed to this silly hike that now didn't seem so foolish anymore. But nothing had changed. If anything, his life was in more danger because of her, and if she gave in, if she took everything he was offering without thinking of the consequences and something bad happened to him, she'd never be able to forgive herself.

She let go of his shirt and pressed her palm against his chest. This time to push him away. Definitely to push him away. She eased back enough to suck in air. "Mitch. This isn't a good idea."

"Your good ideas haven't exactly panned out, sweetheart. Time to try someone else's."

He lowered his head once more, and panic snaked in. A panic that told her if he kissed her again, she might not have the strength to stop him. "Mitch—"

His mouth closed over hers before she could get the rest of the words out. And then his heat was there, sliding across her lips, dipping inside to tangle with her tongue, filling her senses with every inch of *him*.

She groaned, and her fingers curled in his shirt once more, this time to pull him closer. It was stupid. It was reckless. It was everything she shouldn't do. But she wanted. Hadn't stopped wanting. And had no more resistance left to fight him.

"Mitch…"

Her tongue brushed his, slowly at first, then with more insistence. She let go of his shirt, slid her hand up his neck and around the back of his head, her fingers combing through his soft hair, pulling his mouth more firmly down to hers. He answered with another groan, and the arm around her shoulder slinked lower, down her back, pushing her up. Then he was lifting her, tugging her, shifting her body so she was straddling his hips, then sinking down onto his lap and the glorious bulge in his jeans that told her exactly how much he wanted her.

They didn't need the heater now. She doubted they even needed the thin Mylar blanket. Sweat slicked her skin as she trailed her other hand up his chest and into his hair. As she kissed him deeper, again and again. As she felt his hands streaking down her back to guide her up and down as he rocked his hips against her most sensitive spot.

She was breathless. Panting. Couldn't think. Could only feel. Her hands gripped both sides of his face. She pulled away just enough to breathe but didn't let go. His lips pressed against the corner of her mouth, her jaw, trailed a line of hot, wet kisses all the way to her ear. She trembled as he blew against her neck. Desire and a need to feel him everywhere, curled tight, wicked fingers all through her belly, shooting electrical charges straight to her breasts and down into her sex.

"Ah God, Simone." He pushed away from the wall and sat up. One hand slinked up her back and into her hair. The movement forced her hips into closer contact with his, and the hard length of his erection rubbed against her mound, making her see stars. "I've been going mad without you."

He dragged her mouth back to his and kissed her deeply, his lips on fire, his tongue hot and wet and sinful. Everything she remembered it to be.

She was going mad too. Was absolutely wild right now from the taste of him.

She kissed him again and again. His mouth turned greedy, wanton against hers. She moaned against his lips, wanting so much more. The hand in her hair slid down her neck, across her collarbone, and brushed her breast. Electrical charges shot all through her body. She groaned against him. Kissed him deeper. His fingers found the tip of her breast and pinched her nipple through her shirt, a mixture of pleasure and pain she felt everywhere.

"Mitch…"

"I'm right here, baby." His other hand found the snap on her jeans and flicked it free. "Give in to me, sweetheart. I need you."

She needed him too. He had no idea how much. But when his fingers grazed the soft flesh of her lower belly, a little of the sex fuzz filling her mind cleared. Just a tad. Just enough so she became cognizant of what they were doing. Of what doing this with him would mean. Of what kind of danger that would put him in down the line.

Her hands landed against his shoulders, and she pulled her mouth from his, gasping for air, grappling for some kind of control. "Mitch, wait."

"No waiting. I'm done waiting. You want me. I can feel it."

His lips pressed against her neck. His hand slinked lower. He rocked his hips until pleasure ripped through her pelvis, and she knew if he did that again she wouldn't be able to stop herself. But she *needed* to put a stop to this. Not for herself, but for him.

"Mitch…no."

"Yes."

He held her tight, but she put all her strength in her arms, pushed away from him, and stumbled to find her footing. Her boot slipped, and she nearly fell into him, but caught herself at the last second and broke free. Breathing heavily, she held out her hand and moved back a step, unable to see anything in the pitch-dark room, even her own fingers. "I said stop."

She could feel his stare piercing her flesh even if she couldn't see him. No sound echoed in the room, nothing but the howling of the wind and storm outside, but with every passing second, she could feel the anger growing inside him, rolling off him in hot waves that drifted across the cool room, centered directly on her.

Long seconds passed, then finally, a low chuckle rumbled from across the room. "You really are the queen of mixed messages, you know that?"

Here it came. And boy, did she deserve it. "Mitch—"

"No, you know what? I get it." Shuffling echoed. She couldn't see what he was doing, but seconds later, the LED lantern flicked on, blinding her with the flash of light. She covered her eyes and looked away. A click echoed, and then the hum of the small heater filled the room, but it didn't ease the chill sliding down Simone's spine. "I always prided myself on being a pretty smart guy, but with you? Not so much. No more, though. I finally get what you've been trying to tell me the past six months."

She hated that she was hurting him—again. Hated that she was in this position in the first place. Hated even more that her heart felt like it was breaking all over.

She never should have let Ryan and Kate convince her to come to Tahoe with him. Never should have thought they could just be friends. They'd never been *just* friends. They'd always been more. And she still wanted to be more, even knowing it could never happen. She swallowed the lump growing in her throat. "I didn't mean for any of this to happen."

"No, you didn't." He tugged off the blanket and tossed it across the floor toward her. "It was all me. I'm the one who talked you into going out with me. I'm the one who pushed the relationship. I'm the one who dragged you all the way up this stupid mountain. You're the one with the psycho past, but yeah… I take full responsibility." He tugged his coat back on and zipped it up to his chin, then settled back against the wall and crossed his arms over his chest. "I give up."

Panic filled her chest and threatened to steal her breath. The same panic she'd felt the night she'd come back from the east coast and broken things off with him. Words hovered on her lips—apologies, excuses, the truth—but she couldn't voice them. In the end, what difference would they make? They'd still be in the same place—his life in danger and her being the cause—and that wouldn't change until she got out of his life for good.

She reached for the Mylar blanket at her feet, rubbing it between her fingers. Minutes ago, it had been warm and cozy. Not it just felt cold and alone. Like her.

"You'll freeze to death," she managed. "We still need to share the blanket."

"I'll survive."

He'd pulled his hood up, closed his eyes, and leaned his head back against the wall, effectively dismissing her. And as his jaw flexed beneath the sexy stubble on his cheek, tears filled her eyes, making her feel like an even bigger louse. "Mitch—"

"It'll be light in a couple of hours. After we get out of here, I'll call Ryan and find out what his guy's discovered. Either way, you don't have to worry. You can stay at Kendrick's. I'll find somewhere else to go."

That wasn't what she wanted at all. The panic multiplied, sending a fierce shooting pain all through her chest. "You don't have to leave."

He laughed again, but the sound held zero humor. "I don't particularly want to stay anymore. You win, Simone. I'm done."

CHAPTER SIXTEEN

All Mitch wanted to do was get the hell off this mountain.

He packed up his gear in silence while Simone sat on the far side of the lookout, her knees pulled up to her chest, her knit hat tugged down low over her head. She hadn't spoken much to him since it had grown light, and he hadn't offered up any conversation either. Was he being an ass? Probably. Did he care? Not a bit. Last night was just one giant reminder that things between them were dead and buried, and the sooner he accepted that fact, the better off he'd be.

Latching his pack, he reached for her snowshoe—the one that had busted yesterday—and fixed the strap as best he could. He handed it to her. "Try to stay out of the powder with this one. Step where I step, and you should be fine."

She accepted the snowshoe, her fingertips grazing his in the process, cold, hesitant, not a bit like the greedy hands that had fisted in his hair last night as she'd kissed him crazy. "Thanks."

Not for kissing her. Not for making her *feel* anything. He was starting to wonder if the woman even had a heart.

Which was stupid because… He needed to stop thinking about her and pull his head out of his ass.

He pushed to his feet and slung his pack over his back. "Let's go."

The air was crisp when they stepped outside, chilling Mitch's cheeks and causing ice crystals to catch in the scruff on his jaw. Three inches of new snow covered the ground, and he was thankful it wasn't more. After latching on his snowshoes, he led the way down the hillside toward the car they'd parked at the gate. The two-mile trek was slow moving, and neither of them spoke, but it wasn't nearly as much work—or as fun—as coming up. The only plus was that the lower they dropped in elevation, the easier it got thanks to the protection the trees provided from the stinging wind.

Simone didn't speak, and once or twice he looked back to see she was doing exactly what he'd said—picking her way down the hill, stepping where he stepped, being careful she didn't dislodge her snowshoe anymore. Occasionally she'd glance around, looking for that bear, he knew, but it didn't amuse him like it had on the hike up. Instead, it pissed him off even more. He was done being such a pathetic schmuck. So he'd misread her in that safe room. There were worse things in life than being rejected.

He turned the corner and caught sight of the gate. It was closed, just as it had been before, but new snow littered the ground, covering everything in a fresh layer of white. Everything but their car.

Fuck. There *were* worse things than rejection.

Simone's coat rustled next to him, followed by her heavy breathing. She drew to a stop at his side and fell silent.

"Um…" Her voice floated on the cool air. "Where's the car?"

Frustration growing, Mitch moved around the Forest Service gate, rested his hands on his hips, and stared down at the fine powder. Tire tracks in the snow meant whoever had taken it had done it after the snow hit. Likely only hours ago.

"Mitch? Where's the car?"

He turned a slow circle and looked around. A couple of footprints in the powder, but nothing more. "Gone."

"What do you mean 'gone'?" She moved around the gate.

"Gone as in… Someone stole it."

Disbelief flooded her chocolate eyes. "All the way up here?"

"Yeah, all the way up here."

Her dazed eyes scanned the area. "Who would do that?"

"Hikers most likely. Someone who'd parked below and was cold and didn't want to keep going. Could be anyone really."

"But…but we're stuck."

He hated that little edge of panic to her voice. Hated even more that it got to him. "We're only about eight miles from the lake. Three at most to the highway." He pulled out his phone. No service. Shoving it back in his pocket, he started walking and gestured for her to follow.

She hustled to keep up. "You're not planning to walk all the way to the lake, are you?"

"Not all the way." Just until he could get a signal and call Ford. Or catch a ride with someone heading toward Tahoe. But in his pissy mood, he didn't feel like sharing much more. She didn't want to share anything. Hell, two could play that game.

They followed the twisting road down the mountain. It wasn't steep, but several times Mitch had to wait for Simone to catch up. Luckily, though, she didn't complain once, and he had to hand it to her, for a city chick—for one he knew was still freaked about running into another bear—she was holding her own. And that fact didn't turn him on, dammit. He was done being turned on by her.

The closer they got to the highway, the more signs there were that others had been in the area. Snowshoe markings, cross-country ski tracks, footprints. By the time they reached the parking lot, tracks were everywhere, and they found three other cars parked near the road. But no sign of their SUV.

Mitch pulled his glove off and reached for his cell in his pocket. His fingers felt like ice as they closed around the small device. Still no service. Frowning, he looked up and around and spotted a man loading cross-country skis in the back of his pickup.

"My feet are killing me." Simone plopped down on a rock to remove her snowshoes.

"Stay here," he said to her.

He crossed to the red Toyota and introduced himself. The guy looked to be in his late fifties, rugged, a total local. Said his name was Judd.

"Are you heading toward the lake or Truckee?" Mitch asked.

"Incline Village," Judd answered. "Just got out for a few hours of fresh air before the missus puts me to work. She's always got jobs for me around the house."

He smiled and winked in a way that said *you know what I mean?* But Mitch found himself scowling instead of smiling back. No, he didn't know what the guy meant. And he probably never would. After Simone, he couldn't see himself getting involved with another woman. Short-term relationships were the only way to go. Less damage to his ego that way. Definitely safer for his heart.

"Our rig was stolen while we were off hiking. Any chance my"—shit, what did he call Simone?— "friend and I could get a ride into town?"

The man glanced past Mitch toward Simone sitting on a rock. To her credit, she waved and smiled, putting on a good show. She'd obviously learned how to do that—pretend like nothing bothered her—and Mitch wondered why the hell he hadn't picked up on that sooner.

Shaking the thought out of his head, he refocused on the man who was saving their bacon.

"Sure," Judd answered. "Might be kind of tight, though. Truck's only got two seats. As long as you and your girl don't mind sharing, the more the merrier."

Simone wasn't his girl, and she never really had been. That was the problem here. For a minute, Mitch reconsidered. Freezing to death didn't sound so bad, not when he was faced with having to cozy up to Simone so soon after she'd kicked his teeth in—again.

He worked up a smile for Judd. Only for Judd. "Perfect. We appreciate it, man."

He turned and motioned for Simone to join them. Judd moved around the truck and climbed into the driver's seat. When Simone reached Mitch's side, she was breathless again, her cheeks rosy, her nose a red little ball in the center of her face he didn't want to kiss, dammit.

"What's going on?" she asked.

"I got us a ride." He pulled the door open. "Judd, this is Simone."

Judd smiled and leaned toward the steering wheel to get a better look at her. "Well, hello, pretty lady." He looked past Simone to Mitch. "You caught yourself a nice one there. Go ahead and toss your gear in the back."

Mitch pulled off his pack and put it in the bed of the truck. As Simone handed him her snowshoes, she whispered, "What am I, a fish?"

He put his snowshoes in the back with hers and shot her a warning look. "No, fish have hearts. We can leave you out here if you'd rather."

She glared his way and moved toward the open door, but when she looked inside again, her eyes flared, just a touch. "There's only one seat."

"I told your husband it would be tight," Judd said, flipping on the heaters.

"He's not my husband."

Mitch came around next to her and climbed into the truck. The way he figured it, the less this guy knew, the better off they'd all be. "Boyfriend." He grabbed Simone's hand and tugged her in to sit on his lap. "Always have to be so technical, don't you, honey?"

She narrowed her eyes and looked down at him while he pulled the door closed. He fixed her with a silent look, telling her to deal with it.

The truck bounced along the snowy gravel as Judd backed out of the lot, then shifted into gear. Simone braced one hand on the dashboard and slid the other around Mitch's shoulder to keep from falling off his lap. Heat seeped into Mitch's skin even through the layers of clothing between them, and her scent filled his head, making him achingly aware of her cute little ass brushing his groin with every single rock of the vehicle.

Stay focused. She doesn't want you, remember?

"You two up here vacationing?"

"We don't look like locals to you?" Simone asked.

Judd slid a look over her spendy parka and new hiking boots, the ones they'd snagged from Kendrick's house, which he kept around for guests. "No, definitely not locals. My guess is San Francisco. Maybe LA, but I doubt it."

Simone tensed against his lap, and Mitch snaked his arm around her waist to hold her in place. The last thing he needed was for her to give this local any reason to tell people about the strange couple he'd picked up on the road. If someone was looking for them, he wasn't leaving a trail. "Seattle, actually. We flew into Reno a few days ago and rented a car. Gonna be a bitch explaining how we lost it to the rental agency."

"Eh, they have those things insured," Judd said as he pulled out onto the highway. "You'll be fine."

Simone turned to look down at Mitch, and the surprise in her eyes told him she hadn't expected him to be able to lie so easily.

See, sweetheart, you're not the only one who can do it.

Tearing his gaze from hers, he looked out the windshield at the wet pavement. The hills on both sides of the road were all covered in snow, making the area look like a winter wonderland.

Her jacket was puffy and thick, but he could still feel her breast pressing sideways against his chest, could still feel her heat radiating into every inch of his body. Clenching his jaw, Mitch told himself to just get through this, then it would be smooth sailing.

"What is that?" Simone asked.

They rounded a bend, and brake lights shone in the distance. As Judd slowed the vehicle, Mitch looked past Simone toward a fire truck on the side of the road and the handful of firefighters hosing down a smoking vehicle. He couldn't tell what kind of car it had been at first. It was nothing more than a blackened pile of burned metal. Then he caught sight of the bumper, lying askew against the pavement, and the license plate angled their direction.

"Oh my God," Simone muttered.

"Ouch," Judd muttered. "Guarantee whoever was in that car didn't make it."

The hillside next to the wreckage was black, the snow all melted. The highway had been closed down to one lane, and police were directing traffic. Mitch scanned the accident scene as they crept by. A black SUV, definitely, just like the one they'd driven.

"Crying shame," Judd muttered.

"Looks like they lost it on the ice," Mitch managed, his throat thick. Though that wasn't really what it looked like to him. It looked like the vehicle had caught fire somehow and gone up in flames.

"That wasn't just ice, sonny," Judd answered. "Looks like a bomb went off."

Simone's head jerked Mitch's way, and he saw the horror in her eyes.

He knew what she was thinking. The same damn thing he was. He shook his head slowly, hoping she didn't do or say anything to give them away.

They passed the accident, and, thankfully, traffic slowly picked up. Tugging the phone from his pocket, Mitch looked down at the screen and silently rejoiced when it registered service. Simone shifted on his lap to see what he was looking at, and sparks of electricity pulsed through his groin on reflex.

Dammit. The sooner they got to town, the faster he could get away from her and her sultry heat. And figure out what the hell was going on.

In town, at the junction of Highway 28, which ran around the lake, Judd asked, "What hotel are you two staying at?"

"We're actually staying at a condo," Mitch said. "If you could just drop us at the Safeway around the corner, we can give our friends a call to pick us up."

"Sure that's where you want to go?" Judd asked, making a right turn.

No, Mitch wanted to get the hell out of here, but it was the best he could do for now. He nodded.

Judd pulled into the grocery store's parking lot and put the truck in Park. Simone popped the door and climbed out, leaving behind a chill that spread over Mitch.

"Thank you so much," Simone said.

Mitch grabbed his pack and their snowshoes from the bed of the truck, then looked back into the cab. "We appreciate it."

"No problem. You two have a great vacation."

Judd waved and pulled out of the parking lot. When they were alone, Simone turned her worried gaze on Mitch. "That was our car."

"Not here." Mitch nodded toward the store. "Why don't you get us some coffee? They've got a Starbucks."

Simone flashed him an annoyed look, but he didn't care.

"I'll meet you out here in a few minutes." He swung his pack over his shoulder and headed away from the store, into an empty area of the parking lot, and dialed Ford's number.

"Ben Ford," a voice said in his ear moments later.

"Hey, Ford. It's Mathews. We need a ride."

"Where the hell have you been?" Ford asked. "I was about to send Search and Rescue up to Martis Peak to look for you. You were supposed to check in hours ago."

Mitch was thankful that hadn't happened. "Sorry about that. We got snowed in at the lookout last night. When we came down this morning, we discovered our car was gone."

"Damn vandals. Nowhere's safe anymore. Where are you?"

Mitch had a sinking feeling it wasn't just vandals, but he wasn't about to tell Ford that. "Tahoe Vista. Safeway parking lot."

"Car's on its way."

"Thanks, man. I do need one other favor, though."

"Shoot."

"Kendrick mentioned you have a contact at the local police department. We passed an accident on the way down the mountain. Can you find out the make and model of the car and if anyone was injured?"

"Yeah," Ford said hesitantly. "You think it was your ride?"

Um, yeah, he was almost positive it was their ride. "I don't know," he lied. "But if it was, it's a rental, and I need to be able to tell the agency what happened."

"Okay," Ford answered. "I'll see what I can find out."

When Mitch hung up, Simone was just walking out the grocery store's automatic doors, two steaming paper cups in her gloved hands. His heart squeezed at the sight of her, and another burst of loss rushed through him, a reaction that only irritated him more. He was done getting his teeth kicked in. Done pretending this wasn't exactly what it was: the worst damn thing he could imagine.

He took the cup from her without looking into her eyes. Yeah, he was done doing that too. "Thanks."

"Did you get a hold of Ford?" She wrapped both hands around her cup and shivered, and he fought the urge to pull her close and warm her with his body.

"He's on his way."

She pressed her lips together and glanced around the parking lot. They were far enough from any other cars, so no one wandering in and out of the store could hear them. "That wasn't a random accident up there, was it?"

"I don't know."

"But there was no other car."

"It could have been any number of things." But even he didn't believe that. His brain had been whirring since he'd seen the wreckage, trying to figure out how anyone had found them. "Let's not get ahead of ourselves."

"But if they know we're here—"

"No one knows we're here. And even if they did know we were in the area, they obviously don't know exactly where. Kendrick's house is still the safest place."

For the time being. But how long would that last?

She didn't continue arguing, and he didn't bother to look at her. Sipping his coffee, he glanced around the parking lot. After several long seconds, she said, "Mitch, about last night… I—"

Oh no. He wasn't going there.

"Don't." He dropped down to sit on the cement base of a light pole. "Let's not rehash something that doesn't need rehashing. You got what you wanted."

"And what is that?" she asked quietly.

He lifted his cup to his lips and built up a layer of ice over what was left of his heart. Maybe Ryan had it right all those years after he'd lost his wife. Being a total ass was the only way to protect yourself from this kind of misery. "You wanted to be done with me? Well I'm way past done. I'm charbroiled."

Simone didn't respond, and as silence stretched between them in the brisk air, Mitch told himself that was fine. That was the way it was supposed to be.

A sleek new Range Rover pulled into the parking lot, heading their way. Mitch's head came up, and he narrowed his eyes to see through the windshield. A frown pulled at his lips when he recognized the face. "Fuck me."

This so wasn't what he needed right now.

"What's going on? Simone asked, turning from the golf course she'd been staring at to the right of the parking lot.

Mitch pushed to his feet and stuffed one hand into the pocket of his jeans. "Our ride's here."

The Range Rover drew to a stop, and Tate Kendrick unraveled himself from the driver's seat. "Dude," he said, glancing over Mitch as he rested his arm on the open doorframe. "You look like hell."

"Tell me something I don't already know." Holding the coffee in one hand, he stepped toward Tate, caught his hand, and tugged him in for a one-armed hug.

Tate chuckled. "You could act sorta thankful to see me, you know."

Mitch was thankful to see him. More than he'd expected. "What are you doing here?"

Tate slid both hands in the front pockets of his worn jeans and shrugged, his shoulders lifting and falling in the gray sweater, his snow boots scuffing the parking lot as he moved. "Ford called last night all wigged out that he'd lost you two. I told him not to sweat it, and that you and Mother Nature had a thing going, but I don't think he believed me."

"So you flew down here to check on me?"

Tate grinned and shook his shaggy dark hair back from his face, bringing all his rock star good looks into Hollywood mode. "I was having writer's block. Change of scenery's always good for me." He glanced past Mitch toward Simone, and his eyes widened. "Hey, there. You must be the sexy lawyer I've heard so much about."

Mitch's jaw clenched. Without looking at Simone, Mitch said, "Tate Kendrick, Simone Conners."

"How do you do," Simone said.

Tate shoved Mitch out of his way and made a beeline straight for Simone. Wrapping both hands around hers, he tugged off her glove and pulled her hand to his mouth for a kiss. "Baby, you're freezing. This jackass doesn't know how to show a girl a good time. Spend a few hours with me, and I promise you'll never think of him again."

Mitch turned to look, then regretted it. Simone's amused expression said she wasn't sure what to make of Tate, but she wasn't pulling her hand from his lips or telling him to back off like she'd done with Mitch.

Irritation got the best of him as he watched Tate blowing his warm breath over her small hand. "Okay, stop mauling her, Kendrick. She's not one of your groupies."

Tate ignored Mitch. Just focused on Simone, pulling her with him as he turned, hooking her hand through his arm and leading her to the car. "He's just jealous. Ignore him." He opened the passenger door and offered it to her. "Your white knight is here, madam."

"Um…" Simone glanced at Mitch, then back at Tate. "Thanks. I think."

"God Almighty," Mitch muttered.

Tate grinned and winked down at Simone as she sat and pulled her legs into the new vehicle. "Was he this much fun on your hike? You poor, poor thing."

Simone didn't answer, and when Tate closed the door and turned back to him, Mitch shot him a glare. "Pouring it on just a little thick, don't you think, music man?"

"Just trying to cheer her up. Someone's got to. I can tell from your peachy mood you didn't."

He rounded the car for the driver's side. "Come on. It's fucking cold out here."

Mitch frowned again and picked up his pack and the snowshoes, then climbed into the backseat. Warmth enveloped him, but it wasn't the warmth he wanted. No, the warmth he still stupidly wanted was sitting in the front seat, angled toward Tate, making small talk about the weather or some other dumb topic.

He watched the scenery as they headed back to Tate's house and tuned out Tate's flirting. Simone was right to worry. Someone did know they were here. He just couldn't figure out how.

By the time they made it back to the house, all that resentment he'd squashed was back full-bore, and this time it wasn't just Simone's fault—and that pissed him off more. All he wanted was a stiff drink, a shower, and a bed where he could crash for a few hours. What he had was a nightmare he knew he had to deal with now rather than later.

They pulled into the garage. Tate killed the engine and popped the door. The guy was too busy telling Simone about the property he'd purchased and his headache with the builder to care what Mitch was up to. After dropping the snow gear in the garage, Mitch stomped the snow from his boots and followed them toward the house. Inside he was immediately surrounded by warmth, but it quickly chilled when Simone stopped talking midsentence. She glanced his way, and a dark look spread over her features, one Mitch wasn't going to feel guilty about.

She turned her attention back to Tate. "I'm going to take a shower. Thanks for picking us up."

"No problem," Tate said with a shit-eating grin. "Take as long as you like."

She disappeared up the stairs.

"Wow," Tate muttered when they were alone. "She really does not like you."

Mitch tugged off his jacket and hung it on a hook near the door, then toed off his boots. "Tell me something I don't already know."

"What the hell did you do to her?"

What had *he* done? Yeah, it was all him. He pushed past Tate and headed for the kitchen. Instead of the alcohol he really wanted, he opted for a soda from the fridge "I'm really not in the mood to talk about it."

Tate followed, pulling his cell from his back pocket. "You might have to in a few minutes."

Mitch popped the top on the can and took a long swallow. "Why?"

Tate held up his phone. "Text from Ford. Harrison and his wife are on their way. Should be here anytime. Think that means they have some answers for you?"

Mitch's hand froze with the can midway to his mouth. Yeah, that was exactly what it meant. And he knew instinctively it wasn't going to be good. Because if it was good news, Ryan would simply call.

His stomach churned with a mixture of fear and dread. Now more than ever, he really needed that drink, but because he needed to keep his head screwed on tight tonight, that wasn't going to happen. "I think that means I'm about to get fucked. And not in a good way."

CHAPTER SEVENTEEN

The shower did little to help Simone's mood.

Wrapped in a towel, she sat on the end of her bed and rubbed her aching forehead. She was making things worse. Every minute she spent with Mitch made his life that much more miserable. She didn't want to hurt him anymore. She wanted him to be happy, and he was never going to be that with her around. A cold reality spread through her chest. She couldn't wait for Ryan's PI any longer. What she needed to do was pack her bags and get the hell away from Mitch once and for all. Then deal with her broken heart in the aftermath.

A knock sounded at her door, and her head came up, nerves rushing though her at the thought it could be Mitch. "Come in."

The door pushed open, and she held her breath, waiting for...she didn't know what. But when Kate peeked into the room and smiled, Simone's excitement turned to confusion. "What are you doing here?"

"I'm happy to see you too." Kate closed the door at her back.

Simone shook her wet head, realizing she was being rude. "I am happy to see you, I'm just surprised." She tugged the towel tighter around her breasts. "Shannon—"

"Shannon's fine, don't worry. I talked to the kids this morning. They're having a great time with Ryan's parents."

A breath of relief seeped out of Simone. As long as Shannon was okay, she could deal with everything else. "When did you get here?"

"A few minutes ago. Ryan's downstairs with the guys. They told me you were up here alone." Kate's green eyes—so much like Mitch's—narrowed with concern. "Are you okay?"

Was *she* okay? That was a stupid question. Even more ludicrous, because Kate should be worried about her brother, not the woman who'd tromped all over his heart. Rising, Simone grabbed clothes from the dresser drawers, then headed for the bathroom so she could get dressed. "I'm fine."

"You don't look fine," Kate said from beyond the bathroom door. "In fact, you and Mitch both look quite frazzled."

Frazzled was a nice way to put it. She tugged on the pants and buttoned them. "Mitch will be fine once I'm gone. This was a dumb idea, coming up here. I never should have let you talk me into it."

Kate's features were drawn and sad when Simone pulled the bathroom door open. "What happened?"

"Nothing." Simone moved for the closet and pulled out her suitcase. Nothing she was going to tell Kate, at least. She didn't deserve her friend's sympathy. Pulling clothing from the drawers, she dropped them in her suitcase, determined not to look into Kate's knowing eyes.

"Something definitely happened," Kate said softly. "Might help to talk about it."

Talk about the way she'd messed things up—again? No way. Simone tugged shirts from hangers and threw them in her suitcase, not bothering to fold the clothing. "Why are you here?"

Kate sat on the end of the bed and sighed. "Ryan's PI found some information we thought you might be interested in."

Did what he'd found really matter anymore? No, it didn't.

Simone threw a sweater in her suitcase. "You could have just called. You didn't need to come all the way up here." She'd left her jacket downstairs. She needed to go down and get it, but dammit, she didn't want to inadvertently run into Mitch just yet.

"Yes, we did. We both agreed what he found you need to hear face-to-face."

Simone's fingers paused against a shirt, and she turned to look at her friend. "What do you mean?"

"I think it's better if Ryan tells both you and Mitch together."

"Why? This doesn't have anything to do with Mitch."

Kate's eyes filled with pity. "Yes, it does. Whether you want to admit it or not, this is about him now too. Running isn't going to protect him from this anymore, Simone. It's too big for that now. If you run, Mitch's life is in danger. It's time you faced this, head-on."

You didn't tell her yet, did you?"

Mitch finished the soda and tossed the can in a recycle bin. "Nope, and neither will you."

On the other side of the kitchen island, Ryan raked a hand through his blond hair. Dressed in loose jeans and a Cal sweatshirt, he looked nothing like the suit he really was. He also didn't look like a total fucking asshole, but Mitch knew he was that too. "Dammit, Mitch—"

"Don't start with me." Mitch eyed the bottle of Jamison Tate had taken out of the cupboard, but was determined not to reach for it. He crossed his arms over his chest instead. "I have my reasons for not telling her, and besides, it doesn't much matter anymore."

Ryan frowned. "That's a chicken-shit excuse and you know it."

From across the kitchen where he was dropping ice into a glass, Tate chuckled. "Those secret-society guys are always full of chicken-shit excuses."

Ryan shot a shocked look Tate's way, then refocused on Mitch. "*He* knows?"

Shit. Here it came. Mitch rubbed a hand over his face.

"I knew when he got tapped, loser." Tate poured a finger of whiskey.

"'When he got tapped.'" Ryan pinned Mitch with a look. "And you still didn't bother to tell me."

Tate lifted the glass to his lips. "You were so pussy whipped back then, Harrison, you wouldn't even have cared." To Mitch he added, "I'm surprised he cares now. Guy's worse than he was before."

For the first time in hours, Mitch felt himself smiling, even if it was a pathetic turn of his lips. "You don't know the half of it."

Ryan scowled. "You two are so funny I forgot to laugh."

Tate took his glass to the kitchen table and kicked back in a chair. "He's seriously spending way too much time with that mouthy kid of his."

"Look," Ryan said, clearly irritated with them both. "Do you want to know what we found out or not?"

"I want to know."

Mitch froze at the sound of Simone's voice and looked toward the stairs. She was stepping off the last step, wearing jeans and a long-sleeved blue T-shirt, her dark hair hanging around her face in a soft fall of silkiness, her eyes as intense and focused as he'd ever seen. And though his stomach tightened with a thrill that warmed his blood at just the sight of her, common sense said anything she wanted to know had nothing to do with him.

"Hey." Ryan crossed the room and pulled her in for a hug. "You hanging in there?"

"Barely."

She dropped to her toes and let go of him. Behind her, Kate sat on the couch and tugged her feet up under her. "Well?" Simone asked. "What did you uncover?"

"Simone," Kate said, "why don't you come sit by me."

Sit down? Dread churned in Mitch's stomach. Definitely not a good sign.

He could see in her eyes that Simone wanted to argue, but she pursed her lips and sat next to Kate. And didn't once look his way. "Okay, I'm sitting. Now tell me what's going on."

Ryan looked to Kate. When she nodded, he rested his hands on his hips. "Did your husband have any strange burns on his body? Any odd scars?"

"One," Simone answered warily. "On the top of his wrist. He burned himself cooking one night in college. Why?"

"How big was it?"

"About two inches long, one inch wide. Ryan, why are you asking? What could that possibly have to do with anything?"

Ryan tugged his phone out of his pocket, paged through screens, and turned it to Simone could see. "Do you recognize this marking?"

Oh shit. From the sound of Ryan's voice, Mitch knew exactly what he was showing her.

Simone studied the image for a few seconds, then said, "No. Why, should I?"

"It's a brand. A brand for an organization known as Cypher and Dagger.

Son of a bitch. Mitch rubbed his hand over his suddenly throbbing forehead. Right now, he was ready to wring Ryan's neck.

"Wait." Simone held up her hand. "Are you trying to tell me Steve was part of a secret society?"

"You've heard of the Cyphers?"

"Who hasn't? I grew up in the northeast. Secret societies have been around for hundreds of years, at all different universities. And the Cyphers rank right up there with the Skulls at Harvard. But

Steve?" She shook her head. "I have a hard time believing he was part of something like that. And he sure as hell didn't have that brand. I would have known."

Ryan sat on the wooden coffee table in front of her. "He most likely had it removed after he joined the witness protection program, which would explain the scar on his arm. It would have given him away to anyone who was possibly looking for him. The partners he turned on at his firm were members as well. But according to info my PI dug up, your husband wasn't just a witness who came across something fishy. He was the society's treasurer, and he'd been doctoring their books for years, long before you met him."

Simone's face paled, and Mitch fought the urge to tell Ryan to shut the hell up, that this wasn't helping matters, but he kept his mouth closed, knowing if he stepped in now, he'd have to explain things he didn't want to explain.

"The Cyphers are involved in…" Ryan scratched the back of his neck. "Well, everything. Every part of government, every part of society, every profession that touches on anything of importance—military, medicine, politics, industry, energy—you name it, they've got a foothold in it. And they don't always do everything on the up-and-up. Eleven years ago, when you met Steve, the Feds were building a case against a key member of the society—Lyle Dobbs. Only they didn't have all the evidence they needed. Enter Steve. He was young, idealistic, and, thanks to his relationship with you, a target."

Holy hell… Mitch felt like a ten-ton flat of bricks had been dropped in the bottom of his stomach. Things suddenly made sense.

Simone drew in an uneasy breath. "You're saying the Feds used me to get to him?"

"It looks that way. My guy couldn't get anyone at the FBI to open up about it, but you were the only thing different in his life at that point. And they did confirm he was adamant that you be offered protection in exchange for his testimony."

Simone stared at the coffee table as if she were seeing it for the first time. "Lyle Dobbs was not one of the three people convicted in Steve's case."

"No," Ryan said, looking over his shoulder at Mitch. "He wasn't." He glanced back at Simone. "When it came to the trial, Steve surprised the prosecution and named the three from his firm, but not Dobbs. The Feds were pissed—understandably. Dobbs had just become the Cypher's chairman, a position he still holds today. They were expecting the big fish. Instead, they got three small ones who didn't do a thing to help their case against Dobbs."

Silence settled over the room, then slowly, Simone's eyes narrowed and her gaze lifted to Ryan's. "Lyle Dobbs. You don't mean Senator Lyle Dobbs from New Hampshire, do you?"

"The same."

Simone's eyes slid closed, and she leaned back against the couch. "Oh my God."

"I don't get it," Tate said from the kitchen near Mitch. "What's the big deal about this Dobbs character?"

Mitch wanted to punch the guy. Yeah, he was fairly bright, but he rarely paid attention to what was going on in the world around him. He was too caught up in his music to care. "Don't you ever watch the news? Dobbs is gearing up to run for president."

"Oh." Tate looked back at Simone. "Oh yeah, that's not good."

Not good didn't even cover half of it. Mitch had been wrong. Dead wrong. The Cyphers hadn't come after him like he'd thought.

"They think Steve told me something that could ruin Dobbs's shot at the presidency. That's why they came after me, isn't it?" Simone asked Ryan, obviously realizing the same thing.

"That's what my PI thinks."

Ryan's words hung heavily in the air. So heavy Mitch felt the weight of them bearing down on his shoulders and chest.

Simone huffed out a laugh and pressed her fingers to her forehead. "I didn't even know he was a Cypher. What does that tell you about my knowledge where all this is concerned?"

"Maybe it's time you started thinking."

"Why?" Simone dropped her hand, but instead of shock, anger filled her chocolate eyes. "So I can tell whatever it is to the Feds? If this is true, then they've been watching me all this time. And they did nothing to help when Dobbs sent those people after me who shot up Mitch's house. I'm supposed to hope they're going to protect me now? That they're going to keep Shannon safe? Forgive me for not trusting them, but I'm not stupid. If they really think I have something that can be used against Dobbs, they're not going to look out for my best interests. They're going to use me and then cut me loose. And then I'll be back in the same situation I'm in now. Running from a group who obviously wants me dead."

She had a point, but Mitch didn't want to believe it. Turning to the Feds could be her only chance now. And his.

Dammit. They were right back where they'd started. Only worse off, because even if he agreed to disappear to get away from all this, he knew for certain he wasn't doing it with her.

"Simone," Ryan started.

"No." She pushed out of her chair. "I'm not running back to the Feds, because I have nothing to give them. Did your PI find out anything else? Anything at all that could be of use to me?"

Ryan's wary gaze slid from Simone to his wife, seated beside her. Simone glanced from one to the other. "Just tell me already."

Ryan rested one hand against his thigh. "There is one more thing, but I don't know how relevant it is."

"Spit it out."

When he hesitated, Kate said, "Ryan, you have to tell her."

Simone waited, her brow lifted, her face expectant. Across the room, the tick of a clock was the only sound that echoed through the vast space.

"My PI got a hold of your husband's medical records," Ryan said. "And while it's true he showed symptoms that are often present in pancreatic cancer patients, that's not what's listed on his chart as cause of death."

"What was?" Simone asked cautiously.

"A blood clot. Which traveled to his brain and caused a stroke."

Several second passed as Simone glanced around the room, clearly not seeing it. "I don't understand. His doctor diagnosed him with cancer. He got sick and passed quickly, but that's what happens with pancreatic cancer. They said his symptoms went unnoticed for months, and that his organs just…shut down." She looked at Ryan. "Are you telling me he didn't have cancer?"

Ryan glanced at his wife, then pushed off the coffee table and stepped to Simone. "I'm not saying he didn't. I'm just saying that the acute onset of symptoms related to pancreatic cancer can be attributed to a lot of different…substances."

"Substances," Simone repeated suspiciously.

"Chemicals," Ryan clarified.

Simone stared at him. And from across the room, Mitch felt her anxiety as if he were standing right next to her. Ryan ran a pharmaceutical empire. If there was anyone that knew about side effects—intended or not—it was him.

Shit. Don't say it…

"Chemicals," Simone repeated. "You mean poisons. Are you trying to tell me Steve was poisoned?"

"No," Ryan said quickly. "There's no way to know that unless Steve's body is exhumed and tests are run. And I'm not saying that's the case here but, from a medical perspective, after looking at his files and everything else, I'm saying…something seems fishy to me."

He reached for a folder he'd set on the coffee table and handed it to her. "Steve's attending physician was a man named Clayton Browers. He got his undergrad degree at the University of California at Berkeley, then did his post grad work at George Washington University in DC. The Cyphers don't have a chapter at George Washington, but they do at Berkeley. They're one of only a handful of bicoastal societies on record. Browers's name isn't listed on any formal charter that we could find, but associates my PI talked to claim he has the same dagger brand all Cypher members have. The fact there's no genetic history of cancer in your husband's family, coupled with the reality that some of his symptoms don't match up with those we see from cancer patients, well, it has me curious."

Simone looked down at the folder in her hand. "This is Steve's medical record?"

"And the info on Browers. Nothing's definitive, Simone. I don't want you to get worked up. I'm just pointing out some inconsistencies and areas of caution."

Mitch watched the color drain from Simone's cheeks, and an uncontrollable need to go to her, to comfort her, consumed him. But he kept his feet rooted in place, knowing if he did, she wouldn't turn to him. And honestly…why should she? If what Ryan's guy had uncovered was true, the Cyphers—his associates—had murdered her husband.

His stomach rolled, a sickness that consumed him from his toes upward. He looked toward the bottle of Jamison on the counter, desperate for a glass.

"I… I think I need a few minutes alone," Simone said, turning for the stairs.

Kate pushed off the couch. "Simone—"

Simone held up her hand to keep her friend from touching her. "No, I'm okay. I just… I want to read through this. I was pretty stressed back when Steve got sick, and I didn't pay attention to everything like I should have. I'm not saying I buy into all this, but…" She swallowed and faced Ryan once more, and even in the middle of what Mitch knew had to be the shock of her life, she pulled up that rock-solid strength she'd always had and faced it. "Thank you. For all of this. For what you've done. I…appreciate it. I really do."

She disappeared up the stairs. Above, a door closed, then silence fell over the room.

On a sigh, Ryan turned in the middle of the living room and caught Mitch's gaze. "Now do you see why I said you needed to tell her? It wouldn't have come as such a shock if you'd at least prepped her a little."

Mitch huffed out a laugh. But the sound held no humor, just a hot burn in the center of his chest, one that ignited a firestorm that felt like it was consuming every part of him. He knew things were pretty much finished with Simone, but if he'd held out any hope he could salvage a relationship with her daughter, that was dead and gone now. As soon as Simone discovered he was a Cypher, she wouldn't let him within fifty yards of Shannon. "Thank you, Ryan. Thank you for everything you dug up and the sensitive way in which you presented it. Ever hear the phrase, 'if you keep digging, you'll dig your own grave?' Well, you just dug mine. Remind me to return the favor some time."

"Mitch, dammit," Ryan sighed.

Mitch moved out from behind the island in the kitchen. Right now he needed a shower. Needed to be alone. Needed to think.

Ryan stepped in his path. "Hold up. I wasn't trying to fuck things up for you."

Mitch clenched his jaw, and his hand flexed into a fist at his side. "Well, you did."

"These aren't the kind of people you screw around with, Mitch. And contrary to what you think, I didn't come here with all this to make things worse for you. I came because I'm worried. If they got to her husband, they can get to you, and regardless of how pissed you are at me right now, I don't want anything to happen to you. I care about Simone, but I care about you more. You're not just my best friend, you're my brother, and while that might not mean much to you at the moment, it means everything to me."

Mitch's jaw tightened. The red haze that had slid over his vision retreated just a touch. Just enough so he didn't plow his fist into Ryan's jaw. But he wasn't ready to get all touchy feely. He was too pissed for that. "I know what kind of people they are."

"Then you know this isn't a game. You're in some serious shit here, Mitch. They'll come after you because of her."

Mitch knew that better than anyone. He didn't need Ryan reminding him of that fact. He stepped around his brother in law. "I'll be fine."

"But you're not fine," Ryan said, looking after him as he headed for the stairs. "You haven't been fine since you met her. What are you going to do?"

Mitch hesitated with one foot on the bottom step. What was he going to do? At this point there was only one thing left he could do. Only doing it meant stepping back into a world he never should have been a part of.

He pushed his feet up the stairs toward his bedroom. "I don't know. Right now I don't have a single fucking answer to anything."

CHAPTER EIGHTEEN

Simone tossed the file Ryan had given her on her bed, closed the laptop on her lap, and raked her hands through her hair. She'd read the file ten times, had researched until her eyes hurt, and was still having trouble processing the information.

Steve had been a Cypher. He wasn't an innocent victim. He'd known what he was getting himself into. And regardless of what had happened to him, whether he'd died of cancer or something more sinister—which she still didn't totally believe—the angry truth was that he'd known the people he associated with would never truly leave them alone. He'd *known* what he was dragging her and their child into the moment he'd asked her to run away with him.

She shifted the laptop to the bed and rose, unable to sit anymore. Brushing the hair back from her face, she looked out at the darkening lake beyond her second floor window. Dusk was settling in, robbing the lake and trees and sky of color, turning everything to a drab gray chill she felt settle deep in her bones.

She hadn't known Steve. Not the real him. That he could have kept something so big from her wasn't just a blow to the sternum, it was a blast to her pride and the carefully constructed life she'd built for her and Shannon. But what really stung, what truly cut through her like a hot, sharp knife was the reality that she'd given up her life for someone she hadn't even been in love with, all while the man she *did* love was suffering because she couldn't be honest about her feelings.

Anger simmered under her skin, then turned to a bitter misery that sank into her bones when she thought of Mitch's face the night she'd come back from DC and told him she didn't love him. Of how angry he'd been last night, when she'd pulled away in that fire lookout after kissing him. Of the dozens of times over the last few months he'd told her he loved her, and she'd kissed him to shut him up or changed the subject entirely because she was too afraid of what *might* happen.

She closed her eyes, hating the truth. Hating that she couldn't change it. It already *had* happened. He *was* in this nightmare. And if nothing else, she knew now he wasn't getting away from it. If these people could get to Steve in the witness protection program, they could get to Mitch through her. And if there was ever anyone she *should* give up her life for, who deserved that kind of sacrifice, it was him.

One tiny burst of hope bubbled up through the murky darkness, forcing her eyes open. There was one way she could fix this. One way to make at least one small part of this right. Maybe she couldn't protect him from what Steve had done, but pretending she didn't care wasn't working. There was a slim chance that if he knew how she felt, if he knew she wasn't just trying to protect herself, that she could convince him to disappear like she'd tried to get him to do after his house had been destroyed. It was a long shot, but at this point, it was the only one she had left.

She opened the door quietly and peered out into the hall. The space was empty, but voices drifted up the stairs from the kitchen. Ryan's, Kate's, Kendrick's, but no Mitch. Nerves humming, she moved quietly down the hall and stopped when she reached his bedroom door.

He could have left, but she doubted it. Ryan wouldn't have let him leave knowing his life could be in danger. She lifted her hand to knock, then thought better of it. She didn't want to give him any reason to tell her to get lost, and she didn't need anyone downstairs knowing what she was about to do.

Her hand closed around the door handle, and she turned it. Quietly, she moved into his room and closed the door behind her.

The bedrooms were all similar, suites rather than simple guest rooms. Mitch's room looked the same as hers but a little bigger—a king-size bed made of knotty pine, two matching nightstands and lamps, a dresser, and a flat-screen TV on the wall. But unlike her room, there was no half-packed suitcase, no clothes thrown across the bed, no sign he was planning to run. Like she was.

She closed the door at her back and looked around. The lights were off, only dwindling moonlight through the sliding glass doors that faced the lake illuminating the space. The bed was untouched, the room empty.

Her heart dropped, and she leaned back against the door, forcing back the defeat. He must have been downstairs after all. She could wait, but she didn't know how long he'd be. And if he decided to leave before she had a chance to talk to him—

The sliding door across the room pulled open, and a burst of cool air whooshed in just before Mitch. Darkness and the hoodie over his head made it hard to see his face, but her breath caught when she saw the way his shoulders stiffened at the sight of her.

He tugged the hood of his sweatshirt off, turned and looked behind him, then pinned her with an irritated look, one she'd seen too many times over the last few days. "I think you have the wrong room."

He was still pissed. And he had every right to be. But instead of running from it, she knew it was time to face the fire.

Hands shaking, she forced herself to step away from the door and move farther into the room. "I-I need to talk to you."

"No, you don't." He shut the slider and crossed the room, heading for the closet on the far side. "We don't have anything left to talk about."

But they did. So much. She moved closer to the bed. "Mitch." God, how did she start this? "I wasn't honest with you. About…way too many things. I should have told you what was going on right from the start but I-I was scared. I thought that by not telling you, I was doing the right thing."

He huffed from inside the walk-in closet. A thump echoed, followed by fabric rustling. "Sweetheart, you don't know what the right thing is."

No, she didn't. He was right about that. But she knew this was better than what she'd done yesterday. And the day before that. "I never wanted to hurt you. I know you don't believe that, but it's the truth. I've lived under this shadow so long, I think I forgot how to open up and really let people in. You're the only person I let get close, and it scared me because… Because part of me was afraid something like this would happen someday. I never wanted you to get sucked into this."

She couldn't see him, and she couldn't hear him moving around in the closet anymore, but she needed him to come out and listen to her.

"Mitch." She sighed, feeling lost, helpless…desperate. "I didn't lie to you because I was trying to hurt you. I lied because I was trying to protect you."

He emerged from the closet, barefoot, wearing only low slung faded denim jeans, dim light glinting off his muscular chest. But instead of the carefree, laid-back man she'd come to expect, this one was fire and malice and clearly didn't want to have anything to do with her. "Why the hell do people think I need protecting? Do I have *imbecile* stamped on my forehead? I don't need you or Ryan or anyone else looking out for me. In case you haven't noticed, I've been getting along just fine by myself for thirty-six years."

"I know you have. That's not what I—"

"And I don't need you coming in here telling me things that don't even matter anymore." He stalked by her, yanked open the dresser, and pulled out a gray T-shirt.

"But it does matter." She tore her gaze from a body she knew almost as well as her own and stepped around the bed, blocking his path to the door, just in case that was where he was headed next. "I'm trying to tell you that I was wrong. I'm trying to tell you that I know I shouldn't have lied to you yesterday or last week, or all those months we were together. But mostly I'm trying to tell you that…"

A lump formed in the middle of her throat, and she swallowed hard, her nerves suddenly jumping with what she was about to say. But it was time she got it out. Time she stopped hiding from it. "I'm trying to tell you that I love you. I was just too afraid before. Too afraid something bad was going to happen and that I was going to put you in danger somehow. But I was wrong. If I'd told you the truth sooner, maybe we could have avoided"—she lifted her hands and dropped them—"this. Maybe things would be different, now and you'd be somewhere safe, away from this entire mess."

He stared at her in the dimly lit room, his eyes narrowed, his jaw hard. Moonlight cascaded over his chiseled shoulders, highlighting muscles and planes she'd touched and licked and kissed so many times she'd lost count. But he didn't say anything. And in the silence, her nerves ticked up even more, because this wasn't the reaction she'd hoped for. It wasn't even one she'd anticipated.

"You love me," he finally said in a low voice.

She swallowed again, because he wasn't stepping toward her, wasn't reaching for her, wasn't even trying to bridge a gap hours ago he would have attempted to bridge. "Yes."

"That's rich, because you didn't love me last night. You didn't love me when I brought Shannon back to you, and you sure as hell didn't love me when you came home from that trip to DC. In fact, I'm pretty sure your words were 'I *don't* love you.' What we had wasn't love, Simone; it was just good sex and nothing more."

Panic pushed in. A panic that told her she wasn't going to be able to make this right. She took another step toward him. "That's not true. I've loved you for a long time. Ever since you stood in the middle of my bedroom and announced that you wanted to buy a stupid minivan. I just…I was afraid to tell you. But I was going to. I planned to tell you the night I came back from DC, but then I got that call from Will, and I…I freaked out. All I could think about was getting Shannon somewhere safe, and I knew if I filled you in on what was happening, you would have come with us. But I didn't want you to do that. Don't you get it? I didn't want you to put your life in danger because of me. So I lied. I told you I didn't care, and I knew as soon as I got the words out they were wrong, but you were so mad and you wouldn't listen, and then all of this happened and—"

"Oh, so now it's all *my* fault?" His eyes widened, and he pressed both hands against his bare chest, the shirt still clutched between his fingers. "That makes sense. Blame this all on me now."

He had every right to be angry with her, but Simone's own temper was inching up every second he wouldn't listen. "I'm not trying to blame you, you jerk. I'm trying to talk some sense into you. You heard everything Ryan said down there. You know what kind of people are after me. I won't be able to handle it if something happens to you because of me. I'm asking you—I'm begging you—just please disappear for a while, until I can figure out what it is they want. You don't have to be a part of this anymore."

Shock raced over his features. "You want me to run?"

"It's not running. It's being smart. It's being safe."

A defiant look filled his eyes. "I'm not tucking my tail and running like a coward."

Like you.

She heard the words loud and clear. As loud as if he'd screamed them. Her blood ran cold, and what little hope she'd had of trying to talk some sense into him withered and died. But the anger—the resentment she'd lived with for far too long—was still there. Bubbling to the surface after everything she'd endured.

"You don't have a clue what it means to live for someone else, Mitch. If you did, you'd know running doesn't always mean you're weak. And it doesn't make you a coward when it's protecting the people you love."

She turned for the door. She was done trying to reason with him. Done feeling guilty. She couldn't physically make him do something he didn't want to do, and it hurt too much to sit back and watch him put his life on the line for something she could save him from. The only thing she had left to do was get to Shannon then, yes, run, at least until she could figure out what it was the Feds thought she had that was so important.

"News flash." His hand slapped against the door, preventing her from escaping. "Running from the man you supposedly love doesn't make you strong, Simone." He grasped her upper arm and jerked her around to face him. "And yes, you are a coward because even though you're standing here professing your so-called love for me, you're still holding back."

Her eyes widened. She yanked her arm from his grip. "Holding what back? I've told you everything."

"You've told me what you *think* I want to hear. Not the truth. Not what's really eating at you."

Simone stared at him, unable to believe what she was hearing. "The fact I love you isn't enough? The fact I *still* love you, even after you slept with someone else hours after we broke up, isn't enough for you?"

"No, it's not. If you really want me to disappear, then tell me the truth. All of it. Tell me what you're *really* afraid of."

"I already told you," she sputtered.

She tried to move away, but he blocked her path. "Just say it. Say the real reason you're always running from me, from us."

"I'm not running. I…" She braced her palms against his chest and tried to push him away, but he was like a solid rock, immovable. He was too big. Too close. Her head felt light. Her pulse raced. Sweat slicked her skin but did nothing to cool her down.

"I don't need this," she fumbled. "I don't need you trying to make me feel things I don't want to feel. My life was just fine before I met you. It was structured and ordered and…and I never had to depend on anyone but me. Can't you see what you've done? You've made my life messy. You've made *me* messy. I had everything under control until you came along, and now I'm a complete disaster. And I don't like it. I can't control it. I can't control you, and I don't want to need you, dammit. Every time I've ever needed someone, they haven't been there for me, even you. So just…just back off already and stop…fucking…pushing me."

She shoved hard, and he finally stumbled back a step. Chest heaving, she took several breaths in the hopes it would calm her raging temper.

Several seconds passed in silence. Then reality hit, followed by a tidal wave of embarrassment. Oh shit, had she really said all those things?

"I didn't sleep with that girl."

Simone's heart stuttered. Unsure if she'd heard him right, she lifted her head, but instead of the fire she'd seen burning in his green eyes moments before, now they were smoky, focused, and just a little bit unsure. "You… What?"

"I didn't sleep with her. I was going to. I was so pissed at you, I thought if I could fuck her, it would prove I was over you. But when it came down to it"—he clenched his jaw—"I sent her home."

She had to be hearing things. The Mitch who'd just laid into her moments before couldn't possibly be saying this to her now. "Wh-why?"

"Do you really have to ask?"

Apparently, she did. Her brain felt like it was short-circuiting. Somehow she'd gone from professing her love, to screaming at him, to confessing her biggest fear—one she hadn't even known was at the root of everything. "Um, yeah. Right now I think I do."

His eyes softened just a touch, just enough to tell her…he still felt something, even if it was only a fraction of what he used to feel for her. "Because she wasn't you."

The room spun. And the blood pumping in Simone's veins turned to a roar in her ears. Her body moved on instinct, before her mind even cued in to where she was going. Her limbs felt like lead weights, but she closed the distance between them and reached for him, needing the connection, needing to touch him, needing…him. "Mitch…"

"Dammit, Simone." He caught her before she fell. His arms slid around her waist. Her fingers found his shoulders, his neck, threaded into the curls at his nape. Then his body was plastered to hers, his head angling down, his mouth closing over hers in a kiss that stole her breath.

She couldn't think. Didn't want to worry about an hour from now or tomorrow or next week. She only wanted him. Her fingers tightened in his hair. Her mouth turned greedy against his. She brushed her tongue over his, again and again, feeling the flames of desire building inside her. Feeling the cracks in her heart slowly mend with every brush and lick and nip and stroke.

He pushed her back against the door until the solid wood pressed up against her spine and his body plastered against her front. He angled his head the other way, kissed her deeper. One hand fisted in her hair, the other slid down her side, under her sweater, brushing the bare skin of her belly.

Every nerve ending came to life. Every inch of skin tingled. She lifted her chin so she could taste more of him, pushed her chest out in invitation so he would touch her. His hand streaked up her rib cage, sending tingles everywhere, then closed over her breast, squeezing through the soft satin of her bra while he continued to feast on her mouth.

Just when she was about to scream that it wasn't enough, he jerked away from her, grasped her sweater at the hem, and yanked it over her head. Cool air washed over her skin, but it was replaced by his warm, solid, muscular chest pushing into hers all over again.

His mouth attacked hers with a fierceness she'd never experienced from him. Warm. Wet. So damn erotic. As if he were starved. As if he were possessed. As if he couldn't get enough. His hands rushed down her back, over her ass, then under. She felt the heat of his groin, heard the brush of denim against denim as she kissed him, and then he was pulling her away from the door, lifting her in his arms, carrying her…she didn't care where, so long as he didn't stop.

Her palms grazed the scruff on his cheeks, her fingers toyed with the silky soft locks of his chestnut hair. He hitched her to his side, somehow freed one hand and unclasped her bra. Air whooshed over her bare back, and then her spine hit the mattress. He yanked her bra free. Startled, she looked up and caught his blazing gaze just before he lowered his head and laved his tongue over her right nipple. Electrical vibrations rocked her body, but in that one look, her pulse thundered and every hesitation she'd had about telling him she loved him disappeared into the ether.

"Mitch…"

"Don't tell me to stop," he said against her breast.

"I wasn't. I won't. Just..." She grasped his head, lifted her torso from the mattress, tugged his face back to hers, and kissed him, hard. He growled deep in his throat, his hands turning greedy, his fingers fumbling with the button on her jeans. At her hip, she felt his erection, already thick and hard, pressing against her. Her hands rushed down his sides, to the denim at his hips. Tangling her tongue with his, she pushed at his waistband, desperate to free him, to feel him, to make him hers once more.

She never should have walked away from him. She'd been stupid to think she ever could. Losing him had hurt a thousand times worse than losing Steve ever had, and now she knew why. Because he was the one. He was hers. He was everything that had been missing in her life for far too long.

"Mitch..." She nipped at his bottom lip, sucked it between her own, tasting him and a desperation that ignited a searing burn in her core. "I need..."

"What?" His hand slipped inside her jeans. "What do you need?"

His fingers found her sex, traced the line of her slit, drew her wetness up, then circled her clit until she saw stars.

"Oh God." She pulled her mouth from his, closed her eyes, opened her legs to give him more room.

His teeth nipped at her jaw. He kissed his way across her throat. Pressed his lips against the soft, sensitive spot behind her ear until she shivered. His fingers continued to circle and swirl, then slid lower, until one thick digit pressed inside. "Tell me what you need."

She couldn't take it anymore. She was a burning inferno on the edge of combustion.

She turned her face back to his and lifted toward his mouth. "You. Just you. Now."

His hands turned wild. He pulled away from her lips and stripped her of her jeans in one swift move. Gasping at the rush of cool air washing over her body, she pressed her palms against the mattress and tried to look up. But all she could see was him—blazing eyes, flushed cheeks, quivering muscles straining, all for her.

She wanted to tell him what he meant to her. Wanted him to know this wasn't just sex, that it was more, that he was more. But she couldn't find the words. And then he was there, pushing between her legs, lowering his hard body to hers, capturing her mouth with his own and robbing her of all ability to think as the thick head of his cock found her opening and he pressed deep inside.

Her eyes rolled back. Pleasure radiated outward from her center. She gripped his shoulders, lifted her hips so he could slide deeper, and groaned at the exquisite feel.

He thrust deep, retreated, thrust again.

Simone dragged her hands down his back, lifted her hips, and grasped his firm ass in her palms. "Oh…

She was in heaven. In hell. She needed to let go. Didn't ever want it to end. Lifting her mouth back to his, she flicked her tongue against his as he plunged deep, gave herself over to him with every rock and glide, hoping he could feel with her desperation what she couldn't express with her words.

He hit that perfect spot. Sweat slicked his skin, dripped onto hers. The slap of flesh echoed through the room, mixing with their moans and the wet slide of their mouths fusing together.

The blaze inside her built to a roaring inferno. She lifted her hips, encouraging him to drive deeper, harder, to make longer strokes. He picked up her cues, knew her body so well, knew exactly what she needed and how to get her there.

He fisted the comforter in one hand, braced his other against the mattress near her head. Her fingers dug into his hips as he filled her again and again, as she moaned, as he kissed her with his rough, greedy mouth until she couldn't take any more.

White light blinded her. The orgasm tore through her pelvis and exploded in every cell. She wrenched her mouth from his and cried out, unable to think, unable to move, unable to do anything but feel.

Him. Just him. Not pain, not loss, not heartache. Just a shimmering bliss she'd always felt only with him.

His body stiffened, grew tight and hot and hard. Then every muscle strained, and he groaned long and deep in his throat, consumed by his own release. And his climax sent a second current of pleasure arcing through Simone's entire body. This one wasn't quite as intense as the first, but just as mind-numbing and so utterly sweet, her entire body shook with satisfaction.

He collapsed against her, a sweaty, slick mess of man she couldn't get enough of. She closed her arms around him and pulled him close. Her hands slid into his hair, and she twirled the silky locks around her fingers, not wanting to think, not wanting to plan, just wanting to go on feeling…nothing but this.

His hot breath fell across her overheated skin, making her flesh prickle. Several heartbeats passed in silence before he said, "I didn't hurt you, did I?"

The first semi-smile she'd felt in days tugged at her mouth. Hurt? He had to be kidding. "No. Definitely not."

He pushed up on one hand and looked down at her. But instead of the sated, relaxed, playful guy he always was after sex, his eyes were hard, his jaw was tight, and the way he was studying her made her feel like he was double-checking that fact as if he didn't believe her.

A slow chill replaced the warmth she'd just been feeling. He pushed off her without a word, the bed dipping with his movements, then disappeared into the bathroom.

Simone's heart beat hard as she stared up at the ceiling, trying to figure out what had just happened. She'd gone from content to unsure in a matter of seconds. Outside, a light snow began to fall, but it didn't lend a dreamy quality to the room. If anything, it made her feel even colder, and she shivered.

She replayed the last few moments in her mind. Sure Mitch had been angry, but they'd had emotionally-charged make-up sex several times after an argument, and he'd never once cut her after with that cold, assessing, almost detached look she'd seen in his eyes just now.

Then her mind flashed back to his words. *"What we had wasn't love; it was just good sex and nothing more."* Words he'd said *before* she'd thrown herself at him and all but begged him to make love to her.

Except…that wasn't making love. Not with the way he'd rolled off her as fast as he could. That was sex, just like he'd said.

She sat up quickly, reached for her underwear from the floor, and tugged it on. She didn't bother with her bra—her hands were shaking too much to get it clasped—just yanked on her sweater and looked for her pants.

The door to the bathroom opened as she was pulling her shirt down. "What are you doing?" Mitch asked.

There was a hint of surprise in his voice, but she wasn't letting it stop her. Her fingers closed around the denim, and she lifted her jeans from the floor where he'd tossed them only minutes ago. "Getting dressed."

She shook the jeans out in front of her, ready to step into them, but his hand captured one leg and pulled them from her hand. "You're running again?"

"I'm not running."

"Sure looks like it to me."

She reached for her pants, but he held them out of her reach. Exasperated, she turned to face him. "What's the big deal? You're not exactly acting like you want me to stay."

"You decided that in what, two minutes? While I was in the bathroom?"

"I don't have to have a master's degree in geology like you to predict when a landslide's about to happen." She reached for her pants again, but he twisted them behind his back. "Mitch, you're being childish."

"Sorta like you streaking out the door as soon as my back is turned."

Her jaw clenched. She drew a deep breath to keep from lashing out, but it did little to settle her nerves. Dammit, she didn't know what the hell to do. Or say. Everything she said or did lately just made things worse. "Mitch—"

"What if I said I wanted you to stay?"

The air grew thick around her. Slowly, because she didn't want to read too much into his words, she looked up. Irritation still lingered in his gaze, but there was something else in his green eyes. A softness. A worry. A confusion she felt in the bottom of her soul and which she was still trying to work out in her own head. "Is that what you're saying?"

He pressed his lips together and slowly lowered her pants to his side. He was wearing nothing but loose gray sweats, his muscular chest reflecting the little light coming from the windows, and though it was foolish, her heart skipped a beat as she waited for his answer.

"I want you to stay. If you want to stay, that is."

Warmth bloomed all through her chest. He still didn't seem completely sure, but he was right. She had been running. And she needed to stop doing that. If by staying she could try to bridge this gap between them and somehow even convince him to disappear for a while, then swallowing her pride—and her fear—was worth it. "Then…I want to stay."

A whisper of relief crossed his features, and seeing it made her pulse beat even faster. He dropped her jeans on a nearby chair, moved for the bed, and pulled the covers back.

More self-conscious than she'd ever felt before, she tugged the sweater down and carefully slid between the sheets. She moved over to her side of the bed, but he climbed in next to her, pulled the covers up, then lifted an arm over her head and tugged her close to the warmth of his body.

Her hand pressed against his chest. The soft fabric of his sweats brushed her bare legs as his thigh pushed between both of hers. She closed her eyes on reflex as his heat seeped through her sweater and into her skin. He smelled of him, of her, of sex, and her body responded with a host of tingles that started in her limbs and raced to her core.

"Mitch, we still need to talk about—"

"I'm tired, Simone." His voice was weary but soft. And in the darkness, he held her close, not letting her move away. "Let's just sleep now. We can talk about everything tomorrow."

Tomorrow.

It sounded like a good idea, but something inside Simone wasn't so sure.

"Tomorrow," she whispered.

"Tomorrow," he repeated, his voice already drifting off.

She just didn't know what the hell either of them was going to say tomorrow that they hadn't already said tonight.

CHAPTER NINETEEN

Mitch glanced at the clock.

Four a.m.

He'd drifted off to sleep sometime after they'd made love, but it hadn't been restful, and for the last two hours, he'd been lying here, staring up at the ceiling, trying to stop his mind from spinning.

Nothing worked.

Simone lay sleeping softly against him, and he looked down. Her eyes were closed, but even in sleep she didn't look particularly relaxed. And he knew it wasn't just what Ryan had told her either. It was everything that was happening between them and the fact neither seemed to know what to do about it.

He stared back up at the ceiling. And her words—the ones he couldn't get out of his head—ricocheted back through his mind.

"Every time I've ever needed someone, they haven't been there for me, even you."

She was right. Not in the way she'd meant at that moment, but she was more right than she could ever know. He'd been telling himself all this time that she was the one who'd messed things up between them, but the truth was that he was just as much to blame. Instead of listening to her when she'd tried to explain, he'd pushed her away all because he'd been hurt. It was no wonder she hadn't wanted to confide in him. And now, when she was willing to try again, there was nothing he could offer her except more heartache and betrayal when she finally realized his ties to her husband and the people who were chasing her.

"I love you."

His heart pinched. How long had he waited to hear those words from her? And now she'd said them, when there wasn't a damn thing he could do to fix this between them. Not when she found out the truth. And that meant he was stuck paying for a stupid mistake he'd made as a kid before he'd realized what he was getting himself into.

Unable to lie still anymore, he gently pulled his arm out from under her, and slid from the bed. She didn't wake, just grunted and rolled to her other side, and breathing a sigh of relief, he crossed to the closet and grabbed a sweatshirt and socks.

The house was quiet and dark as he made his way downstairs. Embers from the fire someone had built last night were still glowing, casting an eerie red light over the great room when he reached the base of the stairs. He crossed to the kitchen and picked up his cell from the counter where he'd left it, then glanced at the screen.

Thirty percent battery. Enough for one call. His stomach twisted as he pocketed the phone and headed back for the front door. Shoving his feet into a pair of boots, he grabbed his knit cap and a coat. After shutting off the alarm, he stepped out into the cool morning air and drew in a deep, crisp breath.

The elevation here was a hell of a lot higher than the bay area, and the mountain air cleared his senses. It had stopped snowing sometime in the wee hours of morning, and his boots crunched over the fresh layer of snow as he cut across the yard toward the garage.

A light shone in the upstairs window. He had no idea if or when Ford slept, but he was thankful it looked like the guy was awake.

He punched in the security code. The lock clicked, and he opened the door. The stairs to his left led up to the second floor and creaked under his boots as he moved. Just as he was about to lift his hand to knock, the door pulled open.

Ford, dressed in jeans, a flannel shirt, and boots, stepped back to let him in. "Good morning. Or almost."

"Hey." The main room of the security center was lined with monitors and keyboards, a high-tech surveillance system that looked like something out of a spy movie.

Ford closed the door and moved toward a counter on the far side of the room. "You want coffee?"

"No. Thanks." Mitch was already wired enough. He scanned the screens. Every inch of the property was visible from different angles, even rooms inside the main house—the kitchen, the great room, the safe room. "You monitor all this from up here? Every room?"

"Not every room." Ford passed a spoon through his coffee and took a sip of the steaming brew. "Kendrick didn't want cameras inside the bedrooms."

"Smart guy," Mitch muttered. "I'd have to hurt him if he did."

Ford chuckled and moved to a leather swivel chair near a bank of monitors. "Every guest would hurt him if he did. There are cameras outside each bedroom suite, though, monitoring the decks and access to the house." He hit a button, and the empty, snowy deck outside Mitch's room popped up on screen.

Mitch scratched the back of his head. "Thorough. I guess that's a good thing." He looked toward the screen showing the upstairs hallway. "That's how you knew I was up."

"No. You punched in the wrong code when you left. That's how I knew you were up."

Mitch cringed. "Sorry if I woke you."

"You didn't. I don't sleep much. And don't worry. I check for that whenever an alarm goes off in here. No need to send everyone running for the safe room when it's nothing." Ford lowered his mug to the counter next to him. "So what can I do for you at four fifteen a.m.?"

Mitch crossed his arms over his chest. "I was wondering if you heard anything about that accident up on Highway 267."

Kendrick reached for a paper next to his keyboard. "Yeah. It was your car. Plates matched."

Shit.

"They didn't find anyone inside, though."

"No one?"

Ford shook his head and handed Mitch the paper. "They're going to need more time to examine the wreckage, but my guy doesn't think this was some random accident. They found a timing device on the asphalt near the site."

Double shit. Mitch scanned the paper. It didn't provide any more information, just confirmed everything Ford had already told him.

"Yeah, I thought that was weird too," Ford said suspiciously.

Mitch swallowed the growing lump in his throat, not wanting to give anything away. "What about the guy who stumbled onto the property the other day?"

"What about him?"

"Did he look like a normal crazed Kendrick fan?"

"None of Kendrick's fans look normal to me, crazed or not." Ford rocked back in his chair. "You seem a little nervous. Is there something going on you want to tell me about?"

No. There wasn't. Not now. Not when in a few hours he'd be out of here anyway. Mitch handed the paper back. "Sorry. Two weird incidents close together just aren't things I normally deal with."

Ford huffed and set the paper back on the counter. "Lucky you. I get to deal with them all the damn time."

Mitch turned for the door, his fingers itching now to make that call. "I'm gonna take a walk. When I come back—"

"Don't worry," Ford said, pushing out of his chair, "I'll make sure I watch for you and shut off any alarms you trip."

"Thanks."

Outside, Mitch took a deep breath that did shit to calm his nerves. He'd gone over it in his head numerous times while he'd been lying next to Simone, and he'd hoped Ford would have different news, but now that he knew where he stood, there was only one thing left for him to do.

The water at the edge of the lake was frozen. It was still dark, but the clouds had parted enough to let a spray of moonlight lead the way. He headed across the rocky beach and didn't stop until he came to a dark section of land at least two miles away, housing nothing but trees, brush and a FOR SALE sign.

Pulling out his cell phone, he steadied his nerves, dialed, and waited. A click sounded, followed by a familiar voice.

"Mathews?" Chris Murdoch, his boss at PreCorp, answered on the second ring. "Is that you? You are in so much fucking trouble."

Mitch pinched the bridge of his nose. A voice in the back of his head urged him to hang up. Chris's phone could be bugged. Someone could be listening. They could be trying to track the call right now. But another voice screamed this was the only chance Simone had left. And after what had happened with that car…they already knew he was in the area. "Yeah. It's me. Listen, I need some help."

"You're damn right you do. They're looking all over for you. I've tried to head them off on my end, but it's not going to take them long to figure out who your friends are."

Chris was talking about Ryan. And Tate. And anyone else who'd helped Mitch along the way. "Chris, you gotta tell me what they want."

"Aside from your head on a platter? Shit, you know the way things work, Mitch. The brotherhood comes first. Before friends, before family, before your job. You didn't just bend that rule, you damn near broke it off. And not just for any girl. For one who could cause serious problems for the entire organization."

Mitch's protective instinct bubbled up, but he worked to keep his voice even and calm. Losing his cool with Chris would only make things worse. Chris was a lot like him in a many ways. He kept to himself for the most part. But because of his management position within PreCorp, a major player in the oil-and-gas field, he was in closer contact with the founders of the organization. And that meant he played by the rules. At least way more than Mitch did.

"Simone doesn't know anything."

"She was Graham's wife."

"He didn't tell her anything. He kept most of the trial secret from her. She didn't even know he was a Cypher until recently."

Chris heaved out a sound that was half laugh, half disbelief. "Do you honestly think she'd tell you what she knows? She's got no reason to trust you. In fact, she has every reason *not* to trust you."

"No, she doesn't. Because she doesn't know I'm part of this."

Chris was silent for a second, then said, "Are you sure of that?"

Absolutely. Simone never would have come to his room last night if she'd known he was a Cypher. Never would have stayed. Definitely wouldn't be sound asleep in his bed now if she did. And that meant he still had a chance. If, that was, Chris helped him.

Nerves ignited like fireworks in his stomach. "Look, I'm gonna make this clear. You tell me what she's got that they want, and I'll get it for you. She trusts me. Instead of hunting her down, they can have it, and this can all be over. But if I do this, I want confirmation they won't go after her or her daughter or any of my friends or family ever again."

"You want to make a deal?" Surprise rippled through Chris's voice.

Yeah, he did. He'd thought about it most of the night, and it was the only way he was going to be able to keep Simone and

Shannon safe. It meant continuing to lie to her, and ultimately losing her, but it would be worth it to know he could put an end to this nightmare. At least for her. "I know you can make it happen, Murdoch."

Silence echoed across the line. Then quietly, Chris said, "They'll bury you. Even after you bring it to them. They won't forget that you went against them, even if they do agree to your demands. Are you ready for that?"

Was he? Mitch thought about his life. About what he was giving up. The thought of leaving behind his friends and family and everything he'd worked so hard for scared him shitless. But what scared him more was Simone paying for something that had nothing to do with her.

"I'll deal with it."

Time seemed to echo across the line. Then finally, Chris sighed. "I'm gonna have to call you back."

A tiny sliver of hope cut through Mitch. It didn't mean he had an answer, but if Chris was agreeing to help him, it meant there was a chance. "Call me on my cell."

Mitch hung up, then stared down at the phone in his hand. There was a chance this could backfire on him. That Murdoch could have traced the call, that someone could be coming for them right now. But his gut said that wouldn't happen. If the organization had gone to all that trouble to flush Simone out and scare her, it meant whatever she had was important. And it meant they wouldn't jeopardize her safety just to get it, not when he was all but handing it to them.

His hand closed around the phone as he headed back toward Tate's house. *Take the deal. Take the deal. Take the damn deal.*

The grounds were silent when he stepped from beach rocks to grass, the lights in the house still dark, save the one small lamp in the kitchen someone had left on before going to bed last night. He went back around the house toward the front door, quietly eased it open, then typed in—hopefully—the right alarm code. Warmth immediately surrounded him, and a shiver raced down his back, making him realize how cold it had been outside. Adrenaline had kept him from feeling it, but now that he was back in the house, he needed something to warm him up while he waited for Murdoch's call.

He rounded the corner into the kitchen, then drew up short when his sister turned from the counter, coffee cup in hand, and lifted her brows. "Someone's up early."

Those nerves came back full force. She didn't know what he'd been up to. She couldn't. He glanced around the dimly lit kitchen, but they were the only two in the room. "I didn't wake you, did I?"

"No." Kate took her mug to the small table near the windows and slid into a chair. "Ryan was tossing and turning. I'd have kicked him to make him stop, but then he'd be awake, and I need some peace from his stressing right now."

Mitch smirked, poured himself a cup of coffee, then joined her at the table. "Not that I know how he sleeps, but I do know how he stresses. I don't blame you for escaping."

"He's worried about you."

Mitch knew that.

"So am I, for that matter."

He knew that too. And he hated that he was causing her heartache. Leaning his forearm on the table, he reached around his mug, squeezed her hand, and worked up the best smile he could. "I'm fine."

"You're not fine, Mitch." When he let go of her hand and sat back, she eased forward, her eyes filled with the same damn persistence he remembered when they were kids, her voice with an emotion that tugged on his heart. "I love Simone. You know that. She was the first person I met when I came to San Francisco, and the first one I felt like I could truly trust. I owe her. A lot. But she's not family. You are. And I hate to see what this relationship is doing to you. Especially now when we found out everything that she's involved in."

"None of it was her fault."

"It doesn't matter. By being with her, your life is in danger."

"Yours is too. You're here right now just like I am."

"I'm not here because of her. There's a big difference. I'm here because of you."

They'd always been close. As kids, he'd looked out for her, and in college, when he'd realized she was dating his womanizing best friend, he'd been willing to do whatever it took to protect her. Even jeopardize his scholarship to play ball just to keep her away from the guy. Until, that was, he'd realized how head over heels Ryan was in love with her. And when they'd lost her, when they thought she'd died in that plane crash, he felt like a part of him had died too. To have her back now was more than he'd ever hoped for, even if she was telling him something he didn't want to hear.

"What do you want me to do?" he asked quietly. "Walk away from her? I can't do that. None of this is her fault. Just like what happened to you wasn't yours. If I leave her now, I'll never be able to forgive myself. Is that what you want?"

"No. But..." Tears filled her eyes. "I don't want anything to happen to you."

Neither did he. But at this point, he was starting to think that was inevitable. He leaned forward again and clasped her hand again. Her palm was smaller than his, but her fingers were the same length, the same shape, and there was a familiarity in her grip. A bond of family that would never be broken. "Everything's going to be okay."

"How do you know that?"

How? Because he had to believe it. Otherwise...he didn't know what he'd do.

His phone buzzed in his pocket. Drawing it out, he glanced at the screen and felt his adrenaline surge. "I have to take this."

He pushed out of his chair and wove out of the kitchen so his sister couldn't hear him. When he reached the den, he hit Answer.

"Mathews," he said into the phone.

"They agreed."

Relief was swift and overwhelming.

"They're giving you three days," Chris went on. "It's a microchip containing sensitive information. All you need to know is that Graham stole it before he disappeared in witness protection, and the organization wants it back. If you can get it for them, you have your deal."

Three days. Mitch's chest vibrated with excitement and hope. And a sharp shot of fear. "Three days isn't a lot of time."

"If you can't find it in three days, it means she got rid of it. And if that's the case, then all bets are off, because she knows what it is."

Mitch tried to recall what Simone had told him she'd done during those weeks after her husband had died—which, admittedly, hadn't been much. She had to have stored his things somewhere. She was a lawyer. She'd know not to get rid of important papers, if for no other reason than to document her time through WITSEC.

The trick now would be getting her to agree to help him look for a microchip he shouldn't know anything about.

He'd work that out later. Right now, he was just thankful he had a chance. "I'll take it."

Chris sighed. "I think you're stupid. But then you already know that." His voice sharpened. "No one from the organization will bother you for three days. I'll be your contact. Call me when you have news. And Mitch?"

"Yeah?"

"Don't fuck with me on this. I went out on a limb here for you. If you're planning to somehow double-cross the society, it'll backfire."

"I understand."

The phone went dead in his ear. He lowered it and stared at the blank screen. Three days. Three days to finish this once and for all.

Nerves humming, he tugged off the knit cap and raked a hand through his hair, already contemplating what he was going to say to Simone when she awoke. His only hope was to convince her Steve had squirreled something away as a backup plan before he'd gone into witness protection, which he obviously had. She didn't need to know what it was or that he was involved. All he had to do was make her think looking through Steve's things was her idea.

When he walked back into the kitchen, Kate was pouring herself more coffee. She looked up from the carafe, her green eyes clouded with confusion and even more worry. "What's going on?"

Keep your cool. Don't do anything to make the situation worse.

He fixed a carefree look on his face. "Nothing. That was just my boss. I had to let him know I was taking a little more time off."

Her eyes narrowed. "Are you sure that's all that was? You seemed…anxious when you took that call."

He was. But she didn't need to be worrying any more than she already was. He crossed the kitchen, slung an arm over her shoulder, and told himself he might not be able to ease his sister's worries in the long run, but he could give her some kind of peace of mind right now. And maybe he could even get her to help him.

"Everything's fine." He steered her toward the refrigerator. "Though I think it might be a bit better if you made a batch of those famous pancakes of yours. Since we're both up, I mean."

Her eyes narrowed even more, but this time it wasn't with concern, it was with speculation and a hint of mischief. "Something tells me you're trying to pull a fast one on me. And that you've done it before."

She might not be able to remember the years they spent growing up together, but she knew him better than she realized. "Who? Me?" He feigned shock. "I would never do something like that."

He pulled the fridge open and handed her a carton of eggs, then smiled his most charming grin, the one he used to distract women and get them to do what he wanted. "I like blueberries in my pancakes. In case you forgot."

CHAPTER TWENTY

Sunlight filtered through the windows, warming Simone's face, rousing her from a deep sleep. Considering everything that had happened the night before, she hadn't expected to sleep at all and was surprised when she opened her eyes to find the sun was already well above the mountains.

Reality threatened to push in, but she didn't want it to. At least not yet. Rolling away from the light, she slid her arm across the mattress, searching for Mitch. Her hand met cold, empty sheets.

She sat up. Blinked several times. Looked around the room only to realize she was alone. "Mitch?"

Silence met her ears. She glanced toward the open bathroom door and darkness beyond. Nothing moved.

A shot of unease filtered through her, followed by the same damn insecurities she'd had last night.

Climbing off the bed, she told herself she was reading way too much into his not being here this morning. It didn't mean he regretted anything. Maybe it just meant he hadn't been able to sleep.

She tugged on her clothes and fluffed her hair as best she could in case she ran into anyone on the way back to her room. What she needed was a shower and a chance to get in control of her crazy emotions. But when she stepped out into the hallway and smelled fresh coffee, sizzling bacon, and heard laughter coming from downstairs, her stomach rumbled, and her need to find out just where Mitch had gone pushed her feet toward the stairs instead of toward her room.

Warmth from the fire someone had built encircled her the moment she stepped off the last step. She rounded the corner toward the great room, and a sense of family encompassed her when she saw the group busily making breakfast in the adjoining kitchen. Ryan stood at the counter, flipping strips of bacon on the griddle, razzing Kendrick about something related to his music. Kendrick was leaning against the counter, a coffee cup in hand, scowling at Ryan like a petulant child. Kate sat at the kitchen table, one leg tucked under her as she flipped screens on a laptop, shaking her head, and Mitch stood on the far side of the kitchen, pouring a fresh cup of coffee, smirking at the ongoing the conversation.

If you didn't know why there were really all gathered together, you'd think it was nothing more than a family ski vacation at the lake. But Simone knew differently, and as she glanced from face to face, finally settling on Mitch's profile, a profound feeling of loss swept over her.

She'd be giving all this up when she disappeared with Shannon. The first sense of family she'd had in…forever. And though that fact hurt her heart, what caused it intense pain was not knowing what Mitch planned to do or if there was any chance of her talking some kind of sense into him before it was too late.

Kate's fingers stilled on the laptop, and she glanced toward the archway that led to the stairs, her eyes brightening when she saw Simone. "Hey. You're awake."

Conversation died off in the kitchen. Heads turned her way. All but Mitch's. Trying not to focus too much on that fact, and realizing she was wearing the same clothes she'd had on last night, Simone inwardly cringed, then told herself not to be so damn self-conscious. "Sorry. I didn't realize how late it was."

"Not that late." Kate pushed out of her chair, crossed the room, and gave Simone a quick hug. "It's barely nine. The guys all just rolled out of bed."

All but Mitch, Simone wanted to say. She wasn't sure how she knew, but she was confident he'd left sometime in the middle of the night, not this morning. And that fact only sent her nerves higher.

"You obviously needed the sleep." Kate let go of Simone and glanced over her shoulder. "Kendrick, don't just stand there, get the poor girl something to drink."

"That woman is so domineering," Kendrick mumbled to Ryan. "And you like that? Dude, you're more twisted than I thought."

Ryan shot his wife a heated look, chuckled, then went back to flipping bacon.

Kate returned to her laptop, and Kendrick crossed the kitchen, then handed Simone a bubbling orange champagne flute. "Guaranteed to cure whatever ails you. My secret is really good champagne."

"Getting girls drunk is Kendrick's specialty," Ryan said from the kitchen. "Be careful."

Kendrick winked at Simone, then turned back for the kitchen, fixing a shocked look on his handsome face. "I'm hurt you think that. I'll have you know women get drunk on my charm and good looks when they're with me, not alcohol."

"Charm and good looks," Ryan repeated, flipping another piece of bacon. "Uh-huh. And the fact you're a rock star and that alcohol's always flowing freely everywhere you go has nothing to do with it."

"Hey. I can't help it if people want to buy me drinks all the time. Besides, you know I have my limits. I barely touch the stuff."

"No kidding," Ryan said, moving bacon to a paper-towel-lined plate. "So instead you're passing it to the poor groupies who follow you around like puppy dogs."

A one-sided grin tugged at Kendrick's mouth. "That's not exactly a crime."

"It is if you're a parent. You ever pull that with my daughter, and you'll find out just how much of a crime."

Kendrick cringed. "Julia's, like, eight."

"Ten."

"Going on twenty-five," Kate interjected from the table.

"Right," Ryan said, pinning Kendrick with a look and pointing the fork in his hand Kendrick's way. "And God only knows why, but she's got a thing for you, so stop pushing alcohol on poor unsuspecting girls."

Kendrick turned wide blue eyes Simone's way. "Am I the only one who thinks these people are nuts? I may need to hire your services soon, angel. Drink up. It's also a cure for the crazies."

Simone wanted to laugh but couldn't. Too much uncertainty weighed on her mind. Glancing down at the tempting beverage in her hand, she wishing a little alcohol would so easily solve her problems. She knew it wouldn't.

"Here," a quiet voice said at her side. "I'll trade you."

She looked down at the steaming mug of coffee Mitch was holding out, then up to his face. He hadn't shaved in days, and what used to be scruff was turning into a dark beard with just a hint of red. His shaggy, too long hair was curling near his ears and the nape of his neck, and she itched to run her fingers through the soft locks, but couldn't bring herself to reach for him. Especially not when she saw his eyes. Not smiling and warm like they'd been when he was flirting with her on their hike. Not sparkling like they'd been the night she'd come home from DC. But unsure, contemplative, and wary. All the things they'd been last night after they'd made love—correction, *had sex*. All the things she felt right this very minute.

"Um. Thanks."

She handed him the flute and took the coffee he offered instead, wrapping her hands around the warmth, hoping it would infuse her with strength. She really needed to talk to him, but this wasn't the time, and though she'd spilled her feelings and shortcomings to him last night, she wasn't about to do it in front of the entire group.

Mitch went back into the kitchen, crossed to the toaster, and started popping bread into the machine. Kendrick had pulled out a pan and was busily scrambling eggs. Not wanting to get in their way, Simone took her coffee to the table and slid into a chair next to Kate. "What are you doing?"

"Research."

"On what?"

Kate bit her lip, then sighed and muttered, "Screw it." Turning the laptop so Simone could see, she pointed to the article in the *New York Times* she'd been reading. "Senator Dobbs isn't as squeaky clean as his campaign's making him out to be."

"What do you mean?"

"He's been involved in several shady business dealings that all raise questions about his affiliations, loyalties, and who he's really serving, the people or himself."

Simone's eyes narrowed as she scanned the article. "Politicians are constantly being plagued with those questions. Doesn't change anything."

"True, but most of them aren't chairman of one of the most elite fraternal organizations in the country. One with ties to creating the whole New World Order. And none of them have a dead reporter linked to a story about their campaign. The same week you were threatened and Mitch's house was shot up."

Kate flipped screens, and another article popped up.

"It's been all over the press," Kate went on. "Have you seen it?"

Simone swallowed and shook her head.

"Basically, media outlets are spinning the story, saying the reporter suffered from depression and alcoholism, and that the stress of the industry got to be too much for her. But a few online sites have made a connection between her death and a story she did linking Dobbs to Cypher and Dagger, and the death of a member who supposedly had dirt that could ruin Dobbs's political career. The article doesn't name the member in question, but it says he testified against key members of the organization eleven years before, then disappeared into witness protection, and then mysteriously then died himself in questionable circumstances."

Simone stared at the screen. The background was black, the words white, making it hard to read, and the graphics were cheesy and cheap, marking it clearly as one of those conspiracy theorist sites. But she knew without seeing names they were talking about Steve. Somehow, this reporter had tracked him down, and that meant Simone had been right not to trust the US marshals and WITSEC.

"The article also mentions political strife within the Cypher organization," Kate went on. "Which means if Steve really does have something that could bring Dobbs down, and if you've got it, then there's a chance you could find a way out of this mess without turning to WITSEC or running on your own."

Simone's pulse beat fast. "If I have it, and I don't even know what *it* is yet, that doesn't solve my problem."

"Yes, it does."

Simone turned to look over her shoulder. Ryan had flipped off the griddle and was leaning against the counter, his arms crossed over his chest.

"Cut off the head, and the body dies. I looked at everything Katie found this morning. According to these articles, there's a whole portion of the Cypher membership that doesn't want Dobbs to become president. If he falls, they're not going to stand behind him. They're gonna run from any association with him. Which means they won't touch you."

Could it be that easy? Simone looked back at the screen. But even as she thought the words, she knew the answer was a lot more complicated. "I don't even know what Steve had that they could possibly want."

"Whatever it is, he had to have stashed somewhere safe," Kate said. "What did you do with all his things?"

Simone raked a hand through her hair, reminding herself just how badly she needed a shower, barely able to believe she was going along with all this. "In storage."

"Where?" Ryan asked.

Simone sighed and dropped her hands in her lap. "Stinson Beach."

"Just north of San Francisco?" Kate asked.

Simone nodded. "Ray and Betty, my…well, they used to be our neighbors in Baltimore who sort of took us all in and became surrogate parent…bought this house there years ago."

Kate glanced past Simone toward her husband, and, Simone knew, to Mitch beyond. "Are you thinking what I'm thinking?"

"I think Simone and I need to take a drive up to Stinson Beach," Mitch said.

His deep voice sent a shudder through Simone. It was the first thing he'd said through the entire conversation, and the thought of being alone with him in the car for several hours made her pulse beat faster.

Slowly, she turned in her chair to look. Then wished she hadn't. Though he was leaning back against the counter, his hands perched on the surface behind him, his stance relaxed, she caught the unease in his gaze. And the look that told her he wasn't so convinced anything they found was going to help in the long run.

"I'm thinking that too," Ryan said. "And while you two are doing that, Katie and I are going to try to track down more info about this reporter. Someone she was working with had to know what she was digging into."

"Great," Kendrick said near the stove with a frown. "Everyone's got a job but me."

Kate pushed out of her chair, crossed to Kendrick, and patted him on the shoulder. "I'd think you'd be thrilled to finally be rid of us all."

Kendrick gripped her hand before she could get away, pulled it to his mouth, and kissed her fingers. "You? Never. Them?" He nodded toward Ryan, then Mitch. "Absolutely."

Kate laughed. From the opposite counter, Ryan muttered, "Not a groupie, Kendrick. Watch it."

Kendrick chuckled and steered Kate toward the refrigerator. "Have you ever had one of my famous mimosas? I think you'll really like it. In fact, something tells me you could all use one."

Simone chanced one last look at Mitch. And suddenly thought the same thing. Because even though there was now a slim chance she could make things right for him, the dark look in his eyes told her everything she needed to know.

Nothing had changed between them. And though she might be able to save his life, there was no way she could fix what was broken between them.

CHAPTER TWENTY-ONE

Mitch glanced across the console toward Simone, asleep in the front seat of Kendrick's snazzy Range Rover. She'd zoned off somewhere after Sacramento, and, at the moment, he was thankful for the quiet.

After showering and changing, they'd both said their good-byes, then headed out, hoping to make it to Stinson Beach before dark. They'd made small talk on the drive through the mountains, but neither had brought up what had happened last night. She was being standoffish with him, and he couldn't blame her. After all, he was the one who'd talked her into staying, then climbed out of bed without a word and avoided her since. But what she didn't know was that it was killing him being close to her and not touching her. And every minute he went on with this stupid charade of not caring felt like another blow to his already battered heart.

He wasn't going to tell her, though. He'd been over it a million times in his head, and every time he thought of returning that love she'd professed for him last night, he came back to the same harsh reality that had been plaguing him since he'd found out this was all linked to the Cyphers. If he told her how he really felt, it would only prolong the inevitable. She was still going to hate him when it was over. And they still weren't going to end up together. So he was doing them both a favor by not leading either one of them on longer than he already had.

He just wished he hadn't been so damn weak last night and had let her leave when she'd tried.

He turned off I-80 toward Novato. As the bay came into view, an ache formed in his belly, one that urged him to drive down to Pacifica and check out the damage to his house. Not that it would matter. Not that he could do anything about it now anyway. A lot like his relationship with Simone.

The sun was sinking low on the horizon by the time he pulled into Stinson Beach. They'd gotten stuck in traffic near Sacramento and again outside San Francisco, but Simone didn't even stir until he turned off Highway 1, heading toward Seadrift where her parents—correction, *friends*—had a house.

She shifted in her seat, blinked several times in the fading light, and looked around. "We're here already? Wow." She brushed the hair back from her face, looking sleepy and sexy and oh so kissable in the fading light. "I was more tired than I thought. Thanks for driving."

He shifted in his own seat, fighting the urge to reach for her again, to kiss her, to lose himself in her for one more night, and focused on the road. "No problem."

He pulled to the security gate. Simone rolled down her window, leaned over him, and handed the security guard a card from her wallet. "Hi." The sweet scent of her perfume rose up in the air around him, her tantalizing breast brushing his arm in the process. "Quiet up here tonight."

"It's always quiet during the week." There was no amusement in the guard's voice, no interest in small talk either. And how the hell the guy didn't look down at Simone's breasts beneath the thin white T-shirt that Mitch couldn't seem to stop fantasizing about was beyond his comprehension. "Address?"

Simone gave the guard the address and waited while he disappeared in the small building.

"Friendly," Mitch muttered.

"Most of the houses in Seadrift are vacation homes." Simone leaned back in her seat, and a wave of disappointment rushed over Mitch. Not that he could handle more, but damn, that had felt good. "The owners come here for peace and quiet, not to be chatted up by the locals."

"Is that what this is? A vacation home?"

"No. The place was pretty run down when Ray and Betty bought it. Ray's an architect. He loved the lines and art deco style of the house as soon as he saw it. They've been remodeling the place room by room for years, whenever they have time off, but he's so worried about preserving the integrity of the original design, he won't just hand it over to any contractor. They're planning to retire here, once it's finally finished, if they ever get around to it."

"Is that why you moved out here? Because of them?"

"Yeah." She glanced toward the security house, looking for the guard. "When I left Baltimore, I didn't really know where I was going. Ray and Betty are the ones who suggested I use their house. They've remodeled the downstairs, but the second floor's still a mess. Originally, I was going to take them up on the offer, but after I thought about it, I couldn't do it. It's their nest egg. Then I figured if I had to go somewhere, at least I could go to a place where I might know someone…eventually."

"And your husband's stuff?"

A troubled look crossed Simone's features as she continued to stare out the window. "I didn't want it at the house. When I was trying to figure out what to do with it all, Betty suggested I store his boxes here, until, at least, they move in."

The logical part of Mitch wanted to ask why she didn't want Steve's stuff at her house, but the emotional part, the part that was still having trouble processing everything, wasn't sure he wanted to hear the answer. He looked out the driver's window, toward the Pacific. Dark clouds were rolling in from the ocean, a storm brewing in the distance, already blocking out the sun and casting a shadow over the beach. "Do you bring Shannon up here?"

"No. I don't bring anyone here. I haven't wanted to be around any of this."

If he'd gone through what she had, he might not want his daughter around the reminders either.

His daughter.

Shannon.

His chest grew tight. She was never going to be his daughter now. And no amount of wanting or crying about it was going to change that fact.

The guard came back and handed Simone her gate card. She nodded and tucked it back in her wallet. The guard pointed directions, then disappeared back into the building, and, seconds later, the gate lifted.

Mitch put the car in gear and turned left onto the street. They wove roughly half a mile down the strand before she pointed to a modern, geometrically shaped house that faced the ocean, with various rooflines and decks. Flowering plants and shrubs rustling in the breeze surrounded the house. Mitch glanced in the rearview for the hundredth time, but no one was following them. For a moment, at least, they had a respite. Something else he was thankful for.

He cut the engine in the driveway. Simone drew a deep breath, reached for her bag at her feet, and popped the door. "Come on."

Wind whipped Mitch's hair back from his face when he stepped from the car. The trees were already blowing vigorously. While Simone found the key, he grabbed their bags and followed her inside.

The walls were white, the floor a rustic sun-bleached pine. The main room was vast, with vaulted ceilings, a river rock fireplace, and a white couch and side chairs that seemed to blend into the background. A few books lay haphazardly on the shelves, a seascape painting leaned against the wall, a couple of mismatched lamps on the wooden end tables gave the room a rustic, outdoorsy feel. A hallway ran off the main room, disappearing toward the master bedroom, Mitch guessed, and a set of stairs led to what he suspected were the unfinished rooms above that Simone had mentioned. The house was definitely old, but Mitch could see the classic lines and geometric shapes, and the view of the beach, the way the designer had obviously engineered the house so it felt like it was an extension of the beach rather than an obstruction, was clear even to him.

"Wow."

Simone crossed to the kitchen and flipped on lights. The counter wasn't regular granite. It was sandblasted, with rough, textured edges showcasing the white and black specks all through the marble. "It's not close to being done, but it's coming along."

Mitch turned a slow circle and took it all in. "It's amazing. It'll be a showpiece when they're finished."

"Yeah. I figured you'd like it. As soon as Ray saw what you'd done with your place, he told me I'd found the perfect guy."

Mitch looked at her, the soft kitchen light picking up the highlights in her dark hair and the soft, creamy texture of her skin. That ache intensified, burning in the center of his chest, urging him to go to her, to be that perfect guy her adoptive father thought him to be. But he couldn't.

As if she'd just realized what she'd said, her face paled, and she turned away, cleared her throat, and brushed a lock of hair back from her forehead. "Steve's stuff is upstairs."

She didn't wait for him, just moved out of the kitchen and headed for the stairs. Drawing a deep breath, Mitch took one last look out the windows overlooking the patio.

Every minute he spent with her, so close to what he wanted but so far from what he could have, his body physically hurt. And as much as he wanted to go with her and find whatever it was her husband had stashed, another part of him wasn't sure he could handle it. Because finding it meant walking away from her for good. And even though his mind was already there, telling him that was the only thing he could do, his heart hadn't quite caught up.

Simone shifted boxes in the attic. Dust swirled in the air, and she coughed, then waved her hand to move the particles away from her face.

A dim light from a bare bulb illuminated the exposed rafters and plywood floor. Since Ray and Betty had yet to totally move in other than basic necessities when they were here working on the house, there was nothing in the attic besides Steve's assortment of boxes. Simone's pulse beat faster as she lifted what she knew was a collection of pictures and moved it away from her so she didn't have to see them. Part of the reason she didn't come here was because she didn't want the memories, didn't want the feelings, didn't want to focus on anything but doing what she had to do next to get through each day.

That was how she'd lived her life since Steve's death. One foot in front of the other, baby steps not toward being happy, but just getting by. Somewhere along the way though, that had changed. As she pulled the lid off one box and stared down at Steve's rugby jersey from college, she realized it had all changed the day she'd met Mitch.

"I've been looking for someone exactly like you …"

The words from that stupid Van Morrison song—the song that had been playing when Mitch had danced her through his entry hall that ill-fated evening—came back and slammed into her, sending a sharp pain of loss through her.

He was exactly what she'd been looking for, too, only she'd been so stupid, she hadn't realized it until it was too late. She'd loved her husband, could have lived happily with him for the rest of her life, but when she was with Mitch, she realized what had been missing from her relationship with Steve. That burst of heat, of chemistry, of uncertainty and excitement at never knowing what was going to happen next. With Steve, it had been safety and stability. And as much as she liked stability, it wasn't what she needed now. Now what she needed—what she craved—was something she'd screwed up so badly, she was pretty sure even if they could somehow get out of this mess, they were never going to be able to fix what she'd broken between them.

Shuffling echoed behind her, and Mitch cleared his throat. "Not as many boxes as I expected."

Blinking several times, Simone pulled the jersey out of the box, dropped it on another box beside her, and methodically began searching every item for something of value. She didn't look at him…couldn't. Was too close to the edge of reaching for him even though he'd made it clear that wasn't what he wanted anymore. "I gave a lot of his stuff away after he died. Only kept a few things I thought Shannon might want someday. Most of the boxes over there"—she pointed to a grouping of five or six—"were from his home office."

Mitch moved that way and pushed the top off a box. "What about items from his work?"

"There was nothing there."

"What do you mean?"

"I mean"—she moved a Snoopy tie Shannon had bought for him for Father's Day one year to the other box—"when I got to his office, his staff had already cleaned everything out."

"No personal pictures? Not even a paperweight?"

"No."

"Interesting."

Simone hadn't thought much about it at the time, but he was right. It was interesting. As if someone had confiscated all his personal belongings.

They worked for over an hour in silence, shifting boxes around, sifting through papers and files, the only sound the wind rustling past the house outside. Pages and pages of numbers filled Simone's head. It was possible Steve had hidden something in a file, maybe even encrypted a message on some of these papers that made no sense to her, but if that were the case, Simone was going to have to hire someone to look through it all. Because to her all it looked like was a giant mess.

She moved the last box in her stack to the floor, sighing when she came up empty, yet again. It was possible whatever they were looking for wasn't here. Depression sank in. If they couldn't find what the Cyphers so desperately wanted, it meant she was back to square one. Trying to figure out where to go next and how to disappear with her daughter.

Brushing a hand over her sweaty forehead, she pushed to her feet, her knees aching with the movement. Mitch was sitting on the floor across the room, a box between his legs, flipping through papers with an intense expression.

Part of her wanted to know what he'd found. Another part just wanted a break. From everything.

"I'm gonna go make some tea. Do you want any?"

He grunted a response, one that could have been a yes but could have also been a no, but didn't look up from what he was currently studying. With no energy to get into it with him at the moment, she headed for the stairs.

Floorboards creaked beneath her feet as she descended into the living room. She could go to Montana. She'd always wanted to see that part of the country. There was lots of open land for a person to get lost there. She crossed to the gas fireplace and kicked it on, hoping to take the chill off the room. She'd banked money, just in case she and Shannon ever had to disappear. But eventually she'd have to think about a job. In a new field, of course. If the Cyphers knew she was now a lawyer, she wasn't going to be able to practice again. They'd be watching.

The thought of starting over in a new career field sent her mood spiraling down even more. Focus. Plan. Execute. That was all she needed to do. She found a teakettle in the kitchen cupboard, filled it with water, and set it on the stove. While it heated, she moved to the pantry and searched for something to fill her empty stomach.

"You loved him."

Mitch's raspy voice slid over her skin, sending a shiver down Simone's spine. Her hand froze against a box of oolong tea on the shelf, and her pulse picked up speed. Slowly, she lowered her heels to the floor, turned from the small pantry, and glanced at him, then wished she hadn't.

The intense look she'd seen in his meadow green eyes upstairs was still there, but now it was fixed on her, his hair ruffled as if he'd run his hands through it several times, his jaw tight and filled with the same damn stress she felt. And in his hand he was holding a picture, one she recognized at first glance without even getting a close look. One of her and Steve and Shannon laughing in the sun at Hershey Park on Shannon's fifth birthday.

It wasn't a question but a statement, and she didn't know how to answer. But she was done lying. And she was done running from uncomfortable situations, regardless of how they made her feel. "I did."

"When we were on the mountain, you made it sound like you went into WITSEC with him because you didn't have any other choice. That you resented him for that."

"I did," she said again.

He held up the picture. "This doesn't look like someone who's resentful."

"I did resent him. For a long time. But eventually"—she glanced at the photo and Shannon's beaming face, remembering how her daughter had squealed in delight on the roller coaster, how Steve had bought them all an ice cream to share, and how, at the time, Simone had felt it was the best day ever—"I grew to love him. He was a good man. Regardless of what he had or hadn't done, when he was with us, he was a different person. The guy Ryan talked about, the one who kept secrets and double-crossed a secret society… I didn't know that guy. I knew the one in that picture. And yeah, I loved him."

Mitch looked down at the photo in his hand. He was clear across the kitchen, but she felt the heat rolling off him in waves, as if he were right next to her, warming her skin, making her ache for his touch even more. She wanted to add that what she felt for Mitch wasn't the same, that it was more intense, more exciting, and so much deeper, but she pursed her lips, holding the words back. Because she'd spilled her feelings last night and it hadn't seemed to help. And right now, this wasn't about her. It was about Steve. And finding a solution for the mess she'd created.

"I want this," he said quietly.

"The photo?" Shoving her emotions into a box where she could lock them away tight, Simone moved to the counter. Outside, sand pelted the windows from the storm but darkness had settled in, making it impossible to see more than a few feet onto the beach. She opened the cupboard and pulled out two mugs. "You can have it, I guess. I don't think there's anything there, though, that's going to help us."

"No. I want *this*. What he had and gave away."

Simone's hand hovered over the kettle. "What?"

For a second, Mitch didn't move, just stared at her, and in the silence, her pulse shot up even higher. Then he set the photo on the corner of the counter, stepped back, and muttered, "Shit."

Something wasn't right. Had he found a file or some kind of evidence upstairs? Her pulse raced, and her hands grew sweaty with anticipation, excitement…and dread. Swiping her palm across her jeans, she moved out from behind the counter, all the while telling herself to play it cool, to stay calm. That his finding something was a good thing, not bad. "Mitch?"

He scrubbed one hand through his already messy hair, rested the other on his hip, and stared down at the floor like he didn't want to tell her. Which only shot her anxiety up even more.

"Mitch, if you found something, you have to let me know."

"I found that." He dropped his arm and motioned toward the photo. "I want *that* even though I don't deserve it. I want photos like that of you and me and Shannon. Together. The way we were before but more. But mostly I just want to make you smile instead of frown and be miserable like you've been with me this whole last week."

Of all the things he could have said, that wasn't what she'd expected. Especially after last night and this morning and the way they'd been avoiding each other all day. Synapses fired in her brain, but they didn't connect, and though her heart was racing against her ribs, her mind was having a hard time catching up.

"I don't…" She pursed her lips, trying to find the words, afraid of saying the wrong thing, because that seemed to be her pattern. "Um… You might have to explain that to me, because I don't think my brain is working just yet."

"I want you," he said quietly. "I want us. I know you're not looking for a husband and that Shannon doesn't need a new dad, and I thought I could be all tough after last night and keep my feelings to myself, because telling you would just confuse things even more, especially with so much still up in the air, but after I saw this…"

He gestured to the photo again. "After I saw it I realized, that son of a bitch was so damn lucky. He had you. He had Shannon. He had everything I've wanted since I met you, and he let you go without a fight. I'm not gonna make the same mistake. I'll hate myself if I do. Even if it makes things worse, I want you to know the truth because it's the only thing that really matters."

He drew in a breath, shifted his weight and focused on her with that intense, heated, single-minded look she knew so well and had come to love. "Simone, there's something I have to tell you. What your—"

She closed the distance between them, her heart pulsing with warmth and so much damn love. Tears blurred her vision as she threw her arms around his neck. "I want that too. I want you." Her fingers grazed the stubble on his jaw, and she pulled his mouth down to hers. "I want us."

Her lips met his, and she kissed him the way she'd wanted to do all day, the way she'd dreamed of doing all week. His arms caught her just as she fell into him, pulling her tight against his body until she didn't know where she stopped and he began. And then he was kissing her back with an urgency that mirrored her own, pressing all his warm, muscular heat against her, encouraging her, consuming her, infusing her with a strength she'd been missing her whole life.

His tongue slid into her mouth to stroke hers with wet, wanton kisses she felt everywhere. One hand drifted up her back and tangled in her hair. He tipped her head and kissed her deeper, until all thought slipped from her mind, and she could focus only on him.

"Simone…"

She wanted to feel him everywhere. Wanted to forget the last few days had even happened. She pushed him backward until his legs hit the table behind him, and yanked his shirttails free of his jeans. He groaned, and her hands slid up his chest to the buttons on his flannel shirt. Kissing him again and again, she flicked the first button free, then the next.

"Simone, wait." He dragged his mouth from hers, let go of her with one arm, and reached for her hand.

"No more waiting. We've been doing too much of that." She wiggled her hand out from under his and freed another button. "Forget everything I said at your house that night. I was stupid. I didn't mean any of it."

His hand stilled over hers, and surprise crept into his normally confident eyes. And right then it occurred to her that what might be tripping him up wasn't how she would react to his announcement, but what he'd seen upstairs. In that photo.

Her fingers hesitated over the next button. "I did love Steve, but it was a comfortable, stable love, the kind that grew from nothing because we were stuck together and because we had Shannon. But it was never like this. Like what I feel for you. This"—she looked down at her hand, hovering near his heart—"scared me, right from the start, because it was so intense and because I couldn't control it. I was afraid of it, of you, and of what I couldn't direct, but I'm not anymore."

She looked back up at him, and one side of her mouth curled just a touch, because what she saw in his eyes wasn't wariness or hesitation, or even confusion. It was love. Everything she felt reflected right back at her. "Mitch, I love that you're laid-back and wild and unpredictable and that you balance out my overbearing need to plan and map out every detail. I need that. More than you could possibly know. And I love that I never know what you're going to do next and that every day with you is an adventure. When it's not there…these last few days without that have nearly killed me. I don't want to go back to who I was before I knew you, because you make me feel alive. And I haven't felt alive in a very long time. Since long before I met Steve. I've been crazy in love with you for months, I was just too afraid to tell you. But I'm not anymore. I love you. So very much I ache from it. And I—"

His hands captured her face, tugging her mouth up to his again, cutting off her words with his kiss. And when he groaned, when he grasped her around the waist and pulled her in so tight, she knew that he felt the same. That this was all they ever needed. That their relationship wasn't broken, just bent. And that they could fix it. Together.

"I love you too. I love you so damn much." His hand flexed against her hip, and he turned her toward the living room.

She stepped back, kissing him, frantically trying to work the buttons free on his shirt again, needing him. "Show me."

He pulled his mouth free from hers long enough to jerk the long-sleeved green T-shirt she was wearing from her body and drop it on the floor. Her fingers fumbled with the last button, and as she lifted her lips back to his, she pushed the shirt off his shoulders and slid it down his arms.

His mouth opened, his tongue licking against hers with a fierceness that matched hers. Her hands slid down the chiseled plane of his torso until her fingers found the button on his jeans. "Faster…"

His arms closed around her again, and then he lifted her. She gasped into his mouth in surprise and wrapped her arms around his shoulders, her legs around his hips. He carried her into the living room, then laid her out on the couch.

The fire cast warm light all over the room. Her skin prickled with excitement and heat. She didn't even care that the storm was brewing outside. Here, now, she felt safe. And wanted. And loved. Even after all the mistakes she'd made.

He leaned into her, and she felt the hard length of his arousal pressing between her legs. She moaned, loving the feeling. But he pulled his mouth from hers again and pushed up on his hand. "You make me crazy, you know that?"

She smiled and reached for him, wanting his weight on her, wanting to feel all of him. Everywhere. "As long as I don't make you hate me. That's all I care about."

His eyes softened, and something sad crept into their depths. Something she couldn't read. "Never."

A chill spread down her spine, but she ignored it. She didn't want to think about what they'd each said and done to each other these last few days. She just wanted to make it right. Reaching for him, she slid one hand into the soft tendrils at his nape. "Love me, Mitch."

But instead of kissing her again, he pressed back against the hand on his scalp and drew farther away. And that look, the one that had brought back a shot of fear, darkened his eyes. "I want to. You don't know how much I want that. But there's something I need to tell you first. Something you need to hear."

CHAPTER TWENTY-TWO

Simone stared up at him with a hint of confusion mixed into the hungry want in her chocolate eyes, and it killed Mitch to know that in a second, he was going to douse every drop of love she'd showered on him. But he had to tell her everything. When he'd seen that picture of her and Steve, he'd known he couldn't take the coward's way out. He wasn't going to leave her without any explanation to wonder and second guess every moment they'd spent together. He wanted her to know the truth about who he was and what he felt for her. Even if it changed everything between them.

"Simone... I..." Shit. This was harder than he thought. He closed his eyes and filled his lungs for courage.

"You're not trying to tell me you're married, are you?"

His eyes popped open. "What? No."

"And you don't have any secret ex-wives I should be aware of?"

The ghost of a smile on her lips told him she was joking, and God, though it relaxed him, he didn't deserve it. "No. I've definitely never been married."

She pushed up on her elbows and brought her mouth to his. "Then whatever you have to tell me can wait."

Her lips parted beneath his, her tongue sliding in to stroke his, to tease his, her taste filling his senses, his heart, even his soul.

God, he could go on kissing her like this forever. He groaned into her mouth and sank into her kiss, wanting this, only this, forever. But he had to tell her. Before he lost his nerve. "Simone..."

She wiggled beneath him and shifted, and then he felt flesh, soft, warm female flesh pressing against his chest, and he realized she'd worked her way out of her bra and that those world-class breasts of hers, the ones he'd been fascinated with from the first, were naked and crushed against him.

He couldn't help himself. He tore his mouth from hers and looked down. Then groaned and couldn't seem to stop his hand from lifting, from closing around one, from leaning down and bringing it to his mouth so he could taste.

"Mm...Mitch." Her fingers sifted in his hair, and she arched up against him, pressing her hips into his aching cock and rubbing until he saw stars. "I need you."

He needed her too. She had no idea how much. But if she kept that up, he was going to forget about everything he needed to tell her. Though it nearly killed him, he dragged his mouth away from her succulent breast and pushed back up on his hand. "Sweetheart, I need you to—"

She hooked one leg around his hip and shifted her weight. And before Mitch could catch himself, he was falling. Simone gasped and reached for him, but there wasn't enough room on the couch, and his back landed with a crack on the thick white rug.

"Oh my God, Mitch." She giggled and climbed over him. "Are you okay? I didn't mean to do that."

"I'm..." What was he? Not hurt. More relieved than anything, because a whipshot of pain up his spine brought everything back into focus and took his attention off his raging hard-on and how much he just wanted to get inside her right this very second. "I'm fine." He looked up at her. "Are you?"

Dark, silky hair fell around her face, and the golden glow from the fireplace made her skin look richer, her eyes even darker. A slow, sexy smirk played with the corner of her kiss-me mouth. "I'm more than fine." She leaned down and kissed his neck, his collarbone, and slowly worked her way across his chest. "I'm hungry."

Her words didn't immediately register. He was too wrapped up in the feel of her to listen. He slid his fingers into her silky hair on reflex, loving having her close, loving the way she touched him. And then he felt her tongue laving the tip of his nipple, and that raging hard-on came back to life.

She did it again, and his cock twitched, desperate to be set free from the confines of his jeans. But he wasn't going to do that. Because he still needed to tell her...something.

Shit. He could barely think when she did that circle thing with the tip. "Simone, wait." Sweat broke out on his forehead, and he closed his eyes, working to stay in control. "I have to tell you—"

"You've suddenly gotten way too talkative." She pressed her lips against his sternum, then trailed a line of hot, wet kisses down his stomach.

Yeah, he had, but for a reason. Before he could get the rest of the words out, though, her hands slid into the open waistband of his jeans, found his hipbones, and pushed his pants down his legs.

"These have to go." Cool air washed over his groin, but it did nothing to stop his erection from springing to attention. "And oh, yeah, that's mine."

Her voice was thick and gravelly, filled with an awe that shot straight to his heart. Dragging his eyes open, he looked down and watched as she moved back and stripped him of his pants. And God, but she was so sexy, taking control with that lust burning hot in her eyes, a lust that was focused only on him. Love pummeled his chest from every direction, and a desperate need to tell her everything so there were no more secrets between them, so they could start over fresh, right here, consumed him.

He leaned up and reached for her. "Simone—"

She shoved a hand against his shoulder, pushing him back onto the rug, then slid down his body. "You talk. I can't promise I'll listen, though."

Her sweet hand wrapped around the base of his cock, and then her tongue was there, sweeping across the tip, sending electrical vibrations all through his hips, and wiping every thought from his mind.

He groaned at the first touch. Then her mouth closed around the head, and she sucked. And whatever protest had been dangling from his tongue disappeared in the ether.

"Oh God," he whispered, flexing against her, trying to get deeper.

She took the hint, and the pressure eased, just a touch, and then her tongue brushed the underside of his cock as she sank down, taking him so deep he couldn't do anything but moan at the exquisite tightness of her mouth.

"Simone…" She drew her lips up to the tip again and circled, then sank down once more, taking him even deeper. The pressure increased, and he felt himself growing harder. Felt his climax racing toward him with the speed of a freight train barreling down the tracks. He knew he wasn't going to last if she didn't stop, but God, it felt good, and he didn't want her to stop. But he also wanted her to come with him. Not alone. Somehow he found the strength to push up on one hand and grasp her shoulder. "Sweetheart, stop. I want you. Not just your mouth."

Her tongue stroked the underside of his cock. Her body shifted between his legs. She moaned, and the vibration shook his body, sending electrical pulses all through his groin. His hand slipped on her shoulder. She lifted her head, then sank back down, taking him deeper, and then she sucked so hard his cock brushed the back of her throat. And when she swallowed, every last brain cell short-circuited.

"Oh, holy hell..." Stars erupted all across his vision. Heat consumed his body, felt like a firestorm igniting in an uncontrollable blaze. He fell back against the carpet. Lifted his hips. Groaned at the tightness, the suction, the utter perfection. But it wasn't enough. It wasn't everything. It wasn't—

The pressure eased on his cock, and then she was there, climbing over him, kissing his belly, his abs, his chest, his neck, finding his mouth in a kiss he would never forget. He reached for her, slid one hand along her jaw, the other at her hip, dragging her close. "I love you," he murmured against her, pulling her down, so thankful she'd already ditched her pants and that she was finally, gloriously naked against him. "So much. So damn much."

Her knees brushed the outside of his hips, and then her hand closed around his cock, drawing it toward her, lining him up. And then she was sinking down, taking him in, drawing him deeper until she was all he felt and knew and needed.

"Come here." He wrapped his arms around her, tipped his head, and kissed her with everything he had in him, everything he couldn't say. She moaned again, stroked her tongue against his, and then she moved, rocking against him, dragging his cock along the tight walls of her channel, stroking him with her body until he could barely breathe.

She pulled her mouth from his, braced her hands on his chest, eased back, and flexed her hips, sliding her body up to the tip, then sinking back down, loving him slowly, deeply, so intensely he felt it everywhere. "Don't let me go again. Just hold on to me. No matter how stupid I am. That's all I want. All I ever want."

He couldn't take it anymore. Every emotion he'd had since he'd lost her condensed in the middle of his chest, opening a chasm inside him, one that only she could fill. He sat up, wrapped his arms around her waist, and pulled her hips tight against his so he could get as deep as possible. "Never. I'll never let you go again. I promise."

His mouth captured hers. He kissed her wildly, with every ounce of passion he had left, and she returned his kiss tenfold, stealing his breath and heart and soul. Lifting his hips, he thrust harder inside her and knew he was hitting the perfect spot when she gasped and shuddered around him. His hips picked up speed. He knew she was close. Knew every one of her tells. She met his upstroke with her downward momentum, grew extremely tight and wet around him.

She licked into his mouth, grasped his face, and eased back. "I love you, Mitch. So much. So much more than you will ever know."

That was it. All he could take. The orgasm exploded through his hips like fireworks roaring across the night sky before he could stop it, before he could make sure he got her there first, before he could do anything but feel. White light flooded his vision, and electrical pulses raced all through his body, making him shake. Everywhere.

Her slick flesh slid over his, her body tight, so tight around him as she continued to ride him, to draw out his climax so it went on and on in a blaze of heat and light he never wanted to end. She was everything. His past, his future, his world. And no matter what, he had to make sure she knew that.

She groaned again, and he knew she was close. He thrust harder, deeper, so badly wanting to feel her release. Then every muscle in her body contracted, she dragged her mouth from his and cried out, and he increased his speed, no longer caring about himself. No longer wanting anything but to bring her pleasure. And when she called his name, it was the sweetest, most perfect sound he'd ever heard.

She collapsed against him, tried to find her breath. Pulling her close, he wrapped his arms around her and closed his eyes, holding on to her like he'd said he would. Praying, as he tried to catch his own breath, that when he finally did tell her the truth, she wouldn't want to walk away. Because suddenly, the only thing he wanted, the only solution that would ever set any of this mess right, was the two of them together. And whether that was here or somewhere far from here where no one could find them, he didn't care. All that mattered was her. And this. And them.

He just hoped she loved him enough to agree.

Mitch shifted beneath Simone, and she tensed, then relaxed when she realized all he was doing was kicking his jeans away from his feet.

"You're not thinking of leaving me like you did last night, are you?" she asked.

He buried his face in her hair and breathed deep. "Not on your life."

She smiled and relaxed against him, snuggling in closer to his heat. When she shivered, he rolled her to her side and added, "But I don't want you to freeze. Since I don't happen to have my magic backpack with me right now, hold on a second."

He sat up and grabbed a blanket from the back of the couch and a pillow from the armrest. Shoving the pillow under his head, he lay back down on the soft carpet, then wrapped his arm around her again, pulling her into the crook of his arm as he spread the blanket over their entwined bodies. "Better?"

She sighed, hooked her leg over his, and rested her hand on his chest, then relaxed back into him, loving the warmth of his skin and that this was a thousand times different from last night. "Definitely better. I like your magic backpack, but I like this more."

Outside, wind and sand and rain whipped against the house, but inside, it was warm and safe, everything Simone wanted. With her head on his chest, she could hear the beat of his heart, and unlike last night, his still-fast pulse didn't do anything but reminder her that he was alive. And not going anywhere without her, at least not anymore.

They lay still together in silence, his fingers tracing a lazy path up and down her forearm on his chest as he watched the flickering flames in the fireplace, her just relishing that there was no more tension between them.

"What are you thinking?" she finally asked.

For a second, he didn't answer, and though she couldn't see his eyes, there was a faraway look on his face, one she didn't like. Was he thinking about where they would go next? She had some thoughts, but she wasn't sure she should bring them up yet. Though she was pretty sure that was their only option at this point. Neither of them had found anything in Steve's boxes.

"I'm thinking I'm hungry. Like really hungry." His brow lowered, forming the cutest wrinkle between his eyes, one she wanted to kiss from his face. "When did we last eat?"

"Um…breakfast. Ryan made pancakes."

"That you didn't eat."

No, she hadn't, had she? She'd been too upset. "I'm pretty sure I saw pasta fixings in the pantry."

His stomach rumbled as if on cue, and his smile widened. "I think that'll work."

Reluctantly, she disengaged herself from his body and reached for his shirt on the floor. It hung past her thighs, but it smelled like him, and right now if she couldn't be in his arms, she wanted at least something of his around her.

He tugged on his jeans, and she pushed her sleeves up, then pulled the two halves of his flannel shirt together and began buttoning it from the bottom up. His hand captured hers before she could get the last three done, and he pulled her around. "Leave those open. I've missed those breasts."

Her whole body tightened at the heat she saw brewing in his eyes, and when he leaned down and kissed her, she wrapped her arms around his shoulders, kissing him back with the same intensity, the same passion. God, how could she have ever thought she could walk away from this? She'd been so stupid. So incredibly, shitacularly stupid. But she was going to make it up to him. No matter what it took, no matter how long, she'd prove to him how much she needed him, even if it took the rest of her life.

Her muscles were quivering by the time he pulled away, her body lax and close to overheating. As she licked her lips, still tasting him, he smiled down at her and tucked a lock of hair behind her ear, the move so tender, so intimate it felt like her heart turned over in her chest. "Show me where that pasta is."

Pasta. Right. She could do that. Not him. Though she planned to do him again, several times, before this night was over. All part of her not-being-afraid-to-need-him plan.

She turned for the kitchen. "I'll grab the noodles, you find a pot."

She rummaged around in the pantry, and when she came back with sauce and spaghetti noodles, he'd already set a pot on the stove to boil. Sliding off her bracelet so she wouldn't get food on it, she set it on the counter, pushed up his sleeves that had already fallen down her arms, and dumped the sauce in another pan to heat.

Mitch found two beers in the fridge, popped the tops, and handed her one. While she fiddled with the burners, he picked up her bracelet and leaned back against the counter, crossing his feet at the ankles. "I always meant to ask you why you wear this and not Shannon. That's her name, isn't it?"

Simone glanced at the gold Hawaiian heirloom bracelet engraved with Shannon's Hawaiian name, Kanona, on the outside. "It is. It was a Mother's Day gift." She stirred the sauce in the pan with a wooden spoon and shrugged. "Well, a belated Mother's Day gift, I guess you'd call it. Steve took Shannon and me to Hawaii on a last-ditch family vacation about three years ago, and they gave it to me there. I guess I wear it because Shannon loves to see it on me. She helped pick it out. Thing's heavy, though."

He turned the bracelet over in his hand. "What are the numbers on the inside? Near the inscription?"

Simone glanced at what he was reading. The inscription was clearly visible: *To Simone with love from Steve and Shannon*, but the numbers, tiny numbers engraved just past those words, were ones she'd never really noticed. "I don't know. A serial number or something."

Mitch turned the bracelet and looked at it closer under the light. "He gave this to you just before he died?"

"Um…a few months, yeah. The trip was kind of a surprise. Why?"

Mitch lowered the bracelet. "Where's the laptop Ryan gave you? I want to look something up. Can you handle the food without me?"

Unease slithered through Simone. "Yeah. I guess. The laptop's in my bag, in the bedroom at the end of the hall. Why? What are you looking for?"

He slid his fingers into her hair and kissed her temple. "Nothing, I'm sure. I'll be right back."

He disappeared down the hall, and as Simone worked on dinner, she told herself whatever he was looking for wasn't a big deal. But her mind skipped back to the day Steve had given her the bracelet, and his words, which at the time hadn't made her think he was feeling anything other than sad about leaving her and Shannon when he passed.

"*This is for you, and Shannon, and the future. Remember how we traveled. Keep it close and think of me.*"

Mitch came back into the room with a cell phone pressed to his ear. "Yeah. Thanks." He hit End and stared at her. "I got it."

"Got what?"

He waved her bracelet. "The numbers. It's a storage unit in Mill Valley just outside the city."

Simone's brow dropped low. "What do you mean? It's not an address."

He stepped around her and flipped off the stove, and as he moved the pasta to a cool burner, she realized it had been about to boil over. "Not an address. Longitude and latitude. I'm not sure what these other numbers are—maybe access codes or unit numbers or something—but I'm pretty sure Steve left you the exact coordinates where he stashed his evidence."

"What?" Simone took the bracelet from his hand and stared down at the small numbers. "Are you sure?"

He slid his arms around her waist and pulled her into him. "Sweetheart, I know longitude and latitude, trust me."

Remember how we traveled. Steve had been telling her where to look, and she hadn't even realized it.

She glanced up, and when he grinned, she felt her own lips turn up just a touch. "We can go get it."

His smile faded. "Not tonight. The storm's pretty bad, and regardless, I think our safest bet is to get whatever it is in the light of day, just in case."

"You're worried someone could be following us."

The same worried look she'd seen when they'd been basking in the after-sex glow in front of the fire flashed in his eyes but faded quickly. "I think it's just safer if we play things cool. No reason to go running off in the middle of a storm if someone is watching, you know?"

She nodded. Though she didn't like the thought of someone watching them in any way, it made sense. But part of her wanted to get whatever it was right now and get on with their life.

The smile spread back over her mouth, this time filling her with excitement and hope. Real hope. She slid her hands up his shoulders and around his neck. "You know what this means, don't you? It means this can finally be over."

She rose up on her toes and kissed him, and he held her tight, kissing her back with the same passion. Burying her face in his neck, she drew in a whiff of his masculine scent and fingered the bracelet behind his head. She'd had it all this time, the key to everything, and hadn't even known.

"Yeah," he said quietly. "It means it'll finally be over." He was silent for a moment, then added, "You know, there's still something I need to tell you."

And there was still something she needed to tell him too. Or, rather, ask.

She drew back and looked up at him. And where there had been fear before, now there was only love. "Will you marry me?"

"Wh-*what?*"

She smiled, because it wasn't rejection she heard in his voice but surprise. The sweetest kind of surprise. "Marry me. As in, for better or worse, though I think we've had enough worse."

He continued to stare at her with that disbelieving expression, and her heart filled. She brushed her fingers over the stubble on his jaw. "I love you. So does Shannon. And we both need you. I was stupid to let you go once. I'm not doing it again, so if you need more time or you're not sure just yet, I can wait. But I don't want to. I want everything we had together before, but more. I want you to be Shannon's father. But mostly…I just want you. For always."

For a heartbeat, he didn't move, didn't say anything, and a tiny shiver of doubt crept in. And then he caught her face in both his hands and pulled her mouth toward his, and as his tongue swept over hers and his greedy fingers pulled her closer, she knew she had her answer.

"Simone…" He nipped at her bottom lip, and all that heat she thought they'd sated between them earlier came flooding back. His hands drifted down her back, and then he was lifting her, turning her, sweeping her out of the kitchen.

He made it as far as the table and set her on the surface, then pulled his mouth from hers and looked down at her with every bit of love she'd hoped to see in his eyes. "Oh my God."

She laughed and reached for him. "Is that a yes?"

His eyes went all soft and dreamy, the food he'd asked for earlier clearly forgotten. "Yes, God, yes. If you still want me when all this is over, that is."

She wrapped her arms around his neck and pulled him down to her kiss. "I will. Guaranteed. I will always want only you."

"Ah, sweetheart. Same here. Always."

Smiling, she kissed the corner of his mouth and freed the button on his jeans once more. "Show me. Again. Right now."

CHAPTER TWENTY-THREE

Simone stretched beneath Mitch, her foot sliding between his on the crisp white sheets. Outside, the storm had died down to a gentle pitter-patter of rain against the roof, and the wind was nothing but a rustle here and there. He grunted and moved his head against her chest, his chestnut hair falling over her breast, his eyes still closed in deep sleep.

Smiling, she sifted her fingers through his silky locks, loving the way the tendrils curled around her hand, enjoying the way he was draped half over her on the bed in the cozy little house, his legs intertwined with hers, his arms wrapped around her as if he never wanted to let her go. They'd made love in the kitchen, refueled with cold pasta, then made it to the bed, where they'd started all over again. He hadn't been able to keep his hands off her, and she hadn't been able to stop touching him either. And as she ran her fingers down his neck and across the relaxed muscles in his shoulders for the hundredth time, she decided she could get very used to this. For the first time in…she couldn't remember how long…she wasn't worried about tomorrow or next week or even next year, because whatever the future brought, she knew she could face it, with Mitch.

A mixture of warmth and happiness formed a cocoon around her heart. She sighed, looked down at him, and smiled at the way his long lashes formed spiky crescent shapes against his tanned skin. They hadn't talked about when they were going to go to the storage unit. Or what they were going to do with the evidence Steve had collected. And she wouldn't even know what they *could* do until she saw it, but right now she was happy not worrying about it. She was getting married. Again. To a man who stole her breath every time she looked at him. To the love of her life in every possible way.

Her fingers drifted down his shoulder and across his arm, and as she reached for his hand, wanting to lace her fingers with his, she realized his watch, the one he always wore and never took off, was loose against his wrist.

She slowly rolled his hand over so she could relatch the clasp she'd obviously hit when she'd been frantic to get him naked. Her fingers grazed the metal. The hook slipped free before she could catch it, and the watch fell against the sheet at her side.

And the world tipped right out from under her.

No, not a campfire burn like he'd told her. A brand. Three daggers, one pointing down, two angled outward to form a cross, with a circle above containing two numbers and one letter. A brand she'd seen before. On that phone screen Ryan had shown her.

She closed her eyes, opened them again, sure her mind was playing tricks on her, only the mark was still there. Small enough to be covered by a watchband, but exactly like the one Ryan claimed her husband once had.

Mitch was a Cypher? No. He couldn't be. That wasn't possible. He hadn't once mentioned any knowledge of or affiliation with the group. When Ryan had been telling her all about Steve's membership in the society, he'd stood in that kitchen and hadn't said a word. If he'd been one of them, he would have—

Her blood ran cold, and the air felt like it was sucked right out of her lungs.

If he'd been one of them, he wouldn't have said a word. He'd have done exactly what he did. Kept his mouth shut. Used her to find out where Steve's evidence was hidden. Then take it—and her—to whoever was after her.

Her pulse turned to a flurry in her veins, and sweat broke out all over her skin, the flight response as strong as it had ever been. Slowly so she wouldn't wake him, she maneuvered her way out from under his body and slithered to the floor. He startled, and she froze, waiting for him to sit straight up and ask her what the hell she was doing, but he only grunted and shifted his head the other way on the mattress, then fell back to sleep.

Her mind was a whirl as she tiptoed out of the room and found her clothes in the living area. Dragging them on as quickly as she could with hands that were shaking, she looked around for the car keys. Where had he put them when they'd arrived? He'd come inside and glanced around…

Panic snaked through her chest, making it hard to think, to breathe, to function. The air closed in around her, and she knew if she didn't get out right this second, she was going to have a panic attack and give herself away. And she couldn't do that. She had to get to the storage unit, had to get Steve's papers, then had to find Shannon and—

Oh shit. Shannon.

A new sense of panic sent her already roaring pulse into the stratosphere. Shannon was with Ryan's parents, and Ryan was Mitch's brother in law. They'd gone to college together. He had to know Mitch was a Cypher. Oh God. He could be one too.

She spotted the keys to Kendrick's Range Rover on the bookshelf, grabbed them and fumbled with her purse where she'd dropped it near the front door. She was halfway out the door before she realized she'd forgotten the bracelet.

She raced back into the kitchen and found it on the table where she and Mitch had made love only hours ago. Sickness rolled through her stomach but she forced it back. As she whipped toward the front of the house, the purse over her shoulder knocked into a cup of water and sent it flying. Glass shattered against the tile floor in a crash that echoed through the entire house.

That panic went stratospheric. She pushed her legs forward and ran for the door. Rain pelted her face as she rushed around the car and fumbled with the remote lock. She didn't look back, didn't try to see if he'd awoken or followed her. All she could think about was getting away. About getting free. About getting to Shannon.

She slid into the driver's seat and dropped the keys in the console. She had to push the ignition button twice before she could get the damn car to start, because her hands were shaking so much. When it did, she shoved the car into Reverse, jerked back onto the street, sending water flying, and tore away from the house.

And told herself this time she wasn't running. This time she was doing the only thing she could.

The sound of breaking glass dragged Mitch from sleep. He pushed up on his hands and looked around the dim bedroom, finding himself alone.

"Simone?"

A car engine revved outside and slowly faded. Water glistened in rivulets running down the windows, and he listened for footsteps or anyone coming toward the house, but didn't hear them. He also didn't hear Simone.

He climbed out of bed, grabbed his jeans from the floor, and tugged them on as he headed down the hall. The wood was cool beneath his feet, and rain pattered softly on the roof, but there was still no other sound.

The living room was empty when he reached it. So was the kitchen. But a broken glass and a puddle of water lay in the middle of the floor.

He turned a slow circle, scanning the room. "Simone?"

Sidestepping the glass, he grasped his flannel shirt, hanging haphazardly from the back of a kitchen chair where he'd tossed it after ripping it off Simone, and slid it on. A shiver ran down his back, the house suddenly too still, too quiet, too empty.

He looked toward the kitchen table where Simone had set her bracelet when they'd made love, but the scarred wooden surface was empty too.

Confusion drew his brows together. He looked around the room again, lifted his hand to run it through his hair, and from the corner of his eye realized…his watch was missing.

He dropped his hand and stared at the burn on the inside of his wrist.

Oh shit. No, no, no, no, no…

He raced to the front of the house, tore open the door, and stared out at the empty drive. Water ran down his face, but only one thing registered.

Panic tightened the space beneath his breastbone. He slammed the door and rushed back into the bedroom, searching for the bag he'd dropped there earlier. He rummaged around inside until he found his cell phone.

"Come on, come on, come on." He hit Dial and lifted it to his ear. Simone's phone went straight to voice mail.

"Shit." He tried again, but the same thing happened. "Fucking answer!"

That panic spread up his chest, squeezing his lungs until he could barely breathe. The phone fell from his fingers to land with a thud against the carpet. Dammit, he should have told her. He shouldn't have let her distract him. He'd been trying to do that last night before she'd rocked his world, before she'd asked him to marry him. His heart pounded against his ribs with a mixture of fear and pain and loss he knew he wouldn't survive this time. And then his gaze landed on his watch, lying against the sheets.

"Goddamn son of a bitch." He picked up the watch and hurled it against the wall. The tinkle of glass cracking sounded through the room, followed by a thud as it hit the floor.

He braced a hand on the headboard and sucked in air, trying to get one good breath, trying to think clearly. He knew how her mind worked. He knew what kind of crazy things she was thinking right now. He'd finally broken through all her barriers, and now he'd fucked it all up by not telling her everything. He had to figure out a way to make her listen. But that meant finding her, and at this point, she could be anywhere. She could be…

His mind locked on her missing bracelet from the kitchen. And he instantly knew where she was headed. He just had to get there before she left.

Frantic, he grabbed socks from his bag, stuffed his wallet in his pocket, and reached for his cell from the bed. From the corner of his eye he saw the watch and a spark of silver interrupted by something dark that drew his attention.

He crossed to the watch, picked it up, and carefully picked out the glass and thin, broken face, which was already falling out. Behind that, the gears shone up at him, along with one small black computer chip that had no business being in an analog watch.

Holy shit.

He lifted his cell and dialed. Three rings went by, and his heart lurched into his throat. On the fourth, Ryan's groggy voice came through the line. "I'm up. I was going to call you in the morning. Did you find it?"

"Where are you?" Mitch asked. *Please say you're in San Francisco.*

"Home. Katie and I came back last night."

Thank God. "They've been tracking me with my watch. There's a GPS chip inside."

"Shit. Are you sure?"

"Pretty damn. They gave me a watch to cover the brand when I was first inducted. Every couple of years we get an upgrade. Dammit, I should have known. I'm leaving it here. I don't want them to know I know, but Ryan, I need you to get to Mill Valley before she leaves."

"Before who leaves?"

"Simone."

Fabric rustled, followed by footsteps and Kate's sleepy voice asking, "Who is it?"

"It's Mitch," Ryan said softly. "Everything's okay. Go back to sleep, babe." Footsteps echoed again, then a door softly closed, and Ryan's voice came back stronger. "I thought Simone was with you."

Mitch raked a hand through his hair. He had a giant *I told you so* coming from Ryan, but he didn't care. "She just left. She's heading for a storage unit." He read Ryan the address as he shoved his feet into his boots near the front door, grabbed his jacket from the chair where he'd tossed it, then moved into the garage. "You've gotta get to her before she takes off for good."

He flipped a switch on the wall. Light flooded the garage. Mitch looked around the empty bays, and another shot of panic rushed through him; then he spotted the motorcycle leaning against the wall under a drape.

"You didn't tell her, did you?" Ryan asked.

Here came that *I told you so.* He crossed to the bike and tugged off the drape. It was a Honda, red, old, beat up from off-road use, but his saving grace at the moment. "She saw the mark on my wrist before I could." *Please let there be gas…*

"Dammit." More rustling echoed over the line, followed by Ryan's distant voice again. "Dude, wake up. We're taking a drive."

"Now?" a sleepy voice echoed. "Will there be hot chicks? If so, I'm in."

"Kendrick's there?" Mitch asked.

"He came down with us. Was worried about you, with good reason. What's in the storage unit?"

Mitch found the helmet, opened the garage door, and rolled the bike out into the rain. "Whatever evidence her husband stashed. Ryan, if you get there first, you can't let her leave. I'm at least fifteen minutes behind her."

"I'll do my best. Mitch, one thing before you go. That reporter? The one who wrote that article about Steve? Katie and I did some checking. Her source was the US marshal assigned to Steve's case. Holdt. She was dating him. He was a Cypher."

"Shit."

"It gets better. You know how Katie discovered there's a whole faction in your organization who wants to see Dobbs taken down?"

"Yeah."

"Do you have any idea who's in line to take his place if he falls?"

Mitch wiped the rain from his eyes, seriously tired of the twenty questions. "No, who?"

Ryan sighed. "It amazes me how little you pay attention."

It amazed Mitch too. If he'd been tuned in to what the hell had been going on in his own organization, he'd have known they were looking for Simone right from the start. "Just tell me, dammit. I don't have time to play games."

"Chris Murdoch."

It took a full second for the name to register, but when it did, disbelief followed quickly on its heels. "*My* Chris Murdoch? As in…my boss?"

"One and the same."

Mitch glanced from the puddle in the drive to the street, empty and dark but for an orange triangle of light from the lamp above, illuminating a section of shiny pavement. Chris wasn't protecting him. Not like he'd said. He wanted Simone's evidence. And that meant he could be watching this house and was probably—right this minute—following Simone, hoping she'd lead him to it.

A new sense of panic clawed at Mitch's soul. "Ryan, you gotta get to that storage unit."

"We're heading to the car. Relax, Mitch. We'll get her."

Mitch couldn't relax. Not until he knew Simone was safe.

CHAPTER TWENTY-FOUR

Simone pulled into the dark parking lot of the storage facility and reached for her bracelet from the passenger seat. She stopped at the gate, rolled down the driver's window, and looked at the engraving on the inside of the bracelet, hoping the numbers she was focused on were an access code and unit number.

Holding her breath, she punched the code into the security panel and waited. A hum echoed, then the gate began to roll to the right. Pulse racing, she pulled through the entrance and watched the gate close behind her in the rearview mirror.

She'd called Ryan's parents' cell phones, but neither had answered. Frantic, she'd left messages telling them not to let Mitch or Ryan take Shannon anywhere if they came after her. She knew she'd sounded paranoid, and that once they woke up they were going to wonder what the hell was going on, but there was nothing she could do about that now. First she had to get Steve's evidence, then she'd head right to the airport and get on a flight. And in a couple of hours, she and Shannon would be as far from this nightmare as they possibly could be.

Her eyes searched numbers on the buildings as she passed, her windshield wipers brushing the raindrops away. Her hands grew sweaty as she swept by unit after unit. She didn't have time to waste looking. She needed to get it—whatever it was—and leave. Her pulse shot up when her gaze landed on 27B, and she slammed on the brakes.

Steve's unit wasn't one of the outside ones with the giant garage door. No, of course it couldn't be that easy. Frowning, she shoved the car into park, killed the ignition and grabbed the keys. After pushing the door open, she ducked her head in the rain, slammed the door, and raced toward the main door in the middle of the building that led to the inner units.

Luckily, the outer door was unlocked, the entry illuminated by fluorescent lights above. Stepping inside, she shook the rain from her hair, then quickly scanned the cement walls and headed to the right, looking for 27B.

Locked, silver garage-style doors lined both sides of the hall. She searched numbers, not finding hers, and reached another heavy steel door.

She pulled it open and reached for the light switch on the wall. Lights clicked on in this section of the building, illuminating the next hallway. She took two steps, then spotted it, three doors down on the left.

Her pulse was a whir in her ears as she reached for the lock waist-high on the edge of the door. There were no other numbers on the inside of the bracelet. Hands sweating, she dialed in the same access code to the storage site, hoping it worked on the combination lock too.

The lock clicked and slid open. Surprised, she pulled it from the hook, grabbed the handle near the floor, and tugged the door up and over her head.

The unit was empty but for one box sitting on the cold concrete in the middle of the massive room. She moved inside, slid the bracelet onto her wrist, and swiped her sweaty palms against the thighs of her jeans.

Emotions swirled inside her—anger for what Steve had put her and Shannon through, betrayal that he could have kept so much from her, stupidity that she'd fallen for it all. But mostly disbelief that he hadn't just told her what was really going on. Was she so unbending that he thought she wouldn't understand? She'd known he'd loved her and Shannon. That kind of emotion couldn't be faked, even if he'd lied about everything else. Yeah, she might have been upset at first, but she would have worked through it and could have actually helped him. He had to know that she'd never just abandon him.

Isn't that what you just did to Mitch?

Simone's stomach rolled, sending an icy chill along her skin. Slowly, because her head was suddenly spinning, she knelt in front of the box, leaned back on her heels, and stared at the cardboard.

This was different. Mitch was a Cypher. Part of the same organization that was willing to kill for whatever was in this box.

So was Steve.

Mitch had lied to her.

So did Steve.

Sweat broke out across her forehead, and she swiped at it, her stomach shifting all over again. Steve had lied to keep her safe. The less she knew the better… That was what he'd always said. Mitch had purposely kept secrets from her, right from the start. Because he wanted what was in this box.

Words he'd said last night, when he'd come into the kitchen with that photograph in his hand, echoed in Simone's head.

"He had you. He had Shannon. He had everything I've wanted since I met you, and he let you go without a fight. I'm not gonna make the same mistake."

Tears burned her eyes, and she closed them quickly, fighting back the doubt. Her heart felt like it was breaking all over again, only this time, she didn't know what to do next.

She opened her eyes, blinked through blurry vision, and focused on the box again. Something deep inside told her Mitch would never hurt her, that he loved her, that he had a reason for not being honest, but her mind, that logical part that needed evidence to prove an argument, warned she'd let her emotions lead her once before, and that was why she now found herself in the middle of this nightmare.

Blowing out a slow breath, she reached for the box lid, hoping something inside would tell her what she needed to know.

She lifted the lid and set it on the ground. Inside, there was one small file folder, a metal box, and a key.

She reached for the key and slid it in the lock on the metal box. Her breath caught when she looked inside. A gun and a box of ammunition.

Her hands were sweating when she sat back. Steve had owned a gun, but it wasn't this one. His was a Beretta, in a lockbox in her house. This was a Smith & Wesson, black, sleek, brand-new, and—as she looked closer—fully loaded.

Swallowing hard, she reached for the folder, pulled it out, and opened it on her lap.

There was a note at the front, scribbled in Steve's handwriting, but she bypassed that and flipped through the pages behind it, her brow wrinkling when she realized it was medical records. *His* medical records. He'd circled doctor's chart notes and marked in red next to them, questioning the diagnosis and treatment plan, suggesting other alternative causes for his illness. And everywhere the word *arsenic?* popped up.

Bile slid up Simone's throat. She paged faster through the records, then stilled when she found the e-mail correspondences at the end. Numerous printouts from a L.D. to a W.H. Some cc'd to a C.M., but not all. Each one, though, was centered on a discussion about Steve, how he'd turned on the Cyphers and what they were going to do about that. She couldn't find the word arsenic in any of the e-mails, but she did see three words that made her blood run cold: *accident*, *home invasion*, and *poison*.

Her fingers shook as she flipped back through the file and found Steve's note.

Simone,

If you found this, it means things didn't end as I'd hoped. William Holdt, the US marshal assigned to my case, is a Cypher, but don't worry, he's on our side. The Cyphers have members everywhere, and though he was originally tasked with getting rid of me, he helped me instead. Not everyone within the organization is tainted, darling, only a few bad apples near the top who are hungry for power.

I haven't been able to figure out how they got to me, and neither has Will, but we know my illness isn't really cancer. It's something else, though we haven't been able to pinpoint what. I saved all this for you, just in case, and I have faith you'll be able to figure out what I couldn't. It's the best defense you have in case they come after you because of me, but I'm hoping you don't need it. The gun is unregistered. No one will ever connect it to you. Keep it with you at all times.

I loved you, Simone. I know you don't believe that right now, but it's true. I only ever wanted you and Shannon to be safe. If I could go back and change one thing, it would be that I would have walked away the day you told me you were pregnant. Not because I didn't want you or the child we created, but because it would have kept you safe. I'm sorry I was selfish. I'm sorry that I put you through all this. But mostly, I'm sorry that I'm not with you now. You made my life worth living, and everything I did from the day you became my wife, I did because I was trying to protect you. If you only believe one thing, darling, please believe that.

~Steve

Simone blinked back tears, read the letter again, then a third time, still trying to process everything. Her mind skipped back to the conversation with Ryan in Tahoe about Steve's doctor and how he'd suspected from looking at Steve's records that something about his illness hadn't been right. She should have questioned those doctors. If she'd done that…

If she'd done that, she might be dead now too. Her stomach pitched again, and her eyes focused on Steve's note. *Not all within the organization are tainted…* Closing her eyes, she drew a deep breath and thought of Mitch.

"Simone."

Simone's eyes popped open at the sound of the voice directly behind her. Adrenaline surging, she reached for the gun, closed her hand around the grip, scrambled to her feet, and whipped around.

"Whoa." Mitch stood feet from her, his hair wet and plastered to his head, his jacket slicked with rain. He held up both hands, his eyes wide and very surprised. "Hold on a minute. I'm not gonna hurt you. You know me."

Simone's hand shook. She did know him. Her heart did at least. But everything was so jumbled in her head, she wasn't sure what was real and what was a threat. "You lied to me."

"I didn't lie. I just…" His lips pressed together, then he added, "Okay, yeah. I did. But I tried to tell you last night. I really did. I was gonna tell you everything, but I got…distracted."

Distracted. By her. Kissing him. Making love with him. Proposing to him.

God, she felt like such an idiot. She swiped at a stupid tear sliding down her cheek. "Just tell me this. Was it all a setup? Did you pursue me because you knew who I was?"

"What? No." The color drained from his face, and he dropped his arms. "God, no. Simone, I didn't know who you were until a week ago, after my house got shot up and we were in Ryan's office and you told us all about being in witness protection. Ryan did some research after you and Shannon fell asleep on the couch, and when I realized this was all linked to the Cyphers, I was as shocked as anyone. I know I should have told you everything right then, but I didn't, because…because I was afraid you were gonna cut and run and that you wouldn't listen once you found out. And things were already so messed up between us, I needed to fix that first. But I swear to you, I didn't ask you out as part of some elaborate setup. I wasn't with you because anyone told me to be. I'm with you because I love you."

Though Simone still held the gun in front of her with both hands, her fingers shook against the cool metal with uncertainty, and her arms lowered just a touch.

This was Mitch. The guy who, as of an hour ago, had been the man of her dreams. But there was too much buzzing in her head. Too many uncertainties. And she didn't know what to believe.

"Did you know Steve?"

"No. I promise I didn't. I joined the Cyphers my senior year of college. It's a bicoastal organization. I don't know most of the people in the society, and especially not past members. I'll admit it was fun and exciting when I was in school, but it quickly lost its charm for me. It's not who I am. In fact, I don't interact with anyone outside my one yearly commitment. I should have gotten rid of that stupid brand a long time ago, I just…I didn't because I couldn't."

Because no one left the society. She'd done enough of her own research on the Cyphers the last few days to know that much. A lump formed in her throat when she realized what that meant.

"Sweetheart." He took a small step closer, and the misery she saw swirling in his eyes rivaled the turmoil churning inside her. "You know me. You know who I am. I'm not like those people. I love you, Simone. I love Shannon. None of that has changed. If anything, it's gotten stronger because of all this." He moved even closer, and she saw the wet sheen of tears in his eyes. "Please, please, you have to believe me. I don't care about what's in that box or what you want to do with it. It's yours. I swear I'd never do anything to hurt you."

She did believe that. In her heart she did. But there was still so much she wasn't sure of. She truly believed

Steve had never intentionally set out to hurt her, but she'd ended up here regardless.

"They have to know about you," she whispered, tears tracking down her cheeks now, unwilling to be held back. "If what you're saying is true, they have to know about us. They're not going to just let that go."

"I don't care." His hand closed around her wrist, and he pushed the gun down to her side, then slowly tugged it from her hand. "All I care about is you."

The gun grazed her fingertips and then was gone, and as she looked down at her damp palm while he set it back in the box, she felt like every bit of strength left her body with it.

"I've got you."

She didn't feel herself falling, but she did feel Mitch's arms close around her. And when his warm breath fanned her cheek and neck, tingles spread through her entire body. The same tingles she felt every time he held her close.

"I've got you," he said again into her hair. "You told me to hold on to you, and I am. I'm not letting you go, because I can't. God, I can't. I need you too much, Simone. Please." His arms tightened around her. "Please give me—give us—another chance."

All her life, this was what she'd wanted. Someone who could deal with her ups and downs, who knew how to balance her irrationality and stubbornness, and who would love her enough to put her first no matter the situation. She'd had that in Steve, only she hadn't realized it until it was too late. And now she'd found it in Mitch, a man she hadn't been looking for, but whom she wanted. And needed. More than she'd ever thought possible.

All the uncertainty slid to the wayside. It didn't matter what he'd kept from her. It didn't even matter that she still didn't know what to do next. All that mattered was that she loved him.

She lifted her hands to his sides. Closed her eyes. Started to wrap her arms around his lower back. "Mitch—"

"I was afraid she was going to be a problem."

The voice coming from the doorway caused Mitch to go stone still against her, but Simone felt the way his pulse shot up. She couldn't see who'd just arrived, and she didn't recognize his voice, but some sixth sense told her Mitch did.

"Dammit, Mathews," the man said in an exasperated tone. "I didn't want it to end this way. I really didn't."

Mitch braced both hands on Simone's shoulders, then turned, putting himself between her and the newcomer. But before he did, Simone caught a glimpse of his eyes. Wide, guarded, and frightened.

"Murdoch." Mitch held out his hand. "The box is yours. Just take it."

Simone took a step out from behind Mitch so she could see. The man in the doorway was tall and dark, wearing jeans and a navy jacket, and though she didn't recognize his voice at first, she did know that face. Chris Murdoch. Mitch's boss at PreCorp.

Holy shit. C.M. The initials that had been on those e-mails in Steve's box.

Chris rubbed his left eye with a gloved hand. "We're both smart men here, Mitch. You know that can't happen now." He dropped his hand and looked down at the open box. "Graham was stupid enough to put it on paper. She already read what's in there."

Simone stepped out from behind Mitch. "No one has to know. They're yours. You can have them."

"Simone," Mitch warned.

"That's all of it," she said, ignoring Mitch. "There's nothing else. Just let us go, and no one will know any of this happened."

"I tried that," Murdoch said to Mitch, not her. "That reporter, then Holdt. Did you know if Holdt hadn't been fucking her and hadn't talked, she never would have written that article, and we still wouldn't know where Graham's wife was?" He nodded toward Simone but kept his gaze on Mitch, almost as if she weren't there.

Simone's adrenaline spiked. *No one leaves the society*. The words echoed in her head as Murdoch pinned Mitch with a hard look.

"Dobbs wanted to just let it go after the society took care of Holdt and the reporter," Murdoch went on. "He wanted to let *her* go. He said she wasn't a threat after all this time. And I tried to go along with him, but then I found out she was right under my nose, and I just….couldn't."

"Yes, you can," Mitch said. "You still can. Just take the box and go."

"It was supposed to be an easy exchange," Murdoch said, shaking his head as if Mitch hadn't even spoken. "I flush the girl out, you step in to play hero—"

"Shooting up my house isn't flushing anyone out," Mitch snapped.

"No," Murdoch agreed. "Those thugs I hired were a little too aggressive. I'll give you that. Obviously, toning things down worked way better. I got you to offer to get me the file without even asking."

Simone was having trouble keeping up, but everything that had happened since William Holdt's call—Mitch's house getting shot up, the security breach at Kendrick's cabin, their stolen, charred car—it all started to make a sick sort of sense.

"You can still have it," Mitch said. "We can all walk away from this."

"Ah, Mitch." Murdoch rubbed a finger over his brow. "Always the optimist. I want you to know I was going to let it go once I had the file, I really was, but you had to go and fuck it all up, and now I can't do that anymore."

He pulled out a gun. A shiny black gun that was bigger than the one Simone had found in Steve's box, and pointed it right at Mitch.

"Mitch." Simone gasped. Reflex had her stepping toward him.

Murdoch swiveled the barrel her way.

"Chris, dammit." Panic snaked through Mitch's voice. "If you hurt her, I swear to God I'll kill you."

"In a minute, I promise you won't care."

Simone sucked in a breath just as Murdoch pulled the trigger.

CHAPTER TWENTY-FIVE

The gunshot exploded though the room with the force of a cannon. Simone screamed. Mitch slammed into her, knocking her off her feet. Her spine hit the concrete floor; her head snapped back and cracked against the unforgiving ground, sending pain shooting across her scalp. Mitch landed on top of her.

She opened her eyes to a flurry of red. She wasn't sure where she'd been hit, but there was blood. A lot of blood. Then she saw Mitch's face above her, contorted in pain.

"Mitch?" She struggled out from under him. "Mitch. No. Oh God. Mitch?"

"Son of a…" He grunted, rolled off her, and landed on the concrete floor. Blood oozed from a wound in his side, already seeping through his jacket.

Simone yanked his coat back and pressed her hands against the wound, frantic to stop the blood. Mitch's eyes fell closed. He hissed in a breath and winced.

"Stay with me, do you hear me?" Her chest squeezed tight, so tight she could barely speak. "Mitch?"

His head rolled on the floor. Simone pushed down on the wound. "I need help." There was so much blood. Oh, God… There was too much. "I need help, dammit!"

Murdoch sighed somewhere behind her. "His number was up the minute he called offering that deal. But I was ready to live up to our bargain until tonight. You hear me, Mathews? I was going to just delete my name from those e-mails and let Dobbs take the fall, but I can't do that now that she knows. She'll always be a liability, and if there's one thing I've learned in life, it's that liabilities are best dealt with swiftly."

Simone focused on Mitch's face. Love and heartache exploded inside her. "You idiot," she whispered. "You made a deal with him for me? What were you thinking?"

"Was thinking…about you," Mitch managed, having trouble breathing. "I didn't know…it was him," He lifted his hand and set it over hers against his wound.

Simone knew that. Tears filled her eyes. She knew he'd never do anything but try to protect her. She'd been so stupid about so many things.

"That's really romantic," Murdoch said. "Too bad you two were doomed from the start."

Mitch squeezed Simone's hand, opened his eyes, and rolled them to the left. And without turning her head, Simone glanced the direction he indicated.

He'd kicked the box toward her when he'd thrown himself in front of that bullet. Steve's gun was inches away.

"I love you," he whispered.

Links clicked into place in Simone's mind. She calculated the distance, the angle, the time it would take to grab the weapon. Her chances were slim, but she wasn't going to let Mitch die without a fight.

"I know," she whispered back.

Footsteps echoed in the hallway, followed by voices. Mitch let go of her hand. When Murdoch turned to look toward the door, Simone didn't hesitate. She let go of Mitch, lurched for the gun, turned, and fired.

The bullet caught Murdoch in the shoulder. He grunted and fell back against the wall. Simone fired again, not even sure where she was aiming. Another gunshot rang out, this one not from her gun. Mitch's raspy voice echoed, then he slammed into her again, taking her down to the ground.

Her hand hit the cement floor, and the gun went flying. A crack echoed from across the room. More voices. But Simone couldn't see what was going on. Mitch was on top of her again, only this time he was like dead weight. Immovable.

"Mitch." Panic pushed her muscles forward. She fought against him but couldn't get him to move. "Oh God, Mitch!"

"Tate." Ryan. That was Ryan's voice. "Help me."

Strong hands lifted Mitch from her. Simone scrambled to her feet, then gasped when she realized Mitch had been hit again, this time in the shoulder.

"Holy shit," Kendrick muttered.

"Call 911," Ryan yelled.

Kendrick whipped out his phone and started talking frantically. Across the room, Murdoch was out cold against the far wall, his gun yards away on the ground. Ryan tugged off his jacket and shoved it against the wound in Mitch's side. "Simone, hold this here while I try to get at his shoulder."

Simone's bloody hands pressed against Mitch's side.

"Son of a bitch." Ryan yanked at the sleeve of Mitch's shirt. "If we hadn't gotten stuck behind that accident on the 101, we would have been here long before this happened."

Simone tried to see what Ryan was doing, but everything was blurry. All she knew was it was bad. Mitch wasn't answering. He wasn't even moving.

"You sure have a knack for finding trouble," Ryan muttered. "You know that, Mitch?"

"Ryan." Simone stared at Mitch's chest, a new sense of fear rushing in. "He's not breathing."

Ryan's fingers froze against Mitch's blood-soaked shirt.

"Buddy? Oh, don't do this to me right now." He leaned over Mitch to listen for his breath. Fear filled his eyes when he leaned back. "It's not your time, do you hear me?" He squeezed Mitch's nose, tilted his chin up, then blew a breath into his mouth. Shifting down, he felt along Mitch's chest, clasped his hands together, and pressed down, starting CPR compressions. "Kendrick? I need that ambulance, now, dammit!"

"They're almost here."

Sirens sounded outside.

Fear closed Simone's throat. She couldn't lose him. Not now. She didn't know what she'd do without him.

She reached for Mitch's hand, lying near his side, while Ryan kept at the CPR. "Mitch? If you can hear me, hold on to me, okay? You promised you would." She choked back a sob. "You promised, and I'm holding you to that one. Please, please, please, just hold on to me."

CHAPTER TWENTY-SIX

Mitch?"

Struggling to get his still-bandaged shoulder and arm into the damn hoodie, Mitch grunted from the cramped bathroom in his hospital room and rasped, "I'm in here."

Footsteps echoed from beyond the door, then Kate's gentle voice said, "Are you okay?"

That was a loaded question. Sweat slicking his forehead, his spine, nearly every inch of his skin, he glanced in the bathroom mirror, then looked away in disgust. His face was pale, his cheeks sunken, and the beard on his jaw had passed scruffy, even for him, and was now heading toward mountain-man scary. Not to mention he was so weak he couldn't even get his own fucking sweatshirt on. No wonder Simone hadn't been by to see him in days. He looked like death warmed over and felt like it too.

Repulsed by himself, he kicked the door open and took one step into the hospital room where he'd spent the last week. "Does this look okay to you?"

A ghost of a smile curled Kate's lips, and she laughed at the hoodie half hanging off his body and twisted around his back, then quickly covered it with a frown. "Sorry. It's not funny. I didn't mean to laugh. Come sit and I'll help you."

Grinding his teeth, he shuffled toward the bed—shuffled, fuck, he couldn't even walk like a normal person thanks to the pain still radiating up his side and the shortness of breath from his damaged lung. And oh great, he was sweating all over again, just from that little effort.

The TV was running a news program in the corner of the room, the sound on low. Dropping onto the side of the bed, he groaned, hating the smell of the room, the feel of the mattress, hating everything about this goddamn place.

Kate unzipped the hoodie, then moved around his back to gently bring the garment over his bad shoulder. "Let me guess, Mom picked these up for you."

Mitch glanced down at the matching navy sweatpants he'd managed to tug on. "What gave it away? The cheap fabric or the fact the damn zipper doesn't work?"

Kate pulled something from the back of the hoodie and held it up for him to see. "The price tag. We all know how much she loves Walmart."

Mitch rolled his eyes. His mother had brought him three different sweat suits just like this, all in different colors, and while he appreciated the thought, once he got out of this godforsaken place, he wasn't going to be caught dead in any of them. "Before I forget, I wanted to say thanks so much for calling them. Mom and Dad have been camped out in this room since I woke up, driving me batshit crazy."

"You're welcome. I'm just returning the favor. Remember how they rushed down here when you called and told them I was in town?"

"That was different, and you know it."

"As I remember you saying, 'it's time you started pulling your weight in this family.' Well, they've been hovering over me for six months. Now it's your turn."

He couldn't argue with that. Their parents hadn't wanted to let Kate out of their sight, and though he couldn't blame them—after all, finding out your long-lost daughter was actually alive would spur anyone to do a little hovering—a tiny part of him felt guilty for enjoying the respite from their meddling.

"Where are they, by the way?" she asked.

"Talking to my doctor, I'm sure. Making sure I'm not going to inadvertently puncture the other lung by leaving. I swear they think I'm still twelve."

Kate smiled. "You'll always be their baby, Mitch. No way around that for a parent."

He wouldn't know. He wasn't a parent and probably wouldn't ever be one. His mind shifted to Shannon, and he wondered where she was and what she was doing. He hadn't seen her since Ryan's parents had brought the kids back to San Francisco, and while he knew a hospital wasn't exactly a place for kids, he missed her.

"Do you want the sling inside or outside your sweatshirt?"

"Outside." The weather had decided to kick into gear, and it was fucking cold outside. No way was he heading out there in his condition with an open hoodie.

Kate helped him slide his arm through the sleeve. Pain pinched his shoulder where he'd been shot, but it wasn't nearly as bad as the pain in his side every time he twisted. And it didn't even compare to what was happening in the center of his chest each time he thought of Simone.

By the time she finished and helped him tug the zipper up the front, he was sweating buckets. "God Almighty, I'm fucking useless."

"No you're not. You're just injured. You've gotta give yourself time to heal." She sat on the bed next to him and reached for his hand. Her fingers closed around his, strong, sure, familiar. "It's going to be okay. Have a little faith."

He frowned her direction. "Don't patronize me."

"It's the same thing you told me, and you were right."

"I was blowing smoke up your ass. You should have been smart enough to see that. Simone obviously was."

"Mitch—"

"No, you know what?" He let go of her hand, knowing he sounded like the scorned lover and hating himself even more for that. "It's fine. I'll get over it. Forget I said anything."

Kate was silent at his side for a moment, then said, "She's been here. You've just been sleeping a lot."

Right. Yeah. Sleeping. Not every moment, though. And while he did remember her being here when he'd first come out of surgery, groggy and half out of it from the anesthesia and pain meds, he didn't remember seeing much of her since. "It's fine, Kate."

"She's also had to deal with Shannon and all the fallout from the press once the story went public. That's exhausting. Trust me, I know."

He knew that was true. He'd caught clips of it on the news. Simone had turned the file over to the Feds, who were running a full-scale investigation on Senator Dobbs, Chris Murdoch, and PreCorp, which included exhuming Simone's late husband's body and testing it for various poisons. And though no link to the Cyphers had been made by the big news outlets yet—the running story was simply a senator in bed with big oil, and his accountant who'd turned on him—conspiracy theorist websites were bubbling over with speculation about the secret society and the organization's future.

"Ryan said you got a visit from Paul Messing yesterday," she said quietly.

Mitch focused on a square tile on the floor and nodded. "He's the new acting chairman of Cypher and Dagger. He was a few years ahead of me in school. I met him a couple of times at various functions but don't know him well."

"What did he say?"

"He apologized for everything that's happened, if you can believe that. Said Murdoch was acting on his own and that the society didn't know anything about Holdt or Dobbs or Steve's death. He also said the society isn't standing behind either of them."

"Isolating themselves from the drama, like Ryan said they would."

"Yeah." Too little too late, in Mitch's opinion, but…whatever.

"You know why they're doing that, right?" Kate asked.

"Because they're not stupid."

"Because Simone held back part of the evidence in Steve's box."

Mitch looked her way. "What are you talking about?"

"There was more in there besides Steve's medical files. He was the Cypher's treasurer for several years. All that evidence the Feds thought he had linking the organization to money laundering, racketeering, and bribery? He really had it. On a zip drive in the bottom of the box. He just never let it go public for fear of retaliation against Simone and Shannon. Simone, Ryan, and Ryan's team of lawyers met with Messing two days ago and laid it all on the line. So long as the organization backs off and leaves all of us alone, you especially, she won't release what Steve collected. But if anything happens to you—to any of us—it'll go public with one click. Ryan said she was a force to be reckoned with in the meeting. Even his high-paid team of legal whiz kids was impressed."

Awe rippled through Mitch. She was always a force to be reckoned with in a legal setting. Negotiations were her strong suit, and in a business environment… Yeah, he just bet she was a shark waiting to strike.

He couldn't be mad at her for not being here. Not when she was dealing with all that. And not when he now knew she was the reason Messing had given him the option of staying in the society or leaving for good, something he'd wanted for years.

God, he loved that woman. Ached for her. Wished like hell she was here right now. And didn't want to think too much about what it meant that she wasn't.

"Speaking of your obnoxious husband," he said, wanting—needing—to change the subject. "Where is he?"

"Talking to your doctors too. You scared him, Mitch. You scared all of us."

He nodded, not wanting to think about that. Because if he had it to do all over again, he'd put his life on the line for Simone's in the exact same way.

The door to his room pushed open, and Ryan poked his head around the curtain. "You decent?"

Mitch frowned. "As decent as I'm going to get."

"Cool," Ryan said, "because I got all your discharge papers. You're set to go."

"Thank God," Mitch muttered.

Kate pushed to her feet, then moved around the bed to grab Mitch's bag.

Ryan backed into the room, dragging a wheelchair with him. Mitch's frown turned to a scowl. "I'm not using that."

"Yes, you are," the nurse said behind Ryan. "Hospital policy. If you want to leave, this is your flying carpet."

Ryan grinned. "She said I could push, if that makes you feel any better."

Joy. Bracing his hands against the mattress, Mitch grunted and finally balanced his weight on his feet. But it took several tries, and he knew he looked like a wimp. "You'll probably run me into a wall and enjoy it."

Ryan chuckled and helped him into the chair. While the nurse fixed the footrests for him, Ryan leaned down and muttered, "I'm hurt. I really am. Especially after that kiss we shared."

Kate barked out a laugh, then covered her mouth with her hand.

Mitch's face twisted in disgust. "That wasn't a kiss, dipshit, it was CPR, which, thankfully, I don't remember. And I'll be washing my mouth out with Listerine for the next year, thanks to you."

Ryan's laugh deepened, and he steered the wheelchair toward the door. "You liked it. You were begging for more. I gotta say, though, I don't know why the girls are always falling over you. Your sister kisses way better than you do."

"Ryan," Kate warned.

"What?" he said, feigning shock. "It's true. Your kisses are hot, babe. His? Not so much."

Resting his elbow on the armrest, Mitch rubbed his suddenly aching temples. "I'm gonna be sick. I really am."

"Well, that's because you're a girly man who's always getting hurt," Ryan jabbed. "Cheer up, though. I'm sure we can find some pathetic woman to play nursemaid to you. There are still a few out there who like you."

Mitch wasn't so sure. And just any woman wasn't going to do it for him. Not anymore. The only one he wanted obviously no longer wanted him back.

Mitch closed his eyes on the drive to Kate and Ryan's house. A tiny part of him had held out hope Simone would show up as he was leaving, take him to her house, and nurse him back to health like she'd done after he'd suffered that head injury six months ago. But now that he was settled into the front seat of Ryan's Mercedes, his arm resting in the sling at his chest, his head kicked back against the headrest, and his eyes closed, he knew he had to buck up to the fact that little fantasy had crashed and burned, big-time.

The car made a right-hand turn and slowed. At his side, Ryan muttered, "Is that Kendrick we just passed on a bike?"

Mitch didn't open his eyes. The last thing he wanted to see was someone having fun.

"I think so," Kate said from the backseat. "And there's your daughter ahead. They are two peas in a pod, aren't they?"

"I told him to stay away from her. The son of a bitch doesn't listen."

Kate sighed. "She likes him, Ryan. There's nothing wrong with that."

"There is from the other side. He flirts with her."

"She's almost a teenager. Get used to it. Lots of boys are going to be flirting with her soon."

"Not full-grown men."

"Maybe he just likes kids."

"Maybe it's just wrong."

Kate let out an exasperated sound. "Mitch, was he always like this with Julia? Overprotective and unreasonable?"

"Always," Mitch said, his eyes still closed. "And I'm with him on this one. Kendrick's a player. He might not be interested in Julia now, but give him eight years. Or six."

"Do not even joke about that," Ryan warned.

A tiny smile tugged at Mitch's mouth. The first one he'd felt in days. But it quickly faded when he thought of Shannon and the fact he wanted to be that for her. Not exactly the domineering father Ryan was, but her dad, yeah. Worrying over her like any real dad would.

The car made another right turn, and something about the direction Ryan was heading felt off. Slowly, Mitch's eyelids lifted, and he looked out the windshield.

He stiffened in the front seat, and the motion caused a stab of pain to slink up his side. "I thought we were going to your house?"

"Pit stop first," Ryan said.

Unease floated through Mitch's gut. "I'm not really in the mood to see my place."

Shit, was Ryan trying to depress him more? The last thing he needed on top of a gunshot wound—two gunshot wounds—and a broken heart was to see his house, the house he'd remodeled with his own two hands, full of holes he didn't have the strength to fix.

"Pull up your big-girl panties, Mathews. You might be surprised at what you find."

Ryan made the last turn, and Mitch tensed as his house came into view. But instead of bullet holes and broken windows, what he saw sent a flutter of surprise straight through his belly.

New windows, new trim, new siding, even a fresh coat of paint. The porch that had been damaged had been rebuilt. The bushes he knew had been trampled, replaced. There was a new front door, this one black, trendy, the kind of door he'd been looking for for months but hadn't been able to find, with three small panes of glass across the top. Someone had even mowed the lawn.

Ryan pulled to the curb and killed the engine. Shocked, Mitch looked from the contractor's van parked in the drive to the house, unable to believe it was the same place. "How did you—?"

"Surprise," Ryan said.

Voices echoed behind their car, but Mitch was still too focused on the house to turn and look. Laughing, Kate popped the door and hollered at Julia and Kendrick, who went whizzing by on their bikes.

"I...don't know what to say," Mitch said to Ryan when they were alone.

"Don't say anything to me. I didn't do this."

Mitch dragged his gaze from the house and finally looked at his best friend. "My parents?"

Ryan shook his head. "Not Katie either. Though when she found out about it, it was all I could do to keep her from spilling the beans." He pulled something from his pocket and tossed it into Mitch's lap. "This time, don't fuck things up, okay?"

Mitch stared down at the small, black velvet box in his hand, having trouble processing Ryan's words. Before his brain could click into gear, Ryan opened the door and climbed out of the car.

"Oh, and one more thing, Mathews. When you go in there, cut the woman a little slack. She's kicked some serious ass this week while you've been parked on yours. And she did it all spending every damn night in your hospital room, sleeping on that uncomfortable couch while you were high on painkillers. I wouldn't have done it, even if you did kiss me. She's a keeper. But then, I'm pretty sure you already know that."

Ryan closed the door, shouted something at Kendrick Mitch couldn't make out, then took off across the street. Silence settled over the inside of the car. A silence that was broken only by the sudden pounding in Mitch's ears. Slowly, he popped the top on the small box and looked down at the engagement ring he'd bought for Simone and never given her.

His gaze shot back up to the house. And, adrenaline surging, he found a strength he was pretty sure he'd lost the last few days.

It took him longer than he liked to walk up the path, and he was sweating by the halfway mark. Pausing to catch his breath, he looked up at the house. Before he could take another step, red curls filled his vision, and a small voice exclaimed, "Mitch!"

Shannon rushed toward him, wrapped her arms around his waist, and held on tight. Her arm knocked into the bandage on his side, and he winced, but the pain was worth it. Warmth flooded his chest. He wanted to drop to his knees, take her into his arms, but he wasn't sure he could get back up if he did. And he didn't want to look pathetic.

He rubbed a hand over her hair and smiled down at her. "Hey, you. Miss me, did ya?"

Shannon laughed and looked up at him. "Yes. We had so much fun. We went swimming and snorkeling and got to sleep on this really cool boat. I can't wait to tell you all about it."

And Mitch couldn't wait to hear it. But he needed to make it inside the house. Pulse racing, he looked back up at the open front door, not wanting to be disappointed, not wanting to hope too much. "Is your mom in there?"

"Yeah, Mom's been bossing people around all morning. Man, your house was such a mess! Whoever broke in did all kinds of damage. It's a good thing you weren't home. I mean, there were holes everywhere."

Shannon's hurried voice echoed in Mitch's ears, but all he could focus on was the fact Simone was here. She hadn't left San Francisco. She hadn't run away. She was still here, and that meant—maybe—they had a chance.

A lump formed in his throat, and he pushed his feet forward. Sweat slicked his spine when he got to porch, but excitement urged him on. Keeping his good arm wrapped around Shannon while she continued to babble on about her trip, he stepped through the open door, barely able to believe the change.

The house looked exactly the way it had before. Someone had even reframed his signed Mariner's jersey that had fallen off the wall in the entry and crashed to the ground in a pile of glass during the attack.

Voices echoed from the kitchen. A man's. Simone's.

His pulse skyrocketed.

Mitch headed that way, his heart pulling him, his pulse pounding. When he reached the great room, he froze.

Simone stood in the kitchen, pointing something out on the ceiling to a man wearing a ball cap and tool belt. The man answered whatever she asked, jotted a note, pointed at something else. And though Mitch could hear their words, he couldn't focus on what they were saying. All he could see was her, standing in his kitchen, fixing what he'd broken, doing all this for him.

As if she sensed him, she turned abruptly. Shannon's voice died off as he stood staring at her mother. Surprise flashed in Simone's eyes, followed by… Yeah, that looked like excitement, didn't it? "Mitch."

The breathy cadence of her voice sent a shiver down his spine. God, he loved the sound of her voice. Loved the way she said his name. Missed it. So damn much.

The contractor turned too, said something Mitch didn't catch. In a daze, Mitch lifted his good arm from Shannon in a pathetic wave. The man muttered something about the laundry room, then excused himself and disappeared down the hall.

"You're earlier than I thought you'd be," Simone said, rubbing her hands on the hem of the blue T-shirt that accentuated her breasts and made him remember how he'd worshipped them the night they'd stayed in Stinson Beach. She moved out from behind the island quickly, rushing toward him, but drew up short a foot away. "I wanted to be at the hospital, but there was too much going on here. I thought we had at least another hour."

If she'd wanted to be at the hospital, that was a good sign, right? But she wasn't moving into him. Wasn't reaching for him. And though he wanted to pull her close and reassure himself everything between them was okay, he didn't know if he should. Didn't know where they stood. And, man, that was more pathetic than anything. "You did all this?"

Simone glanced up and around. "Yes. Well, no, I didn't do it. I just…directed."

"Mom's good at directing," Shannon said at his side. "I think the contractor's a lot afraid of her."

"Shannon," Simone muttered, glancing down at her daughter. "Why don't you go outside with Julia for a few minutes and let me talk to Mitch alone."

Shannon cast a worried look between them, but eased away from Mitch. "You're not going to disappear again, right?"

Even in the middle of the biggest surprise of his life, the kid could still get to him. His throat grew tight. "I won't. I promise."

He watched Shannon head down the hall toward the front door, his chest and head vibrating with emotions he was afraid to let free.

In front of him, Simone twisted her hands together and bit her lip. "How do you feel? You look a little pale."

He slid his gaze back to her. How did he feel? He wasn't sure yet. But he'd be a hell of a lot better if she kissed him. "I'm…fine. I—"

A very familiar string instrument floated out of the speakers in the ceiling, cutting off Mitch's words.

Simone cringed. "That's Shannon. Sorry."

Mitch wasn't. Van Morrison. "These are the Days." The song that had been playing the night she'd come home from DC.

He just hoped like hell this time things ended better than they had then.

"I can't believe you did all this," he said.

"Well." She dropped her hands to her sides. "I broke this. It was my job to fix it.

She was talking about more than just the house. *God, please let her be talking about more than the house.* "No, you didn't. It was my fault too. I'm the one who should be doing the fixing."

Her eyes held his a long heartbeat, but she didn't answer. And in the silence, every fear he'd had since that awful night came rushing back.

Tears pooled in her eyes, and her kiss-me lips parted, just a touch. "Mitch, I…"

Say you miss me. Say you want me. Please say you still love me, even after everything that's happened."

One single tear rolled down her cheek. And then she was moving toward him, grasping his face, pulling it down to hers, shaking with the same emotions he felt. "Don't you dare put me through that again. I can't lose you. Not now when I finally found you."

Her mouth lifted to his. She wrapped her arms around his neck. And even as pain shot through his shoulder and side at the jerky movement, he groaned, opened to her kiss, wrapped his good arm around her, and tugged her as close as he could.

His legs went out from under him. He dropped to his knees on the hardwood floor. Simone pulled her mouth away and gasped. "Mitch? Oh God, I'm sorry. I didn't mean to hurt you. I didn't mean—"

Yes, he hurt. And yes, he was in pain, but this pain he could live with because it would pass. Losing her wouldn't. "I'm fine. Just kiss me, Simone." He lifted his mouth to hers. "Ah, God, just kiss me."

She sank to her knees with him, and he swept his tongue between her lips, kissing her again, deeply, passionately, with every bit of love swirling inside him. And when she groaned and kissed him back just as fervently, that heart that had broken and cracked right here in this very room fused back together.

The twinge in his side eventually got to be too much, and he dragged his mouth from hers, but he didn't let go. Burying his face in her hair, he held on tight. "I missed you. Damn, but you have no idea how much."

"I missed you too," she whispered. "I was so scared. I shouldn't have run from you. I'm sorry. I thought… Oh it doesn't matter what I thought anymore." Her fingers sifted into his hair, and she held him so close he could feel the beat of her heart against his own, just where it was supposed to be. "All that matters is that I love you. So much. And I won't run again. I promise. I only want you. If, that is, you still want me."

He lifted his head and looked down at her. "I've always just wanted you. You and Shannon and a stupid minivan. You're everything to me, Counselor. You always will be."

Her eyes softened, and very gently, with her hands cupping his face, she pressed her lips to his. "I'm so glad to hear that. But"—she eased a breath away—"there's just one thing. How sold are you on the whole minivan thing?"

"Why?" A whisper of doubt rushed in. "What are you getting at?"

She bit her lip, looking sexy and cute and way too damn perfect. "It's just… I don't quite know how to tell you this." Her cute little nose wrinkled. "I don't think your Defender's going to make it."

His Land Rover hadn't been in the driveway. He hadn't realized that until just now. Which meant it probably had as many, if not more, holes than his house.

And, wow, he didn't even care. What did that say about him now? But he could tell from the mischievous little smirk on her face that she wanted him to play along.

"Ouch. I think that hurt more than being shot. Twice."

She laughed, the sound as sweet as bells, and stroked her fingers against his scruffy jaw. "How about I make it up to you?"

Arousal speared through his belly. An arousal that obviously wasn't deterred by gunshot wounds or surgery or killer pain meds. "That depends on what you have in mind."

Simone grinned and pressed her lips against the spot she'd just been stroking. "Well, I was thinking, if you'd consider upgrading to something a little sportier, I might be willing to go hiking with you now and then."

"That does have potential." He thought of the fire lookout and all the things he'd wanted to do to her in that cozy little room. His blood warmed as she trailed her lips to his ear and gently bit down on his lobe. "Even if there could be bears on our hike?"

"No bears."

He chuckled. "That might be hard to guarantee. What else are you offering?"

"Hm… Well, if the vehicle's big enough, say…like Kendrick's Range Rover…then how about a car seat. Or two?"

Kids. She was talking about more kids. Smile fading, he drew back and looked down into her mesmerizing eyes. "Are you serious?"

"Yes," she whispered. "But only if you marry me first. Because I still want to marry you. Desperately."

He hadn't thought he could fall more in love with her, but he did, right there. And this time his shortness of breath wasn't from his still-healing lung, but from all the emotions tightening his chest. "Ah, sweetheart. I'm pretty sure I'm making out better in this deal than you."

"Not a chance." Her smile returned, and she lifted her lips back to his. "I'm a lawyer. I know how to negotiate a contract to my advantage. So what do you say?"

He let go of her with his good arm, pulled the ring from his pocket, and held it up. "I say…yes."

Her eyes went all soft and dreamy when she looked down at the princess-cut diamond, and one tear turned into several. "Oh, Mitch. Where did you get that?"

"Shannon helped me pick it out. Weeks ago."

"Weeks ago," she whispered. Her eyes slid closed, and she drew in an unsteady breath. But when she opened them again, they were warm and glistening with tears he knew were filled with happiness, not despair. "It's beautiful. I love it."

He slid the ring on her finger, then tipped her mouth back up to his. And as the music shifted to "Someone Like You," he kissed her until she was breathless. Until he could no longer think. Until she was all he could see and feel and know.

"I love you, Mitch Mathews." She wrapped her arms around him. "And I promise I won't ever let you go, so long as you hold on tight to me."

"I will." That was a promise he knew he could keep. "Guaranteed."

Read on for a sneak peek at
EXTREME MEASURES
The first full-length Aegis Security book coming
July 8, 2014

Being prepared for any scenario is the trademark of any good CIA operative, and Eve Wolfe is one of the best. But when her latest mission literally explodes in her face, she wakes up labeled a traitor and—even more surprising—in the custody of elite Aegis Security operative and ex-lover Zane Archer. Although she still secretly has feelings for Zane, he's now demanding the one thing that she can't give him: the truth.

When he caught her breaking the rules years ago, Zane let Eve walk away without an explanation. Now someone has not only sabotaged Aegis but also turned an American city into a war zone, and all signs point to Eve. Zane needs answers that can come only from Eve's still-tempting lips, and he finally has the elusive operative right where he wants her—at his mercy.

The first book in bestselling author Elisabeth Naughton's new steamy romantic suspense series brings a spy in from the cold…and sets her heart ablaze.

CHAPTER ONE

Guatemala
ETA to extraction: Twelve minutes and counting.

Zane Archer scanned the darkened compound from the trees just beyond the perimeter wall and tried to ignore the sweltering jungle heat.

Too bad it didn't work.

Sweat gathered under his fatigues and beneath his helmet, but he knew soon the temperature would be the least of his worries. Wiping a hand over the moisture dripping into his eyes, he looked through the scope. At this hour—nearly three A.M.—the only lights flickering were in two windows on the second floor of the Mediterranean-style mansion. A guard roamed the portico outside the first floor, and other than a few howler monkeys chirping in the jungle canopy nearby, no other sound besides leaves and palm fronds rustling met his ears.

He glanced at his watch again. *ETA to extraction: Eleven minutes, Twenty-five seconds.*

Nerves fluttered in his belly, but he ignored those too. Keeping the M4 carbine rifle trained on the guard, he tipped his head toward the com unit near his shoulder. "Look alive, boys. We're coming up on go time."

In his earpiece, the radio squawked. "You're sure he's in there?"

Jake Ryder's skepticism was nothing new. But on this, Zane was confident. "Carter's intel is sound."

"It'd better be," Jake muttered. "Our balls are dangling out here in the breeze, Archer."

Zane bit back the smartass comment because Jake had let him take the lead on this one and looked through his scope again, scanning the perimeter once more.

His heart picked up speed, and adrenaline flooded his system. Ryder and Hedley should have their men in position on the far side of the compound by now. Though Zane was confident this extraction was going to go down without a hitch, he knew Jake Ryder—CEO of Aegis Security, the private company comprised of Zane and a handful of elite specialists from around the globe—wasn't so sure. Jake didn't know "Carter" from a fart in the wind. And though he was aware Zane and Carter had teamed together during Zane's five years with the CIA, he still questioned the fact this whole op hinged on the intel Carter had passed along to Zane. Intel that said one Adam Humbolt, Ph.D. and specialist in chemical weaponry, was being held in this Guatemalan compound by a gang of thugs who worked for Central American drug lord Roberto Contosa.

"Humbolt's in there," he said into his com unit. "Trust me, Carter and the Company want this guy free as much as we do."

Not as much. *More.* Humbolt "officially" didn't work for the U.S. government, but word on the street was the scientist knew some super top secret shit the U.S. didn't want shared with anyone—Central American drug lords included. And though logic said this extraction probably should have fallen to a SEAL or DELTA team, because the State Department didn't want this op on record, the job had been handed off to Aegis with its superior track record. Their orders were simple: get the job done quietly and quickly and with no link back to the U.S. government whatsoever.

Ryder didn't respond, and Zane knew his boss was thinking, *we'll see,* but facts were facts. Sure, there were a whole lot of people who wanted the science percolating in Humbolt's genius mind, another bunch who'd like to see him dead, but the ones who mattered just wanted him back in the States alive and in one piece.

Time ticked by slowly in the oppressive early morning heat. Zane could all but feel the adrenaline from his teammates stationed around the compound. And though he tried to stay focused as he waited, he couldn't stop his mind from drifting back to the last time he'd worked with Carter. To being stuck in that run-down apartment in Beirut he'd shared with Carter and Juliet. To the months of running surveillance, blending in, fighting back the boredom. To the nights he'd been alone with Juliet when Carter had been out. To the laughs, the looks, the heated moments that never should have happened.

"Jesus," he whispered. "You are such a fucking moron."

"You say something?" Hedley piped in his ear.

Shit, he was talking to himself. He cleared his throat, peered through the scope again, and put all thoughts of Juliet out of his mind for good. "Remember, boys," he said. "Slow is smooth. Smooth is fast."

"Ooh-rah," Landon Miller murmured, the only communication the former Marine had uttered since they'd set up the perimeter.

As the team went black, Zane said a quick prayer they'd be in and out in seconds rather than minutes or hours. Said another that no one got dead.

He shifted his finger from guard to trigger. Lined up the compound sentry in his crosshairs. And just as the last second passed on his watch, he fired once, killing the south end sentry with a barely audible pop. On the north end, he was confident Ryder had just accomplished the same.

He was out of the tree and across the wall before the sentry's body hit the ground, rappelling the cement structure as quickly as possible and bracing his rifle against his shoulder as he crossed the dew-covered grass. At the southwest corner of the compound, he caught up with Hedley's group coming in from the side and pointed up, signaling the hostage room they'd identified earlier on the second floor.

Miller and Stone tossed ropes up and over the second story balcony, the grappling hooks catching the balustrade and securing tight. Zane followed Hedley to the second floor, waiting in silence as the other two men climbed up and over the railing. As a silent unit, they made their way across the balcony and lined up outside the hostage room.

Hedley signaled with his finger, counted to three, then pulled an M84 flash grenade from his pack. When he got the nod from Hedley, Zane used his rifle to blow open the door of the compound. Hedley jerked the pin from his grenade and tossed it into the room.

A roar shook the building and echoed through the darkness, followed by a blinding flash of light, intended to disorient those inside.

Zane was the first through the door, sweeping the right side of the room with his gun. Hedley came in on his tail, scanning the left while Miller and Stone followed through the middle zone. Shouts echoed around them. Zane caught sight of two hostages, tied in chairs in the center of the room, then the tangos, two on the right, one on the left, all three scrambling for weapons in their confusion.

He fired two double-taps, shifted his weapon to the second target, and fired again. The shots hit dead center in the chest, dropping the captors with quick pops. "Clear right," he said into his shoulder.

To his left, he heard two more pops and saw the last captor go down. "Clear left," Hedley echoed in his earpiece.

"All clear," Miller followed from the middle of the room.

"Who's there?" The man in the chair turned his head from side to side, his vision obstructed by a black bandana tied at the back of his head

"The cavalry." Zane yanked the blindfold from Humbolt's head. The man blinked several times. He was thin from weeks in captivity, and he looked like he'd taken a major beating. Bruises and dried blood covered one whole side of his face.

In the chair beside him, the brunette vibrated with fear. Zane shot her a look and then refocused on the job at hand. "Mr. Humbolt, we're here to get you out."

"Thank God," Humbolt breathed.

Hedley cut the hostages' ties while Zane and the other two got them to their feet.

"How did you find us?" the woman asked in a shaky voice as Zane ushered her toward the door. She didn't look much steadier on her feet than Humbolt, but at least she wasn't black and blue.

Zane didn't know who she was, but there'd be plenty of time for intros later. "We'll fill you in once we're secure. Right now just focus on keeping up."

The woman nodded, and Zane glanced at his watch. Time from start of op to apprehension of hostages: Three minutes, thirty-seven seconds.

They were ahead of schedule.

"We're on our way out," he said into his com unit. "Plus two."

"Roger that," Ryder echoed back.

Slow is smooth, smooth is fast, Zane repeated the phrase in his head as he lifted the rifle to his shoulder again and turned back for the door. Miller and Stone took up position on either side of the hostages. Hedley brought up the rear.

They moved with stealth back to the balcony where Zane and Hedley provided cover and Miller and Stone took the hostages over the railing and down to the ground. In the jungle around them, nothing moved, just like they'd planned. The lack of noise from the front of the compound confirmed Ryder's team had taken out their targets and that everything was downhill from here.

When they were safely on the ground, they resumed position and headed for the southwest corner of the compound again, where Ryder's team of four waited.

Just as they rounded the corner, an explosion rocked the compound. The force of the blast shot Zane's body backward. He landed on his back with a crunch, his ears ringing. Coughing through the smoke pouring out of a giant hole in the first floor, he rolled to his stomach. Gunfire lit up the night sky. Something sharp ripped through his left quad.

He struggled to his feet. Swayed but found his balance. Disbelief rushed through him as he held up a hand to block the smoke and dust from getting in his eyes while he scanned the blown out building. His entire body went still when his gaze caught sight of Humbolt, five feet away on the ground, blood oozing from multiple cuts and scrapes over his arms and face and seeping like a river from the man's ears.

Humbolt's eyes were wide and lifeless, his body limp. Draped over his torso, the woman also lay dead, her eyes staring out into space, a hole the size of a melon in her abdomen.

No. Disbelief churned to panic, then boiling rage. *No!*

"Goddammit, Archer!" a voice yelled from somewhere close. "Get back!"

A hand grasped his fatigues, dragging him tight to the side of the blown-open building. He stumbled then fell to his ass. His back hit the crumbling stucco. A burn like dynamite lit up his left leg, and his vision swam. Struggling to see, he found Miller through the smoke, covered in soot, pulling Stone back in the same manner.

The ringing in his ears prevented Zane from hearing shit going on around him, but he recognized the ricochet of bullets hitting dirt, thought maybe he'd been hit—somewhere—but still couldn't focus on anything except Humbolt lying dead against the earth.

His principal. Four minutes, twenty-three seconds after the start of the op.

"…Humbolt's fucking dead!" Hedley hollered into his com unit. "No. One man down. Leg. I don't know. It's gushing. We need to get the bloody fuck out of here!"

In Zane's earpiece, Ryder's muffled voice rattled off commands, but the words were too dim to make out. They always had a backup plan ready to go in case things went wrong. Their backup in this case was to haul ass out before anyone else got dead, then reconnoiter two klicks south of the compound and rendezvous with the chopper.

How had it gone so wrong? Zane had led the planning phase of the mission himself. They'd known exactly how many guards would be on site, what kind of weapons they'd be up against. The firepower raining down around them and the carefully timed explosion signaled they'd been compromised.

Hedley dragged him to his feet, bracing an arm under Zane's to hold him up. Through the smoky haze, Zane saw Hedley's mouth moving as the Aussie screamed directions, but that fucking ringing was growing louder, drowning out most sound. In the distance, two bodies rushed toward them through the smoke. Zane lifted a hand that held no gun. Shit, where was his rifle? He pointed, had no idea if he screamed or not. Hedley whipped around with his weapon just as Jake Ryder and Pierce Bentley appeared through the debris.

Zane nearly went down as soon as Hedley let go, but somehow managed to prop himself against what was left of the wall. Dirt and sweat slid into his eyes and messed with his vision. His lungs burned. The scent of searing flesh and rubber was all he could focus on. Ryder signaled the roundup as the rest of his team fired back at the tangos spraying bullets from the second floor and the outer wall where Zane and his team had just been. Hedley wrapped an arm around Zane's waist, pulled Zane's wrist over his shoulder, and forced him low as they moved under the balcony and stayed out of the line of fire. Behind him, Stone hauled Humbolt's body through the debris and followed.

Zane lost track of time, wasn't sure how the hell they made it through the jungle and to the chopper alive. All he knew when he got there was that he was sweating like a motherfucker, he couldn't feel his leg anymore, and his principal was dead.

Dead.

Hedley threw him in the Huey, turned and yelled at the others behind them. The chopper's blades whipped everything around them—trees, grass, palms. Seconds later, they were loaded, and the chopper lifted off, banking to the left into the inky darkness. Zane shifted where he was lying on the chopper's floor and glanced out the open door down to the compound below, alive with flames and billowing smoke.

It looked like the world was on fire. One simple extraction had gone violently wrong. His gaze strayed to Humbolt's lifeless body.

Nausea rolled through his stomach. He dropped onto his back again, stared up at the Huey's ceiling, and worked not to lose his dinner. Somehow, he clawed himself free of his helmet, dropped it on the floor, and focused simply on sucking air into his suddenly-too-small lungs. It took several seconds before he realized someone was screaming his name over the whir of the blades. His gaze shifted to the side where Ryder held a sat phone out to him.

"Says they want to talk to you!"

Zane took the phone and pressed it to his ear while Stone cut through his fatigues and started work on his leg.

"I need a tourniquet!" Stone yelled.

Hands moved in unison. Blood spurted. Someone tied a strip of cloth or rubber—or, holy *fuck*, that felt like metal—across his thigh. Pain returned with the force of a Mac truck moving at a hundred and twenty miles per hour. Zane gritted his teeth to keep from screaming just as the familiar voice said, "Sawyer? You survived?"

He knew that voice. He recognized the breathy cadence and the use of his CIA alias. But more than anything he understood the sound of victory.

Juliet.

In that second, he knew. He knew just who'd fucked their mission and why.

"How—?"

"How is not important." Her voice hardened. "It's the why you should really be concerned with. But then you know the why, don't you?"

He pushed up to sitting even though Stone pressed against his shoulder with one bloody hand and hollered at him to lie down. The pain in his leg morphed to a blinding red, which erupted behind his eyes. "When I find you—"

"You won't. I trained with the best, and I never lose." He could almost see those amber eyes of hers when she was in black ops mode, hard and cold and as soulless as any terrorist. No wonder she'd made such a good operative. She was just like them. A venomous black widow, waiting to strike.

The phone went dead in his ear before he could respond. As dead as Humbolt on the floor beside him. Zane dropped back to the ground with a groan. The cell fell from his fingers to roll across the floor. And as they flew over the jungle and Stone packed his leg wound, Zane vaguely heard their medic tell the pilot to haul ass or they were gonna run out of time.

But he didn't care. As his vision blurred and darkness threatened, only one thing revolved in Zane's mind. Only one goal remained.

No matter what it took, no matter how long, he'd find her. He'd find her, and he'd make her pay.

To learn more about EXTREME MEASURES and all of Elisabeth's books, visit www.ElisabethNaughton.com

.

About the Author

Before topping multiple bestseller lists—including those of the *New York Times*, *USA Today*, and the *Wall Street Journal*—Elisabeth Naughton taught middle school science. A rabid reader, she soon discovered she had a knack for creating stories with a chemistry of their own. The spark turned into a flame, and Naughton now writes full-time. Besides topping bestseller lists, her books have been nominated for some of the industry's most prestigious awards, such as the RITA® and Golden Heart Awards from Romance Writers of America, the Australian Romance Reader Awards, and the Golden Leaf Award. When not dreaming up new stories, Naughton can be found spending time with her husband and three children in their western Oregon home. Learn more at www.ElisabethNaughton.com.

85875657R00164

Made in the USA
Lexington, KY
05 April 2018